THE HAT GIRL FROM SILVER STREET

LINDSEY HUTCHINSON

Boldwood

First published in Great Britain in 2021 by Boldwood Books Ltd.

1

A CIP catalogue record for this book is available from the British Library.

Paperback ISBN: 978-1-80280-209-2

Ebook ISBN: 978-1-83889-398-9

Kindle ISBN: 978-1-83889-397-2

Audio CD ISBN: 978-1-80048-858-8

Digital audio download ISBN: 978-1-80048-859-5

Large Print ISBN: 978-1-83889-396-5

Boldwood Books Ltd.

23 Bowerdean Street, London, SW6 3TN

www.boldwoodbooks.com

For my friend Diane Cooper, who bolsters me with sisterly love whenever it is needed.

1

Ella Bancroft looked down at the tangled mess in her fingers and stifled a sob. She pulled at the ruined hat in an effort to rectify her error, but the steaming process had set the blunder in place.

A tear slipped from her eye and rolled down her cheek. This was her second mistake in a week. Her first was sticking her finger with a pin and leaving a blood spot on a piece of white tulle. Ivy had ranted and raved as she had snipped off the offending piece of material to rescue the hat.

Now Ella had spoilt the crown of a felt winter hat, having steamed it into the wrong shape entirely. Thinking quickly, she wondered whether, if she held it over the steamer again, she could re-form it.

About to try, Ella caught her breath as she heard footsteps on the bare wooden staircase. It was too late, Ivy was on her way up.

Ella had been employed at Ivy Gladwin's shop for two years and yet suddenly she had begun making errors. Why? Was it because she was unhappy in her work?

'How are you getting on with that order?' Ivy called as she entered the bedroom, which had been converted to a work room.

'Erm... I...' Ella mumbled as she looked again at the floppy felt monstrosity.

'What the...?' Ivy gasped. Snatching the article from Ella, she held it up between thumb and forefinger. 'How on earth...? Good grief, girl, can't you do anything right?'

The sob Ella was holding back escaped her lips. 'I'm sorry, Miss Gladwin, I don't know what happened.'

'Neither do I!' Ivy snapped, throwing the felt onto the table. 'It's completely ruined! An expensive piece of material at the outset and now it's a – oh, do stop snivelling!'

The sharp slap to her cheek caused Ella to catch her breath and she raised a hand to cover the stinging skin.

Ella sniffed and tried hard to halt the sobs racking her body.

'I... I'm really sorry,' she managed at last.

'Well, you will have to pay for it out of your wages. Now, start again and for God's sake mind what you're doing!' With that, Ivy strode from the room, her long bombazine skirt swishing against her side-button boots.

Ella stared at the hat on the table and thought about the last two years of her life. She had seen the advert in the local newspaper for an apprentice hat-maker. Having applied and been interrogated by Miss Gladwin for over an hour, she was given the post on a month's trial. The pay, she was told, would be one pound and ten shillings a week but she must work a week in hand first. Any damages would be taken out of her money before she received it.

Now she was halfway through this week and already there would be two stoppages from her salary. Ella sighed as she worked out just how much she would have in her hand come Friday.

The gold flecks in her hazel eyes were accentuated as more tears brimmed before falling. Pushing a stray dark curl from her forehead, Ella moved to the workbench. With a sniff and a sigh, she began her work again, this time selecting the correct block to steam the material over.

Ella thought once more about her earnings – would there be enough to feed herself and her father? The food in the larder was running desperately low, and she knew if there was only enough for one of them to eat she would make sure it was her dad.

Thomas Bancroft had worked all his life at the Cyclops Tube Works until he was crippled in an accident three years before. The steel tubes, not having been secured properly on their cradle, had rolled down with a thunderous crash and trapped Thomas's legs. When he was eventually freed, the hospital had told him he would never walk or work again, the bones in his legs having been completely shattered. He was lucky to have survived the devastating accident.

Thomas took it very hard in the beginning, but with love and care from his youngest daughter he had slowly come to terms with his disability, or so Ella thought.

Ella's mind moved to her mother, who had died eight years previously when Ella was only ten years old and her sister Sally was twelve. It had been a terrible blow to them all. Trying her best to earn a few coppers here and there, Ella had taken in washing. Now she was in full time employment, but for how long? She always felt as though she was still on probation and she knew that if she made any more mistakes she'd be out on her ear.

Having spread the material over the block, Ella picked up her thimble and began to insert the blocking pins. Thick and strong, they were hard to push into the wooden block and before long her fingers ached with the strain. Then she steamed the hat and sighed with satisfaction – it had turned out all right this time.

Suddenly the door flew open and Ivy marched into the room.

So intent was she on her work that Ella had not heard her coming.

Peering closely at the new felt on its block, Ivy nodded. 'You can go home now – it's gone seven o'clock.'

Seven! It was late. Normally finishing at six, Ella realised her father would be frantic. He would be hungry, too. Snatching her coat from the stand in the corner, Ella said her goodnight and rushed out into the cold dark night.

* * *

January 1900 was a very cold month, with snow and bitter winds. The little town of Walsall in the heartland of the Black Country saw burst standpipes as the weather thawed before freezing again. Those fortunate enough to have water piped to the house were no better off. Hailstones the size of florins hammered down, sending folk scattering in search of shelter.

With her head down against the icy blast of wind, Ella left Junction Street and headed for her two up, two down home in Silver Street. The district, although spelled Caldmore, was pronounced 'Karmer', and it consisted of small houses tightly packed together. Out on the flanks of the town was where the industry was situated; iron and tube works, galvanising plants, foundries, sawmills and brick works. A little further afield lay massive sprawls of heathland dotted with disused coal pits. The Water Works reservoir sat in the centre of the scrubland. Walsall Union Workhouse stood nearby as if to serve as a reminder to all that one day it could be them hovering at the gate, waiting for admittance.

Stepping carefully on the snow-covered icy cobbles, Ella walked as fast as she dared. It wouldn't do to fall and break a leg or an arm – she had her father to see to.

Walking through the darkness, lit only by occasional pools of light from the gas street lamps, Ella was eager to be home. Her long coat kept her legs warm and Ella pulled her shawl tighter around her shoulders with gloved hands. The cold nipped her nose and as she exhaled the breath showed in a ghostly plume.

Entering through the back door, she called out, 'Dad, I'm home.'

'Where on earth have you been? I was worried to death!' came the answer as Thomas dragged his wheeled bath chair into the kitchen by grasping the doorway.

'I'm sorry, but Miss Gladwin kept me late,' Ella said as she hurriedly removed her coat and shawl, hanging them on the nail in the back door. Placing her bag on the table, she took off her hat and set it on top.

'Why?'

'Hello to you too, Sally,' Ella answered her sister's question.

Sally, two years older than Ella, was married to Edward Denton and lived not far away in Cross Street. In contrast to her sibling, Sally was plain-faced with mousy brown hair. Her spiteful nature was well known, and her lazy, good-for-nothing husband was no better. Bequeathed the house by his parents, Eddy was slowly squandering the little money left to him and considered working for a living quite beneath him.

Thomas watched his girl setting a pot of leftover broth on top of the range to heat through.

'We have a fussy client and Miss Gladwin wanted everything to be just right,' Ella replied. It was not a lie, but it was not the whole truth, either. Cutting some fresh bread, she kept her eyes on the gulley for fear of slicing a finger open.

'Did you mess up again?' Sally asked sharply.

Ella ceased sawing at the bread and nodded, not daring to look at her father.

'Put that down and come over here. Tell your old dad all about it.' Thomas held out his arms and Ella rushed into them and fell to her knees, great sobs heaving from her chest.

Thomas patted her back gently for a moment, whispering comforting words. 'It'll be all right, gel, you'll see. Just do your best, no one can ask any more than that.'

Ella cried out her self-pity and frustration, then dried her tears. 'Thanks, Dad.'

Sally had watched the little scene with scorn written all over her face.

'You need to grow a backbone,' she said nastily.

'Don't you have anything better to do than come here every day and pick flies?' Ella asked sternly.

'I come to look after Dad while you're out at work!' Sally said indignantly.

'You what? You only come to drink tea and gossip!' Ella was suddenly furious at Sally's attitude. The girl never lifted a finger to help; Ella did it all. She worked, cleaned, cooked, washed and ironed as well as saw to their crippled father.

'Enough, girls,' Thomas intervened before the situation got out of hand. 'Sally, it's time you went home to your husband.'

Sally snorted and grabbed her coat. Giving Thomas a peck on the cheek, she left the house without another word.

Whilst Ella served up their meal, she explained her mistake with the hat. 'Miss Gladwin was furious with me,' she said.

'That's because she's a dried-up old hag,' Thomas said with a cheeky grin.

'Dad!' Ella scolded but couldn't help the smile creeping across her face. 'She said I'll have to pay out of my wages.'

'It don't matter sweet'eart, we'll manage.' Thomas shook his head then continued to eat his broth.

Whilst Ella washed the dishes and prepared her father's

lunch for the following day, Thomas made his way in his wheel-chair to the sitting room, which had been converted to a bedroom after his accident.

About to knock on his door, Ella stopped and listened. Inside she could hear Thomas berating himself. Peeping around the door, which stood ajar, Ella covered her mouth with a hand. Thomas was pounding his thin legs as he cursed their uselessness.

'Stupid bloody legs! Why won't you damn well work? They should have cut you off when I was in the hospital, 'cos you're no use to me now!'

Returning to the kitchen, Ella swallowed tears that were threatening to erupt yet again. She dallied as she made a cup of tea, allowing her father time to undress and drag himself into bed.

Taking his tea, Ella knocked before entering his room. 'I thought you might like a cuppa.'

'Ooh, lovely, you're a good girl to me,' Thomas said as he accepted the cup. Patting the bed, he went on, 'Sit a minute.'

Ella smiled and perched on the end of the bed.

'I don't want you to let that woman get you down,' Thomas began. 'You're clever and everybody makes mistakes sometimes, so promise me now you won't worry any more.'

Ella nodded with a smile.

'Tomorrow is another day; go in there with a new attitude. Be confident and don't take any nonsense from that baggage!' Thomas grinned wickedly and looked pleased to see his girl smile. 'That's better. Now you get some sleep, my lovely.'

Ella kissed his cheek and went upstairs to bed.

Thomas reached for the little white pills the doctor had given him for the pains in his chest and swallowed one with his tea. The doctor had explained that his heart was weak and being in the wheelchair all the time was not helping. There was nothing to be done about that, but all Thomas could do was continue taking his medication regularly. He still tried to keep his ailment a secret from Ella by asking Mrs Woolley, his neighbour, to collect his tablets from the doctor, which luckily she was happy to do.

Upstairs, Ella's room was cold, and she quickly poured a little water from a large jug into its accompanying bowl and swilled her face. The freezing water stung her skin and she gasped before grabbing her towel and rubbing her cheeks hard to warm them. Frantically she undressed, threw on a voluminous cotton nightgown and climbed into bed. Her teeth chattered as she pulled the eiderdown up to her nose.

Gradually the warmth wrapped itself around her and she began to relax for the first time that day. She watched the light from the moon filter through the lacy patterned frost covering the window, casting strange shadows on the wall.

Staring at the frosted pane, she considered. She was so lucky to have such a good father. She was knew how his legs made him feel, how they emasculated him. There was nothing she could do about that, but she could continue to love and care for him. She had a roof over her head and food in her belly, which was more than a lot of people had – those who lived on the streets, for instance. She had a job, too, for which she was grateful, but she did wish her employer would be a little kinder to her.

Recalling her father's words, she determined she would take more care and work harder, giving Miss Gladwin no reason to be harsh with her.

With drooping eyelids, Ella finally succumbed to sleep.

2

At seven o'clock on the dot, Ella entered the shop. 'Good morning, Miss Gladwin.'

Ivy nodded and said, 'I hope you're ready to get it right today. Please tell me you remember where I told you to place the flowers and feathers on that hat.' She nodded to the felt Ella had been working on the previous day.

Ella nodded. As she took off her coat and hung it up, she thought, *I've been here two minutes and this woman has already sucked the energy right out of me!*

Gathering the things she needed, Ella trudged upstairs, settled on her stool at the table and threaded a needle ready to start work.

Ivy stood watching, a frown creasing her brow and her hands on her hips. She was dressed in a brown suit, the jacket nipped in to her already slim waist. The skirt fell to highly polished boots. Her titian hair was piled on her head beautifully, and her pale blue eyes held a hardness which never softened. Her skin was milky white and had recently begun to show its age.

Satisfied her apprentice was concentrating, Ivy went downstairs to the shop. She had decided to change the display in the window and so she started by pulling out the hats already on show. Boxing them up, she placed them on a shelf in the back room. Grabbing a rag, she dusted down the window before looking at the new range and deciding which to choose.

Picking up a sinamay cartwheel in a light chocolate colour, Ivy ran her fingers over the huge white ostrich feather. She inspected the silk roses of the same pure white for any faults or flaws; having made them herself she knew it was unlikely there would be any. She nodded and placed the hat on a stand in the centre of the window. It was striking and would draw the eye, she thought. Ivy smiled, certain it would sell quickly. Next she chose a black felt winter hat covered with pink silk roses. Then came a black silk gentleman's top hat, beside which she laid a silver-topped cane and a pair of soft napper gloves. Behind the cartwheel hat she propped up an open white broderie anglaise parasol.

Working quietly, Ivy Gladwin hoped her window would bring a touch of class to the drab little town, which was still covered in a blanket of snow.

Upstairs, Ella snipped the cotton, having put in her final stitches. She turned the hat this way and that, admiring her work. She had done a good job even if she said so herself. She just hoped Miss Gladwin would think so too.

Tidying her work bench, she glanced at the tin clock on the mantelpiece. Mid-morning – it had taken three hours to complete her project. Now it was time for tea, so she made her way downstairs.

'I thought you might be ready for this,' Ella said, proffering the cup and saucer.

'Thank you,' said Ivy, taking the beverage and placing it on the counter. 'Stand in the window area while I view it from outside; it may need adjustment, although I sincerely doubt it.' Grabbing a thick woollen shawl, Ivy stepped out onto the cobblestones, which were slick with ice, and gazed at her handiwork.

A moment later she was back indoors. 'It's fine as it is, but then I knew it would be.' Picking up her cup, she asked, 'How did you get on with that order?'

'It's all finished,' Ella said with a small amount of pride.

'I'll drink this,' Ivy held up her cup, 'then I'll come and inspect it.'

The two drank their tea in silence before climbing the stairs to the work room. Ella passed the hat to Ivy who took great lengths to examine the stitches then with a nod she said, 'Right, box and label it. I have a parasol which needs a lacy trim attaching – something even you can't make a mess of!'

Ella winced at the comment and watched Ivy pull open the long drawer beneath the work counter. Taking out a white umbrella, she thrust it at the girl. 'Let me know when it's done.' Shoving the drawer shut, Ivy left the room.

With a sigh, Ella collected the lace trim and picked up an already threaded needle. Would it have hurt Miss Gladwin to say 'well done'? A simple word of praise was all Ella wanted, but no – clearly it was too much to ask. Knowing she had done a good job was one thing, but being told was another entirely.

Pinning the lace in place around the edge of the parasol, Ella snipped off the end before sewing it in place. Her eyes returned to the hat still lying on the counter. *I'd better box that before poison Ivy comes back*, she thought. Immediately she berated herself for being so unkind to the woman who was her employer. Placing the hat in a box, she pinned the label on and tied it with string, then returned to the umbrella.

The fire was low in the hearth, but Ella ignored it. She was working with white lace and couldn't risk smudging it with coal dust if she fed the embers. That would have to be her next task.

* * *

Whilst Ella was endeavouring to keep her stitches as small as possible, her father was sitting in his wheelchair, staring out of the kitchen window. There was little to see, a tiny patch of waste ground and the privy block, but Thomas's eyes didn't register either. His mind had, like so many times before, taken him back to his accident. Unconsciously he winced as he recalled the excruciating pain he felt once the steel tubes had been removed from his shattered legs. Although he no longer suffered the agony, the memory was all too real.

Looking down at his thin bony knees, Thomas sucked in a breath desperately trying to stem his tears. Black Country men didn't cry, he told himself. Born and bred to be strong and fearless, the men of Walsall worked hard all their lives to provide for their families. For Thomas Bancroft, however, there would be no more work.

Raising his eyes to the window once more, he wondered – was this all that was left to him? Would he die in this wicker chair? Could he ever be useful again?

Thomas hated the fact that he had become a burden to his daughters. At eighteen years old, Ella should be enjoying her life – not looking after her crippled father. At least Sally was married, even if it was to Eddy Denton. Thomas had never liked that young man but Sally had fallen in love and so he had relented, agreeing to the wedding. His eldest daughter continued to visit three or four times a week. Although he enjoyed seeing her, he often wished she would curb her acidic tongue, especially where

Ella was concerned. Sibling rivalry was common, he knew that, but there was jealousy, too, which had carried through from their earliest years.

The old saying referring to children sprang to mind, *you never get two the same*, which in this case was true. Sally, ordinary looking with a spiteful nature and a sharp tongue which she never could keep behind her teeth, and Ella, pretty as a picture with a loving and kind nature. He loved them both there was no denying that, but he wished they would cease their constant bickering.

As his thoughts roamed, his hand went subconsciously to his chest to rub at the pains he had learned to live with.

So many times he had considered joining his wife in the afterlife, but the thought of his girls had brought him to his senses. With each day that passed, Thomas knew his depression was growing deeper, and keeping it from Ella was taking its toll. He worried that one day he might succumb and take his own life.

Thomas Bancroft! You need to find something to do! Stop moping about and make yourself useful again! But it was easier thought than done. He was stuck in this chair, unable to get out and about by himself. There *had* to be a way of finding a job that didn't need the use of his legs. His upper body was strong from pushing and pulling the chair around, so maybe he could do some work with his hands.

Suddenly Thomas realised he was thinking positively for the first time in a very long while. Picking up the newspaper, he looked for anyone who might be hiring staff. There was nothing, and feeling despondent again he pushed the paper across the table. The only thing he was good for was peeling the potatoes for their evening meal.

Covering his face with his hands, Thomas finally let go of his pent-up frustration, anger and sadness. He wept as though his heart was breaking.

* * *

That evening, as father and daughter ate their faggots and pota-toes, Ella instinctively picked up on Thomas's mood.

'What's wrong, Dad?'

Thomas shook his head but Ella persevered. 'Come on, I know when there's something amiss. You always taught me to share my problems, thereby halving them.'

Pushing his empty plate away, Thomas took a breath. 'You work so hard to keep the wolf from the door and what do I do? Nothing! I sit around all day feeling sorry for myself. Ella, I *have* to find a job or at the very least a hobby!'

Ella was surprised at the emotional outburst and then she said, 'I can understand that. I suppose you've scoured the paper?'

'Yes, there's nowt doing,' Thomas replied sadly.

'Dad, what about the harness manufacturer? Maybe they'll have some work,' Ella said with encouragement.

'How will I get there? This bloody chair is too big for a cab! Besides, it would be too dear to travel that way every day.' Thomas shook his head, feeling the despair settling on him once more.

'I wonder if they employ outworkers,' Ella mused. 'I could call in and ask on your behalf if you'd like.'

'It wouldn't hurt, I suppose,' Thomas answered with a grim smile.

'I'll go after work tomorrow. Fingers crossed they'll have something for you. Now, you get to bed and I'll bring you a nice cuppa.'

Ella watched her father struggle his way through the doorway before closing her eyes.

Please, God, let there be a job for my dad. I promise not to ask for anything more.

Then she made the tea, hoping against hope that her dad would be employed before too long.

3

The following evening, Thomas tried his best to hide his disappointment. Ella had broken the news gently that there was no work to be had, even for an able-bodied man. Now he watched his daughter practising tying a neat bow with a length of ribbon. Time after time she endeavoured to get it right and in the end she slammed it on the table in frustration.

'I'll make some tea,' she said. Placing clean cups on the table she stared in astonishment at Thomas's deft fingers producing a perfect bow.

'How...?' she gasped.

Pulling the ribbon ends the bow unravelled.

'Watch carefully,' he said and again a bow appeared in an instant.

'That's amazing!' Ella said. 'I had no idea you could do that.'

'Neither did I,' Thomas said. 'Now, you try.'

Ella beamed her pleasure when her bow matched her father's.

'There you go, it's easy once you know how,' he said.

'I still have to master pleats,' Ella answered with a grimace.

Thomas pulled out his handkerchief and passed it to her. 'Show me.'

Ella did her best, but her pleating was uneven and messy.

'Fetch your pins,' Thomas said as he took back the large square of cotton. 'Right, try it like this.'

Ella watched with fascination as Thomas folded the material into a fan, pinning it as he went.

'Dad, you should have been a milliner!' Ella said at last.

'Your turn,' Thomas said.

Ella quickly grasped the idea, laughing at how simple it was.

It warmed Thomas's heart to hear his daughter giggle, it had been a long time in coming.

Ella locked up for the night, banked up the fire in her father's room and went to bed. She lay thinking about what she'd learned in a couple of hours spent with her dad. Then a thought struck. What if Miss Gladwin could hire Thomas to make the bows and silk flowers which would adorn her range of hats? It would have to be outwork, for he wouldn't manage the stairs to the work room.

As she considered the idea further, Ella's excitement grew. She could bring home the haberdashery for Thomas to assemble and take the finished articles back the following day. Her father could earn a wage and feel useful again, and Miss Gladwin would have perfect attachments for her hats.

It was a win-win situation as far as Ella was concerned. Now all she had to do was broach the idea with her employer.

That same evening, Sally had raised the subject yet again of Eddy finding a job.

'I ain't working!' he said. 'If anything, folks should be working for me!'

'That's not likely, seeing as you have no business,' Sally retorted. 'You should have used that money your folks left you to buy into a little going concern instead of piddling it up the walls of every boozer in the town.'

'Don't start, Sal. I've told you before I'm considering my options,' Eddy replied, giving the newspaper he was reading a shake.

'Your options, ha! What are they? Whether we starve or not because you're too lazy to get off your arse and work!' Sally flicked her fingers against the paper held up in front of her husband's face.

'Give over, Sal,' he muttered. Then, laying his reading material in his lap, he said, 'Anyway, it won't matter 'cos when your dad's gone we can sell his house and we'll be in the money.'

'What about our Ella?' Sally asked.

'She'll have to rent a room somewhere,' Eddy replied with a shrug.

'I suppose she could, but the problem there is – they rent that house!'

'Oh, bugger, I forgot about that.'

'So, Mr Cleverclogs, you'll have to find another way to bring in some money.'

'For God's sake, woman, give it a rest!' Eddy picked up the paper once again as a grinning Sally set the kettle to boil for their evening cocoa.

* * *

Ivy Gladwin was reading the newspaper when Ella arrived at the shop early the next morning.

'There's been an outbreak of influenza in London,' Ivy said, 'I hope it doesn't come here.'

'It's possible. After all, people travel more these days. It would only take one person...' Ella responded.

'You're a little ray of sunshine this morning!' Ivy cut her off.

'I was just saying,' Ella defended herself.

Again, Ivy interrupted. 'The British soldiers are still fighting in what they're calling the second Boer war.'

Ella chose not to answer for fear of being shouted down again. Instead, she picked up a length of red ribbon and began to tie a bow like her father had shown her.

Ivy watched from the corner of her eye as Ella laid the completed article on the table. 'You've been practising,' she said.

'Yes. Miss Gladwin, can I ask you something?' Receiving a curt nod, Ella proceeded. 'My father showed me how to do this,' she picked up the bow again, 'and I was wondering – would it be possible for...?'

'Spit it out, girl, for goodness' sake!' Ivy's patience quickly ran out.

'Could you give my dad a job making bows and decorations?' Ella's words came in a rush.

Ivy's mouth dropped open as she stared at her young apprentice. Then, folding the paper neatly, she slapped it on the table.

'Why, pray tell, can your father not go out and find a job like other men?'

'He had an accident in the tube works and now he's confined to a wheelchair,' Ella answered sadly.

'I see. Well, that's a shame, Ella, but I can't possibly afford to take on another worker. Besides, having a man work here, a cripple no less, is completely out of the question!' Ivy's words were sharp and her eyes glittered like cracked ice in the grey light of the morning.

'Please, Miss Gladwin, I could take the ribbons home and Dad could make them into bows, then I could bring them back the next day,' Ella pushed her point.

'I don't have the funds to pay, and I'm sure your father would be horrified at the idea of working for a woman,' Ivy retaliated.

'He wouldn't mind if it meant he was being of use again.'

'The answer is no, Ella. Now let that be an end to it. We have a lot of work to get through today, so I suggest you make a start. The underside of the brim of Mrs Swallow's hat needs pleating, and please ensure you do it properly.' Ivy got to her feet and marched from the room.

Ella swallowed her tears as she picked up the white silk and began.

Downstairs, Ivy was still in shock at being asked to employ a man, let alone one who could not walk. She realised she knew next to nothing about her employee, but then the girl's life outside of work was not her concern.

Busying herself by arranging a straw boater on a pupae – a linen covered wooden head form – Ivy couldn't get the conversation out of her mind. Yesterday Ella couldn't tie a decent bow to save her life and yet this morning she had tied one perfectly. She found herself wondering what else Mr Bancroft could do. It would be most unusual, but the man could have a natural artistic flair, in which case he might well be an asset to her business. Maybe he would have some new ideas, too, which could be taken into consideration.

The pros and cons of the notion waged war in her mind all morning as she worked, tidying and dusting.

Just before lunch a young woman entered the shop and looked around.

'May I help you?' Ivy asked, painting a smile on her face.

'I was looking for something a little more modern,' the woman said.

'In which style?' Ivy bristled.

'Riding hats.'

Ivy nodded and, pushing the ladder on its rollers along the shelves, she stood on the bottom rung. Pulling out a small hatbox she stepped down and placed it on the counter before removing the lid. Lifting the hat from its resting place she held it up for the woman to see.

'Hmm, not quite what I had in mind.' The woman frowned and shook her head. 'I don't like all this... drapery.' Her fingers played with dangling ribbons and massive feathers. 'It's not really a proper riding hat, is it? Looks like someone went a bit mad with the decorating of it. No, I'll leave it, thank you.' The woman gave a grim smile and left the shop.

Ivy glanced down at the hat sitting on the counter. She had thought it one of her finest creations, but the woman had sneered at her efforts.

Snatching up the offending article, she marched upstairs. 'I want all this lot taken off!' Ivy said as she threw the hat onto the table.

'Why?' Ella asked innocently.

'Because I said so! I don't have to explain myself to you!' Ivy yelled, then stomped from the room.

Ella sighed. Ivy was in a foul mood. Was it to do with being asked to employ Thomas? Or had something else happened? Either way, it would pay Ella to keep her mouth closed and follow orders.

Deciding to finish the pleating task first before unpicking the stitches to release the décor of the other hat, Ella resumed her work quietly.

Mid-afternoon, Ivy arrived in the work room just as Ella had taken the last feather from the so-called riding hat.

'What do you want doing with this now?' Ella asked.

'Hmm.' Ivy could not envisage how the item should look in its final state. 'What would you suggest?'

Ella was surprised at being asked for her opinion. Was Ivy at a loss and so moving the onus onto her assistant?

'I would simply tie a length of soft net around the crown, leaving the ends to fall to the back. I really think that's all it needs,' Ella said tentatively.

Ivy nodded as Ella completed the task. Boxing the hat, Ivy left to place it in the shop.

An hour later, Ella heard the bell tinkle and, having little to do, she crept to the top of the stairs. Listening to the conversation taking place between customer and vendor, Ella's mouth dropped open.

'I really think that's all it needs.' Ivy was using the exact same words Ella had spoken earlier; the woman was taking credit for Ella's idea!

Tiptoeing back to her stool, Ella seethed. She made up her mind there and then that she would be keeping her mouth firmly shut in future. Any notions she had regarding hat design or decoration she would be keeping to herself.

'Another happy customer,' Ivy said as she breezed into the room.

Ella ignored the remark as she collected up the blocking pins and stored them away.

'On to the next,' Ivy muttered happily as she checked the order book.

4

When Ella arrived home that night she was horrified at the mess in the kitchen. Wood chippings and shavings littered the floor, and on the table sat two blocks rounded to perfection. Thomas was busily working shaping a larger one.

'Dad! What on earth...?'

'I've made these for you – to practice on,' her father said proudly.

'Do you think I need practice?' Ella asked.

'No, sweetheart, I should have chosen my words more carefully. I meant to say – to work with.'

Ella and Thomas grinned at each other as she stroked the wooden head forms.

'How did you get the wood?' Ella asked as she fed the range after hanging up her coat.

'Mrs Woolley next door. She came calling and I asked her to fetch some off-cuts from the sawmill on Midland Road,' Thomas answered.

'They would have been heavy to carry,' Ella said stroking a hand over one of the blocks.

'Muscles like a navvy, that one,' Thomas laughed.

'Where did you get the money from?'

'Mrs Woolley bullied the foreman and got them free, I believe.' Thomas grinned.

For the first time in years Ella saw enthusiasm light her father's eyes.

'Are you pleased?' Thomas asked.

'Oh, Dad, I'm thrilled! Thank you.' Ella flung her arms around Thomas's shoulders and kissed the top of his head.

Sweeping up the debris, Ella threw it into the fire in the range.

'This one is for men's top hats, and those...' he pointed to the table, 'are for ladies. I can make more if you need them.'

'I think these will be enough, thank you, but I would need a pupae too.' Ella explained about the padded head block covered in linen.

'Not a problem,' Thomas grinned, 'I'll sort that out for you tomorrow. What else will you need?'

'Blocking pins, steam kettle, thimbles, pins, needles, thread, material and accessories,' Ella said with a smile to match her father's.

'Not much then,' Thomas said as he scratched his head beneath his flat cap.

'I know where to get them from, but it won't be cheap, and my wages have to cover the rent and our food as well as gas and fuel,' Ella said.

'We'll manage,' Thomas replied.

'Don't forget I'll have two stoppages out of my money, too.' Ella's smile slid from her face as she remembered her errors at the shop.

'Bloody woman!' Thomas grumbled. 'Everybody makes the

odd mistake; she shouldn't punish you for it, she should show you how to do it properly in the first place!'

'Pig's trotter for tea?' Ella asked, wanting to change the subject.

'What about you?' Thomas asked.

'Ooh, no thanks!' Ella replied. 'I prefer leftovers.'

'You don't know what's good for you,' Thomas said with a smile as he saw his girl wrinkle her nose.

Busying herself with their meal, Ella said, 'I get my wages tomorrow and I've got Sunday off.'

Thomas grunted as he sanded down the block, causing fine dust to fly when he blew on the wood.

Ella sighed inwardly, realising how much more work she had still to do cleaning up Thomas's mess. Then, as she watched him concentrating, she thought, *It doesn't matter. I'm just so pleased he's found something to do which makes him feel useful again!*

The following morning, Ivy handed Ella her wages. 'I have deducted the amount to cover the hats you ruined,' she said curtly.

Ella gasped as she opened the small brown envelope. 'You took ten shillings!'

'Yes. There was nothing I could do to salvage that one hat and I did warn you this would happen.' Ivy stood ramrod straight, her hands folded at the front of her black skirt.

'I know but – ten shillings! How am I able to pay rent and feed us out of one pound?' Ella's heart hammered in her chest at the prospect.

'You should have thought of that before and been more careful!' Ivy snapped. 'I warn you now, any more errors and you'll be out. I'm sure there are many girls who would be eager to take your place.' Turning on her heel, Ivy left Ella to think on what she'd said.

Dropping onto her stool, Ella looked at the money. How could she explain this to her father? Would this paltry amount last them a week? Was there a way she could make it stretch until next Friday?

Sighing loudly, Ella shoved the money into her drawstring bag. Turning to the counter, she picked up a large ostrich feather and stared at it. She wanted to crush it and slap it in Miss Gladwin's hand before telling her she could stick her job up her arse!

With a little giggle at the thought, Ella picked up her needle and began sewing the feather in place.

All day Ella worried about how to tell her father she had worked hard for a week for a single pound. How would he react? Would he be furious with her? Thomas had never been angry with her as far as she could recall, but there was always a first time. She was dreading going home and, despite constantly checking the clock, the day seemed to fly past.

Before she knew it, Ella was walking through the dark streets, the cold nipping at her nose. Clutching her bag as if it contained the Crown Jewels, she was afraid someone might steal her hard-earned money. It was all that stood between them and starvation. Increasing her pace, she rushed home to face the music.

'Ten bob! That's daylight bloody robbery!' Thomas boomed after he had listened to what Ella had to say.

'I'm sorry, Dad,' she said tearfully.

'It's *not* your fault, gel, it's that woman. She's a thieving mare!' Thomas was furious – but not with Ella. His anger was directed at the woman who employed his child.

Ella stifled a sob and Thomas held out his arms. Folded in the comfort of her dad's loving embrace, Ella allowed her tears to fall.

Letting her cry out her misery Thomas said, 'Right, tomorrow you go in there and tell *Miss Gladwin* you've quit.'

'Dad, I can't! What will we do for money?' she asked as she moved to sit at the table.

'You let me worry about that. When you've told her, you take ten bob of that pound and you go and get as much as you can from the haberdashery.'

'Dad! That money is for rent and food!' Ella was shocked at the thought.

'Do as I say, sweet'eart, cos your old dad has a plan.' Thomas grinned as he tapped the side of his nose.

'What plan?' Ella asked suspiciously.

'You and me – we're going into the hat business!' Thomas nodded to the pupae he'd made for his daughter that day.

Ella sucked in a breath. She'd been so worried about the cash flow problem she hadn't noticed it sitting on the table. Stroking the padded head, she breathed, 'It's beautiful, Dad!' Then she asked, 'What happens if we can't sell any hats? How will we live with no money coming in? Where will we sell from?'

'I have it all worked out,' Thomas said, 'but it will mean hard work for you in the beginning. Are you up for giving it a go?'

Ella hesitated. Were her skills good enough to produce items to be sold? She must be, she'd made hats for Miss Gladwin – albeit for only a couple of years. However, they were still sitting in the shop waiting to be sold. Was that because they were not a high enough standard of work? No, Ella believed it was due to their being fashionable years ago and people wanting more up-to-date designs. Thinking hard about the proposal her father had put to her, Ella knew she had to grasp the bull by the horns and make it work, for both their sakes.

'Yes!' she said eventually. Seeing her father all fired up was reason enough for Ella to agree to embark on their new adventure together.

* * *

'You can't just walk out!' Ivy said the following morning when Ella said she was leaving.

'I can and I will,' Ella said, still standing in her outdoor clothing.

'What will I do for an assistant?' Ivy said pitifully.

'You should have thought of that before,' said Ella, using the phrase Ivy had spoken the previous day.

'Before what?' Ivy demanded to know.

'You have been rude to me ever since I began working here. You took my idea and passed it off as your own.' Seeing Ivy blanch Ella went on. 'I heard you tell that customer exactly what I'd said to you regarding that riding hat. Then to top it all you stopped my money, and, in my opinion, far too much!'

'I had to cover my expenses, you stupid girl!' Ivy spat nastily.

'I am not stupid! I understand about accounts but to my mind that was excessive – in fact, it's tantamount to stealing! I wonder how the constabulary would view it,' Ella said raising her eyebrows.

'There won't be any need to...' Ivy moved to the till and a second later held out her hand. 'Here, take this to help out as I know you have to feed your crippled father.' Ivy handed over two half crowns.

They both knew the money was not to ease Ella's situation at all but was to cover the woman's duplicity. Ivy did not want the police on her doorstep because of her greed; she had known the stoppages were far too high. What she hadn't reckoned on was the girl's challenging it.

'Thank you,' Ella said with a glare, 'but I'm still leaving. You said there would be plenty of girls who would be glad of my job –

good luck with that, I hope you find one. Goodbye, Miss Gladwin.'

Leaving the shop, Ella suddenly felt free. Filling her lungs with cold air, she did a twirl right there in the street, much to the amusement of passers-by.

Five shillings better off now, Ella made her way to the drapers with a spring in her step. Taking her time to choose her materials, Ella formed images in her mind of the hats she would make. With everything she needed in a box tied with string, she set off for home.

That afternoon, Ella and her father excitedly drew up plans for their new business. They sketched their ideas on brown paper begged from neighbours and Ella couldn't wait to get started.

'Mr Potts from two houses up sent this old kettle,' Thomas said as he lifted it from beside his wheelchair.

'That was nice of him. Could you find a way of tilting the lid and holding it in place for the steaming process?'

'Yes, a bit of wire will do the trick,' Thomas answered. His heart leapt with pleasure at being asked to find solutions to Ella's questions.

Suddenly Ella's hand covered her mouth for a second. 'Dad, how can we display what we make? Miss Gladwin had a window to show off her hats.'

'Use the sitting room,' Thomas answered simply.

'How? That's your bedroom now!'

'I'll have to learn to climb the stairs again, won't I?' Thomas responded, hoping his smile would ease his daughter's misgivings.

'Dad – it's not going to work! You can't manage the stairs, you know that.' Ella saw their dreams melting away before her eyes.

'I have two strong arms and a backside. I'll manage.'

'And how will you get down again?' Ella asked.

'Same as I went up. Now stop fretting 'cos tomorrow Mrs Woolley is coming round to help you take my bed back to my proper bedroom.' Thomas rubbed his hands together and the gleam in his eye shone bright.

'You have everything worked out, don't you?' Ella asked.

Thomas nodded.

'You know, Dad, I think this might actually work,' Ella said with a laugh.

'What will?' Sally asked as she stepped into the warm kitchen.

Thomas explained about the business they were about to undertake as Ella made tea for them all.

'Of course it won't work,' Sally said at last with a shake of her head.

Ella sighed loudly. No matter what she said Sally would argue with it.

'Who is going to buy a hat from a dingy backstreet house when they can go to the big shops in Birmingham or London?' Sally shrugged her shoulders.

'Why do you always do that?' Ella asked.

Sally raised her eyebrows in question.

'You frown on everything I do! Just for once can't you do something sisterly like say, "Well done for trying"?' Ella's temper was rising and it was all she could do to keep it in check.

'I was only stating my opinion,' Sally replied, feigning hurt.

'Well don't! No one asked you for it!' Ella was fuming now.

'Girls, please – must you disagree about everything?' Thomas gave a weary sigh.

'I can see I'm not wanted here, so I'll go home.' Sally grabbed her hat and coat and slammed the kitchen door behind her as she left.

Father and daughter released a long drawn-out breath in relief.

'What if she's right, Dad?'

'Only time will tell, but I have faith in you. Now, let's have our tea in peace and quiet.' Thomas gave his daughter a cheeky grin as he nodded to her to lock the back door.

5

Two days of hard work resulted in a transformation Ella would never have thought possible. The sitting room was bright and clean, and the furniture moved back to its original place in the house. The windows sparkled and in their bow stood pupaes Thomas had fashioned for displaying the finished hats. Whilst Ella had been busy cleaning he had, with the help of a young lad who lived over the road, made himself a trolley of sorts. In exchange for a cake baked by Ella, the lad had scavenged all that was needed. A wooden seat with a backrest and two short sides had been attached to axles. Four old perambulator wheels were fixed in place. This was to be kept at the top of the stairs. Now Thomas had an easy way to get to his bedroom and his wheelchair could remain downstairs.

In the evenings after supper, father and daughter worked together, their designs coming to life before their very eyes.

'You will have to decide on how much to ask for these,' Thomas said one night.

'Oh, I hadn't thought...' Ella replied.

'Start with your costings. Take into account what you spent

on materials and frippery; how long it took you to make the article and a bit on top for profit,' Thomas instructed.

Ella blew out her cheeks. There was more to running a business than she had expected.

'You'll have to keep ledgers as well – incoming, outgoing; order books and receipts for happy customers, as well as opening a bank account. When you're ready to open for business, you'll need a snippet in the paper telling folk who you are, what you do and where you can be found.' Thomas laid down the bow he had just finished and looked at his girl. 'Close your mouth, there's a steam train coming.'

Ella burst out laughing then said, 'I'm worried about it, Dad. What happens if no one buys our hats?

'*You'll* go hungry.' Seeing the shock on Ella's face, Thomas let out a belly laugh that rang around the small kitchen.

'Oh, Dad, it's so good to hear you laugh again,' Ella said quietly.

'It feels good, too,' Thomas said patting her hand.

Ella watched as Thomas wheeled himself to the stair's door, which was held open by a metal hook and eye. With practised ease, he lowered himself onto the bottom step. Giving a little wave he pulled himself up the stairs. Ella heard the trolley trundle along the short landing and she smiled.

In a week she had quit her job, her father had found he was useful after all and together they were starting up a business.

Tonight, as every night now, Ella prayed that their new venture would be successful. Her eyes shot to the ceiling as she heard her father whistling a little ditty. It was something she hadn't heard in an age – since her mother had died, in fact.

It lifted her heart and, as she banked the fire for the night in the sitting room to stave off the damp, she sang along to the tune.

Dousing the lamps, Ella continued to sing as she made her way to bed.

Thomas's laughter boomed out. 'We make a good pair,' he called out.

'Like father, like daughter,' Ella replied.

Before long, the house was dark and quiet, and Ella thanked her lucky stars for having such a loving father.

* * *

As Ella climbed into bed, her sister was doing the same over in Cross Street. Lying next to her snoring husband, Sally began to calculate. It had been four months since she'd seen her monthlies, which could mean only one thing – she was pregnant.

Having said nothing to Eddy, she thought the time had come for him to know he was going to be a father. How would he take the news? Would he be pleased or would he see it as a drain on their coffers? Whatever the outcome, he had to be told. To be truthful, Sally wasn't sure how she felt about it herself. A baby would take a lot of looking after and it would be expensive. The idea of disturbed sleep filled her with dismay, for it was certain Eddy would not help with night feeds should the little one not take to the breast and need a bottle.

Sally grimaced in the darkness when she realised her figure would swell out of proportion, and a shiver overtook her at thought of the pain of childbirth. She knew the time had passed for her to rid her body of the child she wasn't at all sure she wanted. She had to look forward and try to come to terms with the fact that before too long she would be a mother and responsible for a helpless being who would depend on her for everything.

Turning over, she snuggled against Eddy in an effort to steal the warmth of his body. She would see what tomorrow would bring.

* * *

Ivy Gladwin had found no one to help with her business. All who applied for the post were not at all suitable. One girl had a constant dewdrop on the end of her nose, which she sniffed at with an horrendous noise. Another had no idea what a needle was for and yet another asked if she could bring her knitting with her! Ivy despaired of ever finding anyone who could replace Ella.

Fortunately, Ivy had enough stock to see her through, but over the last six months sales had fallen. Had women stopped buying hats or was it her designs that were at fault? She recalled the lady who searched for something more *modern* in the riding range.

Looking around the shop, she realised she'd had some of the hats on display for years. It came as quite a shock and Ivy wondered how she could rectify the situation. She was surrounded by all of her ideas, and each hat she made turned out very similar to one already completed.

Somehow she had to breathe new life into the contents of her shop. The problem was that she didn't know how to do it. She needed Ella, that girl was the only one who could boost her sales. Ella was full of ideas and Ivy had driven her away.

Cursing her bad luck, she wished she had been kinder to the girl. She didn't even know where Ella lived so she couldn't visit and try to entice her to return to her job – with a pay rise as incentive of course.

Now she was alone with a shop full of old and tired hats. Closed for business as it was Sunday, Ivy decided to go for a walk.

Maybe she would espy new designs as she passed others out for a stroll.

Donning her winter coat, Ivy set off for Palfrey Park. No matter the weather, there were always couples meandering the pathways through the trees. All morning she traversed the park, keeping a keen eye out for something to spark her imagination. But nothing stood out from the walkers or riders enjoying their time at leisure, and Ivy returned home none the wiser.

* * *

Unbeknown to Ella, Thomas had cajoled his neighbour into taking an advertisement to be placed in the *Walsall Observer*. He had used the rent money, hoping that once the business took off he would be able to catch up on the arrears. He was excited as he waited for publication day of the weekly newspaper. Ella would be thrilled, he felt sure.

'I think you should open for business tomorrow,' Thomas said that evening.

'We're not ready!' Ella gasped.

'Tomorrow is Monday and folk will be passing on their way to work. They will see your display and tell others. You have to do it sooner or later,' Thomas said gently.

'But what about...?' Ella protested. Suddenly her courage failed her, and her misgivings loomed large in her mind.

'Sweet'eart, I didn't want to say anything but – we'll need money for rent and food.'

'Oh dear, yes. I'm sorry, I got caught up with it all and I quite forgot this is a business.' With a deep breath Ella added, 'Tomorrow it is, then.'

That night, sleep evaded Ella as she lay in her bed, the covers pulled up to her chin. What if this venture failed? She'd have no job and no money – just a house full of hats. Would her designs sell? Were they over-priced? Questions with no answers swirled in her tired mind. Moonlight shone through the window, opaque with frost, and Ella shivered. She would only have one chance at this – she *had* to make it work.

Early the next morning a newspaper boy, almost frozen to the bone, shoved the paper through the letterbox and banged the door before moving on.

'I'll get it,' Thomas said.

Ella nodded as she poured tea for them both.

Thomas eagerly turned the pages until he found what he was looking for. Placing the paper on his knees, he wheeled himself back to the kitchen.

'There!' he said pushing the article in front of Ella.

'Dad! Oh my...!' Ella was dumbfounded. 'How did you...?'

'Read it out, I want to hear it as well as see it,' Thomas cut in excitedly.

Drawing a breath Ella began.

Ella's Hats. New designs at reasonable prices. Bespoke hats for every occasion. Need something special? Then visit 24 Silver Street and speak with Ella herself!

'They'll be banging on the door in no time.' Thomas nodded, pleased with his wording. It was expensive to advertise so he'd kept it short and sweet.

'I hope so Dad, I really do.' Ella was not at all sure her father was right.

* * *

Over in Junction Street, Ivy too was reading an article in the paper. The Boers had slowly surrounded the town of Ladysmith in South Africa, where British soldiers were garrisoned. Launching a sortie in October 1899, the result had been a disaster for the British. Now, four months later, 20,000 British troops had invaded the Orange Free State.

Tutting loudly at men killing each other over land, Ivy turned the page. Suddenly she sat forward as she saw the advert for Ella's Hats. That little witch! *No wonder she quit working for me,* Ivy thought, *she's taken everything I taught her and...!* Ivy felt betrayed.

How had Ella raised the cash to set up her own business? No bank would loan money to an unemployed person, especially a woman. Reading the advert again, Ivy's anger mounted. Throwing the paper aside she paced the shop, her hands on her hips. She threw out her arm and swept a hat from the counter.

'Bloody girl!' she muttered.

Coming to a halt, she wondered. Would Ella take trade from her? If so, Ivy would have to close down and look for work elsewhere. Her shop had been here for twenty years and she would not allow a chit of a girl to steal her customers.

With one hand on her hip and the other over her mouth, Ivy resumed her pacing, her eyes scanning the floor as she thought hard about the implications of all this.

She could visit Silver Street and have it out with Ella, but what good would that do? The girl was breaking no law in setting up on her own.

Eventually Ivy came to a conclusion: there was nothing she could do but hope Ella's business would fail. However, if by some chance it proved to be successful, then a rethink would be needed.

Ivy Gladwin would have to find a way to ruin Ella Bancroft.

* * *

Monday morning in the Denton household was fraught with tension as Sally watched her husband's reaction to her news.

'When – how?' Eddy asked.

'Bloody hell, Eddy! Are you pleased or what?' Sally asked, feeling full of trepidation.

'Well, I'm surprised. I thought we'd been careful – I mean – are you happy about it?' Eddy immediately pushed the onus onto his wife.

'I don't know,' Sally said as she nursed a cup of tea.

'Me neither,' Eddy muttered. 'How far gone are you?'

'About four months,' Sally replied already knowing what he was thinking. 'It's too late to...'

Eddy waved a hand dismissively. 'This is going to cost us.'

'I've made a list of what we'll need,' Sally said as she produced a sheet of paper from her apron pocket and pushed it across the table.

Running his eyes over the list, Eddy gave a low whistle. 'I ain't sure we can afford this little lot.'

'We'll have to somehow,' Sally said quietly.

Eddy looked into his wife's eyes and knew he had no option – it was time to look for work.

6

Ella worked quietly in the kitchen, thinking how kind the neighbours had been bringing her their old clothes for her to wash and cut up and use in her hat making. Some were beyond redemption, but she had accepted them gratefully nevertheless.

Thomas had ensured the whole district was aware of the enterprise via Mrs Woolley's loose tongue. Hats, caps and coats were piled into an ottoman in her bedroom and Ella had more than enough to be going on with. Her accoutrements, however, were running low and feathers in particular were expensive to buy.

Thomas was binding a lady's top hat crown with a length of mauve silk, which he tied in a neat bow at the back, leaving the remainder to hang just past the shoulder. Every now and then he glanced up at his daughter and saw the worry etching her fine features.

'It will happen – any minute now somebody will hammer on the door,' he said as he picked up a length of ribbon. Pinning as he went, he formed it into a small rose.

'That's clever,' Ella said. 'How it is you know how to do all this?' She spread her arm to encompass the whole table.

'Dunno, gel, seems I just have the knack,' Thomas replied. 'How's about we have a cuppa?'

Ella stood and placed the kettle on the range. Then they heard it – a sharp rap of the knocker. Ella spun round, her eyes as big as saucers meeting those of her father. The sound came again.

'Well, go on before they change their mind!' Thomas urged.

Ella patted her hair and walked swiftly to open the front door.

'Would I be addressing Ella, perchance?' the haughty voice asked.

'Indeed you are, madam. Won't you come in out of the cold?'

Ella led the woman into the sitting room. 'How may I help you?'

'I saw the advertisement in the *Walsall Observer*. I'm looking for a hat for my son's wedding in the summer.'

'How lovely – a wedding. Did you have a particular design in mind, madam?' Ella enquired.

'My name is Eléna Fortescue, m'dear, and no, I hadn't decided.'

'Well, Mrs Fortescue, although my range is limited here, I have a couple you can look at. If you don't see anything you like, we can draw up a design to your own specifications.' Whilst she was speaking, Ella opened a box to reveal a white top hat, the crown of which was wrapped with black open weave lace. The edge of the brim was finished with black ribbon and white feathers were attached to the side.

'Oh, I say! That's rather nice,' Mrs Fortescue gushed.

Ella lifted out another box, which contained a white bowler hat covered in fine cream netting, the front of which formed a short veil. Cream silk roses were placed on the side and two small white ostrich feathers lay lazily between the flowers.

'My word, Ella, these are beautiful!'

'Thank you,' Ella replied, a thrill coursing through her body. 'I have other designs, too.'

For an hour, Mrs Fortescue inspected every ladies' hat Ella had made. Eventually she chose the white bowler.

As Ella boxed it up, Mrs Fortescue said, 'You really should charge more, m'dear. People will pay a fortune for these because there's nothing like it in close proximity. In fact, I'd wager they couldn't be matched even in London.'

'Thank you for the compliment, Mrs Fortescue, and for the advice,' Ella said with a smile. Then she gasped as the woman paid double the asking price.

'Mrs Fortescue, I can't accept...!' Ella began.

'You can and you will. Now increase those prices today because I will be sending my friends here and it's about time they spent some of their money on something worthwhile.'

'Thank you so very much,' Ella said as she saw the woman out.

'Oh, by the way, do you do for men too?' Mrs Fortescue asked as she pulled on her soft leather gloves, the hat box hanging over her arm by its string handle.

'Yes. Top hats, bowlers, caps – I can do them all,' Ella answered.

'Good. I'll send my son along. Expect him tomorrow. Good-bye, dear.' Mrs Fortescue waved as she climbed into a waiting carriage.

Ella waved back and closed the door.

Thomas was there as she turned. 'I told you! And I said you were undercharging!'

Ella laughed and hugged the man she loved with all her heart. 'Thank you for believing in me.'

Pushing the wheelchair back to the kitchen, Ella chatted excitedly to her father about working on some new designs.

It was later in the day when Sally arrived to share her news.

'That's wonderful! Dad, you'll be a grandfather and I'll be an aunt. I'm so pleased for you, Sal,' Ella said as she hugged her sister.

'You don't seem overjoyed about it, Sally,' Thomas said gingerly.

'It's a big responsibility, one I'm not sure I'm ready for,' Sally said by way of explanation.

'You will be by the time the baby comes,' Ella put in.

'How has Eddy taken the news?' Thomas asked.

'Not that well, especially when he saw how much it was going to cost.'

Thomas nodded. He knew Eddy Denton only liked spending money on himself. Even Sally didn't benefit much, as could be seen by her old clothes.

'You'll have to keep an eye out for second-hand stuff like a perambulator,' Thomas suggested.

'Eddy won't stand for that, he'll want all new, I'm sure,' Sally said, pushing her nose in the air in an act of defiance.

'I'll knit some baby clothes for you when I get time,' Ella added.

Sally nodded her thanks as Ella went to answer the knock of an impatient customer.

Returning to the kitchen a while later, she said, 'Another sale!' She noted her sister had left during her absence.

The following morning Ella answered the door to a very handsome young man. He entered the sitting room and glanced around. 'Forgive me, Mother didn't say it was your... sorry.'

Seeing Ella's crestfallen face, he apologised. 'Can we start again? I'm Harper Fortescue and I'm very pleased to meet you, Miss...?'

'Bancroft – please call me Ella,' she said with a smile. 'Now, how can I be of help?'

'I need a topper, Ella – it seems I'm to be married.'

'Seems? Aren't you sure?' Ella asked before she could stop herself.

Harper laughed and began to explain. As he spoke Ella took in his features. Hair so dark as to appear black, he had eyes the colour of molten chocolate and a voice like velvet.

'It's Father's idea and, if I'm to inherit the family money, I have to toe the line.' He gave a shrug.

'I see. I'm sorry, I didn't mean to pry.' It was Ella's turn to apologise.

'So,' Harper said on a drawn-out breath, 'What can you show me?'

Ella gave herself a mental shake when she realised she had been brazenly staring at him.

'Erm, did you have a preference regarding colour?' she asked.

'Isn't there only black?' Harper answered with a question of his own.

'No, you can choose any colour you like. For instance, I have this one.' Ella pulled out the box from the pile on the floor. Taking out a pure white silk top hat she passed it to him.

'Now that's a topper!' Harper said as he plonked it on his head.

Ella giggled as it slipped down to cover his eyes.

Lifting the front with his walking cane, he peeped at her from beneath the brim and his silky voice laughed with her.

Finding a black one, which was smaller, Ella gave it to him to try. It fit much better and he gazed at himself in the mirror on the wall.

'Smart, but I have to say I prefer the white, it's... unusual.' Taking off the hat, he handed it back to her. 'Could I order white in my size?'

'Of course, I'll just have to take your measurements.' Ella was a little flustered and glanced around for her tape measure. As she worked, her heart began to pound; the only man she'd ever been this close to was her father.

Noting down his name and size in her order book, Ella told him the price.

Harper waved a hand and nodded, clearly it was of no consequence. 'Mother showed me her hat, it's beautiful. You are very talented, Ella.'

Flushing to the roots of her hair, Ella mumbled her thanks. 'I can have this ready for you in two weeks' time.'

'Splendid,' Harper answered as he looked around at her display.

'Was there anything else?' Ella asked.

'Hmm? No, thank you. I look forward to our next meeting.' Harper held out his hand and, as Ella extended hers, he turned it over and kissed the back.

Ella's blood rushed through her veins and she smiled timidly.

'Until then,' he said walking through the door Ella held open for him.

'Yes,' she breathed. 'Goodbye, Mr Fortescue.'

Closing the door, she leaned her back against it while she calmed herself. She was totally unaware Thomas had been just the other side of the door to the kitchen and had heard every word. A feeling of unease crawled all over him as he wheeled himself away.

* * *

Whilst Ella had made a few sales in as many days, Ivy Gladwin had seen no customers. Rising early, she decided to change her window display yet again, hoping that it would entice someone to come into the shop.

Ivy worked all morning rearranging hats until at last she was satisfied. Sitting on a stool behind the counter, she fixed her eyes on the window.

Two women stopped to gaze in, and hope rose in her. They chatted and one pointed but the other shook her head and wrinkled her nose. Then they moved on, leaving the shop owner feeling deflated.

Making herself a hot drink, Ivy resumed her counter top vigil. By lunchtime she was bored beyond belief.

The more she thought on it, the more she believed Ella Bancroft was to blame for her shop having no customers. That girl was stealing her clients! It could be the only explanation. She pushed aside the suspicion that it was, perhaps, that her hats were outdated. She didn't want to see that the black and brown felts were dowdy. Ivy had relatively few colourful hats in her range; she'd had no call for them in years gone by. 'Make what you know' had been her mantra and she found no reason to change now.

Her mind on Ella, she wondered what designs the girl was producing. How could she find out without actually visiting to see for herself? Was she displaying? And if so, where? It had to be from the house.

Making her decision, Ivy closed the shop and snatched up her coat. A little foray to Silver Street was called for.

7

Walking the three streets from her shop, Ivy came to the end of Silver Street. Slowly making her way, she glanced right and left. The houses were squeezed together, allowing no light to pass between them. The brickwork was dirty, as were many of the windows. Curtains twitched as eyes peered at the stranger casually strolling along.

Suddenly Ivy found herself outside of Number 24 and she stopped to gaze into the window. Her hat was pulled down low and a scarf covered her mouth and nose to keep out the cold. It also helped to ensure her identity was kept hidden lest she be seen by Ella.

Staring at the contents of the window, Ivy's heart fell to her stomach. How could she compete with this? A black top hat complete with walking cane, gloves and cravat sat centre stage. Next to it was a white sinamay teardrop creation covered in the softest cream net. Small white feathers stood proud at the back with tiny white and cream roses at their base. A folded parasol in cream silk with white lace trim lay beside the hat pedestal. Lying across the umbrella handle were a pair of long white fine lace gloves. To one side was a mauve teardrop bridesmaid's hat to match the bride's, and to the other side a 'mother of the bride' wide-brimmed satin hat in deep plum and white. The whole window screamed spring and summer weddings.

Ivy turned away and walked on, a feeling of abject misery weighing her down.

* * *

For the next couple of days, customers came to Ella and went away happy. During the evenings, she and her father worked furiously in an effort to keep up with demand. Ella wanted to make sure she had enough stock and a good range to present to her callers. Any spare moment was spent thinking up new designs, the sketches of which were kept safely hidden away in a drawer of the small dresser in the kitchen.

Ella was putting on her coat to rush out for more supplies from the haberdashery when a knock came to the back door.

Looking at her father, she saw the colour drain from his face. Opening the door, she was faced with the rent man.

'Come in, please, don't stand out there in the cold,' Ella said.

'Thomas,' the man said with a nod.

'George.'

'Two weeks owing,' the man said as he opened his ledger and laid it on the table.

'Two? I don't understand,' Ella said looking to her father.

'It's right,' Thomas said.

Ella frowned but, not wishing to discuss the reason why in front of the collector, she pulled out the rent card for George to mark it as paid. Then she handed over the amount owed.

'Ta very much. I'll see you next week,' George said as he

dropped the coins into his leather satchel and amended his register.

Closing the door as he left, Ella turned to her father.

'I'm sorry, gel, I was going to tell you but what with us being so busy...' Thomas's voice trailed off.

Ella took off her coat. There was no point in going out now, the money for her supplies had just been given to pay the rent arrears.

'I'm listening,' she said quietly. There was no anger in her voice as she spoke, and sitting at the table she placed her hands in her lap.

'I used the money for the advertisement,' Thomas began. 'I knew we could catch up once the hats started to sell, and I was proved right.'

'But what if they hadn't sold? How would we have managed? Dad, I'm grateful for all you've done for me and are still doing...'

'But?' Thomas interrupted.

'We have to be honest with each other – we must discuss and agree on decisions before they are made,' Ella answered.

'If I had told you what I planned you would have said no, so I went ahead anyway.' Thomas watched his daughter's face crinkle into a tiny smile.

'You're right, I would have said no. So, in the future can we make sure we share the responsibility?' Ella asked.

'Yes. I feel badly that you can't afford your accessories now, but I'm glad the advert served its purpose. By next week the coffers will have swollen enough to get what you need.' Thomas was confident that more clients would rush to purchase the millinery Ella was turning out.

'I hope so. Now I do believe it's your turn to brew up,' Ella said with a cheeky grin.

They were still laughing when Sally bustled in through the back door.

'Something funny?' she asked as she removed her hat and coat.

'No.' Ella glanced at Thomas warning him to keep their discussion to themselves. She didn't want to have to deal with her sister's snide remarks on top of everything else. Besides, it was none of Sally's business.

'Are you making tea?' Sally asked.

'No, I'm not,' Ella answered truthfully.

'I will,' Thomas said as he manoeuvred his chair into place.

Sally sat at the table and glanced around. 'What's this?' she asked, picking up an old drawstring bag.

'It's mine,' Ella said, holding out her hand.

With a snort, Sally handed over the bag and Ella set it on the table next to her cup.

'How are you feeling today?' Thomas asked.

'I'm all right,' Sally answered sullenly. 'Eddy's not happy; he knows he has to go and look for work now so he can support us.' She laid a hand on her stomach as she spoke.

'Quite right, too.' Ella could not restrain herself from making a comment.

Sally shot her a disdainful look but nodded her thanks for the tea passed to her.

'How's your little business going?'

Ella bristled. Yes, it was a *little* business at present, but she felt sure it would take off as soon as she became better known in the town and surrounding areas.

'So far, so good.'

'If I can help in any way, let me know. I would need paying, though, of course,' Sally said.

'We're managing nicely, but thank you for the offer,' Ella

responded. There was no way she would tell her sister she couldn't afford to take on paid workers. Besides, Sally had probably realised this and her comment had been used as a taunt.

There were no more customers during Sally's visit and Ella began to fret, but she made sure she showed no outward signs of her worry.

Eventually Sally donned her outdoor clothing and said her farewells.

When she had gone, Ella picked up the drawstring bag someone had kindly dropped off the day before, and tipped its contents onto the table.

'Dad, look at this.' Ella's fingers spread out the old jewellery. Some of it was broken but usable, the rest could be taken apart easily.

'Blimey!' Thomas said as he placed Ella's freshly made tea next to the glittering hoard.

'This is going to open up a whole new world for our hats,' Ella said. Picking up a cameo brooch, she held it against a piece of fawn material before sticking a brown and cream feather behind it.

'That will work beautifully,' Thomas said. 'What else is there?'

Picking through the assortment, ideas formed and were quickly transferred into sketches. Thomas grabbed his small toolbox from its home under the sink and began to take apart the jewellery.

Ella fetched a lady's black bowler she had recently made, which had been awaiting decoration. Sorting through her collection of feathers, she chose three of roughly the same size; two white and one black. Stitching them onto the side of the bowler in a fan shape, she then picked up a large white stone set in a gold surround. Slipping it from its chain, she gave it a clean before deftly sewing it in place at the base of the feathers. She smiled as the stone shone in the light from the window.

With a satisfied nod, Ella laid the hat on the dresser. She watched as Thomas separated the pieces that could be used. One by one she gave them a good cleaning and threw away the bits left over.

Ella had realised the small teardrop hats were quick and easy to make and she had a number in different materials and colours. Now she had something with which to make them special; to add a touch of class.

She planned to work on these during the afternoon but, as the hours marched on, Ella found she would have no time to do so, for from lunchtime until six o'clock that evening Ella had customers constantly coming through her door.

She was thrilled to have sold so many hats, and as she dropped onto a kitchen chair she was aware she needed to restock, and quickly.

Whilst Ella had been busy with her new clients, Thomas had prepared their evening meal.

'Thanks, Dad, this has saved me a job,' she said as she tucked in hungrily.

Later, as they sat together fiddling with jewels, they discussed how the day had gone.

'I would never have believed it!' Ella said.

'Well, you better had, 'cos I've a feeling it will only get busier.' Thomas grinned as he passed her a brooch of coloured stones set in a flower pattern.

Ella shook her head. 'No, those for this one I think.' Laying a string of fake pearls along the edge of the teardrop point she nodded. Carefully, she pinned them in place and picked up her needle.

Thomas watched as she sewed. 'I'm so very proud of you, Ella.'

'I'm proud of you too, Dad,' Ella said with a beaming smile.

'It won't be long before you own your own shop.'

Ella laughed. 'It will be years, Dad, but I'm happy working here with you.'

'Me, too. Now, don't be too late getting to bed.' Thomas gave his daughter a kiss and headed for the stairs.

Watching him lever himself out of his wheelchair and drag his dead legs up the steps to his bed, Ella thought, *The world would be a much nicer place if there were more in it like my dad!*

* * *

All the time Ella had been seeing to her customers, Ivy Gladwin had sat in her shop, praying for the bell over the door to tinkle. It had not, and as she locked up for the night and retired to her sitting room at the back she sighed loudly.

With no appetite, Ivy made herself a cup of coffee and sat thinking. Rather than make new hats, maybe she could renovate some of those she already had. She couldn't copy Ella's designs exactly, but she could steal a few of the girl's ideas.

Going to the work room and lighting the gas lamp, Ivy grabbed a piece of red woollen cloth and a block. Stretching the fabric over the wood, she shoved hard on the blocking pins. Once steamed into shape, she could put her expertise into action.

For the first time that day, Ivy felt her excitement build. She would produce millinery as good as Ella's, if not better. Then, when she needed fresh inspiration – she would stroll down Silver Street once more.

8

Ella held the finished white top hat she had made for Harper Fortescue close to the window. She felt a sense of pride as the light picked up a shimmer on the silk. Placing it in a box, she tied on the label.

Just then the knocker rapped, making Ella jump. Opening the door, she was surprised to see who stood there.

'Mr Fortescue! I was just thinking about you – please come in.' Ella was suddenly dreadfully flustered.

'I hope they were good thoughts,' Harper said as he stepped inside.

'I wasn't expecting you until next week, sir,' she replied formally.

'I thought I'd pop in and see how you were getting on – with my hat, I mean.'

Harper's honeyed voice seemed to float on the air and Ella caught her breath.

'Actually, it's finished,' she said.

Passing over the box she stood back and waited.

Harper lifted out the hat and held it up to admire. 'Very nice indeed!' Going to the mirror he placed it on his head. 'Perfect.' Checking the price on the label, he drew out his money clip and paid Ella.

'Thank you.' Ella boxed the hat once more and deftly tied it with string. 'I'm glad you like it,' she added.

'I do indeed, I just wish it weren't for... no matter. Have you been busy?' he asked, changing the subject quickly.

Ella nodded. What was it he was about to say? Was it that he wished it were not for his wedding? 'Yes, extremely. I've had customers every day.'

'Well, you will be having more in no time. I believe Mother is bringing her entourage of friends to see you very soon.'

'I look forward to meeting them.' Ella smiled and her hazel eyes glittered in the light. Then she realised Harper was staring at her and she blushed. Taking a quick step backwards she said, 'I hope your wedding goes well and that you will both be very happy.'

'Thank you, but I doubt that we will.' Harper moved to the front door and added, 'I'm sure we will meet again, Ella.' Taking her hand, he kissed the back of it, and then he was gone.

As she closed the door, Ella thought, *I wonder what all that was about.*

For the rest of the day, in her quiet moments Ella's thoughts wandered to Harper Fortescue. Try as she might, she couldn't get him out of her mind. On the periphery of her focus, his velvety voice floated languidly. Occasionally she found herself staring into space and had to snap her attention back to the task in hand.

Thomas had watched his daughter closely since that young man's visit and he was sad to realise his little girl had grown up. When had that happened? How had he missed her transformation into a beautiful young woman? One thing he did know – he would have to be mindful of men now and protect Ella from those who might try to entice her into lying with them before tossing her aside. He prayed that, when the time came, she would choose a good man to be her husband. He wanted for her always to be happy, but somewhere in the back of his mind something told him this would not be the case. He had a feeling Ella would have to fight hard every step of the way to achieve true happiness. Inwardly he frowned. If anyone could do it, Ella could.

* * *

Ivy watched the woman admiring the red hat in the window. *Please come in and buy it*, she thought. As if in answer, the woman entered the shop.

With a smile, Ivy greeted the customer. 'Can I help you, madam?'

'I'm no madam,' the woman said gruffly, 'but you can show me that.' She pointed towards the centre piece.

'Certainly mad...' Ivy lifted out the hat and passed it to the woman.

'I like the colour but I ain't sure about this.' The woman's fingers slid along a large pink feather. 'It's too big for this little Titfer.'

'Excuse me?' Ivy said.

'Titfer tat – hat,' the woman explained.

'Yes, I know what it means, I was just querying why you think the feather is too large.' Ivy was instantly in a huff at the criticism of her work.

''Cos it is, and another thing – red and pink don't exactly go together, do they?' The woman screwed up her face.

'In my opinion they match perfectly,' Ivy bristled.

'Nah, if you take my advice, you'll change your supplier. There's a nice young wench down in Silver Street as meks her own. You could try buying from her. Bostin' designs in her winder.' The woman dropped the red hat on the counter and added, 'I've changed me mind about this'n. I think as I'll go and visit Silver Street instead.'

Ivy's blood boiled as she watched the woman leave her shop, banging the door behind her, causing the little bell to tinkle loudly.

Moving her eyes to the hat, Ivy glared at it. In her mind it was every bit as good as those Ella was producing. However, that customer had thought differently. She placed the hat back in the window. *Well, at least it drew someone in even if it didn't sell*, she thought.

Deciding to work in the back room so she could hear if anyone came into the shop, Ivy reluctantly unpicked the attachments on a few more hats. The massive feathers she was so fond of were put aside and replaced by shorter ones. The huge silk flowers were changed for smaller more delicate ones. Looking at the finished articles, Ivy frowned. They looked bare and, before she could stop herself, she sewed on more and more flowers until they looked like tiny gardens. Happier now, she began to fill the window with her new creations.

Take that, Ella Bancroft! she thought with a perfunctory nod.

Returning to the back room, she continued rejuvenating the old-style millinery.

* * *

Whilst Ivy was up to her eyes in hats and feathers, Ella decided to make a mad dash down to the haberdasher's.

The snow had finally begun to melt, leaving dirty puddles everywhere. Stepping over one such pool, her skirts lifted to avoid wetting the hem, Ella nodded to a chimney sweep who sidestepped out of her way. Soot drifted from the brushes held over his shoulder and landed on the wet cobbles. His face, as black as pitch, split into a wide grin, showing his white teeth.

Hurrying on, Ella heard laughter from children splashing about, heedless of getting soaked through and cold. Horse-drawn carts passed her, and the smell of manure filled her nose. The call of the rag and bone man echoed through the street, which was soon replaced by the steady clip-clop of Shire horses pulling the dray cart loaded with barrels of beer.

Shopping quickly, Ella rushed home for fear of missing customers. Hearing voices as she stepped into the house, she was surprised to see her father in the sitting room surrounded by a gaggle of women. All high society ladies, they were billing and cooing over her latest designs. Thomas, for his part, was pouring out compliments one after another.

'Ah, Ella, there you are,' he said with a smile of pure relief.

Ella greeted her clients and thanked her father as he wheeled himself out of the room, glad to be leaving the ladies to it.

'Mrs Fortescue, it's so nice to see you again,' Ella said.

'Likewise, m'dear. My friends were eager to see what you have on offer.' Pulling a young woman by the arm she continued. 'This is the bride-to-be, Darcie Newland. Darcie, meet Ella Bancroft, the bright new talent in this Godforsaken town.'

'I'm pleased to meet you, Miss Newland,' Ella said.

Darcie nodded and turned back to the hats.

'Don't mind her, she has far too many airs and graces,' Mrs Fortescue muttered as she patted Ella's arm.

'What about this one, Darcie?' one of the other women asked.

Ella watched as Miss Newland shook her head. 'I don't like it. I really don't think there will be anything for me here.' Darcie looked around with a grimace.

'You liked mine well enough,' Mrs Fortescue snapped.

'Yes, but—' Darcie began.

'You thought it had come from a fancy big shop in London, is that it?' Mrs Fortescue cut across.

'Well, I did assume that is where you had purchased it, yes – not from a little backstreet house in Walsall!' Darcie did nothing to hide her disdain.

The other women stared at her, then looked to Mrs Fortescue to intervene. She shook her head very slightly. She wanted to see how Ella dealt with the spiteful Miss Newland.

Ella took the hat Darcie was holding, saying, 'If there's nothing here to suit you, may I suggest you try elsewhere!' Feeling cut to the quick, Ella turned away to hide the tears stinging her eyes.

'I'm sure the quality will be better in London or even Birmingham. It might be as well to look there.' Darcie turned to the others for support. 'Don't you think?'

The two friends exchanged a glance then one said, 'Do what you like, Darcie, but I'm having this one.'

'And I'm buying this,' the other said.

Ella grinned. 'Thank you, ladies, both wonderful choices.' Turning to Darcie, she added, 'I can see why you are unable to shop here, and forgive me for saying so but the shape of your head is rather... unusual.'

Mrs Fortescue threw back her head and let out a great belly laugh. 'That told you, Miss High and Mighty!'

Ella struggled to conceal her own mirth as she boxed the other ladies' purchases and took their money gratefully.

Darcie harrumphed and headed for the door.

'Miss Newland, I must apologise. That was very rude of me,' Ella called out.

'I should think so, too.' The haughty voice was sharp as the young woman turned on Ella. 'That's certainly no way to treat your customers!'

'I agree and I'm sorry. However, I have to add that, firstly, you are not one of my customers as you haven't purchased anything, and, secondly, you too were very rude. There is nothing wrong with this little backstreet house, it's where I grew up in a loving family.' Ella held her temper in check as she spoke.

'Bravo!' Mrs Fortescue gushed and clapped her gloved hands.

Thomas, hiding behind the door to the kitchen which stood ajar, shoved a fist into his mouth to prevent himself laughing loudly. *Go on my girl, you put her straight!*

Miss Newland snorted. 'I come from money, Miss Bancroft, something you wouldn't understand.'

'*New* money,' Mrs Fortescue intervened. 'It really doesn't count. You have to come from *old* money as we do to have any influence around here.'

Ella clamped her teeth together in an effort not to gloat.

'My father owns a string of businesses, as well you know!' Darcie was furious at being humiliated in front of everyone.

'I do indeed. I also know he raised a spoilt brat for a daughter. Now, ladies, if you have all you need, I suggest we leave Ella to *her* business.' Turning to the girl in question as Darcie silently fumed, Mrs Fortescue continued, 'Thank you m'dear, I shall ensure more of my friends visit your delightfully quaint establishment.' There was no disdain in her words as Mrs Fortescue ushered the women to the door. While they filed out, she turned to Ella and said in a whisper, 'Well done! It's nice to see that one put soundly in her place.' With that she strode away, leaving Ella feeling more than a little relieved.

Closing the door, Ella turned to see her father there. 'I wish you wouldn't keep creeping up on me,' she said with a start.

'I can't creep anywhere with these,' Thomas said patting his knees. 'Good on yer, girl, you certainly showed her!'

'I'm afraid I was rude and it may have cost me more custom,' Ella replied as she pushed the wheelchair into the kitchen.

'It won't, lass, have no fear on that score. I will say this, though, you've made an enemy of that one, so beware.'

Ella nodded with a sigh. 'I'll have to get cracking – I need to replace those two hats I sold today.' She may well be at odds with Darcie Newland but felt gratified she apparently had an ally in Eléna Fortescue.

'I'll make a cuppa,' Thomas answered.

As he clattered cups on saucers, his mind went over the previous conversations. Miss Darcie Newland could cause major problems for Ella if she were of a mind. She could spread gossip detrimental to their little business, then where would that leave them? Despite his worry, Thomas was proud of his daughter and of how she wouldn't be put on by the likes of that sharp-tongued young woman.

Whatever happened, Thomas would always support his girl – she and Sally were the only things in the world he loved more than life itself.

9

Harper Fortescue sat in the parlour of The Cedars, his parents' large house across town. He stared out of the window at the looming dark clouds threatening more rain. He welcomed the bad weather; it suited his mood. It also meant the summer would be a while in coming. That would be the time he would have to sign his life away to a woman he didn't love. If truth be told, he wasn't sure he even liked Darcie Newland very much.

The girl he was to wed had been ruined by her parents. They had given in to her every whim and desire. When she had shown an interest in Harper, her folks had approached his with the proposal of a wedding.

He had protested loudly but to no avail. It was a good match, his father had said. Harper had refused point blank to be tied to someone he barely knew, and that was when the ultimatum came. Marry Darcie Newland or he would be disinherited.

His father's words sounded again in his mind. *The Newland businesses will be yours one day... It's all arranged now... If you don't wed the girl then I'll cut you off without a penny!*

Harper was under no illusions; he had no idea how to survive without having cash at his fingertips whenever he needed it. Therefore, having no inheritance would mean he would need to work. And with no useful training it would be impossible to find a position of employment. Besides, he enjoyed immensely the things money could buy. He revelled in being able to attend balls, parties and soirees, as well as mixing with the higher echelons of society.

Would it be such a bad thing to marry Darcie? She was pretty, he couldn't deny that, but her whining when she wanted her own way would soon wear him down. He would be very rich in his own right once her parents had passed, but was that a big enough prize to set him on the road to eternal misery?

Now, if it were someone like Ella Bancroft he was betrothed to, Harper would have been elated. There she was, the milliner, in his thoughts again. He had tried to dismiss her from his mind, but she would rise unbidden when he least expected it. He constantly compared Darcie to the young beauty with the gold-flecked eyes. In his opinion, the hat-maker won hands down every time.

An image formed as he closed his eyes and he smiled. Her dark hair shone, and her voice was soft and gentle. Other than her profession he knew nothing about her. What he *did* know, however, was that his heart rate increased rapidly when he was in her presence.

Harper had realised he was trying to find reasons to visit her again, hence his calling early to see his top hat. He could, of course, order new hats, and if he had them made to measure then maybe there would be fitting sessions.

Opening his eyes, he jumped.

'Daydreaming again, Harper?' his mother asked.

'Oh, Mother! You gave me a start. How was your shopping trip?'

Over tea Eléna regaled her son with the tale at Ella's house. Harper grinned. 'So, Miss Bancroft has backbone, then.' *Yet another thing to admire her for*, he thought.

'Definitely,' Eléna said as she poured herself more tea. 'I do so like the girl and her talents with millinery are beyond compare. In fact, I think I shall call again tomorrow and buy myself a few more of her fabulous hats.'

'May I come with you? I was thinking to replace my bowler and maybe get a boater while I'm at it,' Harper said.

'Good idea, my boy,' Eléna said as she picked up the newspaper.

Harper smiled, and as he enjoyed his tea he allowed his thoughts to centre once more on the delightful Miss Bancroft.

* * *

The following morning, Darcie Newland was most put out. 'Why are you visiting that dreadful little place again?' She had arrived unexpectedly at The Cedars, hoping Harper would treat her to lunch somewhere expensive.

'I have to replace my old hats,' Harper said simply. Grabbing his outdoor coat, he added, 'I'm sorry you've had a wasted journey. Had you let me know you were coming...' He allowed his sentence to drift away into nothing.

'I'm here now! You could go shopping another day!' Darcie snapped.

'I'm afraid it's all arranged; I'm going with Mother.' Harper raised his eyebrows as he strode past her towards the parlour door.

'Harper! What about me?' Darcie whined.

'Go home and I'll see you – whenever,' Harper replied. As he stepped into the hallway, he heard the girl stamp her foot in temper and he rolled his eyes. With every meeting he grew more frustrated with his betrothed. He was ever more sure that the whole idea of marriage to Darcie would be the biggest mistake of his life.

Following him into the foyer, Darcie was fuming at being treated so badly. She saw Eléna standing at the mirror hung on the wall, where she was stabbing a long pin through her hat and into her neatly piled hair.

'Ready, Harper?' Eléna asked and as she turned, she saw Darcie. 'Oh, hello dear, I didn't realise you were here. We're just on our way out...'

'So Harper tells me!' Darcie cut across sharply. 'He told me to go home!'

'Very good,' Eléna said absent-mindedly. Pulling on her gloves she added, 'Our carriage awaits, Harper.'

'Coming, Mother,' Harper replied as he picked up his silver-topped walking cane.

'Harper!' Darcie's voice rose an octave.

Harper sighed. 'Look, why don't you come along with us?'

'To that – backstreet house?' Darcie wrinkled her nose.

'Please yourself, but I'm going with Mother,' Harper said as he held the front door open for Eléna.

'Do stop bickering, children, and let's get on, for goodness' sake.' Eléna climbed into the carriage and settled herself, closing her eyes tight as she heard Darcie screech for them to wait – she would be joining them after all.

As the wheels rumbled over the cobblestones, Eléna eyed the girl sat opposite her. Was it fair to condemn her son to a life with Darcie? The animus radiating from the girl was palpable and Eléna knew she and her son were completely incompatible. Looking at Harper, she wondered if she could persuade his father to free him from the engagement. If not, did she have the courage to stand against her husband for the sake of her boy?

The carriage drew to a halt and in a matter of moments all three stood in Ella's front room.

'It's lovely to see you again – and so soon!' Ella gushed before her eyes landed on Darcie. 'Please make yourselves at home.'

Darcie sniffed and remained by the door.

'Is there anything I can show you, Miss Newland?' Ella asked, feeling decidedly uncomfortable under the woman's gaze.

'No!' Darcie snapped and turned her head towards Harper. Her breath caught in her throat as she saw the look on his face. He was blatantly staring at the milliner. Striding over to him, she threaded her arm through his, her nose in the air.

Ella smiled inwardly. The girl was jealous and had felt the need to make sure Ella knew Harper was her man and belonged solely to her.

Harper extricated himself from his fiancée's firm grip and moved to Ella. 'I find myself in need of a new bowler, and a boater also.' He smiled widely as he took in her fine features.

'Certainly. I have your measurements, but I'll show you what I have.' Ella returned his smile and went to the pile of boxes in the corner.

Despite looking at the hats on show, nothing had escaped Eléna and she smiled. It was evident that Ella was attracted to her son, and that it was reciprocated. It was also clear that Darcie was aware of the fact. She watched as Harper admired the hats Ella produced. They chatted quietly and stood just a little too close as Ella adjusted the boater on Harper's head. She saw their fingers linger on a touch as he passed the hat back. Then she heard a loud sigh and her eyes moved to Darcie, who was tapping her foot.

'Do hurry up, Harper, then we can go on to have lunch!' Darcie's words were sharp.

'I did suggest you go home,' he answered as he tried on a black bowler.

Ella turned her attention to Eléna. 'Can I help you with anything, Mrs Fortescue?' she asked, pointedly ignoring the petulant girl.

'I'll just try a few before I decide,' Eléna said.

'That bowler makes you look like an old man, darling,' Darcie said. 'It's not – right. It just isn't you.'

Ella bristled but kept her counsel.

As Harper tried the boater again, Ella saw Darcie shake her head. 'I don't think so.'

'What's wrong now?' Harper asked exasperatedly.

'It looks cheap,' Darcie replied spitefully.

Ella clamped her teeth together rather than lose her temper.

'Well, I like it.' Harper smiled at Ella. 'Now what else do you have?'

Pulling out a stovepipe she passed it to her customer.

'Oh my goodness! Harper, you can't buy that!' Darcie was aghast.

'Why not?' Harper asked.

'I will not be seen out with you wearing such a monstrosity!' Darcie replied sharply.

'Then I'll take one and you can stay at home,' Harper said flippantly.

'Harper!' Darcie was furious at being humiliated yet again.

Ella added the order to the others, trying to suppress the mirth threatening to erupt.

'What do you think to this one, Harper?' Eléna asked.

'It's awful, Eléna, surely you can see that,' Darcie put in.

'Did I ask for your opinion?' Seeing the girl shake her head Eléna went on, 'Exactly! Box it, Ella, if you would be so kind.'

For an hour Ella was the perfect saleswoman and orders were given. She had tried her best to include Darcie, but the girl was having none of it and eventually Ella gave up. If Darcie wanted to sulk, then let her. Ella was too busy pleasing her best customers to care.

With thanks, Ella saw her clients out. Harper kissed her hand and her heart hammered. Darcie was irate at the open display of affection and stamped to the waiting carriage. Eléna grinned at the girl's childish behaviour as she bid Ella farewell.

10

'Shall we drop you at Dundrennan House?' Harper asked as the carriage rolled away.

'I don't want to go home!' Darcie wailed.

The large house was set back from Wednesbury Road and stood in its own gardens. Darcie's parents had bought it from its previous owner Mr Enoch Evans, having paid over the odds for it. Immediately her mother had set about redecorating it in the most ostentatious and gaudy fashion.

'I had thought we might take luncheon in Birmingham,' Darcie added.

'Cook will have prepared our lunch,' Eléna said as she stared out of the coach window, 'so I suggest you do return home.' With that, Eléna banged on the coach roof, having snatched Harper's cane. 'Dundrennan House please, my good man!'

Darcie glared at Eléna who was passing the cane back to her son. 'Harper?' she asked pleadingly.

'Best do as Mother says,' he replied and patted her hand.

The rest of the journey passed in silence and on reaching its destination the carriage drew to a halt. Darcie alighted, saying, 'Will I see you tomorrow, Harper?'

'No, I have things to do,' he replied and banged on the roof telling the driver to move on.

Darcie sniffed and ran down the driveway. Harper closed his eyes and sighed audibly. Eléna watched her boy and saw the stress on his face as he tried to relax. This couldn't go on, she decided, it was time to speak with his father about finding a way of releasing Harper from the terrible predicament he was facing. It wouldn't be easy and Eléna knew she would have to present a very strong case if she was to help her boy.

Glancing out of the window once more, she set her thoughts in motion. One way or another she would see Harper free of Darcie's clutches and if it caused a scandal – so be it.

* * *

Sitting in the kitchen, Ella's mind was reliving Harper's fingers touching hers; his smile which lit up his face, and his kiss on the back of her hand. She felt her stomach flip as she remembered his dark eyes, which seemed to burn into her very soul.

A small piece of crin in her hands, Ella absentmindedly pulled a thread at the corner. Seeing it begin to ruffle she did the same on the other side. Pulling both tight together she tied three little knots. Liking the effect, she wondered what to do with it now. Her mind once again on Harper Fortescue, she subconsciously started picked at the loose edge. Eventually the crin looked like fronds waving in the wind. Stitching it onto the side of a teardrop hat she smiled. It gave a softness which would frame the face beautifully and was a lovely alternative to feathers. The stitches were hidden beneath a small cameo brooch sewn carefully in place.

'That's gorgeous!' Thomas said.

'Hmm,' Ella replied.

'Ella, it wouldn't work sweet'eart.'

'What wouldn't?' Ella asked as she glanced up at her father.

'You and him – he's engaged already.' Thomas spoke quietly.

'I don't know what you mean,' Ella replied. But, of course, she knew exactly who and what Thomas was referring to.

'He's middle-class, gel, and we're not. I don't mean to upset you, but you have to see that his parents would never allow it.' Thomas sighed as he watched his girl.

'I know, Dad, and I—' Ella began.

'Have to forget him and concentrate on the business,' Thomas cut in quickly.

Ella nodded. She knew her father was right, but pushing Harper from her mind was proving very difficult. She was well aware of the different social status and his being betrothed, but her heart told her she was in love. And, at that moment, she felt she could never care for another in the same way.

'That's my girl. Now, what to do with this?' Thomas asked as he waved a large feather beneath her chin.

Ella laughed as it tickled her, then said, 'It would be more fitting on one of Ivy's hats, I think.'

'I agree.' Thomas laid the feather on the table before they continued with their work, both lost in their own thoughts.

* * *

Over at Dundrennan House, Darcie Newland was banging around in her bedroom. She was still seething about being dismissed by Harper and his mother. They had not even invited her to lunch with them; instead they had sent her home like a naughty child. Well, that would all change once she and Harper were married. She fully intended to put her foot down and rule her own household with a firm hand. The thought made her smile, but her happiness quickly disappeared as her mind moved to the milliner.

Darcie had caught the look that had passed between Harper and the girl and she bristled. Harper's roving eye needed to be addressed – and soon. In fact, when she saw Harper next, she would take him to task about it. She would remind him that he was soon to be a husband and should be acting respectfully towards her.

Recalling the visit to Silver Street, Darcie saw in her mind's eye Harper and Ella laughing together. That was something else she'd put a stop to – his shopping at the dreary little house. In future they would purchase items together in Birmingham or London, and Harper *would* take her advice regarding what suited him and what did not.

Glancing into the long cheval mirror, Darcie ran her hands down her body. Turning this way and that, she smiled. She was beautiful, there was no denying it, and it was time Harper paid her a little more attention. He would, too, providing she kept him away from that milliner.

Each time she thought of Ella, she felt the jealousy burn. Was this how it would be for the rest of her life? Would she be suspicious of Harper throughout their marriage? What if his eye continued to rove? She would just have to ensure that it didn't.

Patting her fair hair into place, she thought, *We will be happy together, I'm certain. How could Harper not be when he'll be married to me?*

Turning away from the mirror, Darcie decided to take tea in the parlour with her mother. She could see how the hunt for a house for the couple was progressing; it was to be a wedding gift from her parents.

Bright and early the following morning, Darcie arrived at The Cedars. She was shown into the dining room, where Harper was enjoying his breakfast.

'You're up and around early today,' he said by way of a greeting, although he kept his eyes on his boiled egg.

Darcie smiled. 'I wanted to catch you before you left to do – whatever you have planned.'

Harper sighed and his eyes moved to Eléna, who folded the newspaper and picked up her coffee cup. 'Good morning, Darcie,' she said before taking a sip.

'Hello, Eléna. I thought I should tell you that Mother thinks she may have found us a house, Harper.' Darcie removed her gloves and sat at the table, then poured herself a cup of tea.

Eléna raised her eyebrows at the girl's forthright manner. 'Help yourself,' she said pointedly. The sarcasm was missed by Darcie but Harper grinned.

'The old vicarage has come onto the market and Mother is sure it will suit our needs!' Darcie was excited about the prospect of being mistress in her own home.

'When I leave this house, it will be to live in one I have chosen for myself,' Harper said with quiet authority.

'But Harper, Mother has spent so long looking...' Darcie began.

Harper held up his hand. 'Stop! Darcie, understand me now, I will not have your mother interfering in my life!'

'I can't believe you're saying this!' Darcie retaliated.

'Well, you'd better, and I suggest you go home right now and tell your mother exactly what I've said.' Harper's temper began to rise as did his voice.

Eléna's eyes flicked from face to face as she watched the argument rage.

'But that's so ungrateful, Harper! We are to be married in a matter of months and as yet we have nowhere to reside!' Darcie's whining tone was grating on Harper and he pushed his plate away, his peaceful breakfast time ruined.

Closing his eyes, he breathed through flared nostrils as he endeavoured to keep his anger in check. Then, looking at the girl, who was dabbing at her eyes, he drew a breath. 'Stop snivelling, woman! I am telling you now, Darcie, if you and your mother continue to try to run my life, there will be no wedding!'

Eléna almost choked on her coffee, drawing both sets of eyes to her. With a napkin to her mouth she coughed, then waved a hand to say all was well.

The betrothed couple's eyes returned to each other, then Darcie burst into tears. Harper threw down his napkin and got to his feet. 'I can't be dealing with this right now, I have an urgent appointment.' He marched from the room and, grabbing his hat and coat, he left the house. He was going somewhere he knew he would be made welcome; to someone who would make him feel so much better.

'Come on, it's time you went home,' Eléna said as she helped Darcie to her feet. Leading the sobbing girl from the room, she inwardly praised her son for standing his ground. The more time went on, the more Eléna knew the marriage would be a very big mistake.

11

Meanwhile, in Silver Street, Ella gather-stitched a piece of net around the edges and pulled. Binding off, she spread out the gathering evenly and sewed it in place. The cream netting formed a birdcage veil, and over the stitches she glued a few small feathers, which she stripped to leave only the tips. Running her thumb and forefinger along the feathers' spines, she smiled as they curved gently. A silk flower, small and delicate, was attached to cover the base of the feathers. Perfect. Happy with her creation, she placed it in the window to be admired by passers-by.

She'd had her mind on Harper Fortescue and was hoping it wouldn't be too long before she saw him again. Every time someone knocked on the door, Ella's heart leapt with excitement. Despite the disappointment of it not being Harper on her doorstep, she greeted her customers with enthusiasm.

It was mid-morning when Ella's patience was rewarded. Opening the door, she flushed as she ushered Harper into the small sitting room.

'It's so nice to see you,' Ella said truthfully. 'If you'd be kind enough to wait for just a moment...' Ella held out a hand to indicate her latest customer.

Harper smiled and nodded.

Going back to the woman, who couldn't make up her mind between two black hats, Ella asked, 'Are we any closer to a decision, Mrs Grainger?'

'Nah, not really, wench.'

'I see. May I ask what the occasion is?' Ella was trying to concentrate but all the time she could feel Harper's eyes on her and it made her shiver with delight.

'Funeral,' the woman answered.

'Oh, I'm so sorry,' Ella was wishing she'd never asked.

'I ain't. It's my brother-in-law and he's died not before bleedin' time if you ask me. Had I had my way we'd have planted him years ago!' Mrs Grainger shook her head.

Ella exchanged a brief glance with a grinning Harper.

'Any road up, I like this 'un, but I can't afford it.' Mrs Grainger plonked the hat in question on her head.

'If I may be so bold,' Harper cut in, 'I feel sure it will get lots of attention.'

Mrs Grainger frowned at the young man addressing her.

'A lady of your tender years is bound to have use of a black hat for a very long time to come, also.'

Mrs Grainger smiled as she placed the hat on the counter. 'Charming as well as a looker; hang on to him, gel, you have a good 'un there.'

'Oh, I... it's...' Ella spluttered.

What made the woman think that Harper was her sweetheart? How had she reached that conclusion?

'I keep telling her the same thing,' Harper said with a cheeky smile.

'Right, I'd better take the cheaper one 'cos my pennies won't stretch.' Mrs Grainger placed her money on the table and glanced longingly at the more expensive hat.

'Mrs Grainger, I have a favour to ask,' Ella said. At the woman's nod, she went on as she placed the favourite hat in a box. 'Please don't tell anyone what you paid for this.' Passing the box to her client, Ella smiled.

'Ooh, gel! You're a bloody diamond! I won't breathe a word, except to say where I bought it, of course.' Mrs Grainger's laugh echoed around the room as she accepted the box. Turning to Harper she added, 'Wed this lass afore she changes her mind.' Then, with grateful thanks, she was gone.

Closing the door, Ella turned to face Harper and both burst out laughing. Composing herself, Ella said, 'I'm sorry about that. Now, what can I do for you?'

'As I'm here I'd best buy another hat.'

Ella nodded as she went to the stack of boxes in the corner. Surely that was why he'd come here in the first place, wasn't it? Or was there another reason? Had he come to see her? Dismissing the thought as wishful thinking, Ella placed the boxes on the table.

'How is your mother – and Miss Newland?' Ella asked as she watched him examine her products again.

'I've left them both at home. I had to get out of the house.' Harper glanced at the dark-haired girl as he realised what he'd said. 'I must apologise, I'm sure you don't want to hear about my problems. Now, what about this?' Placing the other black lady's hat on his head he turned this way and that.

Ella howled with laughter at his antics and removed the hat to re-box it.

'You have a lovely laugh,' Harper said suddenly.

Flushing scarlet, Ella mumbled her thanks. Her heart was beating rapidly and her stomach felt all fluttery.

'I shouldn't have come, I'm sorry, Ella. I didn't mean to make you feel uncomfortable.' Harper made to leave when Ella spoke.

'Mr Fortescue, forgive my asking but – what's wrong?'

Before he knew what was happening, Harper's words poured out in a rush. He told her about the marriage of convenience to a girl he could never love. He explained about the contretemps regarding the house her mother had found for them to live in. Dragging his hands through his hair he finished with, 'I don't know what to do!'

Ella had listened with mounting sorrow for the young man she had fallen in love with. Her heart ached for his distress, but more for knowing she could never have him. The social divide was too great. And he was betrothed to another, whether he liked it or not, and the thought chipped Ella's armour; the protections with which she had tried to surround herself.

'A cup of tea might help,' she said not knowing how else to deal with the distraught fellow. 'Come through and meet my father, maybe he can advise you.'

Ella led Harper into the kitchen and introduced him to Thomas.

'Sir, it's my pleasure,' Harper said as they shook hands.

'Sit you down, lad. Ella, tea and cake please,' Thomas said as he eyed the young man. 'Now then, I heard what you said…'

'Dad!' Ella snapped.

'Ella, you're my girl and it ain't fitting for you to be alone with a man, no matter the reason,' Thomas said as he turned his upper body to look at her.

'Quite right Mr Bancroft,' Harper concurred.

Ella sighed and Thomas nodded.

'Tell me, why was this marriage arranged for you, then? Don't your folks trust you to find your own wife?'

Harper knew it was no good to lie as Thomas had already

overheard everything. Taking a deep breath, he plunged in. 'They think it a good match for our family. Her father has a string of businesses which would come to me eventually.'

'And how do you feel about that?' Thomas asked.

'I don't care about it, sir, I just want to marry for love and be happy.' Harper's eyes flitted to Ella as he spoke.

The movement was not lost on Thomas who said, 'Call me Thomas, lad. What happens if you don't marry your intended?'

'Father will cut me off without a penny.'

'That's a bit harsh.' Both men nodded their thanks to Ella for the tea placed before them. 'So, I expect you'll be chucked out with no money, nowhere to live and without a chance of work, am I right?'

'Yes, sir – Thomas, that's about the long and short of it.' Harper said, looking forlorn.

Thomas blew out his cheeks and, lifting his flat cap, he scratched his head before replacing it.

'Well, you're in a proper pickle and no mistake. Seems to me you have to decide between money and matrimony; possible destitution and freedom.' Thomas raised his eyebrows as he sipped his hot tea with a slurp.

'Indeed. If I call off the engagement there would bound to be a scandal which would put my parents in an awkward position to say the least.' Harper pursed his lips in consternation.

'True. But the thing about all this is – your parents ain't got to marry that termagant!' Thomas said sharply.

Harper laughed loudly. 'I see you've met the lady in question, then.'

'I've heard her and that was enough for me,' Thomas replied.

'Dad, you shouldn't be...' Ella began.

'Look, gel, you brought him in here for my advice, did you not?' Seeing Ella nod, he continued. 'I don't pull my punches, lad,

I say it like it is. I can't tell you what to do but think on this. If you wed that girl you'll be a long time in misery afore you're dead. Yes, you'll have money and lots of it by the sound of things, but is that enough to be unhappy for the rest of your life? And another thing – you'll have to father an heir. How do you feel about that?'

Ella gasped at the forthright question, and felt the heat rising to her cheeks.

Harper shuddered. 'That's something I hadn't thought about.'

'Once you're in that situation, there would be no way of finding the love of your life like I did, and there's not a day I don't miss my beloved wife,' Thomas said quietly.

Harper saw the sadness cross the face of the man who was speaking so much sense. 'I'm sorry for your loss.'

Thomas nodded. 'You need to weigh all these things up and soon. Once you've made your decision you have to stick to it.'

Harper sighed audibly. 'Thank you both for the refreshments and the wise words. I apologise for invading your private space and unloading my problems upon you both,' he said as he got to his feet.

'You're welcome, any time. Look after yourself, young man,' Thomas answered as they shook hands once more.

'I'll see you out,' Ella said.

Thomas watched them go, a heavy feeling descending on him. There would be trouble there, as well as scandal, and without her even being aware of it, his daughter would be the catalyst.

12

Ivy Gladwin fiddled with a piece of grosgrain before throwing it down in temper. She had sold nothing all week and the worry lines showed clearly on her face. Putting the kettle on to boil she thought back to her trip down Silver Street. Another beautiful hat was displayed in all its glory in Ella's window – how had the girl produced the fronds on that cream centrepiece?

The girl had a natural talent for millinery, there was no disputing that, and Ivy was the one suffering. She was willing to bet Ella Bancroft was not in the same predicament as herself. She was certain that girl's sales must be through the roof.

Making tea, she wandered back into the shop and looked around. What more could she do to draw custom in? Placing the cup and saucer on the counter, she stared at the shelves lined with boxes.

Ivy considered; she had money in the bank so she could shut the shop and retire, but then what would she do with herself? If she didn't work she'd go mad with loneliness. She could sell up and move away, but having no family she would still be on her own. No, somehow she had to make her business begin to pay once more.

Grabbing a shawl, she stepped outside to look at her window display again. Maybe inspiration would strike. Staring at her hats, Ivy had no idea how to show them off any better.

She heard a voice as she shivered in the chilly wind whistling down the street.

'Bloody freezing again, ain't it?'

Ivy turned to face the woman who spoke. 'It is indeed.'

'You gonna buy that red monstrosity, then?' the woman asked, tilting her head towards the window.

Shaking her head, Ivy bristled at the woman's description.

'Don't blame yer, it's bloody awful.'

'Can I ask what you don't like about it?' Ivy asked, full of indignation.

'It would be easier to ask what I *do* like about it and my answer would be – nothing.' The woman screwed up her nose. 'Red and pink together – nah, and that feather is all wrong. There's too many flowers an' all, it looks like a bleedin' allotment! Well, I ain't got time to stand here yakking. Ta-ra.' The woman hurried away, leaving Ivy feeling cut to the quick.

Rushing inside, she snatched the hat out of the display and, grabbing a pair of scissors, she cut it to shreds in a rage. Looking at the bits lying on the floor, she felt the tears sting her eyes.

'Bugger, bugger, bugger!' she said as she slammed the scissors on the counter. Dropping onto the chair reserved for customers, she allowed the hot tears to roll down her cold cheeks.

A short while later, Ivy swept up the mess littering the floor and then searched for something to replace the destroyed hat.

Sitting in the back room, Ivy glanced at the frippery lying on the table. What did Ella have that she didn't? Why did people prefer Ella's hats to her own?

Picking up a large peacock feather, Ivy brushed it against her cheek and revelled in the feel of it. Ella's millinery didn't sport much in the way of decoration. Was that the answer? The edict of 'less is more' came to mind but Ivy couldn't allow herself to believe it was that simple. There had to be more to the fact that Ella was selling more hats than she was, and Ivy determined to discover just what her secret was.

* * *

In the parlour of Dundrennan House, Darcie was wailing loudly. Her mother, Verity, was doing her level best to calm her daughter down.

'It doesn't matter, darling. If Harper wishes to choose your house then so be it.'

'Mother! He was so rude! He all but threw me out! If I disagree he'll call off the wedding!' Darcie paced the floor twisting her handkerchief in her hands.

'Sweetheart, you know Daddy would never let that happen. Now, sit down and stop worrying,' Verity said soothingly.

Darcie threw herself into a large, overstuffed armchair with an explosive sigh.

'That's better. Now, how about we go shopping for your wedding gown while we wait for Daddy to come home?' Verity clapped her hands like a young child.

'No, I'm not in the mood. I want Daddy to take Harper to task about the way he treats me. He must be made to understand that my happiness is paramount.' Darcie's mouth turned down in a sulk.

'Of course it is, darling, and I'm sure your father will do as you ask. Now come, let's go and spend some of Daddy's money.

That always makes you feel better.' Verity got to her feet in a gesture of brooking no more argument.

Harper, in the meantime, was gazing out of the parlour window of The Cedars. Nature was still in slumber, but it wouldn't be long before she awoke and the cycle of new life would begin again once more.

With a sigh, Harper knew he would have to tackle his father regarding the forthcoming wedding. He slammed his bunched fist on his knee as he thought, *I cannot marry Darcie Newland!*

Rafe Fortescue would rant and rave when he learned his son was reneging on his promise, but Harper would have to grin and bear it. He could put forth his reasons and hope his father would understand. The questions that plagued him were whether firstly to mention Ella Bancroft, and then tell his parents she was the one for him. If he were to wed anyone it would be Ella, otherwise he would remain a bachelor, he was sure of that now. And if that was the case, that would mean there would be no grandchildren for his parents to dote on and he wondered how that would affect them. He was sure his mother would be bitterly disappointed, but would the threat bring Eléna round to his way of thinking, and would his father care? Surely she knew Harper was not in love with Darcie, so whose side would she take – her son's or her husband's?

Harper watched the wisps of smoke drifting from the chimneys of the houses that lined the tramway across the patch of heathland. The people living in those dwellings had little money, but Harper was willing to bet they were happier than he was at this precise moment.

Dragging a hand through his thick dark hair, Harper was dreading having dinner with his parents that evening for that would be the time to tell them. All together over a meal – the perfect opportunity to inform them he was breaking his engagement to Darcie Newland and hang the consequences. He snatched up the newspaper in the hope of taking his mind off his predicament for a while.

* * *

That afternoon brought Royston Newland on an unexpected visit. Tall and austere, his hair was as black as a raven's wing. His eyes were brown but so dark as to appear black, and his moustache and beard were neatly trimmed.

Harper welcomed the man and called for high tea to be brought down to them.

'It must be something important for you to call on me mid-afternoon,' Harper said as they settled themselves in the parlour.

'I consider it to be,' Royston answered.

The two men eyed each other in silence as the maid delivered tea and cake.

Once the girl had left the room, Harper poured the tea and spoke again. 'What can I do for you?'

Accepting the cup and saucer with a nod of thanks, Royston answered, 'Darcie and her mother called into my office today whilst out on a shopping trip.'

Harper thought he knew what was coming, but held his tongue and waited.

'Darcie is unhappy at the way she is being treated by you, Harper. She tells me you dismiss her like an errant child.'

Harper inclined his head and sipped his tea.

'Therefore, I have come to warn you that this behaviour simply cannot go on,' Royston added.

'Forgive my forthright manner, Royston, but I speak as I find. Darcie is a spoilt young woman; used to having her own way at all times. Now, I tell you – it simply cannot go on.' Harper's eyebrows raised as he watched the man inwardly fume at his audacity.

'You choose to mock me in the face of my daughter's distress?'

'Not at all, I am merely pointing out the root of the problem. If I am to marry Darcie then she will have to change her ways.'

'In what way, pray tell?' Royston asked endeavouring to control his temper and so keep the meeting as civil as possible.

'Darcie only ever thinks of herself; what she wants and how to go about getting it. She never once considers anyone else or their feelings. She is rude and spiteful, and doesn't take the time to consider facts and others' opinions before making a judgement,' Harper replied as he picked out a small coconut cake from the array on the three-tiered stand.

Royston cleared his throat noisily. 'Verity and I brought Darcie up to be a strong character and to take no nonsense from those of a lower class.'

Harper saw in an instant where Darcie had inherited her haughtiness from.

'Well, it would seem you did a fine job in that regard.' Harper saw a tiny smile grace the lips of the man sat opposite him before a roaring fire. 'However, Darcie appears unable to know when the time is right for her to – how can I put this? Well, to shut up.'

Royston's nostrils flared as he drew in a long breath. 'How dare you speak about my daughter in such a way?'

'My apologies if you see it as an insult but I assure you it was not meant that way. I see it as speaking the truth and if that hurts...' Harper allowed the sentence to go unfinished.

'You will treat Darcie with more respect in the future, young man!' Royston retorted.

'Or what?' Harper asked sharply. 'As I recall it, it was you who approached my father regarding this wedding.'

'You agreed to it!' Royston exploded.

'Ah, in point of fact that was also my father – not me,' Harper said with a shrug of his shoulders.

'What are you saying? Do you intend to *jilt* my daughter? Because should that be the case—'

Harper held up a hand forestalling the other man's outpouring. 'I'm telling you now so you are under no illusions that I will put up with Darcie's malicious tongue and frightful paroxysms of weeping. When she is my wife she will do as she is told or she will be returned to your care.'

Royston scowled, placing his cup and saucer on a small side table. Then he rounded on Harper. 'You wouldn't dare!'

'Let her push me further and you will see exactly what I dare to do,' Harper said quietly but firmly. 'Now, was there anything else?'

Royston shook his head as Harper pulled the cord to summon the maid.

'Mr Newland is leaving, please see him out,' Harper said to the girl, who bobbed her knee.

Royston left without so much as a backward glance.

* * *

A few hours later, Harper eyed his father over the dining table. 'Father, I need to speak with you about a very important matter.'

'Oh, yes? And what would that be?' Rafe asked.

An older version of Harper, Rafe had maintained his good looks. His dark hair was now beginning to grey at the temples, giving him a distinguished air. Tiny laughter lines had formed at the corners of his eyes, providing him with a constant smile.

'It's about the wedding,' Harper proffered.

'Hmm?' Rafe nodded as he continued to eat.

'Well – the thing is – there's not going to be one.' Harper's words came out in a rush and he waited for the inevitable barrage of abuse which was bound to follow.

Rafe coughed and dabbed his mouth with a napkin. 'What did you say?'

'I can't do it! I cannot tie myself to someone I don't even like!' Harper's breathing became rapid as he fought to control his emotions.

'But it's all arranged, Harper! You have to learn to take responsibility and grow up!' Rafe leaned back in his chair and stared at his son.

Harper looked from his father to his mother, who had remained still and quiet.

'Don't expect your mother to save you this time. Harper, you know what will happen if you call this wedding off – there will be hell to pay with the girl's parents! Not to mention the scandal your poor mother and I will have to face. Darcie will be heartbroken!' Rafe was furious and threw the napkin onto his plate in a rage.

'She won't be. Darcie will get over it soon enough, but I will never be happy again if I marry her!' Harper's temper began to rise also.

'I told you before, Harper, I'll cut you off without a shilling!' Rafe said as he grabbed his wine glass and took a drink.

'I don't care!' Harper exploded. 'I don't give a hoot about the money!'

Eléna watched the argument rage across the table but kept her counsel.

'Why now?' Rafe asked with utter frustration.

'Because I can't live this lie any longer!' Harper answered sharply. 'Also, Royston Newland called this afternoon to take me to task about how I treat his daughter, and I sent him off with a flea in his ear!' Harper drew in a breath and went on in a quieter tone. 'You must understand, Father. You and Mother married for love. Why can I not be afforded the same privilege?'

'Harper, I don't think you realise what's at stake here...' Rafe began.

'I do, Father!' Harper cut across quickly. 'I know exactly what's at stake, and I don't want the Newland businesses.'

'You can say that now, but what about the future? You will never want for anything once those businesses come to you,' Rafe argued.

'Father, what's the use of all that money if one is too miserable to spend it? Besides, Darcie would drive me insane with her incessant whining.' Harper closed his eyes tight for a second in an effort to compose himself.

Rafe looked at his wife and said, 'What do you make of all this, Eléna?'

'Well, dear, I think Harper is right. He should not be forced into a loveless marriage, one that I feel sure would not produce grandchildren.'

Harper sighed with relief that his mother had pre-empted his next strike.

'I see.' Rafe drummed his fingers on the table as he searched the faces of his wife and son. Clearly they were of an accord, both believing they were right and he was wrong.

'I will not see my son do without, Rafe. The money willed to me by my father will go to Harper sooner or later anyway,' Eléna said quietly.

'What about the scandal? You may be sure there will be one as soon as the Newlands are told,' Rafe countered.

'Do you really think a little scandal will affect me? I can withstand that as long as my boy is happy.'

Rafe pursed his lips as he considered what had been said.

'Well, then, if you are set on this, Harper, then it must be you who informs the Newlands of your decision. I don't doubt they will be on our doorstep the moment they know so you will stay close to home. I will not have your mother subjected to any bad feeling from those people. Fine, then, but on your own head be it.' Rafe pushed back his chair and strode from the room.

'Oh, thank you, Mother,' Harper said with a relieved smile.

'I agreed with all you said, but it's my fear that now you may think you've reached the top of the hill, only to realise you are actually faced with a mountain.'

'I don't understand,' Harper said with a frown.

'You still have to tell your father about Ella Bancroft, and that it is she who holds your heart.'

13

The door to Ivy Gladwin's shop flew open and in marched a rather large woman. Striding to the counter, she spoke even before Ivy could greet her.

'Nice hats, it's about time you 'ad some decent stuff in 'ere.'

'How may I help you?' Ivy asked, trying to ignore the comment.

'I like that black 'un in the winder, the one with the little white rose on the side.'

'I'll lift it out for you to try,' Ivy said, praying she would make a sale.

'Ta,' the woman replied as she looked around.

Passing over the item, Ivy indicated the mirror on the wall.

'I don't want it to look like a fly on a pile o' shit, you understand,' the woman grinned, showing teeth that were sorely in need of dental attention.

'Of course,' Ivy muttered with a wrinkle of her nose.

'Oh, hey, that's bostin', aye it?' The woman inspected it from every angle.

'Very nice. It really suits you,' Ivy commented, but her

thought was it looked exactly like the woman's description of earlier.

'I'll tek it! Do I get a box an' all?'

'You do, madam. It's all part of the service, and I must say your friends will be envious when they see you wearing it.'

'Ta very much,' the woman said as she paid and left the shop happily.

Ivy looked at the money in her hand then, clutching it tightly to her chest, she closed her eyes, savouring the moment.

For the rest of the day women came and went and Ivy's sales soared. As she locked up for the night she realised Ella's edict of 'less is more' was correct after all. Ivy had stripped the decorations from her hats, leaving very little to adorn them. As much as it had pained her to do so, she had persevered, and common sense had finally won through.

Once she had eaten, Ivy knew she had a lot of work ahead of her. There were many more hats to be redesigned ready for the window the following morning.

Sitting with a cup of tea, Ivy smiled to herself. *Thought you could best me, did you, Ella Bancroft? I don't think so!* Her smile spread into a huge grin. She had another even better idea – as well as keeping an eye on what Ella was producing to steal her designs, she could undercut Ella's prices into the bargain. The girl had made a big mistake in having price tickets in the window display.

Then an even better idea struck, and Ivy laughed out loud. She could also accuse Ella of stealing *her* designs! A word in the ear of each customer would see gossip spread like wildfire, and before she knew it Miss Bancroft would have no more clients.

Ivy hummed a little tune as she set to dismantling an old hat. Tomorrow her display would be dazzling.

* * *

The following morning, Ella was unaware that her bread and butter customers were shopping elsewhere and for less money. She also had no way of knowing that Harper Fortescue was about to have the worst day of his life.

Given admittance by the maid, Harper was shown into the sitting room of Dundrennan House, where Darcie was taking coffee with her mother.

'Harper, how nice to see you!' Darcie gushed, instantly forgiving his past behaviour towards her.

'Darcie, Mrs Newland,' Harper returned.

'Will you join us for coffee, Harper?' Verity asked.

'Thank you, no. I can't stay long, I have business to attend to.' Harper perched himself on the edge of a heavily padded chaise longue.

'Well, I'm thrilled you are here, if only for a short time,' Darcie said with a huge grin.

Harper swallowed the lump in his throat and took a breath. 'I have something I wish to say.' His words came out in a croak and he cleared his throat before continuing. 'Darcie, I'm sorry but I can't marry you.'

Verity spluttered coffee onto her dress and wiped her bosom with a napkin. Darcie sat with her mouth hanging open, her cup seemingly suspended in mid-air.

'I thought it best to tell you now rather than wait any longer.' Harper's voice broke the spell hanging in the room.

'But Harper, I've bought my gown!' Darcie screeched at the top of her lungs. 'Mother and I went to Birmingham yesterday – what will I do with it now?'

'Return it?' Harper asked and winced even as he spoke.

'Young man, this really will not do! You can't come in here

and *jilt* my daughter just like that!' Verity snapped her fingers. 'No word of explanation? No begging forgiveness? God knows what Royston will have to say about all this!'

The predictable paroxysm of tears had overtaken Darcie and she wailed like a siren. Harper grimaced at the racket as he glanced at the girl whose heart he was breaking.

'Look what you've done! My daughter is in a dreadful state because of you!' Verity raged.

Harper held up his hands to endeavour to quieten the women. 'Mrs Newland, I am not, nor have I ever been, in love with Darcie.'

'Then why did you agree to marry her in the first place?' Verity snapped.

A fresh bout of wailing issued forth as Darcie stamped her feet like a child having a tantrum.

'It was my father's doing, not mine.'

'Then I think we should meet with your parents to see what can be done about this.' Turning to her daughter, Verity yelled, 'Will you cease that noise!'

In an instant the room fell silent. Except for the ticking of the grandfather clock which stood in the corner, and the crackling fire, there was no other sound. Harper sighed at the peace and quiet but knew it would not last long.

'Mrs Newland, my parents are aware of my decision and are in agreement that I should marry for love and not money.'

Darcie's crying began again, but, with a sharp look from her mother, she brought the noise down to little sobs.

'I see. Well, I hope they will be ready for the repercussions of this debacle because, when word gets out, your parents will be held responsible. They will be shunned in polite society and the newspapers will have a field day.' Verity's sigh was explosive.

'I imagine they are prepared for the backlash, Mrs Newland,

which they will cope with admirably, I'm sure.' Harper spoke with quiet determination.

'I expect Mr Newland will wish to call on your father at the earliest opportunity. Now please leave my...' Verity's words trailed off as Darcie cut in.

'It's that girl, isn't it, Harper?'

'I'm sorry? Which girl would that be?' he asked, knowing full well who she was referring to. He had hoped to escape before having to explain himself further, but clearly that idea was scotched now.

'That hat-maker!' The hatred in Darcie's voice was palpable as she stared at him with fire in her eyes.

Harper drew in a breath, not quite knowing what to say. Yes, he was in love with Ella, but she had no idea of his feelings towards her. Should he admit it and watch the fallout taint Ella's reputation too? Or should he deny it until he could declare his love with honour and so save her heartache?

'You have it all wrong, Darcie,' he began.

'Nonsense. I saw you making cow eyes at her!' Darcie was on her feet, leaning forward with her bunched fists at her sides.

'You are mistaken...' Harper tried again.

'I'm not! I saw you! Laughing and giggling. You ignored me in that filthy little house!' Darcie had taken a step forward. Seeing the threat, Harper stood up abruptly.

'The house was as clean as a new pin Darcie, and well you know it.'

'See – defending her!' Darcie took another step towards him, her eyes screwed up in absolute disgust.

'I did not come here to discuss Ella!' Harper shot back, his temper well on the rise now.

'Who is Ella?' Verity asked.

'Oh, Ella, is it? What happened to Miss Bancroft? On first

name terms already, I see.' Sarcasm dripped from her words as Darcie breathed heavily, totally ignoring her mother's question.

'I have said all I came to say and now I will bid you – I will be on my way.' Harper corrected himself as he realised bidding them a good day was not appropriate in the circumstances.

As he turned to leave, he felt a great weight land on his back, forcing him to the floor. Darcie was on him, punching and scratching at him in her anger. Her screams reverberated around the room and, as Verity jumped to her feet, the door opened and in rushed the maid.

'Don't just stand there – help me!' Verity yelled at the maid and between them they managed to drag Darcie off Harper.

'Get out!' Verity shouted and Harper took her at her word and fled, glad to be out of the mad household.

14

Ella's customer was debating the price of the hat she had asked to see.

'I do luv it but it ain't half expensive!'

'If you want good quality and one-off designs then the price will reflect that,' Ella countered.

'These ain't one-off,' the woman said as she gave the hat back to Ella.

'These are my designs, madam...' Ella began.

'Well, Gladwin's have the same but cheaper,' the woman said with a nod. 'So, if it's all the same to you, I'm gonna buy one from Ivy.' The woman left Ella's front room with a swish of her long skirt.

Back in the kitchen, Ella explained when her father asked about her sudden change in mood.

'I don't understand, Dad, these are our designs. How can Ivy have the same?'

'She's obviously discovered we are in the same business – she's bound to have seen the advertisement in the paper.'

'Yes, but that lady said Ivy's millinery was the same as ours.' Ella frowned as she spoke. 'She's undercutting our prices, too!'

'Right, the first thing you do is get them price tags out of the window. Then we'll have a cuppa and discuss this.'

Ella did as she was bid, then, over tea, Thomas voiced his thoughts. 'I'd noticed you weren't selling as much lately and I wondered why. Well, now we know. It's my guess that old bat has had a gander in your window before going on to pinch your ideas.'

'Oh, no! Dad, what can I do? I can't drop my prices any lower! How can I stop her stealing my designs?' Ella was wringing her hands as she thought about the consequences of the lack of sales. There would be no money for food or rent; they would be thrown out onto the streets to starve. An image of the Union Workhouse formed in her mind and she shuddered. She could not see her father in there, no matter what happened.

'Ella, if Ivy *is* taking your designs there's not a lot you can do about that,' Thomas reasoned.

'But Dad!' Ella gushed, her eyes twinkling in the gaslight as tears formed.

Thomas held up a hand to quieten her. 'I know, I understand completely but as long as your hats are on show – Ivy can carry on thieving your designs.'

'If I don't display them, how can I sell them?' Ella began to pace the kitchen floor, her anxiety mounting. She could envision everything they had worked so hard for disappearing in the blink of an eye.

Thomas could see his premonition of Ella fighting tooth and nail to make her business a success was beginning. He ached for his girl, who had put her heart and soul into everything she produced. Now, because of that spiteful Ivy Gladwin, he worried it could all go to waste. They had to find a solution – and quickly.

'You could leave the same hats in the window, then Ivy would be flummoxed,' Thomas said.

'People will think there are no new hats to be had,' Ella countered as she dropped onto a kitchen chair.

'What about if you took everything out of the display and put a sign up instead?'

'What sort of sign?' Ella asked.

'Something along the lines of "Come in and have a look at what's on offer". You can word it better, of course, but if Ivy can't see your hats, she can't copy them.' Thomas rubbed his whiskers as he spoke.

'Hmmm, that might work. And I suppose it's the only option open to us now.' Ella sighed loudly. 'I'll go and empty the window.'

Thomas watched her go with sadness in his heart. Wheeling himself to the dresser, he pulled out paper, pen and ink. Laying them in his lap, he pushed back to the table, where he laid them out. Thinking for a minute Thomas began to write out a sign in beautiful copperplate writing.

Secrecy is paramount for bespoke millinery. Let no one see your hat until you reveal it to the world yourself. For top quality and one-off designs come inside and speak to Ella.

When Ella returned to the kitchen and saw Thomas's efforts she gasped. 'Dad, that's wonderful!'

'Ta, lass. Now put that in the window in the centre and surround it with haberdashery. Tastefully, mind.'

Ella grinned as she lifted the paper with care, ensuring the ink was dry. For an hour or more she worked on a display, ensuring it didn't look cheap and nasty. She had to prevent it seeming to be just bits of ribbon and lace hanging haphazardly about.

Bowing ribbons, pleating lace and arranging feathers in fans she placed them strategically around the sign. Happy she had done the best she could, Ella returned to the kitchen.

'I hope this works, Dad, otherwise...'

'We'll see, but you have to give it time,' Thomas replied.

'How will we know?'

'First off, you'll have stopped Ivy's nefarious practice.' Thomas began to tick off the list on his fingers. 'Then you'll see whether ladies come in because of our sign. I'm sure as well that folk will let you know what Ivy's up to. You just have to be patient, and, in the meantime, you keep working on any new notions you have.'

Ella moved to her father and hugged him. 'Thank you. I don't know what I'd do without you.'

Thomas smiled, feeling the love swell in his chest. There was nothing he wouldn't do for his girls and he knew Ella felt the same for him.

As Ella prepared a meal, Thomas winced at the pains in his chest. They were coming more often now, but he still he kept them to himself. He wasn't about to pay a doctor good money to tell him what he already knew: one day his heart would give out. However, before that time came, Thomas would do all he could to see his daughter happy and successful. He hoped to live long enough to see her married. At the thought, his mind shifted automatically to Harper Fortescue and he smiled inwardly. Could a relationship between Ella and that young man work? It was clear even to a blind man how Harper felt about Ella and vice versa, but would the boy's family allow it? The social divide between them was wide but was it insurmountable? Could there be a way to see the pair wed before Thomas met his maker?

Ella was chatting away quietly as she stirred the gravy on the stove, but Thomas didn't hear her words. Clutching his chest as the pain exploded, his eyes rolled back and he slumped forward in his wheelchair.

15

'Good grief, Harper, whatever has happened?' Eléna gushed as her son dropped into a chair in the parlour.

'Darcie bloody Newland! She attacked me!' Harper replied as he tentatively touched the scratches on his face.

Eléna pulled the bell cord by the fireplace before going to her son. 'Those need cleaning, then I think it's time I had some words with that madam!'

The maid arrived quickly and was dispatched to fetch clean water and ointment, as well as hot sweet tea. As his mother tended to his wounds, Harper explained about Darcie assailing him.

'It's to be expected she's upset – but this?' Eléna clicked her tongue.

Harper winced as ointment was applied from a small round cardboard box.

'At least your father will see now what would have been in store for you had you married that harridan!' Eléna said, laying the pot of ointment aside. 'Here, drink this, it will help with the shock.' She passed his tea and saw Harper's hands were shaking.

Going to her escritoire, she penned a short note. When the maid came to collect the crockery, she instructed, 'Please ask the stable boy to take this to my husband straight away. Thank you.'

The maid took the note and bobbed a knee, her eyes flickering to the young master's injuries.

'How are you feeling now?' Eléna asked once the maid had left the room.

'Better. Thank you, Mother,' Harper replied, but truth be told he felt wretched inside and out. His face was sore and throbbing and he had begun to feel terrible about the way he had treated Darcie. It was no surprise, really, that she had reacted the way she had, but when all was said and done, he knew he could never have married her.

A short while later, Rafe Fortescue rushed into the parlour to his family. 'What's going on?' he asked, full of concern. Seeing the injuries his son had sustained, he felt anger replace concern and build to boiling point.

Eléna explained quickly what had occurred and watched her husband's astonished look.

'Darcie did this?' he asked, and Harper nodded. 'I thought you had been fighting. My God, son, I'm so sorry. It seems you've had a lucky escape where that young lady is concerned, after all.' Rafe sat in his armchair beside the fire. 'Do you wish to press charges, son? Shall I inform the constabulary?'

'No, Father. It's as Mother said, Darcie was upset. I hope now you can see why I couldn't go through with the wedding, although I had no idea she had such a violent streak in her.'

'I can indeed, my boy, and you have my sincerest apologies for not listening to you before this.'

Harper smiled inwardly. His father could be a bit of a tyrant when he chose to be, but he was not above admitting when he was wrong. He was also man enough to say he was sorry.

'I expect the Newlands will be paying us a visit this evening, then?' Rafe asked.

'Probably,' Eléna answered.

'Don't worry, my dear, I shall deal with it.'

'Father, we should be there too, don't you think? After all, this was my doing.' Harper pointed to his scratched face.

'Very well, you have my word I will not buckle under any pressure brought to bear. You will most definitely *not* be taking Darcie Newland as your wife!' Rafe waved a hand in a dismissive gesture.

'Thank you, Father,' Harper smiled, then grimaced as his face pained him.

As the three sat before the roaring fire, drinking fresh tea brought by the maid, Harper tried to envisage what the evening would bring when Darcie and her parents came to call as they surely would. One thing was for sure – Harper would keep well out of Darcie's reach.

It was after dinner that the Newlands arrived as expected. Shown into the parlour by the maid, they were asked to take a seat.

'Rafe, you know why we're here,' Royston Newland said as he twisted his handlebar moustache.

'I do,' Rafe answered curtly.

'What's to be done about this situation?' Royston returned.

'Nothing. Your girl attacked my boy,' Rafe pointed to his son as he spoke.

'For good cause!' Royston snapped.

'There is never a good cause for violence such as that, sir!' Rafe's temper flared.

Harper listened with his eyes kept firmly on his father. He could feel Darcie's malevolent glare on him and he shuddered.

He could not bring himself to look at her, knowing she would burn him to a crisp if she could.

'My daughter was jilted, how would you expect her to behave?' Royston asked sharply.

'With far more decorum as befits a lady!' Rafe held his anger in check but it was straining at the leash.

'Maybe so...' Royston began.

'Daddy! Tell Harper he *has* to marry me – he promised!' Darcie interrupted with a wail.

Royston waved for her to be quiet, but Darcie was having none of it. 'You cur! You are betrothed to me! How dare you think you can leave me for some – hat-seller?'

Rafe's eyes widened a fraction. He'd heard nothing of this. Had his son found another to give his heart to?

'I have broken the engagement because I do not love you, nor could I ever!' Harper blasted back.

'Quiet, both of you!' Rafe's voice was menacingly quiet and full of authority.

A silence descended as the two families eyed each other across the room.

'There must be some recompense, otherwise we'll see to it that Harper's name is dragged through the mud. He will be labelled a rake and a scoundrel for deserting my daughter. Your good name will suffer, you must see that.' Royston's head shook as he spoke.

'Your daughter could be apprehended by the police for her attack on my son. She could be sent to jail and then your name would suffer too. Or had you not thought of that?' Rafe responded with raised eyebrows.

'I don't think you would go that far,' Royston said confidently.

'Try me,' Rafe answered simply. 'I warn you here and now,

Newland, if you endeavour to blacken the Fortescue name, I will have your daughter arrested for assault.'

Royston glanced at his bird-like wife and then his daughter, who was fuming. He nodded his acceptance and stood to leave.

'Daddy! For God's sake! What are you doing?' Darcie screeched.

'Come, Darcie,' Verity said as she grabbed the girl's arm.

Darcie's fury burst its banks and she turned swiftly and caught her mother with a resounding slap to the cheek.

Verity dropped back into the chair she had vacated a moment before, her hand rising to her face.

'I want justice! I want Harper to pay for what he's done to me!' Darcie's voice echoed around the parlour as she looked at the shocked faces surrounding her.

'Newland, take my advice. When you get home, you take that girl across your knee. It's what you should have done years ago, but it's never too late,' Rafe said as his eyebrows flicked upwards.

'You shut your mouth!' Darcie rounded on him. 'You should make sure your son honours his promises! Some father you are!'

Rafe jumped to his feet and Darcie took a step back in sudden fear. With his face close to hers, Darcie had to lean back. 'Don't you ever presume to tell me how to raise my son! You are a spoilt brat of the first order, having been completely ruined by parents who have no backbone! Now, Miss Newland, you take heed of what I said to your father because I will see it through myself if I have to.'

Turning to Royston, he went on, 'Please take your family out of my house and don't come back. Remember my words, Newland, for I will not hesitate to see your daughter locked away – jail or asylum – makes no difference to me.'

Royston's head bobbed on his neck as he grabbed Darcie's

arm and tilted his head to his wife. He dragged a struggling Darcie away as his sobbing wife followed closely behind.

Rafe retook his seat with a huge sigh. Harper and Eléna exchanged a look, then their eyes returned to Rafe.

'That went rather well, I thought, what say you?' he said.

Mother and son burst out laughing, then Eléna went to the cocktail cabinet to pour them each a stiff drink.

Darcie railed all the way home in the carriage. 'What Harper's father said is true, you are spineless! Consider this, what if I told you I was pregnant?'

Verity's sobs ceased long enough for her to snap, 'Have you lain with him?'

'Well, no, but...'

'Then you would be branded a liar and one not to be trusted!' her mother growled.

'Darcie, all we have ever done is try to please you,' Royston said.

'Well, please me now – make Harper marry me!'

'You must see this is something I cannot do! The relationship is broken and I can't fix it!' Royston was at his wits' end.

'Fine, I'll just make sure the whole town knows.' Darcie's eyes shot fire in the lamplight coming through the window.

'And you would end up in prison or the asylum. You heard Rafe and I have no doubt he would be true to his word.' Royston shook his head. 'Are you prepared to test the theory?'

Darcie stamped her feet on the floor of the carriage in absolute and utter temper and frustration.

'I thought not,' Royston mumbled. 'Now, for goodness' sake be quiet. I don't want to hear another word.'

Darcie opened her mouth, but as her father raised a finger, she clamped it shut again, content to fume quietly – for now, at least.

16

Ella placed their meals on the table and glanced at her father. Poor Thomas, he'd fallen asleep in his wheelchair. She hadn't realised he was so tired and made a mental note to ensure he took a nap during the day.

'Dad, food is ready,' she called quietly.

When Thomas didn't rouse, she went to him and gave his shoulder a shake.

'Dad?' Suddenly Ella felt cold and was filled with dread. 'Dad!' She shook his shoulder again. With not a moment to lose, she ran out of the back door to seek out her neighbour.

Mrs Woolley shot into the house and went straight to Thomas.

'Fetch the doctor, quick! I'll stop 'ere with him.'

Ella grabbed her shawl and fled. She ran down the street, ignoring the pain in her side. She prayed the doctor would be at home when she got there. Rapping on the front door, Ella shuffled from foot to foot before banging again. The door was opened by a maid and Ella asked to see the doctor urgently.

'It's an emergency, please!' she begged.

'Just a moment,' the maid said and left Ella waiting on the doorstep.

Ella moved aside as the doctor came charging through the house to the open doorway.

'Right, let's be off,' the doctor said as he steered Ella towards his trap waiting outside the house.

Climbing aboard, the doctor snapped the reins and the horse moved off. 'Where to?' he asked.

'Silver Street. My father, Thomas Bancroft – he won't wake up!' Ella cried.

'All right, don't worry, I'll see to him,' the doctor assured her.

Drawing the horse to a halt, the doctor jumped down and helped Ella to alight. They rushed indoors to see Mrs Woolley standing over Thomas.

'Let the dog see the rabbit then,' the doctor muttered as he elbowed the woman out of the way.

Ella and Mrs Woolley watched as the doctor examined Thomas. Ella was beside herself with worry, feeling helpless as she looked on. Tears welled in her eyes and a sob escaped her throat.

'I'm sorry, m'dear, but he's gone.'

Mrs Woolley threw her arms around Ella as her legs gave way and she crumpled to a heap on the floor. Dragging Ella to a chair Mrs Woolley patted her back. 'I ain't half sorry, gel.'

The doctor passed the completed death certificate and invoice to Mrs Woolley and left the house quietly.

'I'll just mek you a cuppa then I'll away and send one of my lads for the undertaker.' Mrs Woolley knew Ella was in shock as the girl merely nodded, her eyes still glued to her father.

Nodding her thanks for the tea, Ella muttered, 'I'll have to let our Sally know straight away.'

Mrs Woolley answered with, 'I'll send our Benny for her and our Josh for the undertaker, then I'll come back here.'

It was an hour later when Ella and Sally watched their father gently lowered into a temporary coffin which was then carried outside to the cart.

'You'll need to...' the undertaker began.

'I know. I'll help them sort it all out. We'll come tomorrow to pay and choose a package,' Mrs Woolley said in barely more than a whisper.

The man nodded, tipped his top hat and left the house.

'Right, I'll leave you two girls in peace. I can come round tomorrow and help with the arrangements at the funeral parlour if you like,' Mrs Woolley said.

'We can manage, but thank you anyway,' Sally replied.

'Suit yerself,' Mrs Woolley said indignantly. Turning on her heel she went home to her own family.

Sally made more tea and sat at the table with Ella.

'What happened?' she asked.

'I was serving our meal and when I turned round he was... I thought he was asleep.'

'Says on here that his heart gave out,' Sally said as she picked up the death certificate.

Ella nodded as if in a trance. Her father's heart had given up beating and she had had no idea he'd had any problems. Certainly Thomas had never mentioned it if he had.

Ella's mind tried to make sense of what had happened. One minute her father was alive and well, the next he was gone. How? Why? Had he suffered? She'd heard no sound from him, but then she'd been talking. Had she missed his call for help? She should have taken better care of him; made sure he rested more often. But it was too late now.

Suddenly the enormity of it all hit her like a sledgehammer, and Ella burst into tears. Her heart had cracked like it was made of glass and the pain was almost unbearable. She cried herself out and her throat was dry and sore.

'Drink your tea,' Sally said as she watched her sister sobbing.

Ella dried her tears and forced her mind to work. They had to organise a funeral so she would have to close her business for a day. Next, she'd need to have the house transferred into her name. She prayed the sign in the window would work, for she needed to pay funerary expenses. How would she be able to work without her father's help? More tears rolled down her cheeks as she realised she was missing him dreadfully already. How would she cope without her dad?

Sally stared at the empty wheelchair and felt the sadness creep around her. She had never been as close to their father as Ella had been and it had caused her jealousy to raise its ugly head on numerous occasions. She knew she would have to be the strong one now, for Ella would be unable to cope with the organisation of the funeral.

'I'll come round in the morning and we'll go to the undertaker together,' she said.

Ella nodded and she mopped away her tears.

'Will you be all right on your own tonight?' Sally asked.

'Yes,' Ella mumbled.

Sally grabbed her coat and hat, gave her sister a quick hug and left the house quietly. Ella spent the rest of the night staring at the chair her father had sat in for so many years.

The following morning, Flossie Woolley came through the back door and shook her head. The poor girl must have sat alone all night. Moments later, Sally arrived and scowled when she saw the neighbour making tea.

'You want me to come with you to sort out the funeral?' Mrs Woolley asked as she poured tea for the sisters.

'No, thank you, we can manage.' Sally nodded her thanks for the hot brew.

Ella shot her sister a glance before saying, 'Mrs Woolley, you've been a diamond, I couldn't have coped without you. Thank you and your boys for your help.'

'It weren't no bother,' the neighbour said, patting Ella's arm. 'Let me know the arrangements 'cos I'd like to say my farewell to Thomas.' With that, she left the girls to it.

'She treats this place like her own,' Sally said snidely.

'Mrs Woolley is a good person, Sally, she's been invaluable these last few years helping us out.'

'Even so, you have to stop her just popping in and out when she feels like it.'

'Sally! I most certainly will not. She has been most kind and I like her immensely.'

'Come on, let's get this over with,' Sally said as she put on her coat.

Ella nodded and picked up her own outdoor clothing. The two women walked into the town to the undertakers. Choosing the cheapest package, Ella paid out of her business monies. Then they retraced their steps back home.

They walked quickly through the railway tunnel and each shivered at the thought of trains passing overhead. Glad to be out the other end, they continued on down Bradford Street towards the Walsall and District Hospital. Keeping to the side of the tramway they passed the almshouses, which had originally been built to house the poor of the town. They both glanced at the massive sand pit next to the sawmill and timber yard. Hearing a tram whistle, they cut into Mount Street and then into Silver Street.

As they approached the house, Ella saw a woman knocking on her door. 'Oh dear,' she mumbled.

'Ella, you have to keep working. You'll be needing the money and Dad would have wanted you to carry on,' Sally said.

'I know you're right but... yes, Dad wouldn't want me to give up.'

Walking to the door and unlocking it, Ella said, 'I'm sorry to keep you waiting in the cold. Please come in.'

'You bin out, 'ave yer?' the customer asked.

'Erm, we were at the funeral parlour, our father passed away unexpectedly,' Ella explained.

'Shame,' the woman answered. 'Sorry for yer loss.'

'Thank you,' Ella replied. 'Now, how may I help you?'

'I need a cheap but cheerful hat; I ain't got much to spend but I want summat different. Your sign says I can get a one-off.'

Sally watched the exchange with interest as the woman began to look around the small front room.

'Indeed.' Ella forced a smile and for the next half an hour she helped her client choose a hat she liked within her price range.

Once the woman had gone, Ella and Sally retired to the kitchen.

'I need to eat something and then get some sleep, but I have to stay open for business,' Ella said.

'Well, you can't do both,' Sally replied. 'Why don't you close up for the rest of the day and get some rest?'

'I was going to close tomorrow as a sign of respect and put a notice in the window to notify customers of my intention.'

'It's up to you, but if you take my advice you'll get yourself to bed for an hour or two.' Sally shrugged her shoulders. 'As for me, I'd best get back to Eddy.'

'Yes, of course,' Ella said, suddenly feeling exhausted. 'Thank you for this morning, it was much easier with you there.'

'I'll come back later and see how you are,' Sally said as she headed towards the back door.

Once her sister had gone, Ella warmed up some leftovers and forced herself to eat. Surprisingly, she felt a little better. Ella sat quietly by the fire, wishing her father were still with her. Her only two customers were dealt with quickly and efficiently, then she locked up the house.

Dragging her weary body upstairs, Ella climbed onto the bed, now realising how badly she needed the rest. What felt like only a few hours later she was woken by noises downstairs. Making her way to the kitchen she sighed, seeing Sally making herself a cup of tea.

'You got some sleep, then?'

Ella nodded.

'Do you want a cuppa?'

'Yes, please.'

Sally brewed up and they sat together at the table.

'How are you and the baby doing? I'm sorry I forgot to ask earlier.'

'We're all right. Eddy still can't find work so I'm not sure how we'll manage but at least he's still trying,' Sally said, by way of conversation.

'I hope he gets something soon and then you can buy the things you'll need,' Ella said.

'Did Dad leave any money?' Sally asked.

Ella shook her head surprised at the question. 'You know full well he had nothing to leave us.'

'All right, I only asked,' Sally retorted.

Ella sighed. This was not the time to be falling out with the only relative she had left, but she was shocked Sally was thinking of inheritance when their father was barely cold.

'It's just that with the baby coming and all...' Sally began.

'Sally, I've already paid for the funeral so I can't help you out,' Ella cut across her sentence.

'I know. I'm sorry I couldn't chip in with that.'

'It doesn't matter, it's done now.' Ella shook her head, feeling tiredness wrap itself around her once more. 'I'm going back to bed, I'm done in.'

'I'll pop in tomorrow and see how you are,' Sally said before leaving.

Ella passed the night fitfully, being constantly awoken by bad dreams. She rose early, not feeling refreshed at all. It was as she set the kettle to boil that she heard the banging on the front door. Clearly someone had not read her notice. With a sigh she went to the door.

'I'm sorry, I'm closed today due to...'

'Ella, it's Harper. Please open the door.'

Pulling back the bolts she pulled the door open a crack. 'Mr Fortescue, I'm afraid I can't let you in unaccompanied...'

'I know. Ella, what's happened?' Harper asked, full of concern.

'My father died the day before yesterday,' she said as she pulled the door open further.

'Oh, no! Ella, I'm so sorry to hear that,' Harper said. He was shocked at the sight of her. Her face was ashen and dark circles surrounded her sad eyes. Her dark hair was untidy and her clothes were creased. He wanted to wrap his arms around her and give her comfort but knew he couldn't. It was breaking his heart to see her so stricken.

'If you need any help please call for me, I will come at once.' His words sounded hollow even to his ears, but it was all he could say. He could see she was suffering unimaginable torment and he could do nothing to ease her pain.

'Thank you.' For all she was pleased to see him, Ella just needed to be alone.

'I will leave you now, but please remember my words.' Harper tipped his hat and turned to walk away. He heard the door close quietly behind him.

17

Ivy Gladwin closed the shop for lunch and grabbed her hat, coat and umbrella. She was going to see what was new in Ella's window.

Grey clouds scudded across the sky and the rain pelted down. Dirty water ran in rivulets down the cobbled streets, forming puddles in uneven dips in the road. The wind gusted, turning umbrellas inside out, and blew the rain into a sideways trajectory. Freezing droplets stung the skin of people hurrying towards their destinations or to somewhere to shelter from the downpour.

Ivy grimaced at the inclement weather, wishing she'd stayed indoors, but she had only an hour to spare for spying. Her shop had seen sales rise quickly over the last couple of weeks, and she couldn't afford to close any longer than necessary.

Reaching Silver Street at last, she grinned. No one would recognise her if she kept her umbrella low over her face against the wind.

But there were no hats in Ella's window, just a sign and a notice. Ivy sighed after reading the one announcing bereavement. It must be her father who had passed. Ivy felt a pang of sympathy for the girl, but it was short-lived as she read the sign. *Damn and blast you, Ella Bancroft!* Now Ivy couldn't steal any more ideas.

Turning swiftly, she stamped away, anger and frustration fusing to blacken her mood further. She had tramped all this way and was soaked to the skin for what? Nothing! Fury increased her pace and helped to stave off the cold as she made her way home. What could she do now? How was she to find out about Ella's new designs? Was the girl still producing millinery now her father had died?

Ivy changed into dry clothing as soon as she walked into her living quarters. She hung up her wet coat in the kitchen to dry out, and after making a cup of tea she opened the shop and sat awaiting custom. It was unlikely to come given the foul weather, but she drank her tea and mulled over what she'd learned.

Ella was no longer showing off her hats in the window. Why? Was she aware Ivy was stealing her ideas? Had someone told her? Were her sales dropping off even as Ivy's were increasing? Did the death of her father feature in this change of sales method?

Ivy tapped her booted foot as she pondered these questions. How could she acquire answers? Who would know? The more she thought on it the more frustrated she became.

Walking to the window, she gazed out at the greyness and heard the patter of raindrops on the glass. She shivered and decided the back room with its blazing fire was a much more comfortable place to be. There she could continue the rejuvenation of hats that had graced her shelves for years. Breathing new life into old millinery would take her mind off Ella and the problem of what to do next.

* * *

Back in Silver Street, Ella sat at the kitchen table, unconsciously drawing her fingers along the spine of a feather. She felt it crack and saw the feather curl into an arc. Shoving the quill into the band of a hat lying on the table, she nodded at its pleasing effect. Then her eyes returned to the empty wheelchair and silent tears rolled down her cheeks.

'Dad, I can't do this alone, I need you here with me!' she cried into the quiet kitchen. Just then, the feather shifted position in the hat band with a tiny rasp. Was this a sign? Did her deceased father move the feather to show he was watching over her?

Ella shook her head at the notion. Of course not, the feather had slipped of its own accord. It was, however, in a nicer position on the hat now, so Ella picked up a needle and began sewing it in place. Before she realised, she had finished the hat. With the completed article in one hand she rubbed her tired eyes with the other.

Making tea and grabbing some bread and cheese, Ella went through the motions of having a late lunch, but her mind was already churning out new creations. With pencil and butcher's paper she hastily sketched her ideas before they became over-whelmed by grief.

Laying down her pencil, she considered. Grief was a strange thing. One minute she seemed fine and could work, the next she was a sobbing mess. The sadness appeared to tap her on the shoulder when she least expected it and somehow Ella knew it would always be this way. She had to try to come to terms with the fact that she was alone in the house now and had to fend for herself. There would be no help forthcoming from Sally or her good-for-nothing husband.

Getting to her feet, she took a deep breath. 'Sorry, Dad, but I know you would want me to move on and make something of myself.' Her words were no more than a whisper as she pushed the wheelchair out of the back door and parked it in the communal back yard. Then she followed suit with Thomas's trolley from the landing.

Going into her father's bedroom, Ella glanced around. It was the room her parents had shared all their married life, and only now did Ella realise how small it was. A little bed, a wardrobe and chest of drawers which held a mirror was all that would fit in. Sitting on the end of the bed, Ella covered her face with her hands and allowed her tears free rein.

It was dark when Ella came out of the trance-like state and wearily made her way downstairs. Clearing Thomas's room was a job for another day; she couldn't face it right now. Lighting the gas lamp, she banked up the fire. She started as a knock came to the back door before it opened to reveal Sally.

'Bloody weather!' she said as she stepped indoors. 'I brought you some broth 'cos I didn't think as you'd be up to cooking.'

'Thank you. Why did you knock before you came in?' Ella asked as she watched her sister place the crockpot on the table.

'It's your house now Dad's gone, so it's only polite. I see the chair is in the yard, good idea; it gives a bit more space in here.' Sally glanced around as she spoke. She chose to ignore Ella's red and swollen eyes from where she had been crying.

Ella nodded. 'I was going to clear his room, but...' Letting her words trail off Ella lowered her head.

'I could help if you like,' Sally said.

'No. I can do it, but it will have to wait. I have more pressing matters to see to, like earning a living.' Ella had no intention of allowing her sister to go rummaging around in their father's room looking for anything that might sell.

'Right, I'm away. I'll have my pot back when you've finished.' Sally gave a quick wave and was gone.

Ella lifted the lid and sniffed the contents. The stew made her mouth water and she stood it on the range to warm through.

Another knock sounded and Mrs Woolley barged in. 'God, this weather is terrible!' she said, shaking the rain from her shawl. 'How are you getting on? Are you taking care of yourself?'

'I'm trying,' Ella said, forcing a little smile.

'That's the spirit. It don't do to dwell; you have to get on with your own life now. None of us know what's in store for us, so mek the best of what you have is what I allus say.' Mrs Woolley folded her arms beneath her bosom and gave a perfunctory nod.

'Yes, you're right as always, Mrs Woolley,' Ella replied.

'As long as you're all right I'll get back before my lot kill each other. Get that broth down you while it's hot,' her neighbour said, eyeing the crockpot on the range. 'Ta-ra, gel.' With that the woman left to return to her own house, which was full of children of varying ages.

Ella dished up the broth and cut some bread. It was tasty and before long she was enjoying the hot soup, having been unaware just how hungry she was.

Washing the dishes afterwards, Ella then sat by the fire, watching the flames lick around the fresh coal nuggets she'd added. Only the ticking of the clock broke the silence, its regular rhythm along with the heat of the fire lulling her into a deep peaceful healing sleep.

18

Harper had returned to The Cedars extremely worried about Ella. He sat in the parlour by a crackling fire, seeing her image again in his mind's eye. The pain of losing her father had robbed her of her vivacity. In a matter of a couple of days she had become a shadow of her previous self.

How could he help her? What could he do to lighten the load of grief weighing her down? In his heart he knew there was no way he could make her feel any better; only time could heal the wounds. He would not abandon her, however, for the love he was feeling would never allow that to happen.

The door opened and Eléna bustled in, followed by the maid bearing a tea tray.

'Ah, there you are Harper, I thought we could take tea together,' Eléna chirped, indicating the table where the maid was to deposit the tray.

'Hmm,' Harper replied, his thoughts still with Ella.

'Something on your mind, son?'

Harper's eyes instinctively moved to the maid, then back to

his mother. The maid bobbed a knee and retreated, closing the door quietly behind her.

Eléna arranged her long skirts and sat to pour the drinks, then she waited. Harper would tell her what the problem was in his own time. Even as a child, he would not be drawn until he was ready to speak, but eventually all would be divulged. She smiled inwardly at the memory.

Accepting tea, Harper settled himself comfortably once more. 'I saw Ella Bancroft today.'

Still Eléna waited, the clink of the teaspoon in the cup and the ticking clock the only sounds.

'Her father has passed away.'

'I'm sorry to hear that, he was a nice fellow from what I remember,' Eléna said as she shook her head daintily.

'The best. He gave me some very sound advice,' Harper replied.

'Oh?' Eléna didn't wish to pry into her son's affairs. If he wanted her to know then he would tell her.

'Yes. When I saw Ella today she looked drawn and tired...' Harper recalled her image again as he went on. 'I'm very worried about her.'

'I suppose it's to be expected. The death of someone close takes its toll on those left behind.' Eléna watched her boy over the rim of her teacup.

'Well, it has on Ella, she looks positively ill!'

'Poor girl, but there's not much you can do to help, Harper.'

'No, there isn't really. But I will offer again the next time I see her.'

Eléna raised an eyebrow. So her son would be visiting the milliner again. Truth be told, she was not that surprised. She wasn't blind to the feelings Harper held for Ella, but in her heart, she wished the girl had been born to a higher class family. That would have made things so much simpler.

'You must do what you think best, darling,' she said with a thin-lipped smile.

Harper nodded with a sigh as he crossed his legs and his gaze fell on his brown boot. Swinging his foot in mid-air, he watched the light from the window flit across the highly polished leather.

As if reading his mind, his mother spoke gently. 'Go tomorrow, Harper. She may need time to come to terms with her loss and I'm sure she wouldn't want anyone seeing her crying.'

'Yes, Mother, you're right,' Harper answered, feeling frustrated he couldn't run to Ella and fold her in his arms.

Eléna nodded. Her son was head over heels for this girl, but how his father would take to the news was anyone's guess.

Early the following morning the weather had turned cold once more. Harper, wrapped against the chill wind, guided his horse to walk down Wednesbury Road, keeping well to the left of the wide thoroughfare. He crossed the bridge spanning the railway line and, unable to face passing Dundrennan House, he cut down into Junction Street.

The sound of the horse's hooves echoed off the tightly packed buildings and Harper looked around him. Rows of houses, each identical to its neighbour, lined the street, and only as he turned into Camden Street did he notice the dirty curtains twitching.

He was almost there when he wondered how he would be received by Miss Bancroft. He knew he wouldn't be invited inside now that Ella lived alone; it would be wholly inappropriate. Gossip would be rife and her good reputation could be tarnished, so he would ask after her health on the doorstep. Harper didn't much care where they were as long as he could see her.

Coming into Silver Street, Harper slid down from the saddle and tied the reins around the gas lamp post. Striding the few steps to Ella's door, he rapped the knocker. As he waited, he felt his pulse quicken, and impatiently he knocked again.

The door opened a crack and Ella's eyes peeped out. 'Mr Fortescue...' she began in a weary voice.

'Ella, I'm here to satisfy myself that you are all right.'

'I am, thank you,' Ella responded with a tired smile.

'How did you sleep?' Harper asked, knowing his question was stupid the moment it left his lips. The girl had just lost her father, so sleep would not come easily.

'Surprisingly well.'

Harper smiled warmly. 'Is there anything I can help you with?'

'No, but I thank you for the offer.' Ella shivered at the icy air blasting through the open door.

'Then I will be on my way. May I call again sometime?'

'Please do,' Ella replied graciously.

Saying their goodbyes, Ella closed the door and Harper walked back to his horse.

On his way home, Harper decided to call in and take morning coffee in the Conservative Club. Here he could sit quietly and mull over the events which had led him to this point in his life.

Back in Silver Street, Ella had returned to her seat in the warm kitchen and fed the small range. Setting the kettle to boil for tea, she pondered young Mr Fortescue's visit. She had no idea why he continued to call; he had purchased his hats, after all.

Her heart fluttered as she recalled his image, then realised he'd had scratches on his face. What had caused them? A playful kitten maybe? Had Harper been in a fight? No, he was too much of a gentleman to be brawling. Ella made a mental note to enquire – discreetly – when he next called round. Would he visit again now he knew she was all right?

Making tea like an automaton, Ella sat at the table and began to roll up a ribbon tightly. Pushing her finger in the centre, the rolls spilled out, giving it the look of a rose. With a tiny smile, she wondered if her father had been guiding her hands.

Then, yet again, her grief at his loss overwhelmed her and her tears dripped onto the rose ribbon in her hand. How long would she be feeling this way? Would she ever get over the death of her father? Maybe she would start to heal once the funeral had taken place; somehow she doubted it. At this moment she felt she would miss her dad for the rest of her life.

Allowing the ribbon to unravel in her fingers, she compared it to her life. She thought this was exactly what was happening to her – everything appeared to be coming apart around her and she was powerless to stop it.

Going upstairs to her father's room, she sat on his bed and glanced around.

'Oh, Dad! It's all going wrong! Why did you have to leave me? I need you to come home!'

Ella lay down where she smelled her father on his pillow. Silent tears rolled from her eyes as she breathed in the scent of the soap Thomas was so fond of.

Closing her eyes, Ella drifted off to sleep, the only sound breaking the silence being an occasional dry sob.

19

'Well, now, it's nice to see you,' Stafford Darnell said as he greeted Harper with a handshake.

Ordering coffee, Harper joined his friend at a table in the corner of the room. Glancing around, he noted older gentlemen of eminence chatting quietly; others were reading newspapers.

'It's been a while since I saw you last,' Stafford said, his beady eyes going to the scratches on Harper's face. 'Been in the wars, have we?' He pointed a bony finger to his own face and waggled it.

'You wouldn't believe me if I told you,' Harper said nodding his thanks to the waiter who delivered the tray of coffee.

'Oh, trouble?' Stafford asked as he settled himself in the hope of hearing the tale surrounding Harper's injury.

'No, it's nothing,' Harper replied whilst pouring his drink.

Harper had known Stafford since they were boys, when he had lived next door at The Hollies. Their fathers were great friends. Sipping the hot beverage, Harper eyed his companion. Tall and thin, Stafford Darnell had a shock of dark hair with beard and moustache to match. His brown eyes were small for his face, and his nose was large and hooked, having been rendered that way after an accident with a rugby ball at school.

Both families were wealthy; old money having been passed down on both maternal and paternal sides. Harper's father was the owner of the Alma Tube Works and Stafford's pater was in saddlery. Neither of the sons had, as yet, been taken into the family businesses.

'So, tell me, how are the wedding plans proceeding?' Stafford asked, but upon seeing Harper's look he added, 'Oh, I see.'

'If I tell you, you *must* maintain your silence,' Harper whispered.

Stafford leaned forward to better hear what was about to be divulged.

'Swear!' Harper urged.

'Not something I usually do, but...' Stafford began with a grin.

'This is important, Stafford.'

'Sorry.'

'I've called the wedding off.'

'Bloody hell!' Stafford muttered and despite the gravity of the situation, both young men laughed.

'Shush!' someone called out before shaking his newspaper in disgust at the noise the young men were making.

Looking suitably chastened, the two then spoke in whispers as Harper related his tale. He did not, however, mention Ella Bancroft or his feelings for her. That was something he felt was best kept to himself.

'Do you think Darcie will keep her mouth shut?' Stafford asked.

'I don't know. She was all for dragging my name through the mud and informing the newspapers until Father threatened her with arrest for assault.' Harper touched his cheek and winced.

'You do get yourself in a pickle at times, old boy,' Stafford said.

Harper sighed. 'Don't I just.' The next pickle he would find himself in would be when he had to tell his father about Ella and his intentions towards her.

Stafford's voice droned on around him and Harper only snapped his attention back when he heard his friend say, '...so Silver Street is the place to go it seems.'

'Sorry, what for?' Harper asked.

'A new hat! Do keep up, Harper, there's a good chap.'

'Oh, yes. I've already been and so has Mother.'

'Did you buy anything?' Stafford probed.

'Yes, a white top hat for the... wedding.' Harper's words were stilted.

'Well, you won't be needing that now. White, you say? How very progressive. I thought to pop along and see what's on offer at some point.'

'Hmm.' Harper wasn't really listening, his mind once again centred on Ella.

'Harper! For goodness' sake man, pull yourself together!'

'What? Oh yes, sorry.' Harper tried to concentrate on what his friend was saying.

'Come on, let's go for a ride on the heath and then we'll lunch somewhere expensive,' Stafford said as he jumped to his feet.

Harper joined him, and together they walked quietly from the room, feeling eyes watching them, peeping over the tops of newspapers.

* * *

In Silver Street, Ella had woken with a headache. It took her a moment to realise where she was, and with a sigh she sat up.

Retreating to the warmth of the kitchen, she hastily made a meat and potato pie and shoved it into the range to bake. Opening the doors to the stairs and front room to allow the heat to circulate, she then made tea.

Tomorrow she would open her little business to the public once more and pray she had some custom. Then she had a thought – perhaps after lunch she could go and see what Ivy had in her window. The woman, from all reports, had been stealing her ideas, so it was time she found out what Ivy had produced.

After a slice of pie straight from the oven, Ella donned her hat and coat and wrapped a thick woollen shawl around her shoulders. Grabbing her gloves and bag, she walked out of the house and bumped into Sally.

'Where you off to?'

Ella explained and Sally invited herself along. Meandering the streets, they noted the sudden cold snap seemed to be keeping people indoors. The freezing air nipped their noses and Ella pulled up her shawl, glad now that she had worn it. They walked towards a man loading a few sticks of furniture onto a cart, while the horse stood puffing out hot breaths, causing steam clouds to appear.

The man doffed his cap and Ella nodded as they passed by; another family moving or being forced out because they were too poor to pay the rent.

Ella shivered as she walked on. If her business failed, she could find herself in that man's position. Her train of thought made her shiver again. No sales – no money – no rent paid – no home.

Turning into Junction Street, Ella wondered if Ivy would spot them walking past the shop. It couldn't be helped, it had to be done. Pulling her shawl up higher over her nose, Ella tugged her hat low over her eyes. Was this what Ivy had done when checking out Ella's designs? Slowly walking to the shop, Ella passed it, her eyes taking in as much information as possible.

Sally, however, stood to gaze into the window.

'Sally! Don't let Ivy see you!' Ella whispered loudly.

'It won't matter, she doesn't know me,' Sally returned with a roll of her eyes.

Ella felt a little foolish at the truth of her sister's words.

Hurrying around the corner into Rutter Street, Ella breathed hard as she walked swiftly towards home, going over in her mind what she had seen. Sally followed along quietly, not wanting to disturb Ella's thoughts.

Happy to be in her warm kitchen once more, Ella stripped off her outdoor clothing and snatched up a pencil. Quickly sketching what was in Ivy's window, she wrote the prices alongside each diagram.

Watching avidly, Sally was amazed as the little drawings came to life on the paper. She'd had no idea her sister was so talented.

'How did you remember all that?' she asked.

'I have to if my business is to survive,' Ella replied.

'I'll put the kettle on,' Sally said.

Ella nodded, her eyes still on the sketches. 'There's some coffee left, I think.'

Ella allowed herself one cup of coffee a day because it was so expensive to buy, and as she stared at the drawings, she felt now was the time to indulge herself.

Savouring her hot drink, she stared at the paper on the table. Undoubtedly these were her designs, but poorly constructed, which the prices reflected. Ella now knew what her rival had in stock, so she not only had to come up with new creations, but also a new sign and window display.

Grabbing the pencil again, she began to doodle with little signs and words. How could she grab the attention of women passing by her window? Then her eyes rested on the ribbon she had rolled into a rose and she smiled.

Searching through her haberdashery, she pulled out all the ribbons she could find. With needle and thread, she began to work.

Sally sipped her coffee as she watched Ella's deft fingers, astonished at what they were producing.

'This coffee is delicious, how can you afford it? We certainly can't,' Sally muttered.

'I bought it as a treat for Dad,' Ella answered and felt a stab of pain as she glanced at the space where the wheelchair had once been.

'Can I do anything to help?' Sally asked.

Ella shook her head as she concentrated on keeping her stitches as small as possible.

'I was wondering what you were going to do with the furniture in Dad's room,' Sally said tentatively.

'I don't know yet, why?'

'Well, I thought – if you don't want it, could I have it?'

Ella looked up from her work with a frown. 'Whatever for? You have nowhere to put it in your house.'

'I could sell it; the money would be useful to buy some stuff for the baby.'

Ella stared in disbelief at her sister's callousness. 'What about me? What would I gain from it?' She didn't particularly want what could be got from selling the furniture but felt obliged to challenge her sister.

'I didn't think you'd mind – it would be for the little 'un, after all,' Sally said feeling maybe she'd taken a step too far regarding her sister's good nature.

'Sally, it's not up to me to provide for your child. Eddy should be doing that!' Ella said sharply.

'I know, but he can't find a job anywhere!' Sally snapped back.

'I'm sorry, but he will have to look harder. Dad's furniture is staying where it is.' Ella was shocked that Sally had asked such a thing, especially as Thomas was not even in the ground yet. 'Was this Eddy's idea?' she asked suddenly.

Sally shifted in her chair, clearly uncomfortable that Ella had guessed the truth of the matter.

'I thought so. Sally, you *have* to be firmer with him!'

'It's not my fault he can't get a job!' Sally's rejoinder was acidic.

'I realise that, but how hard is he searching? He's idle to the bone, Sally, we both know that, so don't try to deny it.'

'That's a bit harsh, our Ella,' Sally replied, although inwardly she had to agree.

'It's the truth, Sally! I'm sorry, but I won't sell off *my father's* furniture to give you the proceeds while he sits on his lazy backside!' Ella's temper flared and she winced as the needle pricked her finger. Sticking the digit into her mouth she sucked hard.

Sally rinsed out her cup and laid it aside to drain. 'I should get back and see what progress Eddy's made, then.'

Ella nodded as she inspected her tiny injury. She sighed heavily as she watched her sister leave. *The cheek of it!* she thought. *Some people have no respect!*

By evening, Ella had an array of beautiful roses. Now to work on a sign. After an hour, she had something she thought might work.

> *Ella's fresh new collection of millinery now available.*
> *Turn heads with your bespoke purchase.*
> *Come in for a warm welcome and find your pot of gold.*

Pausing in her work for a bite to eat and a cup of tea, she then set her mind to a window display. Stringing the ribbon roses together like a rainbow, Ella smiled. She stood and stretched her back, her eyes moving to where Thomas used to sit. Nodding with a smile, she knew at last she had inherited her father's flair for creativity. Sitting by the open door of the range, she felt satisfied with her efforts. She would dress the window first thing in the morning, then all she had to do was wait and see if it worked.

Comfortable and warm, Ella was soon fast asleep.

20

Early the next morning, Ella began by removing her bereavement notice and sign. Cleaning the window and shelf beneath, she then hung her rainbows of ribbons with the aid of fine thread and pins pushed into the surround. At the end of the lowest rainbow she placed a hat box with her name inscribed in beautiful copperplate writing. At the end of the same rainbow she hung her new sign. With a nod of satisfaction, she retired to the kitchen to begin working on sketches of new designs as they came into her head.

Around mid-morning, a knock came, which made Ella jump to her feet. Opening the door, she saw a tall thin man standing there.

'I've come about a hat,' he said.

Ella knew that to have the custom and earn some money she would have to invite the man inside. However, her senses screamed a warning. She did not know this man. Would she be safe alone in his company? What would people say, knowing she was allowing young men into the house, albeit on a business footing? She would quickly gain the reputation of being a wanton woman – a doxy.

'Sir, I'm afraid as I am alone due to bereavement, I would ask you only step into the doorway where you can be clearly seen by others.' It was the best Ella could do if she wanted the custom.

The man nodded and entered. Ella left the door wide open, shivering in the blast of frosty air that accompanied him.

'I am sorry for your loss, Miss...?' Stafford Darnell asked.

'Bancroft – Ella Bancroft.'

'It's a pleasure to meet you, I've heard such good things about your little – business.' Darnell said as he glanced around the little room.

Ella's hackles rose and her instinct told her to be careful with this man.

'My name is Stafford Darnell and my friend Harper suggested I call to see you.' The lie tripped lightly from his tongue.

'Mr Fortescue...' Ella said as she pulled her shawl tighter about her shoulders and stepped away from the open doorway. 'He bought a range from me.'

'Including a white topper, which he will no longer have need of!' Stafford said indiscreetly.

Ella frowned but did not pursue the matter. Besides being none of her business, she wanted this man gone from her house. She was desperate to close the door on the cold world outside.

'What can I do for you, Mr Darnell?'

'I just came to see what's on offer,' he said, his eyes roaming over Ella's body.

Well, I'm not on offer, sir! she thought but said instead, 'If you have nothing particular in mind, may I suggest you call back once you have decided.'

Stafford inclined his head and, as he made to push past her, Ella stepped out into the street to allow him to exit.

With a smarmy smile, Stafford donned his bowler and gave her a small bow. 'I will be seeing *you* again, Ella Bancroft.'

'Good day, sir,' Ella said stiffly, before going indoors and slamming the door shut.

Rushing back to the kitchen, Ella fed the range and sat before its open door. That man had made her feel very uncomfortable – even afraid.

This was ridiculous, she couldn't possibly work this way with all the precious heat escaping through an open door. Then again, she couldn't afford to turn custom away. Caught on the horns of a dilemma, Ella pondered her predicament. She certainly didn't want to be alone in the house with strange men, but she desperately needed the money.

Hearing another knock, Ella shivered. Going to the front room, she peeped through the window. Seeing a woman standing waiting, she hurried to open the door.

'Ella?'

'Yes, please come in.'

The woman walked in with, 'I've come on a recommendation from my friend Eléna Fortescue.'

God bless that woman!

'Ah, yes, she is one of my best clients. How may I help you today?'

'I need a hat for the theatre, noting too ostentatious, you understand,' the woman said as she gazed around the room.

'Certainly, madam. Did you have a particular colour in mind?'

'I have a penchant for pink.'

'Then I may have just the thing,' Ella said. Finding the box she sought, she lifted the lid and drew out a pastel pink pill box hat with a short cream veil and a matching silk rose.

Passing it to her customer, Ella pointed to the mirror on the wall. The woman removed her own hat.

'May I?' Ella asked.

With a nod from her customer, Ella placed the small hat on the side of the head and secured it with a pearl hat pin. Gently she pulled the little veil down over one eye, then motioned to the mirror once more.

'Oh, yes! I like it very much. I'll take it,' the woman said without even asking the price.

'Thank you, madam,' Ella said as she quickly wrote out a receipt, which she placed in the box followed by the hat.

Paid and happy, Ella saw the woman out with, 'Please do call again.'

With a nod, the string handle over her fingers, the woman strode away.

Back in the kitchen, Ella immediately put the money with the rent book in the drawer of the dresser. With the rent covered for another week, Ella now had to look to buying more coal and food as well as paying the gas bill. She would have to sell a fair few hats to manage all that, besides finding a solution to selling her men's range.

* * *

Stafford Darnell had walked away from Silver Street with an amused look on his face. Ella Bancroft was a beauty, despite being in mourning. He laughed inwardly at her efforts to try to act the lady and maintain her dignity. Whoever did she think she was? Clearly she thought herself special; an illusion which, when shattered, would be a bitter blow to her. She was a girl in a tiny two up, two down house in a poor part of the town. She had set up a business in her front room selling hats of indeterminate quality, as far as he knew, for he had not actually seen any. He had been there all of a minute before she threw him out, albeit very nicely. That was when Stafford had seen the fire in her eyes; a deep smouldering which said she could be passionate about people and things she loved. He had spotted the challenge on her countenance as she had indicated he should leave her house.

The more Stafford thought of Ella Bancroft, the more he liked her. Could she provide a little light entertainment for him one of these cold lonely nights? The idea of seeing how long it would take him to entice her into his bed appealed to him immensely. She would be another feather in his cap. Stafford laughed out loud at the pun as he swung into the saddle on the horse he'd left tethered to a lamp post.

As he guided the beast in a turn, he wondered whether Harper would be interested in taking on a bet – one involving Ella Bancroft.

21

'I *will not* attend!' Darcie Newland snapped.

'Darling, everyone of any importance will be here at two o'clock sharp,' Verity said.

'Mother, I don't care!'

'Sweetheart, all the wives of the big business owners are coming to discuss raising funds for the Union Workhouse.' Verity was doing her utmost to include her daughter in the afternoon tea gathering.

'So?'

'I'd like you to be in attendance,' Verity pursued.

'Why?'

Verity sighed loudly. 'Darcie, you cannot hide yourself away forever. You have to face people sooner or later.'

'And have them laugh at me? Poor jilted Darcie Newland – what a shame!'

'It won't be like that, dear,' Verity tried again.

'Yes, it will!'

'They won't know unless you tell them.'

'Mother, we both know that nothing remains a secret for

long. It wouldn't surprise me if I'm not already the talk of the town!' Darcie blubbered.

'Will you *please* do this for me?' Verity begged.

'No, I will not! I do not intend to attend your little meeting, so don't ask me again!' With that, Darcie swept from the parlour, her long skirts swishing as she went.

Verity stared after her daughter and she wondered where she'd gone wrong in the girl's upbringing. At eighteen years old, Darcie should now be betrothed at the very least – and had been until Harper Fortescue had thought better of the idea. Darcie had grown from a wayward child into a wilful young woman, who was proving harder to control as time went on.

Verity stared into the fire as she wished her daughter were married and no longer their responsibility. She knew in her heart that Harper had been Darcie's best chance at becoming a wife, for her reputation for bad temper and spite preceded her wherever she went. How could she arrange a marriage for her daughter now? Was there anyone who would take the girl on? Verity doubted it, certainly not in Walsall, anyway. Maybe if they looked further afield – Birmingham, possibly. Royston had business contacts everywhere so he would have to find a suitable match somehow. Making the decision to leave the whole thing in her husband's capable hands, Verity went to the kitchen to check on the preparations for her meeting.

Darcie was in her room, staring out of the window onto the extensive grounds. Looking down at the long driveway that curled up from the roadway, Darcie moved her eyes to the lawns either side, which were bordered by flowerbeds. It had begun to rain and everywhere was grey and drab, which only served to blacken her mood further. She was angry with Harper for calling off the wedding; she was irate at her parents for allowing it to happen. Tapping her foot with frustration, she knew she could do nothing about it. Rafe Fortescue had threatened her with arrest for assault if she so much as opened her mouth.

Hearing carriage wheels crunch on the gravel of the drive and women's voices greet each other in a false so-pleased-to-see-you tone, Darcie scowled. How could her mother think of entertaining at a time like this? Was Verity deliberately ignoring her daughter's distress so she didn't have to deal with it?

Darcie considered: maybe she should attend the small gathering, if only to remind her mother of how she was suffering. Maybe she could let slip the odd word here and there so the guests might guess at her plight. Then she could not be accused of spreading tittle-tattle.

The corners of her mouth lifted in an evil little smile and her blue eyes glinted like glacial ice. Turning away from the window, her blonde ringlets bouncing, Darcie ran from her room. She had decided she would attend Verity's meeting, after all.

'Ah, Darcie, I'm so glad you decided to join us,' Verity cooed as her daughter nodded a greeting to the women gathered in the parlour. 'Afternoon tea first, I think, then we'll move on to the business in hand.'

Darcie saw all eyes dart to the clock on the mantelpiece and guessed what the women were thinking. Afternoon tea at two o'clock? However, no one challenged Verity's decision and, as the maid produced plates of little sandwiches and pastries as well as three-tiered stands dotted with tiny cakes, the gossiping began.

Darcie waited with bated breath for the chatter to turn to herself and her wedding, as she knew it would eventually.

A woman with a face like an owl glared at Darcie and asked, 'So m'dear, how are the wedding plans going?' *There it was.*

Darcie and her mother exchanged a quick glance before Verity said quickly, 'Darcie has changed her mind and will not now be marrying Harper Fortescue.'

Gasps sounded as accusing eyes settled on her.

'Poor Harper, I expect he was heartbroken at the news,' another of the gathering said.

'How very unfortunate, Harper would have been the ideal match for you, Darcie,' owl-eyes put in.

Darcie bit her tongue to prevent the whole story pouring forth.

'Whatever made you change your mind, dear?' yet another asked as she shook her head, making the feather in her hat wobble precariously.

'That must be a tale for another day, ladies, for today we are all about raising funds for the Union Workhouse,' Verity stepped in quickly. Picking up her pen and paper she went on, 'So, what ideas do we have?'

Darcie fumed inwardly at not having the opportunity to hint at the truth of the matter. She wanted these women to know what a blackguard Harper Fortescue was without actually telling them outright. Her blue eyes held a dark anger as she turned them on her mother, who was fussing with a little table to rest her writing implements on.

There were two ways of looking at this, the first being that Verity had saved her daughter from revealing all and possibly being arrested for assault. The other option, which was the one filling Darcie with frustrated disgust, was that Harper Fortescue had dumped her and was getting away with it scot-free.

Realising her chance of dropping Harper in the mire had passed, Darcie stood up abruptly. With a swish of her skirts she swept from the room, to everyone's surprise.

'Young girls are so fickle these days,' Verity said to cover her daughter's rude behaviour. 'Now, what were you saying, Deidre?'

22

Ella was glad to see the back of Stafford Darnell; he had made her skin crawl. He had behaved as a gentleman should, but there was something about him that made her distrust him.

With a shudder, she sat by the table and wished again that her father was still there. Getting stuck into her work, as grief threatened to overwhelm her again, she glanced up at the brief knock on the back door before it opened.

'How are you, gel?' Mrs Woolley asked, rubbing her hands together to get the blood flowing again.

'I'm all right, thank you.'

'You should think about renting out yer dad's room, you know; it would be safer for you, especially having men coming here.'

'Mrs Woolley, I'm not sure...' Ella began, horrified at the thought of someone else using Thomas's room.

'I know how you feel, Ella, but think on this – you'll lose custom from the men if you can't have them inside,' her neighbour interrupted.

'I understand that. Maybe after the funeral I'll consider it.'

'You do that, lass. If you managed to get a nice young lady it would help with rent and the like.'

'She would have to be working, though, which wouldn't really help with my problem as she'd be out all day.' Ella shrugged, feeling there was no answer to her predicament regarding selling hats to men.

'I see what you mean, but at least it would be company for you if nothing else.'

'I can't deny that would be nice,' Ella admitted, but still couldn't shake the feeling she would be betraying her dad by letting out his room.

As if reading her mind, Mrs Woolley said, 'Yer dad would be happier knowing you weren't lonely, I'm sure. Anyway, I just popped in to see how you were doing.' With that and a quick wave, Ella's neighbour left to return to her brood of children, who were probably running riot.

Ella considered what Mrs Woolley had suggested and, the more she thought on it, the more she liked the idea. It would be nice to have someone to chat to in the evenings, as well as bounce her ideas off for new creations.

Grabbing a pen and paper, Ella wrote out an advert for the newspaper. It would cost her initially, but in the long run she could reap the benefits of having someone to share the expenses.

The knocker rapped and Ella went to take a squint through the front window. With a sigh of relief, she opened the door to a lady customer.

'How can I help you?' Ella asked once her client was indoors.

'I've gorra weddin' to go to in late spring, so I want summat as I can wear afterwards,' the woman said as she blew on her cold hands.

Ella pulled out three boxes and displayed her wares.

'They're lovely but I ain't got a lot to spend.'

'Tell me your budget and I'll see what I can do,' Ella answered with a warm smile.

It wasn't long before the satisfied woman left with her purchase and Ella returned to the kitchen. Putting the money in the dresser drawer, she smiled: at least she was still earning.

As she resumed her work, she wondered how Ivy Gladwin's business was faring. Ivy should be doing well – after all, she had a shop, where Ella only had a front room. It would take Ella a lifetime to save enough money to buy a shop; even renting would be too expensive, but she could continue to dream.

Smoothing a circle of black wet sinamay over a head block, Ella pinned it in place and put it aside to dry out. Then she began to sew tiny pearls on the black veiling ready to be attached. The colours she worked with suited her mood at the moment, drab and dark. Sorting through her feather collection she chose a brown goose quill, a couple of pheasant feathers and a peacock one to complete the ensemble. Cutting them to length, she bound them together with thread and carefully curled them over the steam kettle.

Ella worked steadily through the day, with customers coming and going, and her coffers continued to swell. Turning the sign to 'closed', she retreated to the kitchen for a well-earned rest. Too tired to cook, she grabbed a chunk of bread and a wedge of cheese. With fresh tea she settled to her meal.

As she ate, she made the decision to clear out Thomas's room the following day. Being Sunday, she could take her time hopefully without being disturbed by customers. Then, on Monday morning, she would take the advert for a lodger to be placed in the newspaper, before preparing herself for the funeral later that day. She had requested the interment to take place as soon as possible, and the undertaker had been very accommodating. Ella needed to say her last goodbye to her father in order to be able to move on with her life.

Feeling better for having eaten and now having a plan in place, she began work again on her millinery creations.

* * *

Shown into the parlour at The Cedars, Stafford Darnell was greeted warmly by Harper.

'How do you fancy taking on a little bet, old boy?' Stafford asked with a grin as he settled himself before the fire.

'What are you up to now, Stafford?'

'I've met a real cutie and I intend for her to grace my four-poster as soon as possible.'

'You are incorrigible, Stafford. Who is this *cutie*?'

'No names, it makes it more interesting,' Darnell said wagging a finger in the air. 'The bet is how long it will take me to woo her into my bed. Are you up for it?'

'No, I'm not. That's a woman's virtue you are playing with and it's not right,' Harper said, with a frown of disgust.

'Come on, Harper, take the bet. It's only a bit of fun. She isn't anyone important. Don't be such a wet rag.'

'She's important to someone, Stafford. I'll bet on the horses but not on this ridiculous idea of yours. You should be ashamed at even thinking it, let alone trying to do it.' Harper was trying his best to talk his friend out of the notion of despoiling a woman for the fun of it.

'Ah, well, it was worth a try,' Darnell said.

The maid brought in the tea tray and as they drank Harper eyed his long-time friend. He knew from experience that Stafford would not let the idea go so easily. Never one to back away from a challenge, Stafford would find a way around it. He would probably take the bet elsewhere and there would be nothing Harper could do about it. He pitied the poor girl in question, whoever she was.

They chatted a while over their tea, then Stafford rose to leave. 'I'm lunching at the racetrack today if you fancy joining me.'

'Thank you, no. I have things to do today,' Harper replied. It was his intention to go and see Ella again to assure himself she was all right.

Stafford saluted, as Harper said, 'Forget that silly bet, Stafford. Think how you would feel if it were your sister.'

Harper was left in peace to mull over what had been said. However, his thoughts quickly turned to Ella once more. He could not get her out of his mind; she plagued his days and haunted his nights. He would find any excuse to go and see her and if he couldn't find a suitable reason – he would go anyway. Harper sat quietly for a while, savouring the image in his mind of the girl who had stolen his heart.

23

The day began dull and grey, with banks of dark clouds rolling overhead. It was all Ella could do to rouse herself for the task that lay ahead.

Lingering over breakfast, Ella knew she was prevaricating; the thought of clearing and cleaning Thomas's room made her stomach churn.

Eventually she grabbed a broom, dustpan and brush, a duster and some beeswax and headed upstairs. Opening the wardrobe, her heart sank. A couple of shirts, an old jacket, a pair of trousers and ancient leather boots were all that it contained. It was not much, gathered over a lifetime. Scooping up the items, she piled them on the landing to be thrown out later. Polishing the wardrobe inside and out, Ella began to feel she was doing something worthwhile. The room needed to be spotless if she were to have a lodger.

The chest of drawers held a few undergarments, which were put with the rest. In the corner of the top drawer, Ella found a little box. Lifting the lid revealed a gold wedding band, worn thin over years of wearing.

Sitting on the bed, Ella's eyes brimmed with tears as she held her mother's wedding ring. She'd had no idea Thomas had kept it.

'Dad, I hope you found Mum and you are both happy to be together again,' she whispered. Kissing the ring, she placed it back in the box, which she dropped into her apron pocket.

After polishing the chest of drawers, Ella swept the carpet then finally dusted the furniture once more. She cleaned the window and washed the curtains, which she hung on the towel rack over the range to dry. On a second thought, Ella decided that Thomas's clothes should be given to any who could make use of them.

Back downstairs, Ella sat with hot tea, glad the job was done. Now the room was ready, and she hoped the advertisement would provide her with a good lodger.

The back door opened and Sally bustled in. Spotting the pile of clothes, she raised her eyebrows.

'It looks like you've been busy,' she said as she felt the teapot. Grabbing a cup, she helped herself to a hot drink.

'I thought it was time,' Ella replied.

'Did you find anything of value?' Sally asked, even though she knew it was unlikely.

Ella pulled out the little box and passed it to her sister. 'Mum's wedding ring, it was the only thing he had left.'

'What shall we do with it?' Sally asked.

'I'd like to keep it, it's all we have of Mum,' Ella said sadly.

'We could sell it and split the money,' Sally suggested.

'No, not yet anyway. If the time comes when we need to then we will.' Ella couldn't bear the thought of losing the last tie to her mother, despite Sally not feeling the same.

Taking the box back, Ella slipped it into the safety of her apron pocket once more. 'I've decided to advertise for a lodger.'

Sally's eyebrows shot up in surprise. 'It makes sense, I suppose,' she said, although she was still clearly smarting over the ring.

'I thought so. It will help with the bills and I'll have company.'

'Make sure you only take someone trustworthy,' Sally said.

'I will,' Ella replied, feeling like a child at being told what to do. 'Has Eddy had any luck with finding work?'

Sally shook her head. 'The only thing going was street cleaner up at the market.'

'Did he take it?'

'Do me a favour! Eddy sweeping the streets? Certainly not. He said he was worth more than that, and I agree with him.'

'Sally, it's a job and beggars can't be choosers. What will you do when the baby comes and you have nothing collected for it?'

'We'll just have to manage,' Sally said with a shrug. She had said nothing to Ella about the money left to Eddy by his parents, but she knew that would not last forever.

'Do you have any idea how much it costs having a child these days? And it won't stay a baby for long. Before you know it, you'll have to find money for bigger clothes and shoes.'

'I know that! I'm not a dolt!' Sally snapped. 'Regardless, I'm not having my husband sweeping streets!'

'Have it your own way, but be aware I'm not in a position to help.'

'I don't remember asking you to!'

'I'm just saying.'

The sisters sat in silence, making for an uncomfortable hiatus. Eventually Sally got to her feet. 'I'll see you tomorrow at the churchyard.'

Ella nodded and watched her go. Why was it that her sister had the ability to rub her up the wrong way at every given opportunity? Even when they were children Sally would make snide

comments and cause arguments. How come they were so different? Ella was finding it harder as time went on to hold her tongue
against Sally's spiteful comments and bossy ways. Having to
make her own way in life now, Ella didn't need Sally to tell her
how to do it.

With a sigh, Ella began her work, and it wasn't long before
her thoughts drifted to Harper Fortescue. She wondered why he
no longer needed his white top hat as that fellow Darnell had
said. Had something happened? Had Miss Newland called off the
wedding? Ella couldn't imagine that Darcie would do that, but
evidently Darnell knew something she didn't. Recalling the
scratches on Harper's face, she tried to guess if it was all
connected in some way. She had no doubt all would become
clear in the fullness of time.

* * *

Meanwhile, over in Cross Street, Sally was telling her husband
about her visit to Ella.

'She *should* sell that ring because you are entitled to half of
the proceeds,' Eddy said.

'Well, she won't, so that's an end to it. I'll put some water on to
heat for your bath.'

'What bath?' Eddy asked, a look of horror on his face.

'Ready for the funeral tomorrow,' Sally reminded him.

'I don't need a bath for that!'

'Please yourself, it will save me the bother,' Sally said with a
grimace.

'Good, now leave me in peace to read the newspaper.'

Sally looked at the man she had fallen in love with and was
surprised at how much he had changed in the two years they had
been wed. Whilst they were courting, Eddy had been clean and

tidy; quite the Jack-the-lad. Then, twelve months into their married life, Eddy's mother had died, his father having passed some years before. The sad event had been like a trigger for Eddy, who suddenly saw himself as the lord of the manor. He spent money hand over fist in the local public houses with never a thought for his wife.

Now, as she stared, she wondered if she even liked him any more. There were times when she thought she still loved him, but they were few and far between.

Eddy's shaking of the newspaper snapped her attention back. Going to the kitchen, Sally began to prepare the evening meal. Mixing skinned and finely chopped kidney with suet and breadcrumbs, adding nutmeg, salt and pepper, she stirred in a beaten egg. Pouring the mixture into a thick pottery basin, she set it to steam for an hour. Kidney pudding was one of Eddy's favourites, which would hopefully make him more susceptible to discussing the work issue. One thing was clear, if he couldn't or wouldn't find a job, then she would have to, at least until her birthing time.

Early the following morning, Ella took the advert to the *Walsall Observer* office and paid to have it placed in their newspaper.

On her return home, she brushed down the clothes she was to wear to her father's funeral. She polished her boots and selected a black hat from her 'for sale' range. Her dad would have smiled at her taking the opportunity to show off her creation at his interment.

For the next couple of hours, she worked in the quiet kitchen until it was time to go, all the while trying to stem the tears that seemed to be choking her.

Lost in her thoughts, Ella didn't hear Flossie Woolley come in through the back door.

'You ready, gel?'

'Yes, I think so.' Ella fixed her hat in place and donned her coat. Picking up her bag and umbrella, she glanced around. Then the two women left to walk to the cemetery at the other side of the railway line.

Sally and Eddy were already there when Ella and Mrs Woolley arrived. Few words were spoken between them as they waited for the carriage bearing the coffin. The vicar came to greet them, and moments later they heard the crunch of wheels on the gravel path.

Ella saw the conductor walking ahead of the hearse with slow steps. The mourners followed the carriage to the spot where Thomas Bancroft would be laid to rest.

The coffin was lifted down and laid on the ground over the thick webbing straps, and it was as the conductor bowed his head in reverence that Ella was undone. Her silent tears rolled down her cold cheeks and she made no move to brush them away.

Flossie Woolley place an arm around her waist as Ella sagged; Sally, she noted, was watching with insouciance.

Ella looked up as the vicar took a pause in his reading and she was shocked to see Harper Fortescue standing close by. She returned his nod as Sally's head twisted on her shoulders to take in the scene.

The vicar continued with the short service, but Ella's mind was distracted. How had Harper known when and where to come? She'd said nothing to him regarding the arrangements when she had last seen him. Thomas would have been pleased the young man had taken the time to say a last goodbye.

As the coffin was lowered into the ground, an eerie keening carried across the cemetery. Ella had no idea it was coming from her own lips. The sound echoed and bounced off gravestones that had stood for decades.

Finally, Ella's strength gave out, and she fell to her knees, sobbing violently.

'Dad! Oh, Dad!'

Flossie had been unable to hold the girl upright and stood by, mopping at her own tears. It was Harper who rushed to a stricken Ella and raised her to her feet, holding her tightly lest she fall again.

Sally scowled at the impropriety of the move but kept her counsel. Harper was the one who thanked the vicar before the little gathering walked away.

Sally and Eddy were muttering quietly, their heads close together. Clearly neither had any idea who this stranger was.

Harper pulled Ella's arm through his bent elbow and led them back to Silver Street. Once indoors, he sat Ella down and introduced himself to what remained of Ella's family.

'My name is Harper Fortescue and Thomas was my friend.'

Although they had only met once, Harper had immediately taken to Ella's father, and had he lived, Harper would have been proud to call him a friend.

Shaking hands, Eddy introduced himself and his wife. Flossie Woolley made herself useful making tea as Ella sat in silence. Voices sounded on the periphery of her hearing, but the conversations didn't register with her. Her mind was still reeling from the sadness of the funeral.

'Here you are, Ella, get that down you,' Flossie said, passing over a cup of sweet tea.

Ella nodded her thanks and sipped the hot liquid. Slowly she began to focus on the people around her.

'I didn't know you had invited Mr Fortescue, Ella, you said nothing to me about it.' Sally's mood was sour at not being informed about Harper's attendance.

'I...' Ella stammered, not entirely sure how to explain.

'I was not formally invited, Mrs Denton, but felt the need to pay my respects,' Harper responded.

Sally glanced at Eddy who shook his head; he was of no help whatsoever.

Seeing Sally was about to cavil his presence, he pre-empted her with, 'I considered this very carefully before making my decision. I offer my apologies if I have offended you in any way.'

Sally nodded then turned to Ella. 'Eddy agrees with me that you should sell Mother's ring and split the money between us, don't you, Eddy?'

Put on the spot, he glanced at each face in turn. His wife had embarrassed him in front of everyone and he squirmed as he looked at his shoes.

'This is not the time, Sally,' Ella said, feeling thoroughly exhausted.

'Then I'll come for it tomorrow and take it to sell myself.' Turning to her husband she added, 'Come on, you.'

Eddy followed his wife meekly out of the back door.

'Well, I never!' Flossie snapped.

'I'm sorry about that,' Ella said in a whisper.

'Please don't concern yourself on my account,' Harper said.

'Nor mine,' Flossie muttered.

'Sally needs money for when her baby comes and Eddy won't get a job,' Ella explained. 'But I don't want to sell Mum's ring, it's all I have left of her.'

'Then hide it away, wench, and don't tell Sally where you've put it,' Flossie said in earnest.

'Am I being selfish, wanting to keep it?'

'No, most certainly not,' Harper answered. 'If you take it to the bank, they will keep it secure for you until you wish to retrieve it. You will, of course, have to pay a nominal fee.'

Ella shook her head. 'I can't afford that at present as all of my money is accounted for. I have rent to pay and food to buy as well as haberdashery for my hats. It may be I will have to agree to Sally's demand.'

'I don't see why. If that lazy bugger got off his arse and found a job, you wouldn't need to sell that ring. Be ruled with me, sweetheart, and 'ang on to it, for if you don't you'll regret it for the rest of your days.' Flossie crossed her arms over her chest in a final gesture.

'I'm inclined to agree, Ella,' Harper added.

'That settles it, then. Flossie, I have a favour to ask – would you keep Mum's ring safe for me until I can afford to have it put in the bank?'

'Course I will. Give it here and I'll put it alongside my own mum's stuff. Nobody will dare to touch it.'

Ella fetched the gold wedding band from the drawer in the dresser. Giving it a quick kiss, she handed it over. 'Thank you.'

'I'll leave you in Mrs Woolley's care, Ella, but I will visit again if that's all right?'

Ella nodded. 'Thank you for coming today, Dad would have been touched.'

Harper left the women and made his way home. Flossie and Ella sat with more tea, discussing Sally. Flossie's disapprobation at Sally's treatment of her sister was evident. The difference between the girls was astonishing, and Flossie was glad it was Ella who was her neighbour.

25

The nation was in shock. Their beloved queen was dead. At eighty-one years old, Queen Victoria had passed away, leaving her son Edward to take the throne. The newspapers were splashed with the news and folk gathered in the market and on street corners to discuss what this would mean for them. They would be getting a new king; how would this affect the everyday lives of the population? Victoria had reigned for almost sixty-four years – would Edward VII be as lucky?

Women wept openly at the loss of their monarch and children were bewildered by their mothers' tears. However, as sad as it was, life had to go on and men went to their work with heads bowed in respect.

The papers would keep the populace informed of events over the next weeks and months; the printing presses working overtime to fulfil demand. The town criers called out the sorrowful news to the illiterate and, despite the weather, crowds gathered to share their grief. Grey clouds rolled, adding further misery to those standing beneath them. Rain pattered down, the freezing droplets making people shiver, but still they stood, feeling the great loss as if it were a member of their own family.

A knock to the front door had Ella on her feet. Opening it, she was faced with a girl much her own age. Twinkling blue eyes shone out from a face with a perfect complexion. Blonde curls bounced as she shivered in the cold.

'Can I help you?' Ella asked. She had considered closing for the day as a mark of respect for the deceased queen, but her finances had dictated otherwise.

'My name's Kitty Fiske and I've come about the room.'

'Oh, yes, please come in.' Ella had almost forgotten about the advert she had placed in the paper. Leading Kitty to the kitchen she asked, 'Would you like a cup of tea? I've just made a fresh pot.'

'Ooh, ta, that'd be nice.'

Ella smiled as the girl sat herself at the table.

'What are you making – hats?'

Ella nodded. 'I'm a milliner and I work from my front room.'

Giving her thanks, Kitty sipped the hot drink.

'So, you're interested in renting my spare room?' Ella asked.

'Ar, well – look, I'll be honest with you. I used to work up at Roberts's leather works but I quit. Old man Roberts got a little too – let's say familiar.'

Ella felt her heart sink. Miss Fiske wanted the room but with no job she wouldn't be able to pay rent.

'I see. I really need someone who can pay something towards the household bills.'

'I understand that, but I can get another job.'

'How can you be so sure?'

'Looking like this?' Kitty ran her hands down her figure. 'It shouldn't be a problem.' Kitty laughed and Ella joined in.

The girl had confidence in abundance and Ella could see

why. She had an outstanding beauty, which would turn heads wherever she went.

'I could always help you with your hats – in exchange for bed and board,' Kitty went on, 'I'm a quick learner.'

Ella found herself caught up in Kitty's enthusiasm and considered the proposal. If they worked together, they could make more hats; maybe Kitty would have some new ideas, too. Should that prove to be the case then they would definitely sell more. The other advantage was that Kitty would be on site, so Ella could take gentlemen customers without fear of gossip ensuing.

The two chatted over more tea and Ella said at last, 'I think it could work, so I'll say yes, you can have the room provided you work alongside me making and selling my products.'

Kitty bounced on her chair with excitement. 'Thanks, Ella. I promise I won't let you down.'

Ella had a sudden thought and asked, 'Where are you living now?'

'I... erm... I've been staying behind the mortuary chapel in the cemetery.' The words came out in a rush, and Kitty's head lowered in embarrassment.

'Oh, my goodness! That settles it – welcome to your new home, Kitty.'

Kitty's blue eyes brimmed with tears of gratitude.

'Do you have any belongings?'

Kitty shook her head. 'No, what you see is what you get. I had to sell everything to buy food.'

'Right, come on and I'll show you the room. I have a couple of dresses that might fit you.'

'Ella,' Kitty said as she got to her feet, 'Thank you from the bottom of my heart.' Reaching into her coat pocket, she pulled out ten shillings. 'This is all I have left.'

Ella sighed. 'You keep it.'

Suddenly she felt herself held in a tight grip, and Ella smiled as she returned the hug. She had a feeling they would get along famously.

Later in the day, while Ella was showing Kitty her trade, Sally bustled in.

'God, it's cold out. Hello, who's this?'

Ella made the introductions and waited to hear what Sally would have to say about her taking in a lodger with no job.

'Ella, whatever are you thinking?' Sally made no move to cover her anger. 'You can barely feed yourself, let alone two!'

Explaining that they could increase sales working together, as well as not being alone in the house, Ella saw the acceptance creep over Sally's face.

'Anyway, I've only come for Mum's wedding ring.'

'I've already told you, I'm keeping it.'

'Ella, the money we get for it will come in useful, especially for me and the baby.' Sally laid a hand on her stomach in support of her argument.

Kitty felt uncomfortable as she watched the sisters' battle of wits. 'Maybe I should go up to my room.'

'No, you don't have to, Kitty. Sally and I rarely see eye to eye, so you'd best get used to it from the outset.'

A knock to the back door heralded the arrival of Flossie Woolley.

Sally sighed loudly. 'It's like Piccadilly Circus in here.'

'Hello to you an' all!' Flossie said snidely.

Again, introductions were made as the neighbour was given tea.

'Welcome to the street, Kitty,' Flossie said, but her eyes remained on Sally. 'I'm sure you'll be happy here with Ella.'

'Ta, Mrs Woolley. I think I will be,' the girl answered.

Sally harrumphed. 'Well, if you won't give me Mum's ring, I'll get home to Eddy.'

'Has he found a job yet?' Ella asked.

'No, but he's had a few offers,' Sally lied. 'He's deciding which one to take. I'll see you later in the week.'

After Sally had left, Flossie growled, 'That one needs her arse smacked!'

Kitty's tea spurted from her mouth and Ella burst out laughing as a smirk formed on Flossie's lips.

Suddenly, Ella felt deep in her bones that everything would be all right now. She had a wonderful neighbour and now a new friend in Kitty. Between them they could stand strong against anything that came at them. Even Ivy Gladwin wouldn't be able to break through this invisible barrier to hurt Ella again.

Unfortunately, Ella could not have been more wrong.

26

'Ah, Harper, come and join us for coffee,' Stafford Darnell called.

The gentlemen's club was almost empty at this time in the afternoon. Harper nodded a greeting to Stafford and his friend Oliver Holgate, another man they had grown up with.

Ordering coffee, Harper settled himself into a leather armchair and glanced around. He noted that despite Walsall having electricity, the members of the club had stubbornly refused to have it fitted. They did not hold with new-fangled ideas and had chosen instead to remain married to the gas lamps. Large armchairs and long settees were placed strategically around the room to provide privacy if needed, but also for members to enjoy the company of others. Wooden panelling covered the lower half of the walls and red flock wallpaper graced the upper half. Wall lamps were lit, the gas turned down low and the large chandelier hung in the centre of the ceiling, giving off a calming ambience.

Stewards stood quietly near the door, staying alert to any member who beckoned for service. Then they would move silently around the furniture in answer to a twitched finger and bend to listen to a whispered instruction. With a nod, they would respond immediately.

Harper smiled. It was a comfortable place to be and he was readily accepted by its older patrons.

'Stafford tells me your wedding is off!' Oliver said in an urgent whisper. He peered over the round spectacles balanced on the end of his nose. His dark hair was parted in the centre and greased into place, and his moustache jiggled as he spoke.

'For God's sake, Stafford! It was supposed to be a secret! Who else have you told?' Harper was angry at his friend's betrayal of his trust.

'No one, I swear,' Stafford answered sheepishly.

'Well, keep it that way!' Harper said hotly.

'Remember that bet I offered you about that girl? Well, Oliver has accepted it.' Stafford looked very pleased with himself at changing the subject so quickly, but Harper just shook his head.

'I hope no one does the same regarding your sister, Oliver.'

Clearly his friend hadn't considered this and had the good grace to look embarrassed.

'You can't back out now, old boy, we shook on it,' Stafford said with a laugh.

'Sorry, Harper,' Oliver muttered.

'You're idiots, the pair of you,' Harper replied.

'He won't even tell me who this girl is,' Oliver added.

'My question is – how will you know who wins the bet?' Harper asked.

Stafford and Oliver glanced at each other. This was something else that had not been considered.

'Maybe written proof. She could write me love letters professing her undying love,' Stafford suggested.

'It would have to contain mention of the dirty deed,' Oliver answered.

'Well, I'm sure you will hash it out between you. As for me, I want nothing to do with it. You should both feel ashamed of yourselves.' Harper stood to leave then, waving a warning finger at Darnell, he said, 'You keep your mouth closed about my business, Stafford, or else.'

'I swear, old boy, never fear.'

Harper sighed and bid them both farewell before leaving quietly, exchanging nods with others as he went.

Retrieving his horse from the stables at the back of the building, Harper wondered if he had tried hard enough to dissuade his friends from going through with the bet. Climbing into the saddle, he tossed a sixpence to the groom and guided the mare out onto the street. As he rode home his mind inevitably turned yet again to Ella Bancroft.

* * *

Meanwhile, Ella and Kitty sat in the kitchen chatting as if they had known each other forever.

'Don't you have any family?' Ella asked.

'No, they're all gone now.'

'I'm sorry, I shouldn't pry.'

'You should. You've been kind enough to take me in and it's only right you should know more about me,' Kitty said as she made herself useful putting the kettle to boil. 'I got a job at Roberts's leather works straight out of school, but as time went on Mr Roberts got bolder with his attentions towards me. In the end I told him to stuff his job up his arse.'

Ella burst out laughing. 'I'm sorry, I shouldn't laugh but...'

'Laughing is healthy, Ella; we should all do it more often. I don't get offended easily so you don't have to be guarded. I have no secrets and I'm honest and trustworthy. When I make a friend it's for life – unless I'm crossed, of course.' Kitty grinned as she poured boiling water over tea leaves in a brown teapot.

'I only have my sister now my father has passed away,' Ella said a little sadly.

'Sally? She's nothing like you at all.'

Ella shook her head with a sigh. 'We have never been able to get along, as much as I try. Even as children we fell out. Sally could pick an argument with her own fingernails!'

'Is she older than you?'

'Yes, by two years.'

'I guessed. She seems to have taken on the role of mother or boss, even.'

'I always back down in an argument, mostly to keep the peace, but I wouldn't where Mum's ring was concerned.'

'Nor should you. I thought it a bit cheeky her wanting the money from the sale, if you don't mind my saying.'

'She has a husband who won't go out and find work. God knows what they'll do when the baby comes.'

'That's not for you to worry about, Ella. I know you'll be an aunty but it's up to them to provide for the little 'un. It's not your responsibility.'

'I know you're right, but I can't help worrying.'

Seeing the sad look on Ella's face, Kitty determined a change of subject was in order.

'Right, Madame Ella, time to teach me the tricks of the trade of millinery.'

'Madame Ella, I like the sound of that.'

The rest of the afternoon was spent working closely together on hats and their decoration. Each time a customer called, Ella introduced Kitty as her new assistant. For her part, Kitty proved herself a natural saleswoman and Ella was delighted.

Locking up for the evening, the two girls prepared a meal,

chatting excitedly about the sales of the day. Later they began to work on new designs and Kitty breathed new life into old sketches. It was late when they retired to their beds, both tired but happy.

* * *

That same day, over in Junction Street Ivy Gladwin had opened her shop nice and early and had been thrilled at the amount of customers she'd had.

Girls wanting the post of assistant had applied and been dismissed, unable to meet the criteria set out by Ivy.

Working in the shop by day and rejuvenating stock in the evenings was beginning to tell on Ivy, and she despaired at ever finding a suitable young woman to help with her sales.

It was just after lunch when the bell tinkled and a voice said, 'I've come about being able to help you out.'

Ivy frowned at the mousy-haired girl. It was a strange thing to say. If she was applying for the job then surely she would have qualified that, but saying *help you out*?

'What can I do for you?' Ivy asked feeling perplexed.

'I can give you information on new designs coming from a certain person in Silver Street – for a cost, of course.'

Ivy's frown deepened and she narrowed her eyes. 'May I ask how you would come by this information?'

'The less you know, the better. Suffice to say for the right price you will be given the latest designs, as well as what they are being sold for.' The woman glanced around as she spoke. With a sniff she added, 'This is a one-time offer so take it or leave it.'

Ivy wondered how this stranger could possibly know what Ella Bancroft was making and selling, but the opportunity was too good to miss.

'How much is this going to cost me?' she asked, trying not to sound too eager.

'Two pounds a week,' came the reply.

'What? That's daylight robbery!' Ivy was flabbergasted at the amount being asked.

'Your choice. Make up your mind because I don't have all day,' the woman said as she lifted a gaudy hat from the counter. Turning it in her fingers, she dropped it back in its place with a shake of her head.

That simple action sealed the deal as far as Ivy was concerned. However, she asked, 'How do I know you will be telling the truth? Two pounds a week is a lot for me to be paying a total stranger. You could take the money and run, or give me false information.'

'You will know it's the truth because I am Sally – Ella Bancroft's sister!'

27

Over breakfast the following day, Darcie Newland pouted as she listened to her father.

'I have found you an excellent match for marriage. Felix Stoddard is extremely wealthy and lives in a huge house in Birmingham. He has agreed to meet you and will be coming to dinner this evening so, Verity, I will leave everything to you, my dear.' Royston smiled warmly at his wife before returning his attention to his daughter. 'I expect you to be on your *best* behaviour, Darcie.'

'What if I don't like him?' Darcie asked.

'How many suitors are you expecting to have with a temper and reputation like yours?' Royston asked pointedly.

Darcie blew out her cheeks and blinked hard. 'I should have been marrying Harper,' she mumbled sulkily.

'I will not go over this old ground again, Darcie!' Royston snapped. 'For once in your life – do as you are told!'

Throwing her napkin onto her plate Darcie jumped to her feet and marched from the room.

'Oh, dear. Do you think Felix will have her?' Verity asked.

'I sincerely hope so, because if she misbehaves and he refuses her – God knows what we will do.' Royston gave a little sigh and finished his coffee. Kissing his wife, he left for work.

Verity sat a while, mulling over what had been said. She recalled meeting Felix Stoddard at some function or other and gave an involuntary shudder. Around thirty years old, Felix had confidence in abundance; some may even call it arrogance. He had made his money in the leather trade, if her memory served her well. Tall and slim, he had a swarthy complexion not unlike a gypsy. Dark hair and eyes added to his shadowy persona. For all she would not have wed him herself, Verity prayed her daughter would. It was her fervent hope Darcie would not disgrace herself and ruin her chance with Felix.

Drawing a deep breath, Verity began to plan the evening meal. She wanted Felix to be impressed, so it would have to be something special. Beef or lamb? Dauphinoise potatoes maybe? Fresh vegetables, certainly.

Wandering away to the kitchen she wondered about sweet. Her head was now filled with a list of things to do. Clean the silver, wash the best china and glassware, and choose wines.

Upstairs, Darcie sat on her bed and tried to imagine what a man called Felix Stoddard would look like. Would he be hand-some like Harper Fortescue? He was rich, her father had said, which certainly helped. Gentle and kind, or rough and rude?

In one way, Darcie was dreading the evening to come, not knowing what to expect. On the other hand, she was feeling a little excited at the prospect of becoming wife to a man of means. She would be mistress of her own house at last, with servants to do her bidding. With his money she could shop whenever she chose, and in the expensive stores in Birmingham, too. The more she thought on it, the more she warmed to the idea. Going to her wardrobe, she began to search for just the right thing to wear at such an important dinner party.

* * *

Over in Cross Street, Sally watched with distaste as Eddy shovelled his breakfast into his mouth. Looking away and through the kitchen window, she saw the rain pattering down. Her thoughts meandered to the bargain she had struck with Ivy Gladwin and she smiled inwardly. Two pounds a week for the odd snippet of millinery news would see her a lot better off. She considered whether to tell Eddy what she had done, but thought better of it. If her husband knew he would want the money to waste in the first boozer he came to. No, Sally would hide the money to keep for a rainy day. She smiled at the pun as her eyes followed a water droplet snaking its way down the window pane.

In her heart, she knew it was a dirty trick to play on Ella, but her sister had kept Thomas's furniture as well as their mother's wedding ring. An eye for an eye, she thought. Besides, two pounds a week was a better bet; she could squeeze it from Ivy for months if not years. All she had to do was be careful not to be found out and she could then watch her nest egg grow.

Sally knew she would not be able to spend her ill-gotten gains on the baby as Eddy would be on to her in a minute. She wondered briefly what she would do with her *savings*, then dismissed the thought. She had to acquire the money first.

Sipping her tea, she realised she would have to be wary of what information to give to Ivy. Too much and she would be discovered, too little and the money could be withheld. She would have to ask Ella questions regarding the hats and prices but not too often in case it raised suspicion. With a little sigh, she came to the conclusion that the ruse was not going to be as easy as she had first thought. However, the deal was sealed and she would see how it went. It could always be called off if either party were dissatisfied with the arrangement.

Her attention was drawn back to Eddy as he burped loudly. Sally wrinkled her nose as she watched him slurp his tea. There were times when she really didn't like the man very much.

'You going out to look for work today?' she asked.

Glancing at the rain-spattered window, Eddy shook his head. 'It's piddling down. I'll go tomorrow.'

'Eddy! You have to find a job and quick. We need stuff for the baby as well as food, the larder is almost empty!'

'All right, all right! If I get pneumonia it'll be your fault!'

'Don't be such an idiot, and get your coat on.'

Eddy rose and wandered away, muttering about catching his death of cold.

Sally closed her eyes tight and drew in a long slow breath through her nostrils, her teeth clamped hard together. Releasing the tension in her body, Sally opened her eyes when she heard the front door slam. Now she could do her house-work in peace.

* * *

Harper had broken his fast, leisurely enjoying his eggs benedict, hot buttered toast with jam and a cup of coffee. As always, his mind was on Ella and how she was faring after the death of her father.

'You can't avoid it, you know.' Eléna's voice filtered into his brain.

'What would that be, Mother?'

'Telling your father about your feelings for Ella Bancroft.'

'I know, but there's no rush,' Harper said on a sigh.

'I suppose not, especially as you have yet to tell Ella herself.' Eléna gave a wry smile before pouring herself more coffee.

'Yes, I was wondering how to go about that actually.'

'You open your mouth and words come out – it's easy, really.' Eléna grinned at her little joke.

'Mother, what if she doesn't feel the same?'

'At least you will know, in which case you can walk away.'

'But I love her!'

'I know. Sweetheart, you have a choice. You lay your feelings at her feet and see what her response will be, or you shilly-shally about and hope someone else doesn't beat you to it.'

'I hadn't thought of that!' Harper was aghast at the idea of another suitor vying for Ella's attentions.

'Harper, grasp your courage with both hands and make your declaration. Then Ella will know and she can either reciprocate or not.'

'If she holds no love for me then I won't be faced with having to speak with Father.'

'Precisely. *Carpe diem*, Harper.'

'Right, seize the day indeed.' Harper grinned and, kissing Eléna on the cheek, added, 'Wish me luck.'

'All the luck in the world, my son.'

Eléna watched her boy as he left the dining room. She had meant what she said, for she would dearly love to have Ella as her daughter-in-law. She had been extremely relieved when Harper had called off his wedding to Darcie Newland. She knew it would have all ended in disaster. Not so with Ella Bancroft; it was a match made in heaven and she prayed the girl would return her son's love. There was a social divide between the two youngsters, there was no denying, but no obstacle was insurmountable if you worked hard enough at it. Eléna knew Harper would let nothing stand in his way – once he'd managed to pop the question, that is. She also knew that love crossed all barriers as well as class distinctions.

Helping herself to yet more coffee, Eléna found she was drawing up a wedding guest list in her mind. She shook her head to clear the thought, but it stubbornly persisted, so she let it run its course.

Finally she rose, she had visits to make and dinner to plan with the cook. She had to be sure to be home when Harper returned – he would need hugs of either congratulation or consolation.

28

Stafford Darnell had had Ella on his mind also and decided to pay her another visit. He was surprised to be invited in when Ella answered his knock. Seeing a small blonde beauty also in attendance, he bowed a greeting to both.

'Good morning, ladies.'

'Mr Darnell,' Ella said, keeping her distance.

'I thought to see your range of toppers. I'm told they are the finest in the town.'

Ella reached for a couple of boxes that had been stacked in the corner.

Kitty watched and listened. She was eager to learn from Ella and, although she couldn't say why, there was something about this man that unsettled her. Was she picking up on Ella's mood, noting how she dealt with her customer in clipped tones?

Passing over the hats, Ella waited as Darnell tried them on.

'Spiffing,' he said, 'I'll take this one.'

Ella boxed the hat and tied it with string as she muttered her thanks.

'I shall wear it this evening when I go out to dinner. Would you care to join me, Miss Bancroft?'

Ella gasped in surprise at his forthright manner.

'Thank you, but no.'

'Oh,' Darnell looked crestfallen.

Taking his money, Ella passed him the box. 'Is there anything else, Mr Darnell?'

'Only for you to say you will walk out with me, Ella.'

'Miss Bancroft, if you don't mind,' Kitty put in.

Stafford Darnell inclined his head, his beady eyes moving from Ella to Kitty and back again.

'Please say you will dine with me, Miss Bancroft.'

'I'm sorry, Mr Darnell, but no thank you. Now, if you will excuse me, I'm very busy.' Ella walked to the door and held it open.

Stafford stepped out into the street and said quietly, 'I won't give up.'

'You should, for my heart belongs to another,' Ella said and closed the door.

Kitty applauded Ella's rebuff. 'What a rotter! I didn't trust him one bit.'

'Nor me,' Ella said with relief Darnell had gone. 'Now you see why I need help.'

'Well, I'm here now, so between us we can manage buggers like him!' Kitty's blonde curls bounced as she tilted her head towards the door.

As they went back to the kitchen Ella said, 'He scares me, Kitty.' She rubbed her arms as if trying to rid herself of the feeling.

'No need to be afraid, I'll stove his head in with this if he tries anything.' Kitty lifted the poker kept beside the range. Ella burst out laughing as Kitty took the stance of a sword fighter and brandished her weapon.

Another knock to the door had them both stop short. Replacing the poker, Kitty followed Ella into the front room. She heard Ella say, 'Mr Fortescue, please come in.'

Harper and Kitty were introduced to each other and the lodger soon had the measure of the situation. This young man was welcomed warmly, and shy glances between the two of them told her all she needed to know. This couple were in love, but did each know of the other's feelings? She suspected not as she watched them chat innocently – he asking after Ella's health, and she enquiring about Harper's mother.

Kitty stood by, quietly watching the exchange. She felt Ella would be safe enough with this man but observing the rules of etiquette and propriety she elected to stay in the room.

'Ella, I need to speak with you about something very important,' Harper said as he glanced at Kitty.

'Yes?' Ella frowned.

'Yes. I...' Harper glanced again at Kitty, wishing she would leave them for a short while.

'Yes?' Ella asked again.

'I... never mind, it will wait.' Harper could not bring himself to discuss his love for Ella whilst Kitty looked on. It was something that should be done in private.

'If you're sure?' Ella prompted.

'Yes, I am.' Harper replied. He felt almost cheated. All the way to Silver Street he had rehearsed what he would say, and now he couldn't.

An awkward silence descended and Harper broke it with, 'I just called to assure myself you were well. I'd best be off. Nice to meet you, Miss Fiske.'

Ella saw him out and joined Kitty in the kitchen. 'I wonder what all that was about?'

'Blimey, Ella, you are so naïve!'

'What? I don't understand.'

'Girl, that man is head over heels in love with you and it's my guess that's why he came – to tell you.'

Ella blushed scarlet and busied herself with rattling cups. 'I'm sure you're quite wrong.'

'I'm not. Harper Fortescue loves the very bones of you, and, if I'm not mistaken, you feel the same.'

Ella dropped onto a chair and sighed heavily. 'Oh, Kitty, I do but it would never work. My dad told me that. He said Harper's parents would never stand for him courting a milliner.'

'It ain't up to them though, is it?'

'I'm not sure Harper would go against them, even in this.'

'He would marry you, I'm certain.'

Ella shook her head.

'Look, when he comes again, I'll slip out and give you both some privacy, maybe he'll speak up with me out of the way.'

'Kitty, what about...?'

'Nobody will know. As long as you feel safe being alone with him?' Seeing Ella nod she continued, 'I'll hide behind the door.'

'My dad used to do that.' Suddenly Ella was overcome with grief she thought she had under control, and burst into tears.

Kitty hugged her new-found friend until the crying ceased.

'A cup of char is what you need. Strong and sweet, it's sure to help.' Kitty gave a little smile and set about brewing up.

Ella returned the smile, happy to have found a friend at last.

Whilst Ella was suffering in her grief, Harper rode over to the gentlemen's club, feeling sorely disappointed at not having Ella to himself in order to express his undying love.

Striding through the doors, he nodded to a waiter, who took

his order for coffee. He felt it too early in the day for something stronger.

Seeing Stafford and Oliver wave him over, Harper sighed inwardly. He was hoping for some alone time to re-plan a strategy.

'What ho!' Stafford called out, much to the annoyance of other members.

'Stafford. Hello, Oliver,' Harper said quietly as he took a seat. 'What do you have there?'

'New topper, old boy,' Stafford answered as he lifted the hat from its box.

'Very nice,' Harper said but his gaze lingered on its packaging. It was one of Ella's boxes, he was sure. She hadn't mentioned selling to Stafford, but then why would she? He was just another customer to her, and Harper didn't think she knew they were friends.

'Yes, got it at that little place in Silver Street,' Stafford said, confirming Harper's suspicion.

'I thought so. There's no mistaking the fine quality,' Harper said, not fully understanding why he felt rattled.

'Indeed! There's a gorgeous blonde working there now, too.' Stafford wiped imaginary sweat from his brow and chuckled.

Harper settled to listen to his two friends discussing Kitty Fiske as his coffee was served. It did not sit well with him that they talked about her like as if was a piece of meat. His mind wandered away from their conversation to a much nicer topic, Ella Bancroft, but it snapped back on hearing Stafford's words.

'Her eyes have gold flecks, very unusual.'

He could only be talking about Ella, and Harper cursed himself for not paying closer attention.

'You really should go and see for yourself, Oliver,' Stafford went on.

'I don't need a new hat, Stafford, I have one already.'

'One can never have too many hats, Oliver, especially when served by someone as delicious as Miss Bancroft.'

Harper's hackles rose. 'She's not for you, Stafford,' he said sharply.

The others looked at him as Harper drank his drink.

'Do I detect...?' Stafford began.

'Just remember what I said – she's not for you.'

Stafford pulled the corners of his mouth down as his eyebrows raised. He chanced a glance at Oliver, who shook his head; his way of telling Stafford not to pursue the matter.

'Now, how's that bet of yours going?' Harper asked hoping to change the subject.

'Oh, he's no further on, Harper. It looks very much like I will win,' Oliver said with obvious pleasure.

Stafford frowned. 'Give me time and I'll prove my mettle.' He looked at Harper as he spoke, wondering if what he was thinking was correct. Had Harper fallen for Ella the milliner? If so, it would foul the bet he had with Oliver, for he would be unable to make good on it. He couldn't do that to a friend – or could he? Harper wouldn't know, for the haughty Miss Bancroft would never divulge that she had succumbed to Darnell's advances. He felt sure it would be a secret she would carry to her grave, if he could entice her into his bed in the first place, that is.

Stafford very wisely changed the topic of conversation again as he instigated a discussion around the horse racing track.

After a while, Harper left them to it, saying he was expected home for lunch. Traversing the streets on his trusty mare, Harper's mind dwelt on the conversation with Stafford and his warning for his friend to stay away from Ella. Turning the horse towards home, Harper determined he would keep an eye on Stafford, especially where Ella was concerned.

29

That afternoon, Sally called in on Ella. Kitty was there and Flossie popped in and left a freshly baked cake.

'I see you're still here, then,' Sally said, directing her remark to Kitty.

'I see you're *back* here again,' Kitty returned sharply.

Sally sniffed. 'What's that you're making now, Ella?' She tried to sound nonchalant.

'It's a black teardrop with veil for a client attending a funeral.'

'Hmm. How much do they go for, then?'

Ella glanced up at her sister, who appeared to be taking a sudden interest in her business. 'They vary, why?'

'Oh, I was just wondering.' Sally waved a dismissive hand hoping Ella wouldn't guess what she was about. 'What else have you got?'

Laying down her work, Ella frowned. 'Are you looking for a new hat? A hand-out maybe?'

'No! I was only asking! You are wound like a coiled spring, our Ella, do you know that? Whatever has got into you?' Sally feigned hurt to cover her mistake of pushing too hard with her questions.

'I'm sorry, Sally, I think I'm still a little unnerved by a customer we had this morning.'

'Why, what happened?' Sally asked.

'He asked her to dinner, that's what! Reminded me of a snake, he did,' Kitty supplied.

'You said no, I take it?' Sally asked unable to help herself.

'Of course I said no! What do you take me for?' Ella's temper flared but just as quickly subsided.

'You shouldn't be selling to men, it's dangerous.' Sally couldn't hold her tongue if her life depended on it.

'I need the money, Sally. I have to cover a range for men as well as women.'

'Anyway, I'm here so she ain't on her own,' Kitty put in.

'Oh, well, that's all right then, isn't it?' Sarcasm dripped from Sally's words.

'Sally, please don't start. I'm too busy to be listening to you trying to cause trouble.' Ella snatched up her work and cursed under her breath as the needle stabbed her finger.

'I can see I'm not wanted now you've got your new friend...' Sally yanked on her coat and left via the back door.

'Ella, I'm sorry to say this but your sister is a spiteful mare!' Kitty said.

'I know,' Ella agreed.

Sharing a little grin, they settled to their work once more.

Sally walked briskly over to Junction Street and stepped into Ivy Gladwin's empty shop.

'Well?' Ivy asked.

'Black teardrop with veil.'

'How much?'

'Ella wouldn't say.'

'I need to know prices as well if we are to maintain this arrangement.'

'I'm doing my best. Give it time and I'll get them for you.' Sally suddenly found herself on the back foot, no longer feeling in control of the situation.

'She's got herself an assistant now. Well, she's a lodger really, but she's helping Ella out.'

'Hmm.'

'She's learning the business,' Sally added.

Ivy took two pounds from the till and handed it to Sally. 'Have this because we made a deal, but I'll need a lot more information next time.'

Sally saw her chance to once more take charge, and replied, 'You'll have whatever I can get, and don't think to hold out on me regarding my money.'

'You're a nasty piece of work, Sally Bancroft,' Ivy said with a grimace.

At their initial meeting Sally had given only her Christian name. As she always wore gloves, Ivy had not seen her hands or wedding ring, so surmised she was still a Bancroft, and Sally saw no reason to disillusion the woman.

'I can be, Ivy, so I suggest you watch your step. See you next week. Ta-ra.'

Ivy stared at the door long after Sally had left. She didn't like the girl one bit, but their arrangement could prove invaluable to her in time. Should it not do so, Ivy would simply stop payment. Certainly, she would be no worse off for trying.

Going into her back room, Ivy began to sort out black felt and net. Funerary garb was the order of the day. An evil little smile crept to her lips as she worked. All of Ella's designs would be coming to her and the money she paid for them would be nothing compared to the sales she would enjoy.

Ivy permitted herself a cackle as she set to work with a new-found gusto.

Throughout the afternoon, snow fell in lazy flakes and by the evening people were grumbling as they went about their business of lighting fires and having meals. Only a light covering, the pristine white soon turned to a grey slush before melting away into dirty puddles.

A freezing wind bit to the bone through the ragged clothes of the poorest in the town as they hurried through the market in search of last-minute bargains. The stall holders stamped booted feet in an attempt to keep them warm. Gloved hands were blown on before being shoved back into pockets, and shawls wrapped heads and shoulders tightly.

The half-light of early evening gave the town an eerie appearance, and the rattles and bangs of stalls being taken down added to the almost sinister feel to the place.

Hobnail boots tapped on cobblestones as men in flat caps, mufflers, jackets and moleskin trousers trudged the otherwise quiet streets towards their place of work to join the night shifts.

Darcie Newland saw nothing of this as she excitedly dressed for dinner. Their visitor, Felix Stoddard, would be here soon, but Darcie had no intention of standing in wait of his arrival. She had planned a grand entrance once enough introduction time had passed and Felix and her parents were all enjoying an aperitif.

Although at her age hair was usually worn piled high on the head, Darcie stuck resolutely to ringlets, which bounced as she moved. In a ballgown of pale blue silk with pink bows around the hem, she smoothed her hands down the tight bodice to her narrow waist. Checking her look in the long mirror, she beamed her delight at her reflection. What she saw was an elegant young woman, but the truth was she resembled a spoilt little girl.

Crossing to the window, she peered out into the darkness as she heard carriage wheels crunch on the gravel. A figure alighted and spoke to the driver before turning to walk indoors. The carriage rolled away to the stables behind the house where driver and horse would be fed.

Darcie felt a thrill course through her veins. The stranger was tall and slim from what she could discern in the light from the open front door. Quietly tiptoeing through her bedroom door, she peeped over the balustrade to catch a glimpse of Felix Stoddard.

Drawing a quick breath, she stepped back for fear of being seen. She needed time to compose herself after seeing her handsome suitor for the first time.

Ramrod straight, Felix bowed his head as he shook hands with Royston. Then he kissed the back of Verity's hand. As they moved towards the parlour, Darcie gasped as Felix's eyes flicked to where she was standing. Had he seen her? She wasn't sure. Stepping back into her room, she calmed herself. It wouldn't do to go down out of breath and perspiring.

For his part, Felix caught a fleeting glance at the young blonde girl dressed in an awful shade of blue. He smiled wryly at her antics as he was led into the parlour and shown to a seat by a roaring fire.

Earlier in the day, Verity had hired a cook and maid for the evening from the Servants' Registry. She had hoped to impress their distinguished guest but also to spare herself the hard work of cooking and serving a fine meal.

Conversation was flowing well when the parlour door opened and in swept Darcie.

'Ah, there you are, darling,' Verity gushed.

Felix got to his feet as he was introduced to the girl who had spied on him from the landing a little while before. The couple took in the details of one other, and Darcie smiled widely at the handsome fellow who could be her husband if all went well.

Felix bowed politely as he said, 'I'm happy to meet you, Miss Newland.'

Darcie's heart beat rapidly as she took a seat. With a voice like velvet and eyes as black as coal, Felix was causing a flush to rise to her cheeks as she studied him. Darcie listened as he conversed with her father but heard nothing as she tried not to stare.

The maid announced dinner was being served and Felix held out his arm to Darcie. Laying her hand on his, she was escorted to the dining room. Royston and Verity followed behind and exchanged a nod and smile. So far, so good; Darcie appeared to be enamoured already.

'Forgive my asking, but did I not hear on the grapevine that your daughter was betrothed?' Felix asked as he helped himself to two slices of roast beef from the platter held by the maid.

Verity spluttered as she choked on her wine and Darcie's lips tightened as she frowned.

'You heard correctly, but Darcie changed her mind – very wisely, in my opinion,' Royston answered, hoping the lie would not be detected.

'I see. Clearly not a good match then, what?'

'Indeed.' Royston answered, feeling uncomfortable under Felix's scrutiny.

When everyone's plate was full, the maid refilled their wine glasses and retreated back to the kitchen.

'Royston tells me you live in Birmingham, Mr Stoddard,' Verity said.

'Felix, please. Yes, my estate is rather large and I have a manor house with coach-house and stables. I have an orchard and small vineyard as well as servants and groundskeepers.' It was not a boast, Felix was merely passing the information the family needed to know.

'How wonderful!' Verity clapped her hands and Felix forced a smile. He could see where Darcie got her little-girl ways from. He determined that would change if he decided to take Darcie Newland for his wife.

30

'Tell me, Darcie, how do you fill your days?' Felix asked as the sweet was served.

'Oh, we love to shop, Felix,' Verity put in quickly.

'Mother, he was speaking to me!' Darcie snapped.

Royston clenched his jaw as he thought, *Here we go!*

Turning to Felix, Darcie smiled and said, 'I like to shop.'

Felix nodded, his countenance betraying nothing of his thoughts. He had made it his business to find out all he could about the Newlands, and Darcie's temper had featured heavily in his investigations. He had wondered how long it would take for the girl to show her true colours, but even he was surprised at how soon that was.

'And what do you buy when you shop?'

'Dresses like this one. Isn't it simply divine?' Darcie said on a breath, her eyes dropping to the garment in question.

Felix thought, *It might have been, fifty years ago!* Instead he asked, 'Do you ride?'

'No, I go by carriage,' Darcie answered, shaking her head so hard her ringlets threatened to have her eye out.

'I can see I will have to teach you,' Felix said with a smile that didn't reach his eyes. In his peripheral vision, he saw her parents take a quick glance at each other.

'No, thank you. I don't like horses, they're smelly beasts.' Darcie wrinkled her nose at the thought.

Felix inclined his head as if in acceptance.

'I like to go to soirees and balls but there aren't many in this town,' she added.

'In Birmingham there is a party of some sort somewhere almost every night,' Felix told her.

'How exciting!' Darcie gasped as she hung on his every word.

'It becomes boring after a while, I assure you.'

'I could never be bored...' Darcie began.

'Of course, it's not all fun and frolics, business is conducted too. The ladies attending sit on many committees to raise funds for various organisations such as the workhouse.'

'Oh, I wouldn't want to be bothered with all that. I would be content being the mistress of the house,' Darcie answered.

Royston closed his eyes tightly for a second, wishing his daughter would just shut up. Seeing this, Verity slid her hand beneath the table and squeezed her husband's knee before returning it to her wine glass. It was her way of saying *hold your temper, husband.* Royston gave a tiny nod and gulped his drink.

'Coffee in the parlour, sir,' the maid said as she bent her knee and disappeared.

Retiring to said room, the conversation took a turn, much to Royston's relief. It was short-lived, however, as Darcie began to debate the importance of having a Royal Family. She thought it was outdated and a parliament was sufficient.

Felix rose to the challenge, playing devil's advocate.

Verity and Royston listened with mounting dread that their daughter might be talking herself out of a marriage. Eventually

Royston could stand no more and, getting to his feet, he said, 'Brandy and cigars in the study, Felix?'

'Yes. Thank you, ladies, for a very enlightening evening.' He gave a bow and followed his host out of the parlour.

Once settled in the study, drink and cigar in hand, Royston eyed the younger man. 'Well, that's Darcie.'

Felix nodded as he puffed out a plume of smoke. 'Charming.'

Royston wasn't sure if his guest was being sarcastic and took a swig of brandy in order to gather his thoughts.

'She certainly has spirit,' Felix added.

'Is that what you call it?' Both men smirked at Royston's remark.

'Look, Royston, let's not bandy words here. I know all about Darcie's temper and I tell you now, if I agree to this union all that will stop. I cannot have a wife who will embarrass me in polite society, I'm sure you understand.'

'I do,' Royston concurred. 'Should Darcie become your spouse then the onus is on you to deal with her as you see fit. God knows I've tried – to no avail.'

'As long as we understand each other,' Felix said.

'Tell me, why would you consider Darcie? I'm sure there are many who would suit you better.'

Felix nodded. 'I will be honest with you. I need a wife – I need an heir. Your business will go to her on your demise and so to me according to the law as it stands. I can make that business prosper and so provide for any children we may have. Also being married will make my transition into the higher echelon of society far easier. I already interact with mayors, doctors and lawyers but I'm ready to take this a step further. I have my sights on integrating myself with barons and earls and I would be taking Darcie with me.' Felix had considered a number of other young women from wealthy families as possible candidates to be his wife, but Darcie Newland came up trumps, simply because her father was the richest of them all.

Royston's eyebrows rose at the young man's honesty and ambition.

'However, I *will not* put up with her belligerent behaviour. I will stamp on it from the outset.'

'All I ask is that you do so in as kindly a way as possible. Please don't hurt my girl,' Royston replied quietly.

Felix inclined his head. 'Then we are in accord. Tell Verity to arrange the wedding.'

The men shook hands and Felix got to his feet. 'I thank you for a pleasant evening.' He handed his business card to his future father-in-law.

After seeing Felix into his carriage, Royston looked at the card and noted the telephone number beneath the name.

Time I had a telephone installed, he thought as he closed the front door.

* * *

At mid-morning the following day, Ella was already dealing with her third customer.

'I do like it, but Ivy Gladwin has much the same thing, for a tanner cheaper an' all,' the woman said.

'That's not possible, these are *my* designs!' Ella replied.

'I'm telling you straight, wench, you go and see for yourself.'

The woman gave back the black mourning hat and left.

Ella returned to the kitchen, feeling exasperated.

'Maybe it's a coincidence,' Kitty said, trying to make Ella feel better.

'How can it be? Ivy can't possibly know what we're making, Kitty!'

'Not unless someone is telling her.'

'Who? Who would do such a thing?'

'Ella, women talk. That woman will most likely buy a hat from Gladwin's and divulge your prices into the bargain. It won't be done out of malice, it will just be gossip, the same way she told you about Ivy's hats being sixpence cheaper.'

'I don't know what to do! I have to pay the rent and buy food and I can't without money coming in!' Ella rubbed her tired eyes before she noticed Kitty's sad look.

'I suppose I should move out as I'm not contributing,' she said.

'Certainly not!' Ella snapped.

'In that case, you must have this.' Kitty produced the ten shillings she had offered once before.

'No...'

'Yes! I've used your room, kept warm by your fire and eaten your food and now I need to help where I can.'

Ella relented out of necessity, knowing the money was desperately needed.

'Now that's settled we need to come up with some ideas that Ivy Gladwin would never think of,' Kitty said with a grin.

'Like what?'

After a minute Kitty announced, 'Let's go big!'

After lunch Ella stared at the hat on the table.

'What?' Kitty asked.

'It's so... big!' Ella responded doubtfully.

'Yes, quite different to those piddly little things you usually make.'

'But will they sell?' Ella really wasn't sure about the creation with its flowers and feathers.

'Only one way to find out,' Kitty said as she donned the hat. 'I think it's rather stylish.'

'I think it looks like the hats Ivy had me producing, all frippery as my dad would have said.'

'Maybe it's time for a new look and a new sign in the window,' Kitty said replacing the hat on the table.

'I suppose it wouldn't hurt.' Ella took out paper and pen and wrote neatly.

Ella's new range. Come in and take a look.

With the sign in the window, the girls began work on a new hat, again large but this time in a cartwheel shape.

'People will think I've gone mad when they see these,' Ella muttered as she worked.

'I doubt that. They'll come in droves for these, you mark my words.' Kitty prayed she was right, otherwise all their hard work would have been for nothing.

They were interrupted by a knock on the door at around three o'clock. Ella opened the door as Kitty stood aside.

'Mr Fortescue! I didn't expect to see you again so soon. Please come in out of the cold.'

Kitty took a deep breath and waited.

'Thank you, Ella. Hello again, Miss Fiske,' Harper said as he stepped indoors.

Kitty nodded her greeting then said, 'I'll just make that tea now, Ella.' Before her friend could reply, Kitty went to hide behind the door that joined the front room to the kitchen.

Harper and Ella exchanged a smile before she asked, 'What can I do for you?'

'Ella, I need to talk to you.'

Taking his hat, which he had removed and was mangling in his hands, Ella laid it on the table.

'Thanks. My mother suggested I come... I have something...'

'Take a deep breath then just say what's on your mind,' Ella said with a little laugh, having no idea what was making him so tongue-tied.

'Ella, I love you!'

Standing with her mouth open, Ella couldn't believe her ears.

Earwigging in the next room, Kitty shoved a fist into her mouth to prevent her whooping with delight and giving away her position.

'I'm sorry, I didn't mean it to come out that way. I practised all the way here and then I just made a mess of it.'

'I... I don't know what to say,' Ella said quietly as she looked down at her hands. She felt elated at his words but too embarrassed to reply in the same vein.

Harper looked at the girl he loved more than life itself and his face fell. She didn't feel the same. He had bungled his one chance to tell her how he felt, and had now put her in an awkward position of having to refuse him.

'I'm sorry, Ella, I should never have come.' Grabbing his hat, he shot out of the house.

Ella stared at the door, trying to make sense of the whole thing. First, he declares his love, then apologises and makes a run for it.

Kitty came through saying, 'Well, he did rather make a mess of that.'

Ella could not prevent the giggle erupting, as his words finally sunk in. Harper Fortescue had said he loved her and Eléna had suggested he tell her so.

'Oh, Kitty, you were right!'

'I usually am,' she said with a wide grin. 'Now let's see if I'm right about these bloody big hats!'

Laughing together, they returned to their work in the kitchen.

Harper rode home feeling wretched. How could he have been

such a fool? Whatever would Ella think of him now? Certainly, he wouldn't be able to show his face in Silver Street again. Should he have stayed and tried to explain, or would that have made things worse?

He saw her again in his mind, her head lowered. Tears sprang to his eyes as he walked his horse into the stables. Ignoring the groom's look of concern, he muttered his thanks and sprinted indoors. He needed to speak to his mother; if anyone had an answer to his predicament it would be Eléna.

31

In the meantime, Stafford Darnell arrived at the gentlemen's club. Ordering brandy and coffee, he did not see the look of disgust from the steward as he took himself to a quiet corner of the room. Stafford knew he shouldn't be drinking alcohol so early in the day, but he needed it. He had to find a way to get Ella Bancroft into his clutches and win that bet with Oliver.

Nodding his thanks to the steward, he took a gulp of his brandy, feeling the burn at the back of his throat. He sat back and his mind whirled. Twice now Ella had refused him; there would not be a third refusal if he could possibly help it.

She *would* succumb in the end, even if he had to just take her. The difficulty lay with her blonde bombshell of an assistant being there. Surely they wouldn't be together at all times, one or the other would have to shop for food, for example, so maybe that would be a good opportunity to try his luck again.

Swigging the last of his brandy he picked up his coffee. He would probably have to stand in wait for one of them to leave the house. That could prove awkward as he would be spotted by neighbours who would most likely report him to the constabulary for lurking. Besides, who knew how long he would have to *lurk* before the opportunity arose?

He sighed heavily at his own impetuousness. He should never have suggested the bet in the first place, but it was impossible to back out now for Oliver would never let him forget it.

Harper had said he wanted nothing to do with it, so he'd get no help there. No, this was his doing so only he could solve it. All he knew at the moment was that he was determined to win that bet one way or another.

* * *

Whilst Stafford was drowning his sorrows, Darcie Newland was being congratulated by her mother.

'He's the catch of the century, darling!' Verity gushed, although inwardly she shuddered. She hadn't much liked the man herself, but Darcie had been swept off her feet by his good looks and confidence.

Royston had informed them both that Felix Stoddard had agreed to the match and the women should begin planning the wedding.

In the confines of their bedroom, Royston had said he would arrange a date and time with the vicar, which would be as soon as possible. He did not want Felix to have any opportunity to change his mind. It was time, he said, for the two of them to enjoy life without the temper tantrums of their daughter causing havoc.

Verity had agreed with the sentiment and now in the parlour she and Darcie were drawing up a guest list.

'Of course the mayor...' Verity mumbled.

'I don't know him!' Darcie snapped.

'Prestige, my darling. Felix will expect men of stature to be in attendance and you inviting guests such as the mayor will show your understanding of your future husband's importance.'

'Oh, yes, I see. All right, then,' Darcie said with a little pout.

They discussed at length the details such as the ordering of flowers, hiring a cook and servants to prepare the wedding breakfast, and at last they came to Darcie's gown.

'I know just what I want,' the girl said clapping her hands. 'Our last shopping trip was such a disaster, so I hope this time to find the exact thing!'

'Well, if you can sketch it we can engage the best modiste we can find,' Verity said with a twinge of her own excitement.

Making tea while Darcie worked on the drawing, Verity prayed the wedding would be soon. She loved her daughter but she didn't want the girl living with them forever. Also, she felt Felix Stoddard was her last hope of seeing her girl wed.

Returning to the parlour with a tray of tea and cake, Verity placed it on a mahogany occasional table.

'There!' Darcie exclaimed as she passed her sketch to her mother.

Verity eyed the drawing then unable to contain herself said, 'You'll look like a shepherdess!'

'Mother! It will be beautiful!'

'Darcie, darling, I'm not sure... it's only lacking a crook!'

Darcie stamped her foot. 'It's what I want! It is my wedding, after all, so it should be my choice!' She formed her mouth into a moue.

'All right, if you're sure.' Verity relented rather than suffer yet another of her daughter's outbursts.

'I am! Felix will be bowled over when he sees me in this gown, I'm certain of it.'

Verity rolled her eyes as she poured the tea. *He might just drop to the ground in a dead faint*, she thought. She had noted his expensive clothes at dinner the previous evening, and his finger-nails were clean and well-manicured. His shoes were handmade Italian leather and shone like a mirror. His fob watch and Albert chain were high grade gold, as was his cigarette case. It was evident the man enjoyed beautiful things and she wondered again what his house looked like. If they were lucky, he might invite them for a visit so they would be sure their daughter would have the best of everything.

'Yes, dear,' Verity said snapping her attention back to Darcie's ramblings although she had no idea what she had just agreed to.

'The sooner the gown is made, the happier I'll be,' Darcie said.

Verity smiled indulgently. Clearly she had concurred that they should seek out a competent dressmaker that very day without even realising it.

'I can't wait for Daddy to come home, then we'll know the date. Oh, Mummy, I'm going to be married at last!'

'Yes, sweetheart. You will be Mrs Felix Stoddard and have people bowing and scraping to you.' *Nothing new there!* Verity wisely kept the thought to herself.

'Come on, Mother! I want to get to a modiste as soon as I can!'

Verity sighed and placed her half-finished cup of tea on the tray. Wearily, she dragged herself to her feet. She was not looking forward to this particular trip, and she prayed whoever took on the job of making Darcie's gown had a thick skin and could keep her tongue firmly behind her teeth.

* * *

Over at The Cedars, Harper poured his heart out to his mother. He could not prevent his tears as he explained what had happened at Silver Street.

Eléna's heart was breaking to see her son so upset. He hadn't cried since he was a young boy and it was all she could do not to sob along with him.

'She didn't refuse you outright, my son,' she said.

'No, but she didn't know what to say. Oh, Mother, I don't think she feels as I do!'

'I must disagree. Harper, I have seen you together and it's my contention that girl adores you.'

'Whatever am I to do? I feel like such a fool!' Harper said as he dragged a hand through his hair, his tears having abated.

'We all make mistakes and yours was fleeing the scene. It would have been better to have waited to hear Ella out. She may have surprised you.'

'It's too late now,' Harper said with a sniff.

'Will you listen to yourself? I did not raise you to be a coward, Harper, now get a grip on yourself. Go back to Ella. Tell her again and keep telling her until you get this sorted out one way or another. Now go!' Eléna pointed to the parlour door.

Shocked by his mother's sudden change of demeanour, Harper jumped to his feet. Kissing her cheek, he ran from the room. Perhaps she was right – it was now or never.

Eléna smiled as she watched him go. Her son, the only child born to her, was her pride and joy. She knew she had to be sharp with him in order for him to stir his stumps and get the matter settled. She also knew Ella would be delighted to see him again. She prayed this time he would not make a hash of it.

32

Stirred by his mother's words, Harper mounted his horse and set off for Silver Street. However, by the time he reached the town, his courage had deserted him once again. He decided to stop off at the gentlemen's club for a while to gather his thoughts.

His horse safe in the stable at the back of the building, Harper strode indoors, happy to see none of his cronies were there. He needed peace and quiet to formulate a plan of how to explain to Ella why he had rushed away so suddenly.

Ordering tea and cake, he settled himself in a large armchair. He glanced around the room and returned nods of greeting.

Eléna was right, Harper knew he was not a coward, but when it came to Ella his sensibility went out of the window and his bravery vanished. He just wanted her to know he loved her to distraction, that he would lay his life on the line for her. How was it he could think of all these things but could not voice them? Why was he so afraid? Was it because he feared she would reject him? He had already thought she did not feel as he did and it was like a barb to his heart.

Yet his mother was not convinced he was correct, she

believed Ella did love him. Whatever Eléna thought, Harper could not find it in himself to visit Ella again quite yet. Neither did he feel he could go home and have to explain his lack of action. Maybe he should spend a few days at the club until he was certain he could manage his own affairs. With a nod the decision was made. He'd have to send a servant to fetch him a bag with his night things and a clean set of clothes if he were to stay.

* * *

Ella answered the knock to the back door and smiled as she invited the rent man inside.

'I have your money here,' she said, passing it over with the rent book.

'Thank you kindly,' George said, filling in the amount paid in the little book as well as his ledger. 'I'm afraid I have to inform you as of next week the rent has been raised by a tanner.'

'Sixpence! Why?' Ella asked.

'Gaffer's orders, miss,' George said, a look of sympathy crossing his face. 'Seems he was told you have a lodger and felt an increase was justified.'

'But sixpence a week!' Ella said on a breath.

'My understanding is you should have asked permission to have a lodger, although don't quote me on that.'

'Oh,' was all Ella could reply.

'Ar, well, the gaffer decided upping the rent was better than turning you out.'

Ella sucked in a breath at the thought, immediately recognising she'd had a lucky escape.

'I would be grateful if you would pass on my thanks,' she said at last.

'Miss – be careful. He knows about your business as well and if he's a mind to he could shove your weekly rate sky high.'

Ella dropped onto a chair, suddenly feeling the whole world was against her. 'Thank you, George.'

'Just a word to the wise,' he said before taking his leave.

Kitty took a seat as Ella's face paled at the thought of being pushed out of her home because she couldn't pay the rent. Somehow she had to now find an extra amount and sell her hats without drawing too much attention from the landlord. Ivy Gladwin was undercutting the prices Ella was charging, besides finding out about her new designs and blatantly copying them, and Ella's cash flow was suffering as a result.

Tears began to sting her eyes as she thought her dear father would know what to do, but he was gone and she was left to make her own decisions. The trouble was she didn't know how to rectify these problems.

'Cup of tea, the cure for all things,' Kitty said placing a cup on the table.

'Thank you,' Ella muttered miserably.

'What will you do?'

'I have no idea, Kitty. I need to find that extra sixpence from somewhere, but my sales have fallen dramatically. Ivy is stealing the business from right under my nose and I don't know how she's doing it!'

'Then we need to find out.'

'How?'

'Detective work. We have to become sleuths, Ella, because it's my guess there's more to this than meets the eye.'

'How do you mean?'

'Well, Ivy is being told about your designs and prices, so maybe I could visit her shop and see if I can discover how.'

'It's a thought – in fact, it's all we have to go on right now.'

'All right, there's no time like the present,' Kitty said, grabbing her coat and hat. Then she had a thought and left her hat on the peg hammered into the door. She had to give Ivy the impression she was rock-bottom poor, which was not so far from the truth. 'I won't be too long,' she said as she left via the back door.

The tick of the old tin clock was the only sound breaking the crushing silence, and Ella suddenly felt very alone. Warm tears snaked their way down her cheeks as she stared at the space where her father's wheelchair had been for so long.

'Oh, Dad, I miss you so much. Why did you have to leave me?' Her words were softer than gossamer before she heaved in a great ragged breath. Grief overwhelmed her and she gave in to it, crying like her heart was breaking all over again and she felt she could never stop.

Ella sobbed for a long while before finally being able to control her emotions. The tension released, it left her feeling exhausted. She was drained of energy and she slumped in the chair. Her get-up-and-go had got-up-and-gone; her body felt heavy and she was listless and tired to the bone.

The back door opened and in walked Sally, which didn't help her mood one little bit. The last thing Ella needed right now was a confrontation with her sister, but she knew it would come at some point during the visit – it always did.

Glancing at her younger sister, Sally dived right in. 'What's up with you?'

'The rent is going up and I'm not sure I can meet it,' Ella sniffed.

'Well, crying won't help. You should insist your lodger gets a job and pays her way!'

'There's no work to be had, Sally.'

'That's just an excuse.'

'The same as Eddy gives you?' Ella couldn't stay her tongue and waited for the backlash.

'It's difficult for Eddy, as I've told you before. That girl who's living here rent free should be able to find work easily looking like she does! Where is she, anyway?'

'Kitty popped out, she should be back any minute.'

'You'll have to sell Mum's ring now if you have to pay more rent, and when you do I want half.'

Ella shook her head. No matter what happened she would not sell that ring.

It was a while later when Kitty came through the back door with two small packages in her hand. 'I collected the order from the grocer,' she said, spying Sally sitting at the table. Kitty had rushed back from Ivy's shop with a quick visit to the grocer on her way home.

Ella frowned. There was no order as far as she was aware, but she kept her counsel.

'Tea and sugar – and I'm ready for a cuppa,' Kitty said brightly.

'You should be contributing if you're using Ella's supplies,' Sally said snidely.

'You should be minding your own business!' Kitty snapped.

'It is my business if you're sponging off my sister!'

'What goes on between Ella and me has bugger-all to do with you, so keep your big nose out of it!' Kitty's temper rose. She would not stand for this young woman telling her what to do, regardless of the fact that she was right. Kitty knew she should be helping out financially but without paid employment it was impossible.

Sally huffed and pulled Ella's latest creation from its stand and turned it to inspect it from all angles. 'This is a bit big. Changing your designs, are you?'

Ella nodded, 'It was Kitty's idea to try something different.'

'Any luck selling them?'

'Not as yet, but we're hopeful,' Ella answered, glad that the little contretemps hadn't escalated into a full-blown argument.

With a sniff, Sally left the house.

'I didn't leave an order with the grocer,' Ella said no sooner her sister had closed the door behind her.

'I know, but we were almost out so I got it on tick.'

'How did you manage that?'

Kitty's hands followed the line of her figure and she smiled wickedly as she gave a pose like a model.

Ella laughed at the girl's brazenness. 'What did you find out at Ivy's?'

'Her designs are exactly like yours and her prices are lower, as that woman said. However, she has nothing like our new range so we're in with a chance.'

'We'd best get some more made, then,' Ella said her mood having lifted considerably until she realised she was running low on materials. Another expense she would have to finance.

On leaving Silver Street, Sally went straight to Gladwin's. She had already been paid her two pounds for that week, but she may be able to squeeze a little more out of Ivy for her new discovery.

Ivy sighed as Sally entered her shop. 'What do you want now?'

'I have something you may want to hear,' Sally said as she sidled up to the counter.

'What is it?' Ivy patted her titian hair back in place, having made up her mind she would not be paying her spy any more money.

'It will cost you.' Sally raised her eyebrows as she spoke. 'But it'll worth it, believe me.'

'I refuse to hand over any more of my hard-earned cash. You've had your weekly allowance and told me nothing I didn't already know!'

'Well, you don't know this!' Sally shrugged and sauntered back towards the door. 'Fair enough, but it's your loss.'

Ivy quickly weighed the options in her mind – keep her money and lose valuable information, or pay up and discover what Ella was up to.

'How much this time?' she asked before Sally disappeared through the door.

33

Ella had taken the last of her spare money and visited the market in order to replenish her millinery stock. The weather had taken a turn for the worse and the streets had frozen during the night. Children too poor to attend school were using sticks to try to knock down icicles wherever they could be found. Others stood shivering in the ginnels between the houses, wanting to be part of the fun but too cold to join in. Smoke poured from chimneys in steady great streams as fires roared in their hearths. There was no wind but the cold seeped through Ella's coat and shawl until she could feel it creep across her skin. The icy cobbles were treacherous underfoot, making the going slow. Ella winced as she watched a carter's horse slip, its eyes rolling in fear and its breath pluming before it managed to gain purchase once more.

Finally turning back into Silver Street, Ella breathed with relief, she was almost home. She saw a carriage outside her front door and immediately recognised it as belonging to Eléna Fortescue. She silently prayed the visit would bring more desperately needed sales. She was glad she'd put aside the rent for another week but worried how she would manage after that with no money coming in.

As she bustled in through the back door, she was surprised to see Eléna sitting at the table with Kitty, both enjoying hot tea.

'Ah, there you are, dear,' Eléna said, 'it's terribly cold out there, isn't it?'

Bloody freezing, Ella thought, but answered with, 'It is indeed. It's lovely to see you, though.' Hanging up her outdoor clothes on the peg in the door, she accepted the tea Kitty offered, stealing its heat as she wrapped her hands around the cup.

'I thought Mrs Fortescue would be warmer in here, I hope I did the right thing,' Kitty said sheepishly.

'Of course,' Ella replied with a smile, her facial muscles finally warming through.

'I was wondering if you had seen Harper,' Eléna asked.

'Yes, but it was a couple of days ago.'

'That's what I said,' Kitty added.

'May I ask why...?' Ella began.

'Because I sent him here, my dear.'

Ella frowned.

'Let me explain,' Eléna said as she pushed her cup and saucer towards Kitty for a refill. 'Harper told me of his visit and what he said to you.'

Ella blushed scarlet and dropped her eyes to her own cup.

'He's already betrothed,' Ella muttered miserably.

'Not any more, he's not. He called off the wedding.'

Ella looked up in shock. 'Poor Miss Newland,' she breathed.

'She did rather take it badly. She attacked him and scratched his face.'

Well, that explained that little mystery, Ella thought.

'But why did he call it off?'

'My dear girl, Harper is so in love with you he can't think

straight. I insisted he came to tell you so. Clearly, he made a complete mess of it. Oh, thank you, Kitty.' Eléna sipped her tea before continuing. 'He's under the impression you do not feel the same, although I know better.'

'I... I was taken by surprise, I cannot deny,' Ella mumbled.

'Your naivety is charming, but if you wish to wed my son then you will have to tell him of your love for him. I swear I will bang your heads together if you don't sort this out – and soon!'

Kitty burst out laughing and before long they were all howling with pure relief that the subject was at last out in the open.

Finally, Ella asked, 'If Harper is not at home, where is he?'

'Oh, I can guess. He's probably holed up at the gentlemen's club. Don't worry, I'll get his father to winkle him out.'

'How do you feel about – well, Harper and I...?'

'I'd be thrilled to see you wed, as I think you're just right for him. I can see you are embarrassed, Ella, but please don't be. I always speak as I find and I'd love you as my daughter, never having been blessed with one of my own.'

'But I'm just a milliner...' Ella began.

'Not *just* a milliner, Ella, the best there is, in my book. I understand the class divide and I don't think it should stand in your way – not if you're in love. Now, I have taken up enough of your time but, before I go, would you mind boxing that hat for me?'

Ella was surprised when Eléna pointed to the one she had only finished the day before. 'I haven't priced it up, yet,' she said as she searched for a box big enough.

'That's all right, I know how much I'm willing to pay,' Eléna grinned as she took out ten pounds from her bag.

'That's too much!' Ella gasped.

'I doubt that, so you take it. It would cost twice that in London, so I suggest you get to making more. I wish to lead a new fashion trend and this will do very nicely.' Taking the string tied box she added, 'Expect my friends, as when they see this they will be clamouring for one of their own.'

'Thank you, I'm very grateful,' Ella said. Having seen her visitor to her carriage, Ella returned to the kitchen, where Kitty was sitting with a beaming smile.

'I told you so,' she said.

'About what?'

'About the hats and Harper Fortescue!'

Ella settled down to work, quietly recalling the conversation with Harper's mother. Her heart was soaring to new heights to know Eléna was approving the union between Ella and her son.

* * *

The carriage rolled slowly along the icy streets and Eléna pulled the thick blanket tighter around her knees. She was very pleased with her new hat but not so much with her son.

Harper had chosen to ignore her advice and she felt cross with him. Unable to enter the gentlemen's club herself, she had two options open to her. She could ask Rafe to bring Harper home where she could speak to him, but that would mean explaining her intentions. She felt it was down to Harper to inform his father about his feelings for Ella, but if this proved too much for him then she would take over and convince Rafe it was the right thing to do. Then again, she could visit the club and request the doorman fetch her son so they could converse in the carriage. One way or the other, the whole debacle needed to be resolved. The last thing Eléna wanted was for young Ella to be swept off her feet by another beau.

Banging on the roof of the carriage with her umbrella, she called out to the jarvey. Coming to a halt, he jumped down, and

Eléna gave him a new destination. Knuckling his forehead, the driver climbed back into position, dragging his own blanket around himself once more.

As the carriage came to a standstill, the doorman of the club moved to open its door.

'I wonder if you would be kind enough to seek out Harper Fortescue and request he give his mother a moment of his time.' Eléna handed over half a crown and saw the man smile.

'With pleasure, madam,' he answered, tipping his hat before closing the door.

A few moments later, Harper sheepishly joined his mother in the privacy of the carriage.

'Well?'

'Don't look at me like that, please. I couldn't do it, Mother. My courage failed me at the last.'

'Really, Harper! I'd thought better of you.' Eléna glared at her boy as he hung his head in shame. 'Do you love the girl?'

Raising only his eyes Harper nodded. 'With every fibre of my being.'

'Well, what is stopping you whisking her down the aisle?'

'I'm not sure she loves me enough and it would break me in two if she refused me.'

Eléna saw the torment her son was suffering and her heart went out to him. Her stiff demeanour softened as she said, 'Ella feels as you do, Harper. I've already given her my blessing so all that's left to do is propose to her.'

'And tell Father.'

'You leave him to me. All you need to worry about is Ella. A girl that beautiful will not be short of admirers, so if you don't want to see her snatched away by another then I suggest you stop hiding yourself in there and go and pop that question.'

Harper smiled as he said, 'I do love you, Mother.'

'And I you, so do as I say and get over there right now.'

'I will.'

'Then come home and tell your father and me the good news.'

Kissing her cheek, Harper alighted and spoke with the driver.

Eléna gave a little wave as the carriage began to move.

Harper went back inside to pay his bill before walking to the stables to retrieve his horse.

The time had come to ask Ella to marry him and this time he would not shirk from the task. It was now or never.

34

Ivy Gladwin lost no time in acting upon the information she had paid so dearly for. Sally had waltzed off, happily clutching another two pounds she had extracted from Ivy, but both considered they'd had a bargain.

So Ella was making big hats this time. This was Ivy's forte and so she set to with gusto, working late into the night so she would have something new and exciting for her window come the morning.

Having no idea what Ella was charging, Ivy wasn't too worried. She knew what her own millinery was worth and delighted in the notion that her sales would see a boost yet again.

As she worked, she pondered the arrangement made with Sally. In the beginning she had been unsure whether she would benefit, but now she was glad she'd agreed to it. Not only was she doing very well out of it, but Ella would be suffering and having no idea how or why.

By the early hours of the morning Ivy's fingers were sore, and her eyes ached with the strain of working by gaslight. Getting to her feet, she stretched out her back, wincing at the pain in her cramped muscles. Casting an eye over her new creations, she smiled. They would do very nicely. Turning off the gas lamps, she wearily made her way to bed. Despite being thoroughly exhausted, she felt excitement at dressing her window on the morrow. Hopefully it would result in a stream of customers all eager to own a Gladwin hat.

* * *

That same day, Darcie and her mother stood on the platform waiting for the train to Birmingham. They were going to seek out a wedding gown, or a modiste who could follow Darcie's sketch which she had tucked into her bag. They had tried in Walsall the previous day, but Darcie had dismissed every dress she had been shown.

A cold wind blustered along the track and people pushed their way into the already crowded waiting room.

Verity pulled up her fur collar as she glanced left and right, watching for the train.

Darcie tapped her foot impatiently then gave a little excited cry as she heard the steam whistle.

Suddenly passengers spilled out of the warm waiting room to swamp the platform, jostling to be the first to board. Darcie tutted loudly as a woman with three children barged her way past towards the other end of the concrete walkway.

With clouds of coke-laden steam puffing into the air, the great iron beast pulled slowly into the station, forcing everyone to take a step back. Chugging to a halt, whistles sounded as porters flung open the carriage doors. Men and women poured out onto the seething platform as others caused chaos trying to squeeze into the carriages.

Finding seats in first class, Darcie and Verity watched the

platform empty quickly, most folk heading for third class at the end of the long train. The sound of doors slamming and whistles blowing again heralded their departure and bodies jerked as the train lurched forward.

Mother and daughter settled into the comfortably uphol-stered red velvet seats, their bags placed on the small mahogany table before them. In but a moment a steward arrived, a towel hanging over the sleeve of his white jacket. Verity ordered coffee and the man bowed and rushed away. Not long after he was back with a pot of hot coffee with china sugar bowl, milk jug and two cups and saucers. Verity paid the man but gave no tip, and the steward forced a smile in thanks.

Darcie chatted excitedly about her wedding, which was to be held in three weeks' time; as soon as the banns had been called. Unbeknown to Darcie, the vicar at St John's Church had been only too pleased to agree to the earliest possible date, his palm having been liberally greased by Royston Newland.

Arriving at New Street Station in Birmingham, Darcie gasped at the amount of people waiting to board. Alighting, she and her mother had to push and shove their way to the exit, where they breathed a sigh of relief to be free of the crowds.

Verity hailed a cab and called out an address she had been given by a friend over their new telephone, which Royston had had installed the previous day. There had been much excitement as the women had watched the engineers complete their work.

Gazing out of the cab window, Darcie saw the rich and poor traversing the streets. Top hats and flat caps trundled alongside each other as folk went about their business.

Carts and wagons vied for position as they travelled around the Bull Ring then passed by Smithfield Market. Following the tramway into Sherlock Street East, the women grimaced at the odour emanating from the public slaughterhouse, both holding handkerchiefs to their noses. Moving on into Moseley Street, they saw houses standing cheek by jowl all covered in a layer of grime. The carriage works and horse repository stood on the left then the carriage turned into Bishop Street. Darcie was beginning to feel they would never arrive at their destination.

Eventually the cab halted outside a large shop, its window filled with beautiful wedding dresses. The driver jumped down to open the door and help the ladies to alight.

'Please wait, although I have no idea how long we will be,' Verity said.

The driver tipped his cap before climbing back into his seat. Seeing the shop, he knew it would be a while, so he wrapped his blanket around his shoulders, dragging another over his knees. Pulling out his pipe and baccy pouch, he settled to enjoy a smoke while he waited, happy in the knowledge he would be charging for his wasted time.

Darcie was like a child in a sweet shop as she swept around looking at the dresses hanging up. She *loved* this one then *adored* that one, her sketch completely forgotten, much to Verity's delight.

Saleswomen appeared from nowhere to offer their advice and assistance and Darcie was in her element. Verity took a seat on a comfortable settee and watched the hustle and bustle going on around her daughter. A tray of tea with little biscuits was brought for the customers before Darcie disappeared into a fitting room to try on the first of many dresses.

Verity prayed her daughter would find something suitable and quickly. She couldn't bear the thought of having to endure this all day.

After watching Darcie try on one dress after another, Verity sighed with relief when she heard the words coming from the fitting room.

'This is it! Mummy, I've found my gown!'

As Darcie stepped out, Verity closed her eyes tight for a moment before she smiled tightly.

The gown Darcie twirled around in was exactly like the sketch!

* * *

Whilst the Newlands were shopping, Ella peeped through the front window when she heard the knock on the door. It was a habit she had formed after Darnell's visit.

'Shall I answer it?' Kitty asked.

'No!' Ella's face had drained of all colour.

Kitty looked out too and saw the reason Ella had blanched. Darnell was back.

The knock came again and Ella sucked in a breath. 'If we hide he will think there's no one at home,' she whispered as she dragged Kitty away from the window.

'Ella, just open the door and tell him we're closed today.'

'I can't, he frightens me!'

'Then I'll do it.' Kitty strode across the room and threw open the door.

Ella's hands trembled as she listened.

'I'm sorry, sir, but Ella's is not open today.'

Suddenly the door banged back on its hinges and Stafford pushed his way inside.

'Out of my way! I've come to see Ella!'

Ella stepped back as Kitty closed the door. 'How dare you force your way into my home!'

'I wanted to speak to you, and *she*,' his arm shot out towards Kitty, 'tried to prevent it.'

'Mr Darnell, as a gentleman you should know you enter only

at an invitation. You have not been extended that courtesy so I would be grateful if you would leave.' Ella dragged courage from the depth of her being and stood tall and straight.

'I simply wished to invite you to dinner – yet again,' Stafford said.

'I have refused in the past, Mr Darnell, and I haven't changed my mind in the meantime.'

Kitty had moved to stand next to her friend and watched the man carefully.

'What would it hurt?' Darnell snapped.

'I have asked you to leave and I will not do so again. I will walk out and find the nearest constable.'

Stafford took a step forward and Ella's bravado began to crumble.

'I think you should go,' Kitty said.

In the blink of an eye Darnell flung his arm out and knocked Kitty off her feet. She landed hard and didn't move.

'Oh, my God!' Ella gasped as she saw her friend prostrate on the carpet.

'You will not turn me away again, Ella.' Darnell, in two strides, grabbed the girl tightly.

Ella struggled to free herself. 'Let me go! Take your hands off me!'

Darnell clamped his mouth on hers and Ella tried to fight him by pushing on his chest. She yanked her head away from his, leaning back at an awkward angle. Swinging her arm, she gave him a resounding slap across his cheek. 'You get away from me right now!' she growled.

'Come, Ella, you know you want me as much as I want you,' Stafford said with a leer.

'Let me go or I'll scream!'

'Oh, I don't think you will, my little pussycat.'

Ella felt sick. Her friend was unconscious on the floor and she was trapped by a man who was intent on harming her. She had to get away somehow. Slumping in his arms as if she were giving in to him, she took him by surprise as she lifted her hand to caress his cheek.

'My pussycat,' he murmured again.

'Cats scratch!' Ella ground from between clenched teeth as she raked her fingernails down his face then she let out an unholy scream, almost shattering his eardrum.

Darnell yowled and clutched his injury. Seeing blood on his fingers, he smacked her face hard, knocking her backwards.

Ella continued to scream for all she was worth, fighting and kicking herself away from him.

Suddenly there was another figure in the room and Darnell was yanked backwards before he found himself measuring his length on the floor beside Kitty.

'Are you all right, Ella?'

She heard the voice and saw the face in front of her but registered nothing. She didn't see Kitty dragging herself upright in a daze.

'Ella!'

The shout brought her back to her senses and she breathed relief as she saw Harper's face.

'I'm... yes, I'm all right.' She moved to help Kitty to a chair as Harper pulled Darnell to his feet.

Rubbing his chin, Stafford stared at his friend.

'What the hell...!' Harper raged.

'Harper, old boy, she's just a girl,' Stafford said quietly.

'Don't you dare "old boy" me, Stafford!' Harper was so infuriated he threw another punch and glared at the man he had once called friend, again lying on the floor.

Ella and Kitty stood by, their arms wrapped around each other.

'Get up, you swine, and get out!' Harper yelled.

Stafford scrambled to his feet and staggered past, disappearing through the door and banging it closed behind him.

Harper turned to the girls and ushered them back to chairs in the kitchen, where he set about putting the kettle to boil.

'Harper, how did you know?' Ella asked on a whisper.

'I didn't. I was on my way here anyway.' He passed them both cold wet cloths to hold against their faces where Darnell had struck them.

'How do you two know each other?' Ella said.

'We grew up together and have been friends for many years, until today, that is.'

Just then, Sally walked in through the back door. Harper closed his eyes tight and lowered his head in sheer frustration. Would he *ever* get time alone with the woman he loved? Feeling the thought a little insensitive, he pushed it to the back of his mind.

'Hey up, what's going on here, then?' Sally asked, taking in the situation at a glance.

'Your sister has been attacked!' Kitty said sharply.

'Who by?' Sally said as she eyed Harper.

'A man called Stafford Darnell, who I will be calling on as soon as I leave here. I have further business with him!' Harper said.

'I know him! Eddy used to work for his father up at the saddlery works!' Sally said. 'I heard he had an eye for the ladies.' Glancing at Kitty, she asked, 'What happened to you?'

'He knocked me out!'

'You'll have a real shiner there tomorrow,' Sally said with a shrug.

Kitty felt her skin prickle with dislike at the woman staring at her. 'Tell me something I don't know!'

'Well, is somebody going to tell me exactly what happened?' Sally said taking off her coat.

'I was on my way to call on your sister and when I arrived, I heard screaming. The front door was closed so I raced around the back. I arrived just in time to see Darnell strike Ella.'

'He saved me, Sally. Darnell was about to... to...' Ella was suddenly overcome by it all and burst into tears.

Sally rolled her eyes. 'Did he...?'

'No! But he would have if Mr Fortescue hadn't arrived when he did!' Kitty snapped.

'I warned you this might happen, Ella. I told you not to have men customers. It's your own fault.'

Jumping to her feet, Ella gulped a breath and yelled, 'Shut up, Sally! If you can't, then go home!'

'Well, that's nice isn't it? I come here to see how you're getting on and you treat me like dirt!'

'Sally, your sister is in shock. The last thing she needs is you berating her for something what was not *her* fault at all!' Kitty was on the warpath and was not about to stand for Ella being blamed.

'Whichever way you look at it, I was right! You shouldn't be having men in the house. You'll get yourself a reputation of being a loose woman!' Sally's words were directed at Ella, but her eyes were on Harper.

Ignoring the woman, whose face could sour milk, Harper's attention returned to Ella. 'Shall I fetch a constable? You should press charges for assault.'

'No, thank you. I just want to rest and forget all about it,' Ella replied.

Harper looked at Kitty who shook her head.

'I'm surprised Mrs Busybody from next door didn't come running,' Sally mumbled.

'She must be out, otherwise Mrs *Woolley* would have come to help!' Ella retorted.

'Do either of you need a doctor?' Harper asked, growing more frustrated by the minute with the interfering sister.

'No.' The answer came in unison.

An awkward silence descended on the small kitchen.

Sally glanced from face to face and realised they were waiting for her to go home, and it was clear she would obtain no further news for Ivy today, so she grabbed her coat.

'I'll see you tomorrow,' she said over her shoulder as she walked out.

A collective sigh sounded and Harper stood once more in front of Ella. 'Is there anything more I can do for you, ladies?'

'Yes, you can make another cuppa. I'm as dry as a bone,' Kitty said with a careful grin.

'It's difficult to believe you and Sally are sisters,' Harper said tentatively.

'Ain't it just!' Kitty added. 'Ella, I have to say it, every word out of Sally's mouth causes an argy-bargy! I don't know how you lived with her for so long. She's a spiteful bugger!'

Although surprised, it was all Harper could do to hide the smile coming to his lips at Kitty's outburst as he made tea.

'Now, if there's nothing more, I should be getting on home. May I suggest you keep the doors locked? I'll see you both tomorrow.'

Ella nodded and smiled as she saw him out. Locking the door behind him, she felt she was missing him already.

35

Stafford Darnell climbed into the saddle and dug his heels into the sides of his horse. People leapt out of the way as he rode at breakneck speed along the streets. Men yelled at him but he didn't hear them, he wanted to be away from this place. He needed to find a public house where he wouldn't be recognised and where he could drink himself insensible.

Coming to the Forge Inn on the Pleck Road, he left the horse in the stable at the rear and charged inside. Ordering a double whisky, he barged his way through the crowd to the corner and dropped onto a spare seat, ignoring the grumbles aimed at him.

Taking a gulp of his drink, he savoured the burn at the back of his throat. Breathing hard, he fought to bring his emotions under control.

He had been such an idiot. He touched his cheek where Ella had gouged him and he winced at the sting. He should have called off the bet with Oliver. But it was too late now. He had made a fool of himself; he had hurt a young woman and tried to force Ella to submit to his will. Not only that, but he had been caught in the act by Harper.

How could he have known Harper had thrown Darcie Newland over for Ella? Harper had said nothing of falling for the dark-haired beauty. Then Harper's words came back to him – *she's not for you.*

Stafford instinctively knew his friendship with Harper was in jeopardy now, in fact it was most probably dead and buried, never to be resurrected. He groaned as he realised that on top of everything else, he had lost the bet and Oliver would revel in Stafford's defeat.

Ordering another double, he settled in for a day's heavy drinking. By the evening, Stafford was feeling very drunk. Hailing a cab, he called to be taken home, his slurred words causing him to howl with laughter. As the carriage rolled along, he began to sing at the top of his voice.

The cabbie rolled his eyes and prayed his customer would not vomit in his nice clean cab.

* * *

It was late when Harper arrived at The Hollies and rang the bell. The maid gave him entry when she saw who it was, having known him for years.

'Where's Stafford?' he demanded.

'In the parlour, sir,' the maid said with a bob of her knee.

Harper didn't wait to be shown to the room but marched ahead, his temper rising as he went.

Throwing open the door, he crossed the room with quick strides to where Stafford was sitting hunched in a chair before the fire.

'How could you, Stafford?' he yelled.

'Keep your voice down, old boy, the parents are in bed,' Darnell slurred.

'You attacked Ella Bancroft and you expect me to whisper so your folks don't hear?'

'Look, Harper, I had no idea you had set your sights on her. You didn't say a word. How was I to know?'

'You shouldn't have been there in the first place! I warned you this would turn out badly, but you had to go ahead – for a bet!'

'Harper, calm down. I'm sorry. I didn't know.' Darnell held out his hands trying desperately to keep a drunken smile from rising.

'It was wrong, Stafford, the whole idea was so very wrong. I tried to tell you, but you wouldn't listen!'

'Is she going to press charges, do you think?'

'Dear God! Is that all you can think of? Your own hide and how to save it! You make me sick, Stafford!'

'I've said I'm sorry.'

'It's not enough. This is one thing I cannot forgive. We have been friends for many years Stafford, but no longer. I'm tempted to beat you senseless, but it would not change you. You will always be a selfish swine. I will tell you this, though, if I see you within a mile of Ella ever again, I will hunt you down and thrash you to within an inch of your life! Stay away from her and me. I don't ever want to see your face again!'

Turning on his heel, Harper strode out of the room, his fists clenched in anger.

* * *

Early the following morning, Harper rode across town to visit Oliver Holgate. He needed to know what had occurred and the distress his bet with Stafford had caused Ella and Kitty.

'Morning, Harper, to what do I owe...'

'I need a word in private,' Harper said as he tipped his hat to Oliver's mother, who was still sitting at the breakfast table.

Oliver rose from the table, a frown on his face, and led Harper to the sitting room.

In armchairs either side of a roaring fire Oliver asked, 'What's up, Harper?'

Harper explained every last detail to the young man, who watched him with mounting horror.

'Oh, my God!' Oliver exclaimed when Harper had finished speaking. 'I knew Stafford was intent on winning, but to go that far?'

'Oliver, it was Ella! He was going to... She's the girl I'm going to marry if she'll have me.'

'I'm sure she will, Harper. Bloody hell, I'm still in shock!'

'You are! Think how those girls felt.'

Oliver nodded. 'I'm so very sorry, Harper. Had I known Stafford would take it so far, I would have called off the bet. In hindsight, I should never have been cajoled into it in the first place. Is there anything I can do to make amends?'

Harper shook his head. 'Ella and Kitty have no knowledge of your bet and I'd like to keep it that way. They are under the impression that Stafford's lust got the better of him; I assured them he wouldn't be calling again.'

Oliver blew out his cheeks as he shook his head. Then, looking at Harper he said, 'So is Ella the reason you released Darcie Newland from your engagement?'

'Yes, she is, but I didn't tell Darcie that, of course.'

Oliver shuddered. 'Very wise,' he said knowing full well the extent of Miss Newland's temper.

Ringing for the maid to bring coffee, Oliver's conversation returned to Stafford Darnell.

'I still can't believe he would do such a thing. I know he's a prankster and always up for a jape – but this? What's happened to him, Harper?'

'I have no idea. He's drinking more, that I do know, but other-wise...' Harper held out his hands and shook his head.

'What do we do now? Should I go and see him and let him know I'm aware of what he's done?' Oliver asked.

'It's probably best to leave him alone for a while. Let him think on the whole debacle and maybe he'll come to his senses.'

'Good idea. I'll tell you this, though, that's the last time I will ever be drawn into a bet by Stafford.'

'I'm glad to hear it,' Harper said as he stood to leave, shaking hands with his friend.

Now he had the task of informing his mother before she heard it from anyone else.

Harper found Eléna in the parlour on his return home. 'Mother, I need to speak with you,' he said as he settled into an armchair.

'Have you told Ella of your feelings yet, darling?'

'No...'

'Really, Harper! You must get to grips with this before you lose her altogether.'

'Mother!'

Eléna was taken aback by her son's sharp tone.

'I went to propose to Ella and was shocked to the core when I got there. Stafford Darnell had knocked Kitty, Ella's assistant, out cold and he was attempting to force himself on Ella!'

'Good grief! Are they all right?'

'Yes, although they refused medical treatment.'

'Have you informed the police? I know Stafford is your friend, but...'

'No, Ella didn't want the constabulary involved either.'

'What's to be done, then?' Eléna asked.

'I punched him and threatened a severe thrashing if he ever goes within a mile of Ella or Kitty.'

'Well done, son. I really can't believe it of Stafford! Why ever did he do it?'

'It was all over a bet with Oliver Holgate. I've just come from Oliver's so he's aware of what's happened.'

'A bet? My goodness. Stafford's father should take that boy in hand.'

Harper nodded. 'Under the circumstances I had no opportunity, and did not feel it appropriate, to speak with Ella privately.'

'No, of course not, it was a wise decision. There will be another time when it will be right and then you will have to discuss it with your father.' Eléna gave a tight smile as her son grimaced at the prospect.

Sighing loudly, Harper set his mind to how to approach Rafe and tell him he was intent on marrying a milliner.

36

At the time Ella was being attacked by Darnell, Darcie was staring at her image in the long mirror, twisting and turning so she could see herself from every angle.

'It's perfect! Don't you think so, Mother?'

'No, dear, I'm afraid I don't,' Verity said quietly. 'I really think something a little less showy...'

'I think *modom* looks beautiful,' the sales assistant put in.

'See? I agree, and it fits like a glove too!' Darcie gushed.

'Darling, please, won't you reconsider?' Verity tired again to persuade her daughter from purchasing the shepherdess dress complete with its bonnet.

'No, Mother! I want this one!' Darcie stamped her foot in emphasis.

'So be it, but what your father will say I have no idea, I'm sure.'

With a final twirl, Darcie retired to the back room to remove the dress.

Verity watched as the assistant boxed the gown and bonnet, a sad feeling coming over her. This was not how she had envisaged her daughter's wedding. The man Darcie was to marry had agreed for personal gain and not from any love for her girl. She wondered yet again whether Darcie would ever be happy. She and Royston had been in love when they were joined in wedlock and she still felt the same after twenty years. She just hoped Felix would be kind to Darcie, even if he could never love her.

Leaving the shop, the two women boarded the carriage to journey back to the railway station. Darcie was ecstatic but Verity could not find it in her to join in the revelry. No matter what she thought of the whole idea, it was Royston's decision and she had to abide by it. Now it would be up to Darcie to make what she could of being Mrs Felix Stoddard. The girl would have to find her own happiness somehow.

Verity heard nothing of Darcie's excited chatter as they travelled home; she was lost in her own thoughts of how her daughter would manage her new life.

* * *

It was mid-afternoon the following day back in Silver Street and Ella and Kitty were discussing Darnell, both nursing bruised faces.

'I hope he rots in hell!' Kitty snapped.

'At least Harper arrived in time. He said he was coming to see me. I wonder why?' Ella said as she served tea and toast.

'Ooh, a mid-afternoon snack – wonderful.' Kitty smiled, wary of her aching jaw.

'I think Sally was right, though, about having no more male customers.' Ella shook her head, aware of how much business would be lost.

'You can't let one rotten apple spoil the barrel,' Kitty said.

'I know, but it's dangerous, Kitty! I'm afraid to answer the door now when I hear a knock. I'm beginning to think we should have informed the police after all.'

'Ella, it would be our word against a man – a gentleman at that. Who do you think the constabulary would believe?' Kitty shook her head at the injustice of it all.

'There would be Harper's word, too,' Ella went on.

'The police might think it was just jealousy on his part.'

'I suppose you're right, but I can't help worrying he might try again.'

'Stafford Darnell wouldn't dare show his face here in the future, not after what Harper did to him.'

'No, but there are other young women out there. What if he forces his filthy ways on one of them? I would be devastated to hear of it, knowing a visit from the police might have prevented it.' Ella rubbed her jaw, where a purple and yellow bruise was just beginning to show.

'The bobbies won't do anything, Ella, I've told you. Anyway, we have more pressing matters – like how to sell your men's range safely.'

Ella nodded. She knew Kitty was right in what she said. It was a man's world and, no matter how unfair she felt it to be, Ella could do nothing to change it. She watched Kitty pick up a piece of red satin and an idea sparked. Taking the cloth, she asked, 'Can I use you as a model?'

Kitty nodded, wondering what Ella had in mind. Winding the material around Kitty's head, she pinned it in place carefully. Rummaging in a drawer of the dresser, she pulled out a brooch, which she used to fix a feather to the side of the new creation. Passing Kitty a small hand mirror, she waited for her friend's response.

'Bloody hell!'

Ella smiled. The brightly coloured turban was everything Ella had imagined and she was thrilled. 'The new theatre range?'

'I should say so! Ella, it's beautiful,' Kitty enthused. 'We ought to make a few because I think these will be very popular.'

Ella grinned then winced at the ache in her jaw. Mr Darnell's visit would stay with her for a while yet, at least until the pain ceased.

With renewed vigour, the two girls lined up the head blocks on the table before pulling out what bits of material they had left.

'I'll need to buy more fabric,' Ella said. 'Felt for the caps and satins and silks for the turbans.'

'Well, with what Mrs Fortescue paid for her hat, you can afford it now,' Kitty answered.

'I'll put the rent aside first and some for food and to pay the grocer's bill, but there should be enough left over to get what I need.'

Deciding a trip into the town could wait, Ella and Kitty settled to making up their first turban.

A tap to the back door came, followed by Flossie Woolley.

'What's all this I hear about screaming and carrying on while I was out yesterday?'

Ella and Kitty exchanged a quick glance. It hadn't taken long for the news to get out.

Over refreshments, the girls explained about Darnell's visit and his despicable behaviour.

'What a disgusting little bleeder!' Flossie exclaimed at last. 'I hope he gets his! He certainly will if my Ernie hears of it.' Flossie's husband was a big burly pit worker and spent his days in the bowels of the earth digging coal, and Flossie had no doubt he would paste Darnell good and proper.

'You ought to tell the coppers and have him arrested,' Flossie said.

Repeating what she'd told Ella about their word against his, Kitty saw the neighbour nod in resignation. 'I suppose you'm right. I don't know what this world is coming to when you ain't safe in your own home! Hey, but that Mr Fortescue is easy on the eye. A proper gentleman, and if I ain't mistaken he has *his* eye on you, Ella.'

Ella's cheeks reddened and, wanting to change the subject quickly, she asked Flossie's opinion about the turbans they were making. 'We will have to keep this a secret so Ivy Gladwin doesn't get wind of it.'

'She's been pinching Ella's ideas and undercutting her prices,' Kitty added by way of explanation.

'Good God, is nothing sacred?' Flossie said almost as a whisper.

Just then the back door flew open and in marched Sally.

'Having a mothers' meeting, are we?' she asked with a grin.

'Hello, Sally.' Ella spoke as if she had the weight of the world on her shoulders.

Taking off her coat, Sally sat in the empty chair at the table and folded her hands over the bump now beginning to show. She glanced at the millinery being undertaken. She couldn't as yet make out what they would become eventually, and she sighed in frustration.

It had not gone unnoticed that Sally had not asked after the health of her sister and Kitty, but Ella kept quiet, not wishing to raise the subject again.

'What are you making here, then?' Sally asked, trying her best to look bored.

'Hats, Sally, that's Ella's business, if you remember,' Kitty said sarcastically.

Sally's answer was a snarl. It was clear these two women

disliked each other intensely, and Flossie watched to see whether the contretemps would escalate.

'Has Eddy found a job yet?' Ella asked.

'No, he's still considering his options.'

'Oh, like whether he should bother to look or not?' Kitty could not hold her tongue.

'You mind your business! This is private and has nothing to do with you as I've told you before!' Sally snapped indignantly.

'Can I help it if you choose to bring your *private* discussions out in the open? I live here, in case you hadn't noticed!' Kitty fired back.

'For free, too!'

'Stop it! Sally, why does every sentence spoken have to become an argument with you?' Ella closed her eyes tight for a second then glared at her sister. 'Each time you open your mouth a fallout with someone ensues. If you can't be civil to my friends,' Ella's arms stretched to encompass Kitty and Flossie, 'then I must ask that you don't come here again.'

'Dad would spin in his grave if he heard you,' Sally spat.

Ella was on her feet in an instant. 'Don't you dare bring Dad into this! It's you, Sally, can't you see how spiteful you can be? You have always been the same and I'm sick and tired of it! So, if you can't be nice then go home to your lazy husband and don't bother coming back here!'

Without another word, Sally grabbed her coat and fled.

'Bullies don't like it when they're bullied themselves,' Flossie said. 'Good on yer, girl!'

Kitty and Flossie clinked their teacups, but Ella didn't join in. She immediately began to worry if she'd said the right thing, but it was done now and only time would tell whether Sally would heed her words.

Sally marched away from Silver Street in a huff. She had learned nothing new to sell to Ivy Gladwin and had been yelled at by Ella into the bargain. Now she had to go home to her bone-idle husband who, no doubt, would be reading the paper with his feet up.

She hated her life, having to scrimp and save what she could, which was not much with Eddy out of work. All she had was what she could prise out of Ivy's sticky fingers. She and Ella would never see eye to eye, and she wondered how as sisters they could be so different.

On top of all this she was pregnant, a position she really didn't want to be in. Having thought about it at some length, Sally had decided that once the baby was born she would give it up for adoption. She could not envisage herself raising a child, and Eddy would be of no help whatsoever. It would all be left to her; feeding, changing napkins, and the sleepless nights. No, this was not how she saw her life. She wanted money and status, all the things she could never have being married to Eddy and living in this Godforsaken town. When her offspring was given away, Sally intended to move to another town in the hope of meeting a man of wealth.

Entering the house, she called out that she was home. Walking into the sitting room, she sighed. Eddy was asleep, the open newspaper on his lap and his feet propped up on the footstool.

Sally strode over and pushed his feet down. Eddy woke with a jolt.

'You're back, then,' he said, rubbing his hands over his face.

'It scares me sometimes how smart you are,' Sally retorted as she removed her coat.

Ignoring the barb, Eddy asked, 'What's to eat?'

'Whatever is left in the larder,' Sally responded as she sat in the other easy chair.

'I'll have that, then.' Eddy picked up the paper and shook it.

When Sally didn't move, he peeped over the paper. 'Did you hear me?'

'I did. You can have some bread and cheese. The kitchen is that way.' Sally hooked a thumb over her shoulder.

'All right, what's going on?'

'I'm pregnant with your child, Eddy, so I shouldn't be running around while you sit on your arse.'

'Pregnant don't mean ill. It ain't like you're dying.'

Sally saw red. 'I wouldn't be in this position if you'd been more careful!'

'I knew it would be my fault! It ain't like you had anything to do with it, is it?'

'There's no point in arguing about it now, it's done! The pantry is virtually empty and I can't refill it with no money. You're the head of the family so it's up to you to provide, and what do you do? You sit in that chair all day, then drink yourself half to death at night! I've had enough, Eddy! Either you get a job or I'm off!'

'How many times do I have to tell you – there's no work anywhere!'

'Well, if you want your child to live, I have to eat. As for you – no work means no food!'

Eddy jumped to his feet and slammed the paper onto the chair he had just vacated.

Sally raised an eyebrow as she watched him pace back and forth, his hands in his trouser pockets and his eyes on the rag rug.

'Oh, bugger this, I'm going to the boozer!'

'Don't you come home drunk again because you'll find the door locked and it's freezing out there!' Sally yelled as Eddy disappeared into the kitchen. A moment later the door slammed and she sighed heavily. She knew she had a sharp tongue but did she deserve all this? Wearily getting to her feet, she went to find something to eat.

As she prepared the cheese sandwich, she thought: in a few months her belly would be empty and she could flee, leaving Eddy to wonder what had happened. The money she was earning from Ivy would help her to set herself up in rooms somewhere nice, and then she could begin her search for a rich man to take care of her.

Looking at the food, she thought that time could not come quickly enough.

37

With yet another hangover from hell, Stafford Darnell sat on his bed thinking about what he'd done. He felt wretched that he could have stooped so low, just to win a bet. He had lost more than money; he no longer had the friendship of Harper and, he guessed, of Oliver too. No doubt Oliver was well aware of what had happened, having been suitably informed by Harper.

Stafford groaned as his head pounded and his stomach roiled. Seeking solace in the bottle had not been one of his better ideas, for now his physical health was suffering as badly as his mind was.

Before he knew it, his mistake with Ella and her friend would be being gossiped about all over the town. He had to get away. He needed to go somewhere no one would find him. It was time to grow up and move on. Living with his parents at his age was no longer an option for him: he would live in dread of them finding out he had struck two women and tried to rape one of them. His folks would be unable to hold their heads up once the talk began.

Slowly he dragged out a travelling trunk and began to pack his clothing. He had wanted to see America for a long time and now would be the perfect opportunity. He could catch a train to Liverpool where he could buy passage on a ship bound for the Promised Land.

But, feeling dizzy again, Stafford decided there was no rush to finish packing, so he pulled the curtains closed and returned to his bed. Nausea rolled over him and he reached for the gazunder, holding it close. Eventually he fell asleep, the chamber pot clutched in his arms like a lover.

* * *

'Hello, George. Come in, I have your money ready,' Ella said to the rent man standing at her back door.

Stepping inside, he took the six shillings and sixpence but did not note it in his huge heavy ledger. Instead he passed a letter over to Ella, a dour look on his face.

'What's this?' Ella asked.

'I don't often have to deliver them but when I do, they never contain good news. I'm sorry, Ella.'

Tearing open the envelope, Ella's eyes scanned the words before she dropped onto a chair, her face drained of all colour.

Kitty looked to George, who bowed his head, then back at Ella. 'What is it?'

Ella waved the letter towards her friend.

'He can't do this, surely?' Kitty asked.

'He can. It says right there we have a week to vacate the property.' Ella fought the tears beginning to well up.

'I guessed as much. The boss has a family he wants to move in, and it looks like he's picked your place to do it,' George mumbled.

'But why? We pay our rent every week without fail!'

'I know, but with a family Mr Barton can charge twice what

you pay.' George glanced around the small kitchen, then on impulse he laid the money Ella had given him back on the table. 'Six and six, it might help a bit.'

Ella inclined her head in thanks, unable to trust herself to speak for fear of bursting into tears.

'I'm so sorry, girls. There are some days I really hate this job,' George said sadly as he shook his head.

'What are we going to do now?' Ella asked.

'Well, you'd best be having a word with your sister and see if she'll take you in,' Kitty answered.

Ella closed her eyes, a look of pain crossing her face. 'I can't, Kitty. There's no way on God's green earth I could live with our Sally again.' Looking at her friend she added, 'Whatever we do and wherever we go, it will be together.'

Kitty felt the emotion build inside her and in a moment the girls were hugging and crying. Worried at having nowhere to go, sad at leaving but with the small of joy at staying friends at least, they sobbed out their woes as Flossie Woolley arrived.

Ella told her neighbour the news about them being evicted.

'What a bastard!' Flossie cursed before apologising for her bad language. Then a smile crossed her face.

'What?' Ella asked.

'I have an idea, but it will mean you will have to agree and be uncomfortable for a couple of weeks.'

'In what way?' Kitty asked.

Flossie bent across the table to whisper her plan.

'But what about my business?' Ella said at last.

'You'll have to close up shop for a little while until all this is sorted out,' Flossie answered. 'I'm sorry, wench, but it's the only way if you want to stay here.'

Ella nodded. 'It's worth a try.'

Suddenly the audacity of Flossie's idea had them all in fits of giggles, George's booming laugh sounding loudly around the room.

'You'll have to keep your mouth shut, George,' Flossie said as the man turned to leave.

'I'll play my part, Flossie, don't you worry about that.'

Once the rent man had gone, the women settled down to work out the finer details. All that was needed now was for their plan to work.

* * *

It was mid-morning the following day when Stafford Darnell saw his trunk loaded onto a cab and he turned to hug his sobbing mother.

'Why America? It's so far away! We may never see you again!'

'Mother, it's a land full of promise! I will make my fortune and return a rich man in my own right.'

Climbing aboard, he waved as the cab rolled forward. He knew he had to get away before news got out about his misdeed, and he felt relieved he was finally on his way.

At the railway station, Stafford hailed a porter to collect his luggage whilst he went to the ticket office. Purchasing a fare to Liverpool, he turned towards the platform.

'Running while you still can?'

Stafford looked at the person who addressed him, his blood turning cold in his veins.

'I'm sorry, were you speaking to me?' he asked.

'I was, Stafford Darnell,' came the reply.

'I'm afraid I don't know you or what you are talking about.' Stafford searched for any sign of recognition but found none.

'You may not be acquainted with me, but I know you and what you've done.'

Feeling his colour blanch, Stafford made to push past but the stranger barred his way.

'You must excuse me, I have a train to catch.'

'Wherever you are going, I think you should take me with you.'

'What? Are you mad? Why on earth would I take a complete stranger with me?' Stafford was nonplussed by the cheek of it.

'If you don't, I'll scream for a bobby. Once I tell him who you are and what you did to Ella Bancroft, then you'll be arrested and thrown in jail.'

'Who are you? What do you want from me?'

'I want to get away from this place and you are my meal-ticket. As to *who* I am – I'm Ella's sister. Sally's the name, nice to meet you. Now I suggest you go and buy me a ticket to – Liverpool, wasn't it?'

* * *

Flossie unwrapped the wet fish she'd bought at the market as Kitty unwound the end from the curtain pole.

Ella wrinkled her nose at the smell pervading her front room. 'I'm still not sure we should be doing this, it feels all wrong.'

'Look, wench, what Arnold Barton is doing is what's wrong. Turning you girls out so he can move a family in for twice the rent!' Flossie said firmly.

'I agree he's not being fair, but...' Ella began.

'Well, it's too late now. George will already have told the land-lord there's a foul stench coming from somewhere,' Kitty cut across.

'Barton will be along quick as a wink to see for himself, you see if he ain't,' Flossie added.

Ella wanted to stay in the house she'd grown up in but

couldn't truly condone the way they were going about it. She watched as Kitty shoved the fish inside the curtain pole before replacing the end stop loosely.

'I hope this works because this thing will need a thorough cleaning afterwards,' Kitty said as she went to the kitchen to wash her hands.

'Leave that door open so the smell goes all round,' Flossie said pointing to the door to the kitchen.

'Oh, I must put a closed sign in the window, too,' Ella said grabbing a pen and paper. Just about to place the sign in position, a knock came to the door. Peeping out, she saw Harper. Waving to attract his attention she pointed to the alley directing him to the back entrance. Opening the back door, she invited him in.

Harper was puzzled, but spying the fish wrapper on the table he guessed they were about to eat.

'I apologise for disturbing your luncheon,' he said.

Ella glanced at the odoriferous paper then to Flossie and Kitty. 'Erm, no we had lunch earlier.'

Harper raised his eyebrows in question. It was not like Ella to leave such a smelly paper lying about.

Kitty and Flossie exchanged a glance, both wondering what Ella would say next.

'Take a seat, I think there's something you need to hear.'

Showing him the letter from her landlord, Ella then proceeded to explain their plan.

All three women stared when Harper threw back his head and roared with laughter.

38

Verity Newland sat in the dining room of the swanky hotel, her eyes darting between her daughter and Felix Stoddard.

'It's lovely of you to invite us for lunch,' she said, 'and in such a grand place too.'

Felix waved a hand dismissively. 'My pleasure.' He noted his soon-to-be mother-in-law had eaten sparingly whilst Darcie had a robust appetite.

Verity sipped her wine from the delicate glass in her gentle fingers; Darcie was just the opposite, grabbing and quaffing like the stocks might run dry.

With each glass, Darcie's voice grew louder, drawing glances from other diners. As the waiter moved to refresh her drink, Felix shook his head. 'I think the lady has had enough, thank you.' The waiter inclined his head in acknowledgement and returned to his place on the periphery of the room.

'I want more wine,' Darcie drawled.

'Darling, Felix is right. No more for you today,' Verity said, trying to take charge of a situation she knew from experience could spiral out of control in the blink of an eye.

'Mummy!' Darcie snapped.

Verity flushed scarlet as she heard the whispers around her.

Felix nodded to another waiter. As he approached Felix said quietly, 'Have the ladies' carriage brought around, please.'

The waiter nodded. 'Very good sir.'

Felix signed for the lunches to be added to his account and rose from the table, as did Verity.

Darcie glanced at him and giggled, 'Where are we off to now?'

'You are going home, my dear,' Felix said patiently.

'No! I don't want to!' Darcie banged her hands on the table, making her glass jump.

Bending forward, Felix cupped her elbow tight enough to make her wince, his mouth close to her ear. 'Do not embarrass me more than you have already, Darcie, or I swear you will die an old maid.'

Glancing up at him, she blanched. He was threatening to call off the wedding if she misbehaved. Even in her drunken state she knew she could not endure being jilted a second time. Getting to her feet, she clamped her teeth together and walked meekly to the door.

Behind her, Verity breathed a sigh of relief. Maybe Felix would be good for Darcie after all. Their wedding couldn't come soon enough as far as she was concerned. Giving her thanks and apologies for her daughter's behaviour, Verity climbed into the waiting carriage.

'Please don't concern yourself,' Felix said with a tight smile. 'Good day, ladies, I will see you in a few days once my business is complete.'

Nodding to the jarvey, Felix stepped back as the carriage rolled away. He pursed his lips in anger. That was the first and last time Darcie would humiliate him in public. On his next visit to the Newlands he fully intended to ensure the girl would know her place.

Nodding to his driver, Felix climbed into his landau, his thoughts roaming through the silence of his mind. He didn't *have* to marry Darcie if he chose not to. However, that would mean not getting his hands on Newland's businesses. The old man would be due to retire before long, and with luck he would pass his string of businesses onto his new son-in-law. Felix was well known for buying up dying companies and making them flourish once more.

Having made discreet enquiries into Newland's affairs, he knew the output was far below what it should be; he also knew how to correct that error. However, he would keep that knowledge to himself until the works became his. Once in control, he would watch the profits soar, helping him on the way to his ambition to be one of the wealthiest men in the country.

To achieve this goal, he would have to turn Darcie from a spoilt brat into a compliant wife. It would be a challenge, but one he was certain he could take on and achieve. By the time he had finished with Darcie Newland, even her own parents would not recognise her, but he had to work quickly. He had to cow her before they were wed, for once that ring was on her finger it would be too late. Threatening to call off the wedding was the key and he would turn it as far as it would go, thereby locking everything in place.

His network of informants had discovered the true reason Darcie had not married Harper Fortescue, and she could not risk it happening again. Felix smiled to himself as he neared his home. He would spend the next few hours going over his accounts; he needed to be sure of how much to offer Royston Newland for his businesses should it come to that. Felix would not wait forever and so had constructed a back-up plan. Inherit or buy, either way those works would be his.

* * *

Darnell eyed the woman who sat opposite him in the first-class compartment of the train. The weather had turned dull and the gas lamps had been lit. He watched as she drew her hand lovingly over the plush blue velvet of the seat, a smile gracing her lips. Each train's first-class carriage carried a different colour upholstery, some were red, and others were blue. Her smile widened as a steward served coffee before exiting quietly.

'How did you know I would be at the station?' he asked.

'I didn't. I was there for another reason, one which does not concern you,' she answered. She kept to herself the fact that she had been there only to price a ticket to somewhere as far as her money would take her.

'How do you know me?'

'I just do, all right?'

'What do you want from me?'

'Money,' Sally said simply. 'Enough to ensure I'll keep my mouth shut.'

'What's to stop you blabbing once you have what you want?'

Sally shrugged. 'You'll have to trust me.'

'I don't,' Darnell snorted.

'That's understandable, but I only want enough to live comfortably – well away from Walsall. I don't care where you go from Liverpool, provided you see me right.' Sally rubbed her fingers and thumb together and grinned.

'All right, but only if you promise to leave me alone. I want to see you onto another train, then I'll believe you.'

'Fair enough. Now, how about you buy me lunch?'

The two barely spoke on the long journey and at last the train pulled into Lime Street Station. Instructing a porter to collect his luggage, Darnell asked, 'Where will you go?'

'Home, first, to collect my things, then as far away as possible. Don't worry, Mr Darnell, you won't see me again.'

Going to the ticket office, he purchased a fare back to Walsall and passed it to Sally.

'Money?' she asked pointedly.

Taking out his wallet, turning away from prying eyes, he handed over fifty pounds.

Sally shook her head so, with a scowl, he added another fifty. Nodding, she tucked it into her pocket. 'Nice doing business with you.'

Darnell harrumphed before leading her to the train she was to catch. Seeing her aboard, he waited until the iron beast puffed its way out of the station. Only then did he sigh with relief.

39

It was early evening before George stood in Arnold Barton's sitting room to hand over the day's rent collection.

'The smell at 24 Silver Street is awful, Mr Barton,' George said, wrinkling his nose.

'Why did the tenant not report it to me?' Barton asked, his beady eyes studying his rent collector.

'Scared, most like, but she don't seem to mind it none.'

'What's causing it?' Barton pushed back his greasy hair before stroking his moustache.

'I ain't got a clue, although it could be the drains.' George watched his employer rub his whiskers, thinking the man was badly in need of a shave and a bath.

'I'll have to get down there in the morning and see for myself.'

'I'm not sure the place is fit for a family, Mr Barton. It might be something infectious and anybody with kids ain't likely to want it.'

The beady eyes narrowed to pinpoints as Barton considered the words. 'Bugger!'

'Will you be wanting me to go with you tomorrow, then?' George asked, as casually as he could manage.

'Yes. Nine o'clock.' Barton flicked his fingers in dismissal.

George allowed his grin to spread across his face only when he was outside in the darkness. As he trudged home in the cold, he wondered how their little ruse would pan out.

At nine on the dot the following morning, Ella answered the knock to the back door. George and Arnold Barton walked in to see Flossie and Kitty wrapping cups and saucers in newspaper before packing them in a box.

Barton sniffed before he spoke. 'George told me about the smell.'

'It's not too bad today,' Ella said as she glanced at Flossie, 'although it's a bit worse in the front room.' Ella led Barton through and George remained in the kitchen, his fingers crossed behind his back.

A moment later they were back and Barton said, 'I can't make out where it's coming from.'

'I can only surmise it's from the drains and that, I believe, is your domain,' Ella said as she joined the others to continue packing her things.

'The council should see to it. I'll get on to them today,' Barton retorted.

'The council will have a look, Mr Barton, but if it's the house drain they won't touch it.' George spoke quietly, feeling the women's eyes on him.

'Bugger it!' Barton paced as he began to consider the implications. George was right, no one would want to rent the property with such a foul stench emanating from it. Glancing at Ella, he thought she didn't seem overly bothered by it, and she *was* always on time with her rent. He wondered if he could persuade her to stay, at least then he would have an income from the building. He didn't want to notify the council in case they slammed a condemned notice on the whole house.

Ella watched her landlord closely, silently praying he would change his mind about evicting her.

'The thing is, if you move out I probably won't be able to find another tenant,' Barton said at last.

'It was not my choice to leave. I believe you had a family all ready to move in,' Ella said, trying her best to remain calm.

'Ar, well, they, erm, they found somewhere else, so – you can stay if you want.' Barton's eyes couldn't meet Ella's.

'I can't afford to pay the extra sixpence a week if I'm unable to run my business from here,' Ella said, giving her attention to wrapping yet another cup.

'Pay the tanner and I'll turn a blind eye,' Barton said, thoroughly disgruntled at being bested by this chit of a girl.

Ella held out her hand and Barton was forced to shake on the deal. Turning on his heel, Barton strode out of the house. George gave Ella a wink before he followed.

After a moment, the three women burst out laughing and shared a hug.

'Get some water on to heat and find some washing soda, it's gonna take a lot of work to get rid of that stink!' Flossie said, as she began to unwrap the crockery. 'Kitty, get that fish out and put it in this newspaper. Then we'll set to cleaning that curtain pole.'

'Thank you, Flossie, you're a diamond,' Ella said as she busied with pans of water on the range.

'Just remember, this is our secret. If Barton finds out what we did he'll have us all out – including George.'

'I hope he doesn't get into trouble,' Ella said, whilst dissolving soda crystals in the hot water.

'He won't if we all stay tight-lipped. Now, come on, let's scrub that curtain pole,' Flossie said. Over her shoulder she called out, 'Kitty, get that fish put into the bin for the rubbish men to collect.'

Kitty nodded and did as she was bid, leaving the back door open to rid the house of the all-pervading odour.

An hour later saw the women celebrating their success with a hard-earned cup of tea, the Black Country remedy for all ills.

* * *

Having returned home considerably better off financially, Sally silently congratulated herself. It had been a stroke of luck seeing Darnell at the station – five minutes later and she would have missed him.

Eddy had not enquired as to where she'd been. He probably thought she had visited Ella, and Sally saw no reason to disillusion him. Sitting with tea, she stared at him reading his newspaper as usual. He had finally risen from his bed around midmorning, consumed his breakfast and settled himself for a day of relaxation. Sally's lip curled, seeing his braces over his vest – *too idle to even get dressed properly!*

Sipping her drink, Sally knew she needed to get him out of the house so she could pack her few belongings. She had considered leaving after the child was born, but now she had money she decided to flee as soon as possible.

Eddy shifted in his seat and broke wind loudly. Sally cringed; she could not bear to live with him any longer. She didn't have to be here to have the baby, she could give birth anywhere. Once that was done she would find an adoption agency, and if she couldn't she would leave the kid on a doorstep somewhere.

The question now was – where to go? Hearing Eddy burp, Sally felt her stomach roll and nausea overtake her. Taking her cup to the kitchen to wash it, she wondered whether to tell Ella what she was about to do. No, her sister would try to talk her out of it. What about Ivy Gladwin? Again, Sally decided against it, for Ivy would not be happy at losing her source of information about Ella's business.

Listening to Eddy playing a symphony with his bodily functions, Sally grabbed her coat and walked out. She would visit Ella and see what was new in the hat world. She might as well continue to collect her cash from Ivy while she could.

Although it remained cold, the big freeze had moved on and everyone thought the promise of spring was beginning to show.

Sally still wasn't sure where she could go or what she would do when she got there, but with the money safely hidden away she knew she wouldn't starve.

Ella's house was a hive of activity when Sally arrived.

'What's going on here, then?' she asked.

'We're just spring cleaning the front room ready for our new range,' Ella replied. She hoped the little fib would save her from Sally's sharp tongue.

'It's a bit early, ain't it? Still, I can see the need.' Sally wiped a finger over the table looking for dust, and, finding none, she snorted.

Flossie dug Kitty in the ribs and flicked her eyebrows; Kitty responded with a nod.

'So, what's this new range like?'

Ella pulled a couple of turbans from their wrappings and displayed them proudly on the table.

Picking one up, Sally turned it to see it from every angle. 'A bit fancy for my taste. I'm not sure you'll get much call for them around here.' Plonking the hat back on its wrapper, she sniffed.

'We're aiming at theatre goers and soiree attendees,' Ella said in response.

'I suppose it would depend on what you're asking for them.'

Sally tried not to show too much interest but curiosity was getting the better of her.

'We thought two pounds, ten shillings each wasn't too expensive.'

'Two pound ten! Bloody hell, Ella, folk ain't made of money, especially in this town.'

'Here we go again,' Kitty said with a sigh.

Sally ignored the comment and ploughed in with, 'If you want to sell these – you have to keep your prices down!'

'I can't, Sally, I have to pay the rent,' Ella said, feeling rather than seeing the glance her two friends exchanged. 'We have to eat and buy coal. I couldn't manage if I dropped my prices.'

'You could if *she* went out to work!' Sally pointed at Kitty.

'I can't listen to this again, Ella, otherwise I won't be responsible for my actions! I'm going out.' Kitty snatched her coat from the peg on the back door.

'I'll come with you,' Flossie added, throwing a disdainful look Sally's way.

As they walked away from the house, Kitty growled, 'I'll swing for that one before too long!'

'I'll hold yer coat,' Flossie replied with a grin.

Kitty laughed, her anger melting away.

'Where are we going?' Flossie asked.

'I thought I'd have a peek in Ivy Gladwin's window to see what she has on offer.'

'Good idea. I could do with a good laugh,' Flossie said.

Arm in arm, the two set off at a brisk pace.

Back in the house, Ella and Sally were arguing yet again. Ella worked to get the front room display set up as she listened to Sally's ranting.

'You can't go on feeding and sheltering a lodger who is

supposed to be paying you! You're too soft by half, our Ella. You need to get a grip and turf her out!'

Eventually Ella had had enough. 'Sally, if you can't be civil then just go home! No matter what I do it will be wrong as far as you're concerned.'

'I'm only giving my opinion,' Sally countered.

'I understand that, but has it ever occurred to you that your opinion isn't wanted?'

'I still think you should get rid of that girl – or at least make her pay her way.'

'It has nothing to do with you, Sally!' Ella was becoming exasperated at her sister's interference in her life, which was evident in her sharp tone.

'I'm trying to make you see sense.'

'You're poking your nose in is what you're doing. Now, if you don't mind, I have a lot to do today.' Ella glared at her sister, holding a hat in each hand.

'Fine, I'll bugger off, then!'

'You do that.'

When Sally had gone, Ella sat in the kitchen looking at the space where Thomas's chair used to be. 'I'm sorry, Dad. I do try with our Sally, but she incenses me at times. I know you wanted us to get on together but, in all honesty – it's never going to happen.'

Suddenly the grief she thought she had under control hit her like a thunderbolt yet again. Burying her face in her hands, Ella wept as the crack in her heart split a little wider.

40

Ella wiped her eyes on her apron before answering the knock to the back door.

'I hope you don't mind me coming to the back – Ella, what's happened?' Harper said, on seeing her distress.

Permitting him entry, Ella closed the door quietly and, as she turned to face him, her tears fell again.

Harper was undone and rushed to her, enfolding her in his arms. He kissed her hair as Ella cried on his chest, propriety having gone out of the window.

'I'm missing my dad and I've argued with Sally again,' she managed between sobs.

Suddenly realising they were alone at last, Harper knew he might not get another chance such as this. Holding her at arm's length, he looked into her amber-flecked eyes.

'Ella, I love you with all my heart.' Dropping to one knee he went on quickly, 'Ella Bancroft, will you marry me?'

Looking at the man who held her heart, she nodded. 'Yes, Harper, I will.'

Jumping to his feet, he picked her up and whirled her

around. Ella squealed with delight and as they came to a halt she beamed with pleasure, as her tears turned to tears of joy.

Harper lowered his lips gently on hers and Ella melted into him, her arms snaking around him. They held each other tightly, neither wanting to let go. 'I love you, Harper,' she murmured, and his heart soared to a new dizzying height.

A few more tender kisses later, Harper finally let her go, and as she made tea for them both, his eyes watched her every move.

'I'm the happiest man on earth right now,' he said with a grin like a Cheshire cat. 'I will have to see the vicar to arrange a date. Do you have a preference, my love?'

'As soon as possible,' Ella said, suddenly feeling a little shy.

'So be it. Mother will be ecstatic when I tell her.'

'I hope so. I wish Dad were here to see this.'

'He'll be watching over you, Ella, I'm sure.'

They talked for an hour or more about wedding plans before the back door burst open and in bustled Flossie and Kitty.

'You'll never guess – oh, hello,' Kitty said as she spotted Harper sitting at the table.

'Ladies,' he responded.

'I'm getting married!' Ella gushed, unable to hold back her excitement, which infected her friends as they jumped for joy.

'It's about time,' Flossie said. 'I thought you'd never get around to asking her.'

'I tried many times, but circumstances seemed to get in the way,' Harper said with a grin.

Kitty hugged her friend. 'I'm so happy for you both.'

'What were you going to tell me when you came in?' Ella asked.

Kitty glanced at Flossie, knowing what she had to say would spoil their reverie.

'She has to know so it might as well be now,' Flossie said.

All sitting around the table, Kitty began. 'Flossie and I went to have a look in Ivy Gladwin's window...'

'To see what cack she was selling,' Flossie put in.

'And who did we see coming? Only your sister Sally. So, we popped into the grocer's next door to hide,' Kitty went on.

'Why?' Ella asked, unable to see where this was all leading.

'We wondered what she was up to. So we waited until she left and Flossie went in.'

'I don't understand...' Ella began.

'Hold yer 'orses and you'll find out,' Flossie answered.

'It seems Ivy knows exactly what you are making and selling because Sally is telling her. Judging by the money Sally shoved in her pocket on leaving the shop, it's my guess she's selling your ideas.'

Ella's mouth fell open as she listened. 'I don't believe it!'

'How else could Ivy know what's in your range? Face it, wench, yer sister is selling you out for a couple of quid a time,' Flossie said with a shake of her head.

Ella glanced at Harper, who nodded. 'I think they could be right, Ella. There's no other way Ivy could know. I'm sorry, darling.'

'Sally has shown a bit more interest in my hats of late, I have to admit,' Ella said as she cast her mind back, 'and today she was prying as to prices.'

Flossie and Kitty nodded their agreement.

'What are you gonna do about it?' Flossie asked.

'Well, we need to be absolutely certain Sally is selling my designs before I tackle her,' Ella said.

'You'll know soon enough if Ivy has turbans in her window by next week,' Kitty said, lifting the very hat Sally had handled only hours before.

'So we wait and watch. Kitty, we must protect our creations somehow,' Ella said, her mind in a whirl.

'All you can do is lock the back door and keep the curtains closed so Sally can't see in when she calls round.' Flossie crossed her arms beneath her bosom as she spoke.

'Good idea, Flossie, then Sally will have to knock so we'll have time to cover our work up or move it,' Kitty added.

Ella nodded with a sigh. 'I hate all this cloak and dagger stuff but, until we know for certain, I can see the necessity.'

'What you need, my love, is a shop of your own,' Harper said.

Ella grinned then rolled her eyes. 'I wish. I'll get there one day, but until then I have Sally and Ivy Gladwin to deal with.'

'As well as a wedding to organise. Speaking of which, I must away and give Mother this most excellent news.' Harper gave a little bow to Flossie and Kitty and kissed Ella's cheek. 'I will see you tomorrow, my love.'

'Tomorrow,' Ella said dreamily as she watched him leave.

'Right, to work finishing the front room now that bloody awful smell has gone,' Kitty said, getting to her feet.

'I'm away home, girls, so I'll see yer tomorrer an' all. Congratulations on your engagement, Ella,' Flossie said.

'I can't believe Sally would do that to me,' Ella said into the quiet of the kitchen, when it was just her and Kitty left.

'Well, it looks very much like she has. I'm sorry, Ella.' Kitty patted her friend's shoulder as they moved to resume their work in the sitting room. 'Looking on the bright side – you are soon to become Mrs Harper Fortescue.'

'Ooh, Kitty, I can't believe that either!'

Wrapping their arms around each other, they danced around the room, laughing and singing the wedding march.

41

Darcie rose with a banging head and roiling stomach. She joined her mother in the parlour, where she poured herself some coffee.

'You've decided to get up at last, then,' Verity said.

'Mother, don't start, I have a headache.'

'I'm not surprised after what you drank yesterday.'

Darcie closed her eyes and sighed.

'I warn you now, my girl, Felix will not put up with such aberrant behaviour.'

'For God's sake!' Darcie winced at the pain in her head and she leaned back, resting it on the comfortable armchair.

'You have a week left before your wedding, which is more than enough time for Felix to change his mind.'

'Like Harper did, you mean?'

'You said that, not me.'

'But you thought it!'

'You have to learn humility, otherwise it will be on your own head.' Verity shook her head as she walked from the room.

Darcie considered her mother's words, realising reluctantly that they were true. Felix would leave her if she refused to toe the line. Harper Fortescue had jilted her for, in her opinion, another woman, and although this news had been kept secret, Darcie could not risk it happening again. She still smarted about the way Harper had treated her and would have loved to have outed him to the town. However, the threat of jail time for assault still hung over her. Her hands were tied where Harper was concerned. Felix was another matter, though, he would have no qualms about letting people know he had forsaken her because of her temper and bad behaviour.

Darcie thought about what she could lose; a beautiful house in the heart of Birmingham brimming with servants. Visits to the theatre, parties and soirees as well as mingling with the highest echelons of society.

All she had to do to have it all was to be meek and mild for a couple of weeks. Once she was wed she could return to being herself. Certain she could manage it, Darcie decided for the moment she would go back to bed to sleep off her hangover. Tomorrow would be soon enough for the new Darcie to show herself.

* * *

Whilst Darcie was arguing with her mother, Ivy Gladwin was placing her new creations in the window.

The money paid to Sally the previous day would see good returns, she felt sure. Ivy had worked almost all night to produce turbans for her display. She was tired to the bone but couldn't help smiling to herself. Her window looked beautiful, full of hats large and small. The burst of colour would remind people that springtime was not far away. They would be drawn in to be the first to buy and so lead the fashion trend. The two pounds a week had turned into two pounds a visit, but Ivy didn't mind, the information she received was worth every penny.

Looking again at her display, she nodded with satisfaction. Bright silk turbans adorned her window, all priced at two pounds – ten shillings cheaper than Ella's. With a smug smile, she waited for the shop bell to tinkle, heralding her first customer of the day.

* * *

Returning home two pounds better off, Sally sat in the sitting room with a cup of tea. Eddy was asleep in the armchair with his feet on the stool as usual, and she didn't disturb him; she wanted to enjoy the peace and quiet for a while.

She thought about her money hidden away and cast her mind back to her little jaunt with Stafford Darnell. She could have blackmailed him right there at the station but it was far too crowded. There was also the worry that Darnell could have called a constable and had her hauled off to jail. Thinking on her feet, she had forced him to take her with him. He was running scared, otherwise he might well have sent her packing.

During their train journey Sally had wondered where Darnell would end up, but was wise enough to know he would not disclose his destination to her. She had considered trying to go all the way with him, but on reflection knew he would never have stood for that. It would have been a step too far. And, anyway, it was of no consequence, Sally was happy with her lot.

Her thoughts moved to Ivy and the cash she had handed over. Sally couldn't make up her mind whether it was time to call a halt there now as she didn't want to push her luck too far. There was always the risk that Ella would discover who was selling her out, so maybe she should cut her losses and move on.

For now, though, she decided to wake Eddy and rile him

enough for him to storm out in temper. Once she was sure he was clear of the house she could throw a few things in a suitcase and be off on her travels.

Pushing Eddy's feet off their perch, Sally watched him jerk awake.

'What the...?'

'Wake up, you lazy sod!' Sally yelled.

Eddy rubbed his eyes. 'What's going on?' he asked, glancing around as if he didn't know where he was.

'Get up, get a wash and get out there to find a job!' Sally's anger mounted quickly and she grimaced as she saw him scratch an armpit. 'You are disgusting, do you know that? So much for all the airs and graces you show to everyone else, they don't see you like this do they? Sitting there in your vest, scratching like a dog with fleas – you make me sick!'

'Woah, girl, where's all this coming from?' Eddy asked, perplexed at the sudden outburst.

'I've been patient with you, Eddy, God knows I have, but enough's enough! You find every excuse in the book not to find work and I don't intend to put up with it any longer. Now, you get out of this house and don't come back until you are employed! Don't push me on this, Eddy, because I will leave you and you'll never see your child!' Sally covered her stomach with both hands in a manner which left him in no doubt she was being serious.

'Sally, for God's sake!'

In answer, Sally threw her arm out and pointed to the door, her face stern and murder in her eyes.

Eddy scrambled to his feet, grabbed his jacket and fled the house. As he went, he wondered when Sally had become the master and he her slave. He had not noticed the roles reversing. He should not have become so complacent, but judging by his wife's mood it was too late to worry about that now.

Trudging down the street he thought, *Bloody women! They have no idea how hard life is for a man. How do they expect us to get work when there's none to be had? They have the life of Riley, sitting by the fire all day, having nothing more to do than knitting. It's us men who bring in the money for their wives to spend on whatever they like. Well, I'm fed up with being told what to do by a woman! If she wants to go, let her. Then we'll see how she manages without me to take care of her!*

Eddy made for the nearest tavern as he jingled the coins in his pocket. He intended to drink himself into unconsciousness and sleep where he fell. Sally would worry herself sick when he didn't come home. With a nasty grin, Eddy threw open the doors to the public house and strode in. He was greeted by his pals, who would help him wash away his cares with a good ale.

Marching to the bar, Eddy slapped his coins on the counter as he settled in for the duration.

Meanwhile, Sally was busy packing. She had very little so it didn't take her long. Standing in the kitchen, her hat and coat on and her money safely tucked in her underwear, she glanced around.

Should she write a note for Ella and say where she was going? No, this was to be her fresh start, her new beginning. Besides, she wasn't sure where she'd end up herself as yet. She intended to portray herself as a recently widowed young woman when she arrived at her destination.

But where to go? Where had Darnell gone on to from Liverpool? Had he caught another train or had he booked a passage on a ship bound for exotic lands? She could do that now she had money, especially as she had taken Eddy's savings, which he had hidden in a shoe in the wardrobe. What an idiot! Did he think she would never find it?

Grabbing her suitcase, Sally walked out of the house and

away from the life she hated. She was bound for Liverpool yet again and then onwards to a new life in another country. She had plenty of time to choose which one as she travelled to the port. A cab, a train and a ship, and Sally Denton could be anyone she wanted, once she'd given up the child for adoption. The thought warmed her, and she hurried to find the cab that would take her on the first leg of her exciting journey.

42

Everyone in the town was reading, or having read to them, the article in the newspaper regarding Queen Victoria's funeral. The coffin was to have been drawn on a gun carriage by white horses as per the old queen's express wishes, but was in fact dragged by the Naval Guard of Honour. The Blue Jackets had come to the rescue when the horses broke free of their traces. Quickly attaching ropes, the sailors hauled the gun carriage from Waterloo railway station to Paddington, where the coffin would travel by train to Windsor.

The Queen of the United Kingdom of Great Britain and Ireland, and Empress of India, had lain in the Albert Memorial Chapel for two days before being interred at St George's Chapel in Windsor Castle, next to her beloved Albert.

The weather had turned bitterly cold again but the snow that fell had not deterred the crowds from lining the streets to watch the procession pass by. Thousands of people were in mourning alongside King Edward VII, who had walked sedately behind his mother's coffin. Military bands played as they marched, and the busbies of the Horse Guards could be seen clearly as their mounts trotted along in perfect block formation.

Felix Stoddard folded the newspaper neatly before his mind turned once again to his forthcoming marriage. He had been fitted for his wedding attire but was in need of a new top hat. He could, of course, go to Lock & Co of London, but it was a long way to travel for just one item. He recalled being told of a little place in Silver Street, Walsall, where the head gear was said to be second to none. He decided he would try there first. Grabbing an overcoat, hat and cane, he called for his carriage to be brought round.

On his journey from Birmingham, Felix wondered for the thousandth time if he was doing the right thing in marrying Darcie Newland. He wanted the family businesses, of that there was no doubt, but would taking on a spoilt young woman he didn't love be a price too heavy? He would be tied to her for the rest of his life, which would be a very long time. The pros and cons bounced off each other in his mind as the carriage rattled along the busy streets.

Eventually coming to a halt, Felix stepped down and hammered the door to a dingy house with his cane. A moment later, it was opened by a girl with gold-flecked eyes.

'Miss Bancroft?' he asked. Seeing the girl nod, he went on, 'Then I have the right place. My name is Felix Stoddard and I'm in need of a top hat for a wedding.'

'Please come in out of the cold, Mr Stoddard,' Ella said, allowing him entry before closing the door on the chill wind.

'This is Kitty Fiske, my assistant,' Ella said.

Felix stared openly at the blonde-haired beauty.

'Pleased to meet you,' Kitty said with a smile that lit up the room.

'Likewise, Miss Fiske,' Felix managed.

Ella noted the lingering look shared between her friend and the handsome stranger.

'I will need to take some measurements first, then you can tell me what you are looking for,' Ella said.

'Yes, of course,' Felix muttered, trying to drag his gaze away from Kitty.

Ella bustled about with her tape measure, noting the figures on a sheet of paper. 'Now, what did you have in mind Mr Stoddard?'

'Something different,' he answered, his eyes still glued to Kitty.

'I can make a top hat in any colour you like, black, white...'

'White,' he said.

Ella felt a shiver run down her spine. Harper had ordered a white topper when he was betrothed to Darcie Newland. She made another note, asking, 'And when would you need it for?'

'I need it in a week.'

'A week! Goodness, that doesn't give me much time, but I think I can manage. I take it you are the groom, Mr Stoddard?'

Felix nodded, his concentration completely on Kitty, who was beaming at him.

'I will ensure it's ready by one week from today.'

'Thank you,' Felix mumbled but made no attempt to leave. His eyes ached from staring, but he could not drag them away from the girl whose looks and figure had hit him like a thunderbolt.

'Was there anything else, Mr Stoddard?' Ella asked as she began to feel uncomfortable.

'What? Oh, no, thank you.' Turning his gaze back to Kitty, Felix felt his heart wrench. He began to sweat despite the cold, and he was sure he could hear the blood pounding through his veins. He had to leave, and the thought had him in a state of panic. Kitty Fiske had come into his life a mere ten minutes before and now he must go with the possibility he may never see her again.

Ella walked to and opened the door, saying, 'We'll see you in a week, then, Mr Stoddard.'

Felix nodded and, with a last glance at Kitty, he was gone from the room. The girls watched from the front window as the carriage rolled away.

'Kitty Fiske!' Ella said with a grin.

'What?'

'You know what! That poor man was practically drooling!'

'He's handsome though, eh?' Kitty laughed as they returned to the warmth of the kitchen.

'You certainly turned his head, I just hope it's not away from his fiancée, whoever she is,' Ella said as she immediately began work on her commission.

'It would be interesting to know, wouldn't it?' Kitty asked with a dreamy smile.

'Don't even think about it, just set that kettle to boil then give me a hand here.'

Whilst they were working Ella said, 'It's strange that Sally hasn't called round.'

'It is, she's usually been and gone by now.'

'I hope there's nothing wrong. She could be ill or...'

'She's probably sulking. I wouldn't fret, she'll come when she's ready. I can't believe you worry about her despite the way she treats you.' Kitty shook her head and sighed loudly.

'She's my sister, Kitty,' Ella said simply.

They carried on working until, after a while, their chatter turned once more to the dashing Felix Stoddard.

* * *

Whilst Ella had been serving her customer, Harper had been swamped with kisses when he had told his mother that Ella had accepted his proposal of marriage.

'Now I just have to tell Father,' he said, nervously.

Eléna advised him to wait a while and in the meantime make the arrangements with the vicar.

'Let me sound out your father in the first instance,' she said. 'We don't want him going off half-cocked before he's even met the girl.'

Harper agreed, although he was concerned his father would be furious at his son marrying a milliner. Rafe would surely cut Harper off without a penny and then how would he pay for his wedding? All he could do now was to trust his mother's judgement and wait and see what would happen.

43

Sally stood with her train ticket to Liverpool in her hand. She had wondered about telling Ella what she was doing and had decided against it. Now she thought she would, if only to gloat. Ella would most likely be furious with her for just upping and leaving, but her mind was made up. She was going, no matter what her sister said. Hailing a cab, she climbed aboard, a satisfied smile on her face.

Arriving in Silver Street, she asked the cabbie to wait, leaving her luggage inside. Entering through the back door she was greeted with, 'I told you she'd be back,' from Kitty.

Sally ignored the remark and spoke directly to Ella. 'I've only come to tell you I've left Eddy and I'm moving away.'

Ella stared with an open mouth.

'Bloody hell, that's a turn-up for the books, ain't it?' Kitty gasped.

'Why?' Ella asked, feeling the shock of Sally's announcement.

'I've had enough of the lazy bugger!' Sally snapped, 'So, I'm off!'

'How can you afford it? I thought you were on the bread line,' Ella said.

'Well, I've come into some money and there will never be a better time.' Sally had no intention of divulging where her sudden wealth had come from.

'Oh, yes, of course,' Ella said, her eyes narrowing.

Sally frowned. Ella could not possibly know about her black-mailing Darnell.

'I expect you have a tidy sum amassed by now,' Ella said, trying to control her anger.

'I don't know what you mean.'

'Oh, I think you do, Sally.'

Kitty watched the exchange in silence, excited to see which of the sisters would come out on top.

'Well, I don't. Anyway, I only came to let you know out of courtesy.'

'And to gloat, no doubt!' Ella spat.

'Whatever has got into you today, our Ella?'

'Don't you *our Ella* me! I know what you've done, Sally!' On her feet now, Ella leaned her splayed hands on the table.

Sally blanched at the outburst. How could her sister know? Could she have seen Sally and Darnell together at the station? Possibly, but they could have just been passing the time of day.

'Don't you shout at me!' Sally responded in the same angry tone.

'Why don't you admit it, Sally? Tell the truth for once in your miserable life!'

'The truth about what?' Sally tried to play for time as her mind whirled.

'Where your money came from.'

'It's none of your business!'

'Oh, but it is, because I already know and it concerns me!'

'Actually, it doesn't,' Sally said with a smug smile.

Kitty winced as Ella stood up straight, fully expecting to hear the sound of a slap.

'So you selling my designs to Ivy Gladwin doesn't concern me?'

Sally swallowed noisily. She'd been found out somehow. Thinking quickly, she decided to deny everything.

'I have done no such thing! How could you think...'

'You were seen, Sally!' Ella cut in.

'I... I...' Sally stammered, suddenly at a loss for words.

'How could you do it?' Ella asked, almost in tears of anger and hurt.

'To your own sister an' all,' Kitty put in.

'I've told you before to mind your own business, lodger!' Sally yelled.

'I'll just shut my mouth then,' Kitty said with a little grin.

'Why, Sally?' Ella asked again.

'I'll tell you why! You with your good looks and fine figure; the apple of Dad's eye. Liked by everyone, no one even noticed me. Except Eddy, I suppose, but look how that's turned out. I'm pregnant with the idle sod's child and I don't want to be.' Sally saw shock register on Ella's face. 'You didn't know that, did you? Well, it's true. I don't intend to keep it when it's born, it will go up for adoption.'

Ella drew in a breath. 'Sally, you can't!'

'I can and I will. Then I'll be free to enjoy my life. I can't do that here, always having to live in your shadow. No matter what I do it will never compare to you. I've finally realised that, so I'm going as far away from you as I can get!'

'I didn't know you felt this way,' Ella said quietly, all anger gone from her now.

'You wouldn't because you were always too busy. Even as kids you had no time for me, did you?'

'I tried, Sally, but you were so spiteful all the time.'

'Yes, I was, because no one loved me.'

'That's not true, Mum and Dad loved us both equally.'

'No, Ella, they didn't. For once let's be honest and face up to it. Anyway, now I have enough money – my cab is waiting so I'll say ta-ra.'

'I'm sorry, Sally, really I am.' Ella said holding out her arms for a hug.

Sally curled her lip and walked out, leaving Ella feeling wretched.

'I wonder where she'll go,' Kitty said.

Ella could only shake her head.

'You're better off without her!' Flossie Woolley said as she trundled into the kitchen, taking both girls by surprise. 'I'm sorry Ella, I couldn't help overhearing. I came running when I heard the yelling but thought it best to wait outside until it was all over. I didn't want to go and add my two penn'orth.'

'Thank you,' Ella replied while Kitty was busy with the teapot.

'Now you have only to deal with Ivy Gladwin,' Flossie said.

'I suppose I do, but I'm not sure how.'

'You go up there and tackle her! You have it straight from your sister's mouth Ella, she admitted it!'

'But what good will it do?'

'You have to make Ivy aware that you know what's been going on. It's my guess Sally hasn't told Ivy she's leaving, so at least you'll have the satisfaction of telling her that,' Kitty added.

'I'd threaten to take her to court for stealing, if it were me,' Flossie said.

'That wouldn't work, Flossie, it's still a man's world and they'd laugh us out of the courtroom. Or worse still, have us arrested for wasting their precious time!' Kitty snorted as she rattled a spoon in a cup.

'It's up to you, Ella, but if you decide to visit Ivy, I'd be happy to come with you – just for sport, erm, support I mean,' Flossie said. 'Right, I'm off 'cos I've chores to do.' With that she left the girls to begin their work once again.

* * *

That evening, Harper joined his parents in the parlour, and seeing his mother nod, he knew the time had come to talk to his father about Ella.

'Father, may I speak with you?'

Rafe folded the newspaper he had been reading and nodded. Eléna watched her son gather his courage.

'I have met the most wonderful girl and I am to be married.'

'Congratulations, son,' Rafe said with a beaming smile. 'Who is this lucky girl?'

'Her name is Ella Bancroft and she lives in Silver Street.'

Rafe's smile turned to a frown as Harper continued. 'She's a milliner, Father, and I love her with all my heart.'

'A milliner! Harper, you cannot possibly marry a working girl! Whatever are you thinking?'

Eléna watched her son struggle to convince his father of his love for Ella. She had to give Harper the opportunity to stand up to Rafe, especially over this. She decided she would step in only when it was necessary.

'Father...'

'No, son! I will not hear of it! You should be setting your sights far higher; a girl from a monied family.'

'Ella is...'

'I don't care what Ella is, I forbid it! You will not be marrying a milliner and that's final!' Rafe picked up the newspaper once more but Harper was not about to let the matter drop.

'It's all arranged. She accepted my proposal and I've spoken with the vicar.'

'You've done what?' Rafe's anger was evident as he threw the paper aside. Turning to his wife, he asked, 'Did you know about this?'

'I did.'

'Then you should have discouraged it!'

'Why?' Eléna asked simply.

'Because he should be—'

'*You* think he should be... What about what Harper wants? I would have thought you would be pleased he's found the girl of his dreams, especially after the debacle with Darcie Newland.'

'I admit he had a narrow escape there, but I cannot condone this, Eléna!'

'You don't have much choice, Rafe. Harper will wed Ella with or without your blessing.'

'Then it will be without!' Rafe got to his feet and marched from the room.

'That went better than I thought,' Eléna said with a cheeky grin.

'He won't attend, will he?' Harper asked.

'Possibly not, but *do not* allow that to interfere with your plans, my son. You go right ahead and wed Ella and be happy.'

'Thank you, Mother, for all of your support. I do appreciate it, although I worry how I'm going to afford the wedding in the first instance. Then, in order for us to live fairly comfortably, I suppose I'll have to get work somewhere – doing something.'

'You have no need to concern yourself, son, you won't starve if

I have anything to do with it.' Eléna nodded then went on, 'Does Ella know the date yet?'

'She will tomorrow,' Harper said, his smile radiating his joy.

'Excellent. I will be expecting my invitation soon, then.'

Harper moved to his mother and hugged her tightly. 'I love you,' he whispered.

Eléna's eyes brimmed with tears at the show of affection. Harper said his goodnight, leaving Eléna to consider how to bring her husband around to her way of thinking.

44

Felix Stoddard nibbled at his breakfast, despite having no appetite. He hadn't slept a wink all night for thinking of Kitty Fiske. Having only met her the previous day, he had already become obsessed with her. Throughout the night he had berated himself for allowing his greed to tie him to the Newland's daughter. He had paced his room, searching for a way out of the agreement he had made with Royston, but was left wanting.

The first thing he had to do was discover whether Kitty liked him enough to walk out with him. For all his confidence, Felix felt his chest constrict at the thought she might refuse him. However, he would never know if he didn't ask.

Drinking the last of his coffee, he pushed his plate away. Striding to the hall, he donned his hat and coat, and grabbed his gloves and cane. He climbed into the carriage, which was waiting on the gravel drive as it did every morning.

'Silver Street this morning, please, Albert,' he said to the driver.

'Very good, sir.'

As the landau lurched forward, Felix breathed deeply. The business with Darcie would have to wait. Kitty Fiske came first.

The closer he got to his destination, the more excited he became. He would have to buy another hat as a pretext for being there of course, but with luck he would know how Kitty felt by the end of the visit.

'Mr Stoddard, how nice to see you again,' Ella said with surprise as she answered the door. 'Please come in.'

Removing his hat, he stepped inside.

'Miss Fiske,' he said with a gracious bow. He was rewarded with a beaming smile from Kitty and his heart melted.

'How can I help you today?' Ella asked.

'I find myself in need of a new bowler for business purposes,' Felix answered with barely a glance at the milliner.

As Ella reached for the boxes, she shuddered slightly as a feeling of *déjà vu* crept over her. She had felt it previously when he had chosen a white top hat, but she had dismissed it.

Passing over a black bowler hat, she waited as he inspected it quickly and tried it on.

'Yes, that will do nicely,' he said as his eyes moved yet again to Kitty.

'Should I box it for you?' Ella asked.

'Yes, please do,' he answered.

'Will there be anything else?' Ella asked, while tying string around the box.

'Actually, there is. I was wondering if Miss Fiske would care to dine with me this evening.'

Once more the feeling crawled over Ella, but she kept her counsel.

'I'm not sure I can, Mr Stoddard, after all, I don't really know you,' Kitty replied.

'You will be quite safe, I assure you. Please say you will come.'

'I'm sorry, I'd love to but...'

'I swear I will treat you with the utmost respect.' Felix's heart hammered in his chest.

'I cannot; you are to be married,' Kitty said.

Felix's face fell. 'I'm sorry,' was all he could say as he threw some money onto the table for his hat. He made for the door, leaving the box where it lay and with a last longing look at Kitty he stepped outside.

Closing the door behind him, Ella said, 'I'm glad you refused him, Kitty, because that man is betrothed to another.'

'I know, and that's precisely why I did. I would have loved to go. I know it would have only been dinner and I hated turning down a good feed.'

Ella grinned despite her misgivings. Then she noticed the box he'd left behind. A ruse to earn him another visit, perhaps? She thought Kitty was making light of the invitation and in her heart she knew nothing good could come of this.

Kitty wiggled her eyebrows and they laughed together as they returned to their work.

Felix could hardly believe his bad luck as he travelled to his office, and knew he would have a scowl on his face for the rest of the day.

An hour after Felix had left, Harper was sitting in Ella's kitchen, excitedly revealing the date for their wedding.

'Three weeks! Harper, there's not enough time. I have to find a dress and...'

'Be calm, my love, all will be well. I will take you to find a gown and anything else you might need.'

'I can't afford to buy one, so I will have to make it myself,' Ella muttered as if to herself.

'Fret not, you will have whatever you want. I will ensure you have the very best. Now, who will give you away?'

'Oh, I don't know! Ella was pacing the floor, wringing her hands.

'I know your dad can't but – I can do it,' Kitty said.

'Would it be allowed?' Ella asked.

'It's your wedding, you can have whoever you like, I would have thought,' Kitty answered.

'I'm sorry to disagree, but I'm not sure the vicar would be very pleased if he thought we were flouting tradition,' Harper said a little sadly.

'Then I'll give myself away, but thank you for the offer, Kitty.' Ella's excitement was infectious and the chatter went on to include flowers and whether to walk to the church or take a cab, as well as cover Kitty's disappointment.

Harper wondered whether to inform Ella that it was possible his father would not be in attendance, but he thought better of it. He didn't want to shatter the happy atmosphere in the tiny kitchen, or see Ella's eyes cloud over with sadness.

'As much as I don't want to, I must leave you ladies to your work. I will see you both tomorrow.'

Harper took Ella in his arms and kissed her gently. 'I can't wait to have you as my wife.'

'I'm afraid you'll have to, for a little while anyway,' Ella answered.

Once he had gone, the conversation continued excitedly about the wedding.

'Ella, where will you live once you're married?'

That was something else she hadn't considered, and Ella sat with her mouth hanging open at the thought.

* * *

Whilst Ella and Kitty were excitedly discussing wedding plans, Darcie Newland, who had been expecting to see Felix that evening, had received a note saying he would be unavoidably detained and he would see her the following day.

'He hasn't even said why! Just a cursory note saying he's not coming!' Darcie railed.

'It will be to do with work, darling. You will have to get used to that; Felix is a businessman, and a very successful one at that,' Verity said in answer.

'Mother, I should come before his work!'

'Don't be silly, Darcie. If you want everything he can give you, you must be prepared for him to spend long hours at his work.'

'I suppose,' Darcie said sulkily.

'Good girl. Just think of the jewellery and clothes he will buy you.'

Darcie nodded. Once they were man and wife her demands would be high.

Verity left the parlour, saying she had things to do, and Darcie sat alone with her thoughts.

She should really be more accommodating where Felix was concerned, otherwise she could find herself in trouble. The last thing she needed would be to be discarded for a second time. It still smarted that Harper had left her and she could not risk losing Felix in the same way. Darcie knew it was a marriage of convenience and that Felix didn't love her, but she also knew he was her last hope. If this arrangement fell through she would have to live with her parents until their deaths. It made her shudder to think of it; having to care for them when they grew old. She would never be a wife or have children of her own. She would only be mistress in her own house once her parents passed.

Darcie slowly began to realise how important it was to have

Felix as her husband. She *had* to improve her ways, after all it would only be for a few days more, then she could do as she liked.

Feeling a lot better, she dropped the note onto the fire and watched it burn. She imagined Harper Fortescue sharing that same fate, and with an evil smirk she went to her room to decide what she should take with her to her new home.

45

Whilst Ella had been happily chatting with Kitty, Ivy Gladwin was beginning to fret. She had not seen Sally for a couple of days now and was wondering where she had gone. Maybe the girl had nothing new to report.

Ivy's sales figures had shot up since making the deal with Ella's sister and she was eager to know what new ideas would be coming from Silver Street next. There was nothing to do but wait for Sally to visit – until then, she would have to hope to sell what stock she had left.

Wandering around the shop, her fingers itched to be working on some fancy creations, but she had no notion as to what to make. She suddenly realised she was totally reliant on word from Sally. What would she do if the information stopped coming for any reason? How would she manage? She would just have to return to using her own creative instinct once more. She'd been doing it for twenty years so it wouldn't be a problem, she told herself, although she felt her confidence waver.

Glancing through the window at the snow still falling silently, Ivy pulled her thick woollen shawl tighter about her shoulders.

The sky was bright, foreshadowing a lot more snow to fall before the day came to an end. Watching the large white flakes float lazily from the heavens, Ivy was certain women would not be out shopping for hats today.

The street was quiet and there were no footprints showing in the virgin snow. She considered closing the shop and retiring to the fire in the back room with a nice hot drink. But sod's law said if she did she might miss a customer or two. So she resigned herself to staying open for a while longer yet.

Later, as the daylight began to fade, Ivy finally set the sign to 'closed'. She turned off the gas lamps and strode angrily to stoke the fire in her comfortable sitting room. Another day gone with no sign of Sally and, worse, no sales.

Setting the kettle to boil she muttered, 'Damn you, Sally!'

Picking up the gulley she began to slaughter a loaf of fresh bread in her fury. Slamming a pot of stew on the range to heat through, she banged a cup on a saucer, adding sugar ready for the tea. Pouring boiling water onto the leaves in the pot, she dropped the lid on and pulled a cosy over the whole. Fetching a jug of milk from the cold slab, she removed the bead-weighted net covering and raised the jug to her nose. At least the milk was still fresh. Stirring the stew, she tasted it. Satisfied, she ladled some into a bowl and sat down at the small table. Pouring her tea, she nodded; good and strong, just how she liked it.

After she had eaten and washed the dishes, Ivy settled herself with pencil and paper. She was going to sketch some new designs of her own, certain they would sell quickly.

Sitting with the end of the pencil between her teeth, Ivy Gladwin put her mind to work.

* * *

Felix Stoddard collected Kitty on the dot of seven. They travelled in his carriage to a hotel dining room where he had booked the best table. Taking her coat, he handed it to the girl who hung it alongside a few others, as well as his own.

Shown to their table, Kitty smiled at the glances she drew from other diners, especially the men. Candles burning on each table gave a warm glow to the room, and they could hear the quiet buzz of conversations taking place.

Felix ordered wine and menus were brought. 'I'm so pleased you agreed to accompany me this evening,' he said.

'Well, like I said, there's to be no hanky-panky.'

Felix grinned and beckoned to a young girl with a basket of flowers over her arm.

'Choose,' he said.

Kitty peeped into the basket. 'I can't, there are so many!'

'Then I will do it for you. We'll have those red roses, please.'

Kitty immediately saw the significance – red roses were for love. She thanked him warmly and returned the flower-girl's smile. 'They are beautiful,' she said as she lifted them to her nose.

'They pale into nothing against you,' Felix said.

'This wedding you bought a topper for, would it be yours, by any chance?'

Taken by surprise, Felix lowered his eyes. 'Yes, it was supposed to be.'

'Supposed to be?'

'I will be honest with you, Kitty. It's a marriage of convenience for both parties but...'

'But?'

'How can I wed her now I have found you?'

Kitty gave a little laugh, assuming he was joking.

'I'm serious. I cannot possibly become a husband to another. Kitty, *love hit me between the eyes the first time I saw you, and I knew I had to declare that love before it became too late.'*

Taken aback, Kitty stared at the man she barely knew. She had seen him twice and here he was telling her he loved her. There was no doubt she had been hit by the same thunderbolt, and she would give anything to become his wife, but they should have a decent courtship first. Then there was the matter of the woman he was already engaged to.

'The lady you should be marrying would be devastated if you let her down, and I'm not sure I could live with that on my conscience.'

Terrified he might lose her just when he'd found her, Felix summoned all of his courage. Rising from his seat he pushed it back. Getting down on one knee, he held her hand in his.

Kitty glanced around the room at the smiling diners, who broke into spontaneous applause as they looked on.

'Kitty Fiske, please say you will be my wife as soon as is humanly possible.'

Kitty's other hand flew to her chest as she heard the diners call out for her to accept.

The applause grew louder and a chant struck up. 'Say yes, say yes, say yes!'

Kitty found herself caught up in the jubilant mood as she looked around her, then down at Felix's grinning face. Then, in a moment of gay abandon, she nodded. The noise in the dining room was deafening as Felix rose, lifted her from her seat and swung her round. Kitty threw back her head and laughed, enjoying being in the strong arms that whirled her.

Placing her on her feet, Felix asked, 'May I kiss you?'

A nod signalled her permission, and they shared a gentle kiss to the raucous noise still sounding. For a while afterwards people came to offer congratulations and Kitty revelled in the attention.

In the kitchen, Kitty woke from the sweetest dream she'd ever had, but her heart was heavy. Ella passed over hot tea. 'You nodded off and I hadn't the heart to wake you.'

'I was dreaming about getting married,' Kitty said, forcing a smile.

'It's probably because we've been discussing it for days,' Ella replied gently.

'Ella, I...'

Frowning, Ella thought Kitty was feeling unwell.

'I think I'm in love – with Felix Stoddard!'

Ella's mouth formed an 'O' as she listened to Kitty's feelings pouring forth.

Eventually Ella found her tongue and said, 'Kitty! Are you being serious?'

'Yes,' came the dreamy reply.

'After only having met him twice? You know nothing about him, he could be a murderer! And what about his intended?'

'I can't help how I feel. If anyone knows that, it should be you.'

'Who is the girl he is to wed, do you know?'

'No, and I'm not sure I want to know. Look, Ella, I know you may think ill of me, but I was certain as soon as I saw him that he was the one for me.'

Ella mellowed at the girl's words, for hadn't she felt the same for Harper? Hadn't her father warned her about allowing her feelings to run out of control? 'It's just that I worry for you, I don't want you to get hurt.'

'I understand.'

Ella was still reeling from the shock when she retired for the night. Kitty had said how she had fallen for Felix Stoddard and how upset and miserable she was that he was already betrothed. Settling herself in her cold bed, Ella pulled the eiderdown up to her nose and closed her eyes against the chill of the room.

Tomorrow was another day, and her thoughts turned to Sally and where she might be. For all they had disagreed most of their lives, they were still sisters, and Ella couldn't help but worry about her. From there her mind moved to Ivy Gladwin. Maybe it was time to confront the woman. Ella knew she couldn't let it lie forever. There was a reckoning coming, and the sooner the better – then everyone could just get on with their lives.

Before sleep overtook her, Ella prayed to the good Lord to keep all those she loved safe and well. But something was niggling in the back of her brain. Ella couldn't help thinking that Kitty's feelings for Felix Stoddard would bring trouble to her door and Ella would have to be the one to sort it out.

46

It was barely light when a thunderous pounding on Ella's back door sounded. Grabbing a thick dressing gown, she hurried down the stairs to see who it was.

'All right, I'm coming!' she called as she unlocked the door.

Eddy stood there in the freezing cold, his trouser braces over his vest covered only by a jacket. He was unwashed and had clearly not shaved for days by the look of his chin.

'Come in, Eddy,' Ella said, dragging him indoors. 'I'll make some tea.'

Ella fed the range, leaving the oven door open for the heat to circulate. The tiny kitchen would be warm in no time.

'What's all the bleedin' noise?' Kitty asked sleepily as she entered with a woollen blanket covering her from head to toe.

'It's Eddy, our Sally's husband,' Ella said with a pointed look.

'Oh, right,' Kitty said as she joined him at the table.

'Is Sally here with you?' he asked, looking wretched.

'No, Eddy, she's not,' Ella replied, not knowing what else to say.

'She's finally done it, then,' he whispered before dragging his hands down his face.

'Done what?' Kitty asked.

'She's left me!' Eddy looked at the girls in turn then promptly burst into tears.

Ella felt sorry for him, sad at the way her sister had simply gone without a word. Clearly she'd said nothing to Eddy nor even left the poor man a note.

Eddy fought to bring his emotions under control and eventually said, 'She said she'd do it and now she has. I didn't think she meant it, though.'

Ella and Kitty allowed him to speak without interrupting.

'What about the baby? I'll never see my son or daughter, Ella!'

'I'm sorry,' was all she could think to reply.

'I don't understand how she could go without any money. Where is she? How's she managing?'

'She had money, all right!' Kitty put in.

Eddy looked at the girl who spoke. 'Where from?'

'She was selling Ella's ideas to her rival Ivy Gladwin!'

Eddy's eyes glistened with tears as he muttered, 'I'm sorry, Ella. I had no idea.'

'It's true, I'm afraid, Eddy, it seems she took us all in. None of us had a clue what she was up to.'

'I married the wrong sister, I'm thinking,' he answered with a forced smile.

Ella shuddered at the thought. 'You loved our Sally.'

'You're right, and I still do,' he mumbled. 'I'll get off home in case she comes back.'

With a nod, Ella closed the door behind him as he left, looking sad and forlorn. She knew Sally would not be returning but couldn't face telling Eddy that. She had to leave him his hope, for God knew he had nothing else.

'Poor bugger,' Kitty said as she sipped her hot tea.

'He most likely brought a lot of it on himself, Kitty. He's idle to the bone, but even he doesn't deserve to be treated this way.'

'I wonder where she ended up,' Kitty remarked.

'Wherever it is, I hope she's all right. I don't like to think of her in trouble.'

'If she was, she'd be back here in double quick time.'

Ella nodded and the girls fell into silence, their thoughts with poor Eddy.

* * *

Sally had no intention of returning home, however; in fact, she had already purchased a ticket on a packet ship. She had no feelings either way about the child being born abroad, it was her intention to give it up anyway. She had spent the night in a small boarding house near the docks, and after an early breakfast she left to find the ship that would carry her to a new and exciting land.

The *Esmerelda* lay at anchor with the lowered gang plank busy with sailors carrying goods to be stowed in the hold. Barrels of fresh water, sacks of grain, crates of vegetables, and boxes of tea and sugar, as well as bottles of wine and rum by the dozen.

Feeling the excitement build in her, Sally stood a while and watched the activity. The air was filled with the smell of fish and the noise was deafening. Jack tars called out greetings to each other or whistled as they worked. The occasional curse reached through the racket to her ears and Sally grinned. Seagulls swooped and screamed overhead, hoping for a chance to steal a fish from an unwary merchant's crate.

Sally's eyes moved to the massive ship she was about to board, with its masts reaching high into the sky. The crew scurried across her decks like ants as they went about their preparations for a long journey.

Picking up her suitcase, Sally strode forward. She knew the captain would have to wait for the tide, but she was eager to be aboard and settled in for her voyage.

Nodding her thanks to sailors who waited for her to step onto the ramp, Sally hesitated.

'C'mon, lady, give me that bag then hold my hand and I'll take you aboard.'

Sally grinned at the young seaman, and before she knew it she was on the ship and being shown to her cabin. The room was tiny with a small bunk and a slop bucket. Sally grimaced at the thought and hoped she wouldn't have to empty it herself. Poking around, she found a tall thin cupboard where she could hang her clothes, so she began to unpack, glad now she had brought so little with her.

Sitting on her bed, Sally listened to the creak and groan of timbers as the ship adjusted to the weight of its load. Like a child, Sally clapped her hands silently, a beaming smile splitting her face. It wouldn't be long now before the *Esmerelda* would be on the open sea, her sails unfurled and bellying out to catch the wind.

Leaving her cabin to go on deck to enjoy the bustle of the port, Sally prayed she would not be seasick.

Matelots tugged a forelock as she made her way to the rail at the side of the ship and Sally smiled in response. Ladies and gentlemen strolling the dockside waved to her and she waved back. This was it, Sally Denton was about to embark on a whole new life and the thought made her laugh out loud.

The sailors grinned as they heard her, knowing she wouldn't

be laughing for long if the weather turned and they were battered by storms. Leaving her to enjoy the moment, they scuttled away at a shout from the captain.

Sally was happy for the first time in as long as she could remember and revelled in the noise and smells of Liverpool docks.

* * *

That same early morning had seen Felix Stoddard pacing his bedroom. He had not been to bed but instead had sat up all night, thinking of Kitty Fiske. She set his blood on fire and his heart hammering in his chest like a drum. Never having believed in love at first sight before, Kitty had changed that in an instant. The feeling he experienced was almost a physical pain in his stomach. His appetite had deserted him, as had any desire to sleep. That girl had touched not only his heart but his soul too, and he knew without a scintilla of doubt that if he could not have her, he would never be happy again.

His thoughts then swung to Darcie Newland, the girl he was to marry in a few days' time. He was aware she had been let down by Harper Fortescue, though how his spies had found this out was a mystery to him. He desperately wanted to call the whole thing off so he could court Kitty, but he knew he couldn't do that. As spoilt as Darcie was, he could not find it in himself to betray her. He had made a pact with her father and he would have to stick to it as a gentleman should.

Despite the cold room, Felix felt the sweat form on his brow as his mind envisaged the forthcoming wedding. He felt his chest constrict and he gasped for breath in a panic. Pulling out the chamber pot from beneath the bed, he vomited into it. Dabbing his mouth with a handkerchief, he poured a little water from the carafe into a glass and sipped.

Get a hold of yourself, man! he scolded himself, but somehow he couldn't. He began to worry that he would feel this way for the rest of his life, and die a grumpy old man.

There was nothing he could do other than keep his word to Royston Newland and marry his daughter. Fully clothed, Felix lay on the bed and pulled the covers over his head. Tears fell as he hid away in the dark sanctuary he had found for himself. 'Kitty! Oh, my love, what am I to do?'

47

As the morning moved on, Ella voiced her thoughts. 'I think it's time to pay Ivy Gladwin a visit.'

Her neighbour Flossie had joined them for the usual morning tea after she had seen Eddy come and go. Ella had explained the reason for his visit and Flossie harrumphed her disgust at Sally's treatment of him.

'What are we going to see Ivy for?' Kitty asked, still feeling half-asleep.

'It's confrontation time, soft girl,' Flossie said with a shake of her head.

'Oh, right, yes, I see.' Kitty stretched her eyes open wide then yawned. 'I could have done with another couple of hours in bed.'

'Didn't you sleep well?' Ella asked, full of concern.

'No, I couldn't stop thinking about Felix.'

Flossie frowned. 'Felix Stoddard?'

Kitty nodded.

'Why on earth were you thinking about him?' Flossie asked.

Kitty blushed to the roots of her dishevelled blonde hair.

'The lamp is lit and all becomes clear,' Flossie said. 'You've fallen for him, haven't you?'

Kitty nodded again, a dreamy look crossing her face.

'You know his wedding is any day now? And you know who he's marrying?'

Ella's ears pricked up, and she halted her washing of the breakfast plates. 'No, who?'

'That Darcie Newland, that's who!' Flossie retorted.

The name hit Ella like a slap in the face. 'Oh, goodness! She's the one Harper was set to marry!'

'Bloody hell!' Kitty gasped.

'Indeed,' Ella said.

* * *

Ivy's shop hadn't seen many customers over the previous days, but she put it down to the foul weather. She was still bristling at having no word from Sally as she turned the sign to 'open'. Glancing out of the window, she was relieved to see the snow had melted, leaving dirty puddles in its wake. Maybe now the women of the town would venture out to look for new hats for the coming spring.

Sitting on the high-backed chair by the counter, she sipped her tea as she waited for the first customer of the day. Glancing around, her smile was tight-lipped; surely her new creations would sell. The millinery she had worked so hard on was dotted around on stands, hats with feathers, some with flowers, and others with both. She nodded, assured they would go quickly once the shopping began in earnest.

Taking her empty cup into the back room she stoked the fire and stood a moment to enjoy the heat emanating from the glowing coals. Hearing the bell tinkle, Ivy rubbed her hands together and went back to the shop with a smile plastered on her face.

The sight that greeted her stopped her in her tracks and wiped the smile off her face in an instant. Three women stood in her shop, one of whom was Ella Bancroft.

'Hello, Ivy,' Ella said pleasantly.

'I didn't expect to see you!' Ivy returned, having finally found her tongue. Her eyes had immediately taken in the fine headgear they were each wearing.

'I'll bet you d'aint,' Flossie put in.

'What can I do for you – ladies?'

The word said as an afterthought was not lost on the trio as they looked around at the display of hats.

There's not much changed here, Ella thought, but said instead, 'It's more what we can do for you.'

'Which is?' Ivy asked with a frown.

'To tell you Sally has done a bunk.' Ella watched Ivy's face blanch.

'Sally?' Ivy instinctively decided to deny all knowledge as it became clear she'd been found out.

'My sister.'

'I'm afraid I don't know your sister.'

'Oh, you do, but what name she gave you I have no idea,' Ella said, her voice even and calm.

Kitty and Flossie waited quietly at her side, both wondering how the confrontation would play out.

'Ella, I don't know what all this is about, but...'

'Then let me tell you,' Ella's words cut across Ivy's as her serene exterior changed. 'I know about the deal you made with Sally.'

Ivy gulped loudly and Kitty and Flossie exchanged a grin.

'I know you paid her to spy on me,' Ella went on.

Ivy began to shake her head, but Ella ignored her. 'And I *know* she sold my designs to you. You not only copied my creations, but you undercut my prices into the bargain. What I *don't* know is – why?'

'It wasn't my idea, I swear!' Ivy said in a rush, feeling like a rat trapped in a corner.

'I don't doubt that for a moment. But I ask again, why, Ivy?'

'Sally said she needed the money, and I was trying to help her out!'

'My sister did need the money,' Ella said and saw Ivy relax a little, 'but as for you helping – that's a lie, Ivy.'

'No, it's true, I swear!'

'Swears a lot that one, don't she?' Flossie said before she and Kitty dissolved into fits of giggles.

'How much did you pay her?' Ella asked.

'Two pounds a week.'

Ella nodded. 'Was it worth it?'

'Oh, yes! I mean – my sales improved.' Ivy hung her head in shame.

'I imagine they would with you passing off my work as your own.'

'I'm sorry, Ella, I was desperate! Trade was falling and I didn't know what to do!'

'You could have come to me and asked for help.'

'What, ask advice from a student?'

'You see, that's half your problem, Ivy, you haven't yet realised the student has become the master. I do not say this in boast, but merely as a statement of fact.'

Ivy dropped onto the chair and nodded. 'I think I knew that Ella, but my pride would not allow me to believe it.'

'The question now is – what do we do about all this?'

48

Eléna had tried her best to talk to Rafe regarding their son's wedding but he remained adamant he would not attend. He also said he would disinherit Harper if he went through with it.

Sipping her coffee, she watched her husband shake his newspaper grumpily.

'You can't ignore me forever, Rafe,' she said at last.

Rafe muttered something unintelligible.

'Rafe! Put down that paper and let's have this out once and for all!'

Slamming the sheets onto his knees, Rafe glared at his wife.

'That's better. Now, can we please speak to each other in a civil and polite manner?'

'Eléna, I have told you before...'

'I know you have but now you can tell me what you have against Ella Bancroft.'

'She's a milliner! A working girl!'

'She is indeed, and she's bloody good at it!'

Rafe's mouth fell open at his wife's expletive.

'She's kind, considerate, a real beauty and she's in love with Harper.'

'That's as maybe, but it doesn't change the fact that she's a commoner.'

'Don't be such a snob, Rafe. It's only an accident of birth that made her such. The important thing here is that if you continue along this path you will lose your son. Are you prepared to accept that because of your outdated beliefs?'

Rafe sighed loudly. 'Of course not. But Harper will find someone else, given time.'

'He won't, Rafe. If he should lose Ella through any fault of yours he will never forgive you. She has his heart and soul and he could never be happy with anyone else.'

Rafe's eyes darted around the room as he considered his wife's words.

'Do you love me, Rafe?'

'That goes without saying,' Rafe replied, feeling flustered at being asked such a question.

'That it does. When did you last tell me?'

'I... Eléna, please!'

'Exactly. You can't remember,' she said sadly.

'But you know I do!'

'Yes, but it's nice to hear it occasionally.'

Rafe stared at his wife, her eyes glistening with tears. That was something else he couldn't remember – when he'd last seen Eléna cry.

'Darling...?'

Eléna shook her head before lowering her chin to her chest. Rafe was out of his chair in an instant and by her side on the chaise longue. 'Darling, please don't cry. I love you, with all my heart I love you, and will until the day I die.' He wrapped his arms around her and kissed away her tears. 'I'm so sorry I haven't told you more often, my love, but that will change. From this moment onwards I will remind you often of how I feel about you.'

'I love you, Rafe Fortescue, and I always have. From the first time I saw you I knew we would be happy together.'

'As did I, sweetheart,' he mumbled into her hair.

'Will you promise me something, then?' she asked tentatively.

'Anything.'

'Will you at least meet Ella and think more on what we've discussed?'

'Yes, my love, I will.'

'Thank you, Rafe,' Eléna said with a sniff against his chest. A little smile crept across her face as she gave a dry sob and felt his arms tighten around her.

* * *

Whilst Eléna was cajoling her husband into a meeting with Ella, Ivy stared at the women in her shop and finally said, 'I'm so sorry, Ella.'

'So, I ask again, what are we to do about this?'

'I don't know,' Ivy replied, feeling distinctly uncomfortable.

'I have an idea if you are willing to consider it.' Seeing Ivy nod, Ella went on, 'We could combine forces once more. However, this time it would have to be as partners.'

'What? I'm not sure...' Ivy began.

'Hear me out before you decide. I have the expertise with design, but you have the shop, as well as being the best sales-woman in the town.' Ella was appealing to Ivy's ego to get her point across and she saw it was working as Ivy stood even straighter than usual. 'We could fuse our talents and make this business flourish in no time.'

Ivy was thinking about what she said, Ella could tell. 'Now, Kitty here has been an invaluable asset and I think it would be prudent to employ her as an assistant.'

'I can't afford that!'

'Neither of us can on our own, but together we could.'

Kitty and Flossie exchanged a glance, before returning their attention to Ivy.

'Well...'

'Why don't you give it a go?' Flossie asked. 'You said you ain't been doing too well – at least before Sally came on the scene.'

Ivy frowned at the not-too-subtle reminder of her duplicity. 'We would need to have a contract drawn up by a solicitor.'

'Agreed. I'm sure I can leave that in your capable hands.' Ella tried not to get too excited at the prospect of finally having a shop to display her creations in.

'What if it doesn't work out between us?'

'Then we tear up the contract and go our separate ways,' Ella answered. 'Are we of an accord?'

'All right, we'll try it for six months to see how we do,' Ivy said, feeling relieved the girl wasn't threatening to report her to the police instead.

Shaking hands on the deal, Ella said, 'Let me know when I will need to sign the contract. In the meantime, Kitty and I will work on some new ideas.'

'What should I do?' Ivy asked, suddenly feeling lost.

Glancing around, Ella said, 'It might be an idea to clear a space ready for our new stock.'

'What, close up?'

'No, stay open but gradually shift these old hats out of the way. They could go in the workroom upstairs to be re-used at some point.'

Ivy looked at the hats she'd spent hours and hours working

on only for them to be consigned to a dusty room. But, knowing Ella was right, she nodded her assent, feeling heavy of heart, and already wondering if she was doing the right thing.

'We'll need a new name for the shop, too,' Ella said, praying she wasn't pushing her luck too far.

'Why?' Ivy asked abruptly.

'Partners, Ivy – remember? I thought we could use both of our names.'

'Gladwin and Bancroft, you mean?'

'No. I thought *Ivella*.'

'That sounds really posh!' Flossie put in.

'That's the idea. We are going to take this shop to dizzying new heights. What do you say, Ivy?' Ella asked.

'Actually, I rather like it. It's classy.'

'Right, I think we're finished here so we'll get off. We all have a lot of work to do,' Ella said, then as they turned to leave, she added, 'Will you get the sign-writer in as soon as possible too? Because Kitty and I have a lot of stock to bring over.'

Ivy nodded. After they had gone, she thought through everything that had been said. She had gone from sole trader to partnership in a matter of minutes. However, the benefits to having Ella as her partner would surely prove themselves in the days to come. Ivy would only have half the profits, but if they worked well together those profits could soar beyond her wild imaginings. She could find herself considerably better off financially. She wouldn't be so lonely, either, with Kitty and Ella around the place.

The more she thought on it the more she liked the idea, and for the first time in a long while, Ivy felt true excitement. It was a whole new beginning, and she knew she was very lucky to have been given it. She could have found herself in real trouble had Ella decided to inform the town of her espionage.

The old saying came to mind: *One foot forward and trust in the Lord.*

With a smile, Ivy decided to do just that. She grabbed her coat and hat, locked the shop and stepped out to engage the services of a solicitor and a sign-writer.

On their journey home from Ivy's shop, Ella grinned as she listened to Kitty and Flossie extolling her virtues.

'I can't believe Ivy agreed to it all!' Kitty said in astonishment.

'To be honest, neither can I,' Ella said with a little laugh.

'What would you have done if she'd said no?' Kitty asked.

'I have no idea!'

'Well, it don't matter now, do it?' Flossie said. 'Be warned though, gel, read that contract thoroughly before you put your name to it.'

'I will, Flossie, be assured.'

Back in the warm kitchen, the women celebrated their success with a cup of steaming hot tea. Flossie left the girls to the job of packing up the hats and haberdashery in readiness to be moved to the shop. Some hats were left on display in case they should have customers.

'We have to make this work, Kitty, for I'm sure we won't get another chance to have our own shop.'

'If anyone can do it Ella, it's you.'

'Let's have something to eat, then we'll carry on with putting together a fresh new range,' Ella said.

'It's exciting, don't you think?' Kitty asked with a broad grin.

'I do indeed, Kitty.'

Suddenly both girls were dancing around the kitchen, laughing fit to burst.

The knock to the front door had the girls stop their cavorting. They went together, as usual, to answer it and were surprised to see Felix Stoddard standing forlornly in the street. He looked dishevelled, as though he'd slept in his clothes, and his hair was in disarray.

'Mr Stoddard, won't you come in?' Ella asked.

Stepping into the front room, Felix's eyes instantly fell on Kitty. 'Miss Fiske,' he said, totally ignoring Ella, who was closing the door.

'Your top hat is finished,' Ella said.

'That's fine. Pardon my intrusion, but I came to see...' Felix's eyes remained on Kitty.

'Ah, I'll just move over here and – find something to do.' Ella strode to the corner and began sorting out the empty boxes.

Felix walked closer to Kitty and, in a whisper, said, 'I had to come. You have stolen my heart and I can't eat or sleep for thinking of you.'

Ella closed her eyes tight as she tried her best not to listen in to the conversation taking place at the other side of the room.

'Mr Stoddard, you shouldn't be speaking to me in this way, you are to be married, after all.'

'I know, but Kitty... oh, Kitty what am I to do?'

'Mr Stoddard, please don't make this harder for either of us!'

'So, you feel the same?' Felix could have jumped for joy at the possibility.

'What I feel is neither here nor there, Mr Stoddard. We know nothing about each other in the first place, and secondly I will not come between a man and his fiancée.'

Ella winced at the words, knowing that was precisely what she had done with Harper and Darcie.

'Kitty, you could be my betrothed if only you would agree!'

'I can't! I... We... Please just take your hat and leave.' Kitty saw Ella turn to her and, unable to stay a moment longer, she fled the room.

Feeling awkward, Ella passed over the box containing the white top hat. Felix shook his head in disappointment as he paid for his purchase.

'Thank you. I must apologise for...' he waved a hand at the door Kitty had disappeared through.

'Believe me when I say I completely understand.'

Something in the gold-flecked eyes told Felix she had seen this dilemma before, or even been in the same situation herself. Suddenly a thought struck: was this the girl Harper Fortescue had left Darcie for? It had to be!

'You are most kind,' he said.

'Good luck,' Ella said as he stepped onto the pavement. She watched him climb into the waiting carriage and, as it rolled away, she was sure she saw a handkerchief mop at his eyes.

Going back to the kitchen, she found Kitty sobbing. Wrapping her arms around her friend, Ella waited until the tears subsided.

A little while later the two girls talked quietly.

'I wish I could feel differently, but I can't!' Kitty moaned.

'I know. It was the same for me with Harper.'

'Yes, but Harper managed to get out of his – arrangement!'

'He did, but it had nothing to do with me – it was his decision. He didn't love Darcie Newland, it was their fathers who agreed the union and Harper had little say in the matter.'

'What were the odds of it being the same girl? I can't believe it!' Kitty said with a sniff.

'Millions to one, I would imagine. I'm sorry, Kitty, I truly am.'

'So am I,' Kitty said as she stared at the tea leaves in the bottom of her cup.

Meanwhile, Felix travelled home, sobbing in the privacy of the carriage. Kitty hadn't said she felt as he did in so many words, but he was sure she did. Two people who admittedly were virtual strangers had been hit by Cupid's arrows at the same time, but were now destined never to be together. Life could be unbearably cruel at times and Felix thought he would never be happy again.

On reaching his home, he dashed from the conveyance and ran through the house to his bedroom. He sat on the bed, the hat box next to him as if taunting him. Picking it up, he threw it against the wall before raking his hands through his hair, anger and despair fusing and leaving him feeling exhausted.

* * *

Over at Dundrennan House, Darcie was chatting to her mother about the wedding preparations.

'Do you think Felix will call this evening?'

'Yes, I'm sure he will, darling,' Verity answered.

'Send a note, Mother, will you, inviting him to dinner.'

Verity nodded and moved to her escritoire to pen an invitation. Calling for the maid, she asked it be delivered at once.

'To Birmingham, madam?' the recently hired maid asked.

'Yes!' Verity said sternly.

'Very good, madam.' With a bob the maid left the parlour.

'It's nice to have a servant, but that one has ideas above her station,' Verity said as she took her seat by the fire once more.

'One more day, Mother, then I will be a married lady!' Darcie gushed.

Thank God! Verity thought to herself. 'You must finish your packing, darling, make sure you have everything you need.' *That way, you won't have to come back here!* Verity mentally admonished herself for thinking such a thing about her own daughter, but, if she was honest, she couldn't wait to get rid of the girl now.

Darcie's prattling was lost on Verity as she began to imagine how peaceful life would be in just a couple of days. She and Royston could attend functions without having to worry about Darcie embarrassing them in polite company.

Nodding in all the right places, Verity smiled. *Please God, let nothing interfere with this wedding.*

* * *

Harper had arrived at Ella's beaming with pleasure at seeing her again.

'Mother has invited you to have dinner with us this evening.'

'Oh, I...' Ella began, surprised by the request.

'Father will be there too,' Harper added tentatively.

Meeting Rafe was something Ella had been dreading but she knew it had to happen eventually. Being friendly with Eléna was one thing, but Rafe was the one who could call a halt to the whole marriage, as her own father had told her before he had died.

'Very well.'

'I'll call for you at seven, then,' Harper said, only then seeing Kitty sitting quietly at the table. 'Are you quite well, Kitty?'

Shaking her head, Kitty sniffed as tears again rolled down her cheeks.

Harper looked to Ella for an explanation.

'Kitty had a visitor earlier, which has upset her.'

'I'm sorry to hear that. Is there anything I can do?'

'You can tell him, Ella, I don't mind,' Kitty said amid sobs.

Ella explained about Felix calling in on them and how he was to marry Darcie Newland. Harper was surprised at the revelation and saddened by the news that Kitty and Felix had feelings for each other.

'Oh, Kitty,' Harper began, not really sure what to say that could make her feel any better.

'I know, it's a bugger!' Kitty said, trying to lighten the sullen mood that had descended.

Feeling utterly useless and unhelpful, Harper made his excuses and left the girls to talk it out together. His heart went out to Kitty. After all, he knew exactly what she was going through. Despite himself, he had pity for Darcie too. After what he did to her – dumping her like a sack of potatoes – how could he not? He wondered if Felix Stoddard would do what he hadn't been able to and actually marry Darcie.

It was a while later when Ella and Kitty discussed the dinner Ella was to attend with Harper's family, but there was no enthusiasm in their chat. Kitty was desperately unhappy and Ella was at a loss as to how to help. Eventually they fell to working in silence, both lost in their own thoughts.

LINDSEY HUTCHINSON

That evening, at seven on the dot, Harper arrived. Looking around, he could see no sign of Kitty.

Ella noticed and explained. 'Kitty's gone next door to have a cup of tea with Flossie and play games with the children. I think to try and take her mind off Felix for a while.'

'Ah. So, are you ready to run the gauntlet?' Seeing Ella's face fall, he immediately took her in his arms. 'Sorry, that was in rather poor taste.'

Ella forced a smile and reached for her coat and hat. She had chosen a small teardrop with a little feather, tastefully made to match her burgundy coat.

'You look beautiful,' Harper breathed as he helped her into her coat.

'Right, let's get going. I'm eager to meet this father of yours,' Ella said, although nothing could be further from the truth.

The atmosphere in the carriage ride to The Cedars was strained, as the young couple both knew Ella was nervous. Harper had been honest with regard to how his father had reacted to him marrying a milliner.

It was no more than Ella had expected, for hadn't her own father warned her it might happen? Feeling a sudden pang of grief, Ella mentally shook herself as the carriage came to a halt. They had arrived.

50

Ella was greeted warmly by Harper's mother Eléna, who hugged her like a long-lost daughter. Ella's fears melted away, her initial nervousness forgotten.

'How are you, my dear? It's so nice to see you again. Hmm, I like that hat, I'm thinking I might have to have one too.' Eléna's soothing voice eased the tension as Ella's outdoor clothes were taken by a smiling maid.

'Come along into the parlour for an aperitif, Rafe is waiting for us.' Seeing the look of panic cross Ella's face, Eléna took the girl's arm. 'Don't worry, I have him right where I want him.' Eléna winked and Harper chuckled as he trotted along behind them.

Rafe stood to greet them as they entered, and Harper made the introductions.

'Welcome to our home, Miss Bancroft,' Rafe said.

Ella noted he did not say he was pleased to meet her.

'Thank you, Mr Fortescue,' she replied, deciding not to afford him the same courtesy. She smiled, knowing instantly that the game was afoot. The evening, she guessed, would be spent with

Rafe dancing around the reason she was here. She, of course, would be forced to defend her position of being Harper's fiancée.

Fair enough – let battle begin!

'What will you have to drink?' Rafe asked, going to the cocktail cabinet.

'A little water, thank you,' Ella replied as she sat by Harper on a massive couch.

First point to me, Ella thought, as she saw Rafe's surprised look.

Once everyone was seated with drinks in hand, Rafe started the conversation with, 'I'm told you are a milliner.'

'I am indeed, and a very good one at that.'

Rafe nodded and Ella smiled.

'You live in Silver Street, I believe.'

'I do, extremely happily.'

Harper and his mother exchanged a brief glance as what seemed like an inquisition went on.

'My condolences on the loss of your father.'

It was Ella's turn to be surprised and she conceded the point to her opponent.

'Thank you, he is greatly missed.'

The dinner gong sounded, and they all trooped into the dining room. Pâté was served, and again Ella refused wine.

'What was your father's occupation?' Rafe asked.

'He worked at the Cyclops Tube Works, which is a smaller concern than your own, the Alma Works if I'm correct, until his accident, that is.'

Ella mentally ticked off another point in her favour.

'The unfortunate cost of such work, I'm afraid,' Rafe said.

'Very true but my father, it turns out, was a fine milliner also.'

Ella felt she was on a winning streak and a warm smiled accompanied her words.

Clearly both she and her future father-in-law had done their homework regarding the other. Ella had spent an hour with Flossie, who appeared to know everything about everyone. No doubt Rafe had a *man* who would have discovered all he could about her.

As the roast beef dinner arrived, Ella thanked the waiting staff. Eléna and Harper had watched in silence as Ella held her own under Rafe's stern comments.

'Mr Fortescue,' Ella began again, noting he did not request she use his Christian name, 'Would it be possible to stop beating around the bush and get to the heart of the matter?'

Rafe's fork halted in its journey to his mouth, a look of surprise on his countenance.

'I am here only because you agreed to meet with me. It is not your wish for Harper and me to be wed, and I assume the reason for that is that I was not born into the same class as you.'

Rafe listened as he continued to eat.

'I have to work to live, sir, and my profession is an honourable one. I have recently agreed to go into partnership with Ivy Gladwin of Gladwin's Hats in order to further my career, and have employed an assistant.'

From the corner of her eye she saw Eléna smile her encouragement.

'I am fully aware of the unfortunate circumstances surrounding Darcie Newland and my betrothed.'

Ella swallowed the little laugh that began to rise as Rafe coughed and spluttered.

'Harper proposed to me because he loves me and I accepted because I love him, so a wedding there will be whether you like it or not. I would, however, prefer you give your blessing to our union, and I truly hope to be a part of your family.'

Eléna could contain herself no longer and applauded as she called out, 'Bravo!'

Rafe glanced from Ella to his wife and back again. Eventually he threw back his head and laughed loudly, much to everyone's relief.

'By God, this one has spirit!' he said at last.

'I got it from my father, but please don't speak about me like I'm a racehorse,' Ella grinned widely.

Rafe's laughter boomed out yet again. Harper's mouth hung open as he watched his father warm to the girl he had chosen for his wife.

'Ella, you have surprised me, I cannot deny it. I'm not sure what I expected but it wasn't this. I only have to look at you two to see how much in love you are, therefore you have my blessing. Congratulations, I hope you will both be as happy as we are.' Rafe reached out and grasped his wife's hand.

'Thank you,' Harper and Ella said in unison.

Throughout the remainder of the evening, Ella and Rafe traded gentle insults causing great humour and which heralded the fun that would characterise her relationship with Rafe throughout future years. Ella revelled in being accepted into the Fortescue family.

* * *

Meanwhile, over at Dundrennan House, Felix sat quietly at the dinner table with the Newlands. He had responded to Verity's note with one of acceptance, knowing he could not rightly refuse. However, that didn't mean he had to enjoy himself. He couldn't have done so, no matter how hard he tried.

Darcie rattled on about how divine her wedding gown was and how beautiful it made her look. Verity ate sparingly, clearly uneasy about something, and Royston smiled indulgently at his daughter.

Felix felt like he was drowning, hearing Darcie's voice in muffled tones. His head pounded and his throat was dry. The sight of the food on his plate turned his stomach, although at any other time he would have thoroughly enjoyed the roast duck.

He nodded with a forced smile as he drained his wine glass and watched the maid refill it.

After they had eaten, the women retired to the parlour for coffee and Royston led Felix to his study for brandy and cigars. Pouring the amber liquid into a cut-glass goblet, Royston passed it to his guest.

With a feeling of unease, he asked, 'Felix, are you ill?'

'Well, sir, I'm not quite myself.'

'What ails you?'

Felix fought to find an answer. Could he renege on his promise to marry this man's daughter? Or would he have to go through with the ceremony the following day?

'I...' he began but words failed him as an image of Kitty formed in his mind.

'Are you having second thoughts?'

Felix gulped his brandy then bowed his head.

'I thought so,' Royston said as he dropped heavily into a chair.

'I'm sorry, Royston, truly I am.'

'The question now is: what do we tell Darcie and Verity?' Royston said, as despair washed over him.

51

'Royston, I confess I have met someone very recently who has stolen my heart,' Felix said, then seeing the forlorn look his words prompted he hurried on, 'but I intend to honour my pledge to marry your daughter.'

Looking up sharply, Royston was amazed at Felix's confession but more so by what had followed it.

'You would give up this girl?'

Felix nodded. 'I gave my word as a gentleman and will abide by that. Besides, I cannot be sure the young lady in question feels as I do.'

'But will you be happy with Darcie?'

'Who knows? Maybe time will show her to be the right one for me,' Felix said, even as he doubted his own words.

'I admire you greatly, Felix, for being so honest with me. However, it leaves me with guilt weighing heavily on my shoulders.'

Shaking his head Felix said, 'I did not intend for that to happen, only that you should know that I am first and foremost a gentleman of my word. You may rest assured that I will care for

Darcie as best as I can, but also that I will stand for no nonsense. But I will do my utmost to make her happy.'

'Then let's drink to that,' Royston said as he refilled their glasses. Clinking them together, both men emptied them in one swallow.

'I think it's time to join the ladies,' Felix said, getting to his feet.

Royston nodded, feeling more guilty than ever.

'I was hoping to see you one last time before our big day tomorrow,' Darcie gushed as the men entered the parlour.

'Is everything all right?' Verity asked her husband, seeing his pale complexion.

'Yes, my dear, all is well. I'm a little tired, that's all.'

'Then I will be away. My thanks for your hospitality and the lovely dinner, Verity.' Turning to Darcie, Felix kissed her cheek chastely and added, 'I will see you at the church on the morrow my sweet.'

Darcie nodded with a girlish giggle, and Felix gave a tight smile as he shook hands with Royston.

In the darkness of his carriage, Felix moped silently all the way home.

The following morning dawned clear and bright, but remained cold. The frozen droplets of dew shone like tiny diamonds in the weak sunshine, giving everywhere a look of a winter wonderland. Spring was on its way, but just for today winter seemed to have stolen its way back in. Curls of grey smoke spiralled up from chimneys as the town came awake, and the Newland household was a hive of activity. The maid had lit the fires and was busy preparing breakfast, muttering to herself about not being paid enough for having to do everything.

Darcie was up and about early, calling for her bath to be filled whilst she warmed herself by a roaring fire. Today was her wedding day and she wanted everything to be perfect.

Royston had barely slept a wink, his mind going over his conversation with Felix the previous evening. He was torn over how he felt about the wedding. On one hand, he thought he should remain tight-lipped and watch his daughter wed, leaving him and his wife finally free of her bad-tempered ways. On the other, he wondered if he should speak up about what he knew. It would save young Felix from a life of misery he felt sure was coming his way, but it would quite rightly enrage and distress Darcie. Could he do that to her after she had been so badly treated by Harper Fortescue? In truth, he could not. One or the other of that partnership was destined to be unhappy and there was nothing Royston could do about it.

Over breakfast, Darcie chatted excitedly. 'I know it's fashionable to be late, but I would prefer to be early. I don't want Felix thinking I've changed my mind, so we simply must be on time at the very least. Daddy, are you listening to me?'

'On time,' Royston said with a nod as he forced himself to eat his boiled egg.

'Don't worry, darling, everything is in hand,' Verity assured her daughter.

'Good, because I don't want any mishaps – not today,' Darcie snapped, not noticing her father wince.

For the next hour, she had everyone in a spin ensuring all was going to plan.

*　*　*

Having no knowledge of the uproar Darcie was causing at Dundrennan House, Ella stoked the fire into life and set the kettle to boil on the small range. Judging by the time she'd been given to complete the white top hat, she guessed today would be Felix's wedding day. As if to confirm her thoughts, she heard the church bells begin to peal in the distance.

Laying out cups, she knew Kitty would be inconsolable when she rose from her bed, and Ella searched her mind for ways to ease Kitty's unhappiness. Her heart ached for her friend, knowing it could so easily have been herself in that same position.

The best she could do for Kitty was to keep her busy helping to move the stock over to Ivy's shop. Once Kitty had risen, they collected boxes tied with string and marched them over to Junction Street. Ivy simply stared, making no move to help them as she felt they were taking over her life as well as her shop.

After they had left, she shoved the boxes into the corner of the back room with the toe of her boot. She was tempted to kick them out altogether but thought better of it.

Time after time, Kitty and Ella carried their wares to their new destination, with Ella trying her best to coax conversation from her friend.

It was to no avail. Kitty was saying nothing. She couldn't trust herself to speak for fear of breaking down into tears. She too was aware Felix was probably in the church right now speaking his marriage vows, and the thought all but paralysed her. Keeping her mouth closed was the only way she was able to deal with the raw feelings that were ravaging her. So throughout the day she plodded back and forth to the shop with Ella, her only thought being to get home and retire to her bed where she could cry her heart out.

* * *

Over at St John's Church, Darcie and her father arrived by carriage. She fussed as she was helped down, making sure her shepherdess dress was immaculate.

'Slowly, Daddy, I want everyone to see my gown,' she said taking his arm.

Royston nodded, feeling as though a lead weight was sitting in his stomach. What if Felix wasn't there? He looked at his daughter and prayed her fiancé had not done a moonlight flit.

As they entered the church, Royston breathed a sigh of relief as he spotted Felix with the vicar at the other end of the aisle.

Music sounded from an old pump organ and the bridal procession began. Darcie beamed at the guests as she passed them, too happy to notice the looks of ridicule at her choice of wedding apparel.

She was so wrapped up in herself she didn't see the lack of colour to Felix's cheeks or his frown at her bad taste in gown.

The ceremony began and Royston held his breath when the vicar said to Felix, 'Wilt thou take this woman to be thy wife...?'

He heard the reply, 'I will,' and only then breathed his relief.

Once the ceremony was complete, the bride and groom walked sedately down the aisle to the doors, Darcie with a wide grin and Felix nodding to well-wishers.

It was done. Felix Stoddard was a married man, albeit unhappily.

* * *

Back in Silver Street, Kitty was bawling on Ella's shoulder.

'There will be someone out there who is just right for you,' Ella said feeling helpless.

'But my heart is broken,' Kitty sobbed.

'Kitty, you are my friend and I love you dearly but look at this logically. We're not even sure it *was* Felix's wedding – it could have been anybody.' Seeing her friend nod she went on, 'So dry your tears because I'll need you at my side when we visit Ivy today. We must have our wits about us if we are to sign a contract with her, for I don't trust her an inch.'

'Neither do I,' Kitty said at last.

'Then let's get it over with,' Ella coaxed.

As Kitty went to wash her face, Ella felt her heartstrings tug. Somehow she was desperate to be convinced the man Kitty loved was not married to another woman.

52

Eddy Denton sat in front of the fire, his braces over his vest as usual. He was feeling very sorry for himself. He had stupidly thought Sally would never find the money he had stashed away, but she had. She had taken every last penny with her when she left. Now he was destitute, he had no money, no job and no wife.

The food in the larder wouldn't last long and the coal bunker would be empty in no time. He was still wondering why Sally had gone, hardly believing his refusing to find work could be reason enough. Had she found another man? Were the two of them off somewhere living the high life on his money? What about his child? Would Sally care for it or would she give it up to be adopted?

His misery deepened at the thought of having a son or daughter he would never meet. 'Sally Denton, you are a bitch!' he grumbled.

Unable to see himself as the cause of the problem, Eddy continued to lay the blame at his wife's feet.

He knew he was on his own now and had to try and make the best of a bad job, but how to go about it had him foxed. It was easier to indulge himself in his unhappiness, that way he could stay indoors in the warm. However, the thought that he would have to be earning a wage to live constantly pushed its way into his mind. 'Bugger that, I'll go on the rob first!' he muttered.

* * *

The *Esmerelda* bobbed on the water as she headed out to sea. Sally watched in awe as the young sailors coiled huge ropes, giving her an occasional cheeky wink. The older tars scowled at having a woman on board, sticking firmly to the old superstition of it being bad luck.

Feeling the sting of salt spray on her face Sally revelled in her freedom and daring. The train had borne her to Liverpool and now this beautiful tall ship was taking her to another country to begin a new life.

She had barely given a thought to those she left behind, for she saw it as her past to be buried, never to be resurrected.

Hearing the snap of the sails in the wind, she looked up to see them belly out. The sound of the captain yelling orders carried to her and she glanced around. Everyone was busy with some task or other so she turned once again to watched the land slowly becoming more distant.

The feeling of trepidation at what she was undertaking was far outweighed by the excitement of a sea voyage. The scream of gulls overhead startled her and she giggled in embarrassment. The creak of the rigging echoed across the water as the ship rose and dipped on the waves. She noted the stream of white water the ship left in its wake as it surged forward.

She laughed loudly as she recognised the strange feeling that came over her; it was happiness. Something she vowed she would hold onto for the rest of her life.

* * *

Whilst Sally was riding the waves in sheer ecstasy, Ella read the note delivered to her by the maid from The Cedars. Harper had taken a chill and thought it prudent not to visit and so risk passing it on to her or Kitty. Disappointed and a little worried, she reconciled herself to the fact he would be well taken care of by his mother.

Flossie arrived to help carry the hats over to Gladwin's and was quietly informed about Kitty's sad mood.

'We should 'ave hired a cart for all this lot,' she said as she glanced around.

'We can once the contract is signed,' Ella said.

'Good thinking.'

The three set off laden with string-handled boxes, and it was not long before they bustled into the shop.

'You're here, then,' Ivy said sarcastically.

'Looks that way, don't it?' Flossie spat back.

With a scowl at the retort, Ivy produced the documents to be signed and witnessed, a copy for Ella and one for herself.

Reading them carefully, Ella nodded. Signed and dated, she placed hers in her bag.

The bell tinkled and they all turned to see the sign-writer. 'I have a new sign here for you,' he said.

'You'd best put it up, then,' Ivy said.

They all trooped outside to watch the work being done and in a trice the premises were re-named Ivella.

Ella grinned at the thought of finally being able to sell her own goods from a shop rather than her front room. *You'd be proud of me, Dad*, she thought as they thanked the man and went indoors once more.

'I've cleared that half for your *stuff*,' Ivy said, as she tilted her head.

'Wouldn't it be better to intermingle our *stuff* rather than split the room in half?' Ella asked pointedly.

'Do whatever you like, I'll make some tea.' With that, Ivy strode to the back room.

'Her nose is well and truly out of joint,' Kitty said.

'It's 'cos she knows Ella's hats are better than hers,' Flossie replied.

The three women were working hard to transform the tired old room when Ivy returned with a tea tray.

Stopping for a well-earned rest to sip their hot drinks, Ivy nodded. She had to admit the shop was already looking better. The long heavy counter atop its cupboards had been dragged to stand along the back wall facing the door. Free-standing cupboards had been moved to the space left by the counter and display pupae were placed in good strategic positions.

'That window needs emptying,' Flossie said with a glance at Ivy.

'Would you mind, Ivy?' Ella asked.

'Oh, no, you go right ahead. I don't mind at all that you're taking over!'

'Ivy, I'm sorry, I didn't think,' Ella said, suddenly realising her faux pas.

Ivy harrumphed indignantly.

'It's my fault, I just got a bit over-excited.'

'A partnership means working together and I don't recall you asking my opinion about any of this.' Ivy flung out her arm indicating the rearranging of the furniture.

'You're right, I apologise,' Ella said sheepishly.

'But, as it happens, I like it; it gives a feeling of more space.'

'Then should we carry on?' Ella asked, trying not to smash the toes she'd already trodden on.

Ivy nodded. 'I'll get the window cleared and then we can see what's what.'

For the rest of the day the four women worked as a team, with Ella quietly leading them forward. There had been no customers, although people gathered in little groups to peer through the window to see what was going on. News of the change would travel fast, which would hopefully lead to higher sales figures.

Eventually Ella called a halt, saying they'd done enough for one day. She suggested they start afresh the following morning when they could display the rest of their wares to their best advantage.

Tired and dusty, Ella, Kitty and Flossie bid Ivy farewell and set off for home.

'I ache everywhere,' Ella said as they trudged the streets in the failing light.

'It's a job well done, though,' Flossie said. 'I thought Ivy was going to explode when she saw we'd moved her furniture.'

'Yes, that was an error on my part, and a lesson well learned. The better way to go is to suggest things more gently, and make Ivy think the changes are her idea,' Ella concurred.

'That would make life easier, but if not, you could always bury her under that bloody great counter!' Flossie said as she rubbed her sore back.

Ella grinned, but noted Kitty was again lost in a world of her own.

With grateful thanks they parted company with Flossie, who shot off to feed her brood, and Ella and Kitty went indoors.

Shoving coal into the range, Ella called out, 'I'll warm some meat and potato pie for tea, shall I?'

'Not for me, thanks, I'm not hungry. I think I'll just go to bed,' Kitty said as she headed for the stairs door.

Ella ate alone and her worries increased. Harper was unwell and Kitty was drowning in sadness, but the worst of it was she couldn't help either of them.

Kitty had kept her dolour well-hidden all day, but Ella knew she was probably crying her heart out at that very moment. Ella wondered how Kitty would feel when it was time for her to marry Harper. Would it seem like they were rubbing salt into a wound? Could her friend put a brave face on and push through it?

Knuckling her tired eyes, Ella locked up for the night and went quietly to her bed, her worries laying heavily on her.

53

Over the next few days, Ella and Ivy got the shop up and running, Kitty refusing to leave her bed, saying she was feeling poorly. Ella didn't insist on Kitty getting up, understanding that the girl needed time to come to terms with the possibility of Felix being married.

Early one morning, another note arrived from The Cedars. This was from Eléna, saying Harper had taken a turn for the worse and the doctor had been called in.

Ella wondered whether to visit and see for herself how Harper was feeling or go to her work at the shop, but in the end there was no contest. Grabbing her coat and hat, she set off for Harper's home, leaving a brief written explanation for Kitty, should she decide to leave her bed.

The weather had turned milder and Ella felt warm as she hurried along the streets. Arriving at the house, she banged on the front door impatiently. Finally given admittance by the maid, she was shown into the parlour to await the arrival of the mistress.

'Ella, how lovely that you came,' Eléna said as she entered.

'How is he?'

'The doctor is concerned he could have tuberculosis, which means he will have to go to hospital should that prove the case.'

'May I see him?'

'Would that be wise? I don't want you...'

'Please, Eléna.'

'Very well, come with me.'

Led to Harper's bedroom, Ella was shocked at the sight of her beloved. Harper was as white as his sheets and sweat glistened on his forehead. He moaned in his sleep as if he was in pain and Ella sat next to him and bathed his brow.

Eléna slipped silently from the room to instruct the maid to take tea to Ella.

'My love, please get well. I can't bear to see you thus,' Ella whispered.

Harper's eyelids fluttered open for a moment and he gave a little smile before a spasm of coughing overtook him.

Feeling the heat coming off him in waves, Ella pulled back the bedclothes. With more water from the jug and bowl on the dresser, she sponged his chest. She winced as he shivered at the touch of cold on his burning skin, but she persevered. Harper had a raging fever and she knew she needed to reduce his temperature in the only way she could. She soaked his hair until it was a matted mess and continued to bathe his face and chest.

Finally her ministrations appeared to be working as she watched Harper slip into peaceful rest. Going to the window, she yanked it down hard on its sash. The cool air hit her and only then did she realise someone had lit the fire in the bedroom. Taking the poker she raked it fiercely, stabbing the embers down the grate into the ash pan. Satisfied it would soon go out, she returned to her silent vigil at Harper's bedside.

The maid brought tea and moved to the fireplace seeing the fire was low.

'No! Leave it, please. Harper needs fresh air to cool his fever, the fire will only exacerbate it.'

The maid nodded and left without a word.

Ella began to worry whether she was doing the right thing, but she knew a high temperature was dangerous and she continued to watch Harper carefully for any signs of improvement. She stayed until darkness began to fall and finally relented when Eléna insisted she go home. The doctor was due to call that evening, she was told.

'Go to your shop tomorrow, Ella, you've worked too hard to risk losing it now. If things change here I will let you know immediately.'

'Thank you.' Ella hugged her mother-in-law-to-be and hurried home to see to Kitty. She had to rouse the girl's spirits somehow, as well as find something to tempt Kitty to eat once more. Ella feared for her friend's life if she didn't consume food soon.

Once home, Ella warmed a pan of broth she'd made the day before and took a bowl up to Kitty. Laying it on the cabinet by the bed, she lit the gas lamp, seeing her friend had been lying awake in the darkness.

'I've brought you some broth, Kitty, will you sit up and eat it?'

Kitty shook her head and turned on her side.

Ella sighed. 'You can't go on like this, Kitty, you'll starve to death!'

No answer came from the prone figure in the bed and Ella tried again. 'Just a little, please, for me.'

In the dim light Ella saw tears roll from eyes that had once twinkled with mischief and her heart cracked like glass for her friend.

'Kitty, I'm afraid for you! Please don't do this to me, I'm begging you!'

Watching the silent tears continue to fall, Ella knew she could do no more. As she returned to her own meal, she decided that tomorrow she would call the doctor out and see what he suggested.

Meanwhile, the doctor was shaking his head as he examined Harper. 'This is tuberculosis, Mrs Fortescue. I think it best to have your son taken into hospital where he can be cared for night and day.'

Eléna blanched but nodded her agreement.

Glancing again at his patient, he went on, 'In fact, fetch some blankets and have your carriage brought round. I will accompany him there myself this very night.'

Eléna rushed away to yell her orders then watched as Harper was swaddled and carried downstairs by her husband and the jarvey. She felt Rafe's strong arms around her and, laying her head on his chest, she cried as if her heart would break as she watched the carriage pull away.

'He'll be all right, darling, he's strong. We will visit him tomorrow and you'll see he'll be much better,' Rafe said, not feeling the confidence he was trying to portray.

'Oh, Rafe, he can't die! Please don't let my boy die!'

Rafe tightened his arms around her again in response to her plea and, fighting back his own tears, he prayed that Harper would recover quickly.

* * *

Ella arrived at the shop early the next day, loaded down with haberdashery.

'I'm not staying, Ivy, as Kitty is – unwell.'

Ivy nodded, happy to be left alone to conduct business. She didn't bother to enquire as to what ailed Kitty.

Returning home, Ella pulled out her order book, pen and paper. She had a letter to write, which must be sent in all haste. Searching her book for the address, she copied it neatly onto an envelope then began her letter.

Dear Mr Stoddard,

I write to inform you your bowler hat is now completed. I am in the process of moving my business to alternative premises in order that I can care for my dear friend who is very ill. Please collect your hat immediately as time is of the essence.

Yours sincerely,

Ella

Reading what she had penned, she wondered if Felix would guess at what she had hinted. She needed to be careful in case his new wife opened his post; she knew from experience how jealous Darcie could be. However, she wanted him to realise how sick Kitty was and that she was in danger of losing her life. Would it be enough? Would he come?

Sealing the letter in its envelope, Ella grabbed her coat and set off to the post office. With every step she took, she prayed Felix would visit as soon as he could, for she knew he was the only one who could bring Kitty back from the brink of death.

Having posted her correspondence, Ella returned home to make some soup and try again to coax Kitty to eat.

It was as she ladled the soup into a bowl that a knock came to the door. Rushing to answer it, she was faced with the maid from The Cedars, who shoved a note into Ella's hands and fled.

How very curious, Ella thought, as she returned to the kitchen.

Opening the note, she dropped onto a chair as she read it. Harper was in hospital! He was suffering with tuberculosis, as they had all feared.

Ella's hand covered her mouth as tears streamed from her eyes and her mind whirled. Had she contributed to it by opening the window and allowing the fire to burn out? Had she made things worse by bathing him with cool water? Deep down she knew she had done the right things to help break a fever, but the doubts still remained.

Drying her eyes, Ella tried to compose herself. One thing at a time; the letter to Felix had gone off, now to see to Kitty, then she could visit Harper in hospital.

Taking the soup upstairs, she placed it on the bedside cabinet. 'Kitty, I've brought you some soup.'

She heard a groan from beneath the blankets. With everything she had to cope with, Ella's patience snapped like a twig. 'Kitty! Stop being so selfish! Get up this instant and eat this food! Harper is in the hospital with tuberculosis and here you lie feeling sorry for yourself. I'm run ragged trying to look after you and keep the business going. This is the last time I will ask. If you don't stir your stumps, I will leave you to rot in own misery, and how will that look when Felix comes for his bowler?'

Ella saw her friend's eyes peep out from the huddle of bedclothes.

'Felix?' Kitty croaked.

'Yes.' Ella had not meant to say anything in case the man didn't arrive, but in her temper she had blurted it out.

'Harper?'

'Harper is very sick, Kitty,' Ella said more gently.

'Ella, I'm sorry.'

'Don't be, just get up and eat something, please,' Ella begged.

Kitty nodded and Ella sighed with relief.

Ella helped her friend to sit up and spoon-fed her the soup, all the while bringing Kitty up to date with everything that had happened.

With the food consumed, Ella said, 'Now you rest a while and digest. I must get to the hospital to see Harper.'

'Ella, I'm sorry,' Kitty said again, weakly.

'Don't fret, just get well. I can't manage without you.'

'Will he come?' Kitty asked.

'Felix?'

Kitty nodded.

'I don't know, Kitty, and that's the truth, but I hope so. You two need to talk things through because you can't go on like this.'

Kitty's tears came again and Ella hugged her gently. 'Get some more sleep, you'll feel better for it.'

Ella closed the door quietly behind her as Kitty nestled herself in the warm blankets.

Donning her outdoor clothing, Ella strode out towards the Walsall and District Hospital, praying she would find her fiancé in better health from the last time she saw him.

54

Felix received the letter that same afternoon by special messenger, which he knew was an expensive way to send a communication. Whatever it was, it must be important.

Going to the privacy of his study, he tore open the envelope and read the short note. His brows drew together as he considered the words. In all honesty, he had forgotten he had ordered a bowler, and for Ella to remind him in such a manner had him perplexed.

Reading the note again, the hidden meaning became clear as it hit him between the eyes like a poleaxe.

Dear friend – Kitty! The love of his life was ill, and Ella was calling for him to come!

Dropping the note on the fire, Felix rushed from the room, calling for his horse to be brought immediately.

'Where are you going?' Darcie asked as she joined him in the hallway.

'I have urgent business to attend to.'

'But you promised to spend some time with me!' Darcie said sulkily.

'I will, my dear, just not right now.'

'I don't want you to go out and leave me here all alone.'

'Darcie, this cannot wait! I will return as soon as I can.' With that, Felix strode through the front door and leapt up into the saddle of his waiting horse. Kicking his heels into his steed's flanks he galloped down the long driveway, sending gravel flying in all directions.

He had to get to Walsall as fast as possible, he needed to know that Kitty was all right.

* * *

In the meantime, Ella arrived at the hospital and was told Harper was in an isolation ward.

'I must see him, he's my fiancé,' she pleaded.

'I'm sorry but it's not possible at the moment,' the matron replied.

'Please! Just let me look at him for a few seconds.'

The matron shook her head. 'Mr Fortescue is very ill, but be assured he is being well cared for.'

Ella turned to leave with tears coursing down her cheeks.

'Try again tomorrow. It might be that he's well enough for you to have a quick visit,' the matron said, having taken pity on the girl, who looked tired to the bone.

'Thank you,' Ella replied amid her sobs.

The matron watched her leave and shook her head. *She'll be the next to be in here if she's not careful*, she thought as she walked back to her office.

Ella made her way home, feeling as miserable as it was possible to be. Once indoors, she made tea and took a cup up to Kitty. Her friend was sleeping soundly so Ella left quietly, taking the cup with her. In the kitchen she began preparing a meal she thought might entice Kitty to eat. It was then that a furious knocking had her rush to the front door.

'Oh, thank God!' Ella exclaimed as she allowed Felix entry and led him into the warmth of the kitchen. She explained about Kitty's illness, watching the shock come to his face.

'You are married now?' she asked at last.

Felix nodded, his eyes awash with pain and regret.

'I guessed – and so did Kitty, and I'm afraid it was too much for her.'

'I'm so sorry, but I was honour bound,' he whispered.

'I understand. Kitty is still abed, she's too weak to rise as yet but I think a visit from you will lift her spirits enormously. Come with me.'

Ella led him upstairs to Kitty's room and whispered, 'For the sake of propriety I will remain.'

'Of course.'

Felix stepped into the room with Ella right behind him. She watched as he knelt by the bed.

'Kitty,' he whispered, 'I'm here, my love.'

'Felix?' came the quiet response.

'Yes. Come out from there so I can see you,' he said pulling the cover from her face.

Ella saw the twinkle immediately re-appear in her friend's eyes and she swallowed the lump in her throat.

'You came.'

'Of course. Ella called me to your side and here I am.'

'Oh, Felix!' Kitty smiled for the first time in days and Ella gave silent thanks to the good Lord for his mercy.

Kitty struggled to sit up and Ella helped by plumping pillows behind her.

Felix grasped her small hands and gazed into her eyes. 'You must get well, Kitty, I can't bear to see you like this!'

Kitty nodded and again she gave a little smile.

'Please tell me you will eat and recover your health and strength,' Felix insisted.

'I will, only for you,' Kitty said hoarsely.

'I'm going to make some tea, provided you two behave yourselves,' Ella said with mock admonishment as she dragged a chair towards Felix.

Alone now, Felix told Kitty of his pledge to marry Darcie and why he had made it. He tried to explain as gently as he could why he had had to honour that promise. He knew she was hurting but it needed saying and he brushed away her tears as he spoke.

'My heart belongs to you, Kitty, and will until the day I die.'

'You have all of mine, too,' she said.

Leaning forward he placed his lips on hers, feeling the fire course through his veins. Pulling away he gazed at the woman he loved to distraction.

'One day you will be mine,' he said in all seriousness.

Kitty shook her head, knowing it could never be.

'Trust me, my love. Somehow I will find a way. We *will* be together, you have my word on it.'

They were enjoying another kiss when Ella entered with a tea tray.

'I knew it. I guessed you would be up to no good,' Ella said with a laugh.

The three chatted for a long while before Felix got to his feet. 'I have to go now but would it be possible to visit again?'

'Of course.'

'Until tomorrow,' he said to Kitty.

Downstairs Ella said, 'Thank you for bringing my friend back to me.'

'But?'

'But I worry she may begin to rely on your visits too heavily. I'm afraid that if you were to stop coming she might relapse.'

'That is the last thing either of us want. I have told Kitty we will be together one day and I mean to ensure that happens. I don't know when or how, but I have given her my word. I would like to visit as often as I can, with your permission.'

'Of course. Oh, your bowler hat,' Ella said as she fetched the box, 'in case Darcie should ask.'

'I burned the note, so keep the hat for me.' He took out his wallet and paid her. 'I might need it as an excuse sometime.'

Ella nodded. She was not happy about being part of the conspiracy, but if it helped Kitty get well she would put up with it for now.

'Thank you, Ella. I am indebted to you.'

Seeing him out, Ella leaned her back against the door with a huge sigh of relief.

Returning to her cooking, her mind moved to Harper. She couldn't wait for the following day when she might be permitted to see him, if he was well enough.

55

The following morning, Ella took breakfast up to Kitty early. She was pleased when her friend tucked in eagerly. Clearly the girl was famished.

'I'm going to the hospital in the hope of seeing Harper, but I won't be long.'

'I hope he's better today,' Kitty said through a mouth full of boiled egg.

Ella rushed about, gathering her hat and coat, and set off at a brisk pace.

At the hospital the matron was called, and Ella was given a cloth to hold over her face before she was allowed a two-minute visit.

Looking down on Harper sleeping peacefully, the sweat lining his brow, she muttered, 'Come back to me, Harper, I love you with my whole heart.'

Back in the corridor, she dropped the cloth into a bag held open by a nurse, who sped away to dispose of it.

Turning to the matron, she asked, 'How is he doing?'

'Mr Fortescue is very poorly, Miss...?'

'Bancroft.'

The matron nodded. 'Tuberculosis can be a terrible thing, Miss Bancroft. I think you should speak with the doctor and he can explain. Please come to my office while I fetch him.'

The doctor arrived and Ella's complexion paled as she saw him shake his head. 'It's my thinking Mr Fortescue has had this for some considerable time, Miss Bancroft, and I'm amazed that it has not been passed from person to person. How are you feeling?'

'I'm fine, doctor, I'm just tired.'

'Good. Now, I think you should prepare yourself for the worst; I'm not sure he will pull through, although we'll do all we can to help him.'

Ella gasped, tears springing to her eyes.

'I'm sorry, but I thought you should know. Of course, he could surprise us all and be calling for food in no time, however...' The doctor gave a tight smile.

'He *has* to recover, we are to be married!'

'Be patient, my dear, and let's see how things progress.'

Ella thanked the doctor and matron and walked home wearily, her mind in a whirl.

Entering via the back door, Ella was astonished to see Kitty sitting by the table wrapped in a blanket, Felix by her side.

'Well, look at you!'

'I feel so much better. I thought I'd come down to await my visitor.' Kitty smiled at the man sitting so close to her. 'How is Harper today?'

'The doctor said there's no improvement as yet, but we're living in hope.' Ella tried not to spoil Kitty's joy at having Felix there.

'Kitty has explained and I'm sorry to hear about Harper. I will add my prayers for his swift recovery,' Felix said.

'Thank you. Now tea is called for, I think, because I'm parched.' Ella began preparing the panacea for every ailment known to man as Kitty and Felix chatted quietly.

Kitty was still pale and weak but there was a discernible improvement in her demeanour and Ella was grateful for it. Now all she had to worry about was Harper getting well as quickly as possible, and her business thriving in her absence.

* * *

Having no idea of what Ella was going through, Sally was delighting in her voyage. The *Esmerelda* coursed across the ocean at what seemed like lightning speed as Sally stood at the rail running the length of the ship. She heard creaking timbers and rigging and tasted salt on her lips. Sailors mopped the decks and orders were yelled as their voyage continued. The day was fine, if cold, but Sally didn't feel it, so happy was she that the ship was making good time.

She marvelled at the matelot climbing up the rigging to the crow's nest, his agility a testament to having done it many times. She watched as he scanned the horizons through his telescope before yelling down to the captain standing below him. In a thrice he was once again on the deck, whistling a ditty as he winked at her.

With a grin, Sally returned her eyes to the water. There was nothing for hundreds of miles except sea and sky, which made her shiver. There was little between her and the ocean and, although she could swim, she knew she would never survive so far from land should there be a catastrophe. Pushing the dismal thought away, she turned as a sailor whistled loudly. He hooked a finger and Sally walked over to him.

'Dolphins,' he said, pointing to the water below.

Sally shrieked with delight as she watched the large mammals swimming so close to the bow, then suddenly they were gone. She felt blessed at having witnessed such a sight. Turning to thank the crew member, she realised he had returned to his work, allowing her to enjoy the moment alone.

A little while later the skies darkened, and rain pattered down. The wind strengthened and Sally had a job to stay on her feet.

'Looks like a squall, I'd get below if I were you, miss,' a passing sailor said.

Sally mumbled her thanks and on shaky legs made her way to her tiny cabin to wait out the storm. Sitting on her bunk, Sally felt the ship being buffeted by the ever-increasing wind, and nausea swept over her. Eyeing the pail in the corner, she grabbed it as her food parted company with her stomach.

The *Esmerelda* rose high before crashing down again and Sally retched until there was nothing left to bring up. She moaned as her head ached and tears ran free from the effort of emptying her insides.

Her wonderful voyage had turned to a nightmare in an instant with wind and rain battering the ship. Sally prayed it would all be over soon as she lay on her side, the pail close to hand. She gave a brief thought to the child inside her before nausea claimed her yet again and she retched into the bucket.

* * *

Back on land, Felix said his goodbyes and left with the promise of further visits. Ella began work, which had been put aside whilst caring for Kitty, and with taking her completed millinery to Ivella.

The mini round hat with a narrow brim was made in lemon

crin and was designed to sit on the side of the head secured with a hat pin. Ella gently pushed the brim with her thumb to give it a distressed look, and once satisfied she looked for suitable adornments.

Kitty watched in silent fascination as Ella chose two brown pheasant feathers, working the spines between her fingers so they curved. Happy with the arc, she attached them with minute stitches. Taking a thin strip of crin, she bent it into loops before sewing them in place to cover the quills.

All the time she worked, her mind was on Harper and whether he was out of danger yet. Had he been at home she would never have left his side, but the hospital had strict visiting rules so she must wait until the following day to see him again.

Seeing the worried look on her friend's face, Kitty said, 'He'll be all right, Ella, it just takes time.'

Ella nodded, not trusting herself to speak.

A quick knock and the back door opened as Flossie rushed in.

'It's gone cold out again – bloody weather! So, tell me who the fella is who keeps calling.'

Kitty explained about Felix and Ella told Flossie about Harper being in the hospital.

'Blimey! I leave you girls on your own for a few days and look what happens!'

'Tea, Flossie?' Ella asked.

'Is the Pope Catholic?'

'I don't know, is he?' Kitty asked innocently.

Laughter erupted and for a moment all seemed well with the world.

56

Bright and early the next morning, Ella walked briskly to the hospital. Waylaying a nurse, she requested a short visit with Harper. The nurse blanched and dashed off to fetch the matron.

'Miss Bancroft, please follow me.'

Ella trundled behind the large woman dressed in blue. Once in the office, Ella was asked to take a seat.

'I'm so sorry, dear, I'm afraid I have some bad news.'

Ella's stomach lurched and her heartbeat became rapid.

'I hate to tell you this, but Mr Fortescue passed in the night. Please accept my condolences.'

Ella stared at the woman who was telling her Harper had died. It couldn't be true, she must be mistaken!

'I don't understand, he seemed a little better yesterday,' Ella said haltingly.

'The calm before the storm, we see it often in here.'

'Have his parents...?'

'Yes, they were informed at the time,' the matron said as gently as she could.

'I... I...' Ella's eyes darted around the room as if she were looking for something.

'Miss Bancroft, might I suggest you go home, there is nothing more to be done here.'

Ella nodded and stood on wobbly legs. 'Thank you,' she muttered as she walked home in a daze.

Stepping into the kitchen, she was greeted with, 'How is Harper today?'

'He's dead,' Ella whispered.

'What?' Kitty exclaimed.

'He died in the night.' Ella sat on a kitchen chair in a dream-like state.

'Oh, my God!' Kitty gushed. 'Oh, Ella, I'm so sorry. Tea – you'll need a cuppa.'

Ella merely nodded, still unable to take in what she'd been told.

Placing a steaming cup in front of her, Kitty grabbed a coat and went to fetch Flossie. A moment later they were back.

Ella was staring into space and drinking her tea like an automaton.

Kitty looked at Flossie with a question in her eyes.

'It's the shock, I've seen it before. Sometimes it takes a while to sink in.'

'Then?'

'Then there'll be tears enough to drown in.'

A distressed Kitty looked at her friend, who was in a world of her own, and her heart went out to her.

'What do I do?'

'There's nothing you can do, lovey, you just have to wait for the shock to wear off.'

'And after that?'

'Watch her closely, listen to her ramble and hold her close

when she cries,' Flossie said wisely. Tipping her head to the door, Flossie told Kitty she would be next door if she was needed.

Kitty nodded and watched her go before turning back to Ella, who had begun to mumble. Kitty watched in fear as Ella berated the hospital staff for not saving her betrothed, then railed at God for being merciless before pleading with Him to return her loved one.

Ella banged her fists on the table in outrage and grief, making the cups jump on its surface. She yelled for Harper to come back to her, then suddenly she was quiet.

The sound of the old tin clock ticking was loud in the silence and Kitty waited to see what would happen next, her eyes never leaving Ella.

A low moan emanated from Ella, which grew in pitch and intensity.

'Nooooo!'

The sound tore at Kitty's nerves, reminding her of a wounded animal. She watched Ella rock back and forth as she keened endlessly.

Kitty wrapped her arms around the girl whose heart had shattered like a pane of glass. Tears fell from two pairs of eyes as they rocked on the chair as one.

Neither had seen or heard Felix enter through the back door, wondering what on earth was going on.

* * *

At the same time Ella was sobbing as if her heart would break, out on the ocean the *Esmerelda* pitched and yawed in the gale that threw her around like a toy. The orders being screamed out were lost on the howling wind as sailors scrambled around on deck.

Sally was thrown from her bunk as the ship tilted violently. Too sick to feel afraid, she lay where she landed.

The sound of an almighty crash had her close her eyes before opening them again quickly as nausea swept over her once more. She began to wish she were at home with Eddy and had never set out on such a foolish venture. Groaning, she dry-heaved over and over, her stomach empty and aching. Surely the storm couldn't last much longer? The thought was broken by another loud crash and Sally wondered if she would die out there on the sea.

Rolling about on the floor of the cabin, she prayed. *Lord, if it's my time, then come for me now!*

* * *

Back in Silver Street, Ella's tears ebbed and Kitty let go of her. She was taken by surprise as Felix spoke.

'I knocked at the front door first, but when I received no answer I thought to try the back. Can you tell me what has happened?' he asked, tilting his head towards Ella.

Bidding him to take a seat, Kitty explained the situation and Ella's distress.

'My condolences.' There was nothing more he could say.

Ella sat like a statue, blind and deaf to the goings on around her, before suddenly getting to her feet.

'I have to see Eléna,' she said and rushed out of the house.

Kitty stared at Felix and shook her head. 'She'll be back. She needs to do this, to see this Eléna,' he said.

'It's Harper's mother,' Kitty replied.

'Ah,' Felix said, 'then we'll await Ella's return.'

It was hours later when Ella came home, clearly all cried out. Her eyes were red and puffy and she sniffed as she explained.

'Eléna said Harper is to be interred at the family plot at the cemetery.'

'What about a service?' Kitty asked.

'It will be held at St John's Church, then mourners will be requested to join the family for the interment.'

'How was Eléna?'

'Distraught, as was Rafe. I could barely hold myself together as we discussed everything.' Ella sniffed again.

'Oh, Ella, I feel sorry in my heart for you and Harper's family,' Kitty muttered.

'I can't believe he's gone, Kitty. It all seems so surreal.'

'When is...?' Kitty began.

'Two days' time,' Ella replied, realising how difficult it was for Kitty to ask.

'That's quick,' Kitty said.

'That's money,' Felix added. 'Things get done a lot quicker when wealth is involved. Ella, I'm so sorry for your loss.' He saw Ella nod. 'Now I really must be on my way. Will you ladies be all right?'

Kitty nodded and watched him leave, the love shining from her eyes like a beacon.

The next two days passed slowly for Ella, who mourned her beloved Harper. No thought was given to work or Ivella and it was Flossie who took the news to Ivy Gladwin, who sent back a message of condolence.

Kitty and Ella dressed in black on the morning of the funeral and walked in silence to the churchyard. Ella carried a single red rose, bought from the florist at great cost.

Rafe and Eléna greeted them solemnly as they surrounded the graveside. Eléna hugged Ella and gave a tight smile to Kitty. Rafe was looking pale and tired as he shook hands with both girls.

More people arrived, some of whom Ella was acquainted with through her business dealings with them. She and Kitty stood with the Fortescues as folk whispered their condolences before moving inside the church.

Ella heard quiet conversations going on around her once they were all indoors. Questions were being asked about Harper's demise. How had he died? When had he passed over? The answers were given just as quietly, and eyes turned to peer at her when there was mention of the wedding that would now not take place.

She listened to the vicar but his words did not register with her, for Ella was lost in a world of hurt. On the periphery of it all she could hear Eléna sobbing and Rafe doing his best to console her, but he was drowning in his own grief.

Kitty pulled at Ella's sleeve and she realised the vicar had finished speaking and people were filing out of the doors. It was time to go to the cemetery.

Following along behind Harper's parents, Ella walked as if in a daze. She knew from burying her father that this would be the hardest part for them all. Only when the ground swallowed the coffin would she believe it was real, and then she would grieve all over again.

Ella stumbled and Kitty caught her arm, steadying her.

'Are you all right?'

'I can't do this, Kitty, I just can't!'

'You have to, my lovely. Come on, I'm here with you. We'll do it together,' Kitty said.

Ella nodded and walked on, coming at last to the place where she would say her last goodbye to the love of her life.

Another service began and the vicar faltered as Ella stepped forward to place her rose on the coffin lying on the bier. Looking to Harper's parents, Ella shook her head. They nodded, as they understood she was telling them she could stay no longer. She could not bear to see the casket lowered into the ground.

Turning, Ella walked away with Kitty holding her up as the vicar continued with his service. Ella stopped dead in her tracks as the howl carried across the graveyard. Eléna's voice sounded more like an animal in the direst pain. On and on it went, echoing off the gravestones dotted around.

Falling to her knees, Ella's voice joined that of Harper's mother as she howled out her own agony. Kitty knelt beside her friend and held her tightly as she keened her distress to the world.

EPILOGUE

It was a week later, and Kitty was reading the newspaper aloud.

'The good ship *Esmerelda* sank in a storm, all hands lost.'

There was no way Ella could know her sister and the child she carried had perished when the ship went down.

As the weeks passed, slowly Ella began to work on her millinery again, earning a grudging respect from Ivy Gladwin. The shop was a great success and the money poured in from sales even Ivy couldn't believe.

Eddy Denton never visited Ella again and she heard on the grapevine he had moved to Birmingham in search of work at last. To her mind it was too little, too late.

Darcie had flown into a temper when Felix said he was filing for divorce, and stabbed him in the leg with a kitchen knife. She was quickly transported back to her parents with all of her belongings. Royston and Verity Newland took their daughter and moved to Scotland in an endeavour to escape the gossip.

Kitty waited patiently for Felix's divorce to be granted so they would be free to marry. The only talk to surround Felix was that people considered him very foolish to have married Darcie in the first place, and he was wise in the decision to get rid of her.

Eléna and Rafe Fortescue never fully recovered from losing their only son, and retired quietly from the social scene. Ella saw them often, when they would chat about the boy they had loved with all their hearts.

Ella visited Harper's grave regularly, telling him her news as she changed the flowers in the urn. She could not envisage a time when she would marry and have a family of her own. She felt sure she was destined to become an old maid like Ivy, but it didn't concern her. Harper's memory was with her always. It brought her great comfort and she had no intention of ever being without it. Her love for Harper would travel with her into old age before death took her and they could be together once more.

ACKNOWLEDGMENTS

To The Hat Company, Manchester – where I spent a delightful couple of hours.

MORE FROM LINDSEY HUTCHINSON

We hope you enjoyed reading *The Hat Girl From Silver Street*. If you did, please leave a review.

If you'd like to gift a copy, this book is also available as an ebook, digital audio download and audiobook CD.

Sign up to Lindsey Hutchinson's mailing list for news, competitions and updates on future books.

http://bit.ly/LindseyHutchinsonMailingList

The Children From Gin Barrel Lane, another gritty Black Country saga from Lindsey Hutchinson, is available now.

ABOUT THE AUTHOR

Lindsey Hutchinson is a bestselling saga author whose novels include *The Workhouse Children*. She was born and raised in Wednesbury, and was always destined to follow in the footsteps of her mother, the multi-million selling Meg Hutchinson.

Follow Lindsey on social media:

f facebook.com/Lindsey-Hutchinson-1781901985422852
🐦 twitter.com/LHutchAuthor
BB bookbub.com/authors/lindsey-hutchinson

ABOUT BOLDWOOD BOOKS

Boldwood Books is a fiction publishing company seeking out the best stories from around the world.

Find out more at www.boldwoodbooks.com

Sign up to the Book and Tonic newsletter for news, offers and competitions from Boldwood Books!

http://www.bit.ly/bookandtonic

We'd love to hear from you, follow us on social media:

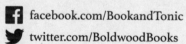

facebook.com/BookandTonic

twitter.com/BoldwoodBooks

instagram.com/BookandTonic